The
Exquisite and Timely
Death of God

Andrew Shannon

ISBN 978-0-6488077-0-4

Andrew Shannon asserts the moral right to
be identified as the author of this work.
Andrew00Shannon.com
Andrew00Shannon@gmail.com

This is a work of fiction. The characters and places in it are all fictional.

Sun 20 Sept 1959 **11:35am**
Jacob's Prelude

A foreign sensation materialised inside Jacob and caused him to lose balance. Thinking quickly he dropped to his knees and fell forward, lying face down on the floor where he could fall no further. It was as if there was a nauseating irritation inside him, in his belly, but no, it was not his belly, in fact now that he thought about it maybe it was in his chest, his head. It did not seem to have a precise location that he could identify.

Was this a heart attack? He was being filled up from the inside with something like a warm light or a wavelength of a particular frequency that his body was absorbing. The light or whatever it was inside him was slowly changing, increasing in warmth and had somehow become audible.

How does light make a sound? Can it? This was no sound that he was listening to in the normal physical sense, it was a note he had never heard, an impossible sound, but he understood it and knew what it was. It was a message. This was a communication straight from a source. And the source was? Jacob's eyes opened wide. The source was…

Gone. But it had left a residual, a mystery within Jacob. A foreign entity was now inside of him, he could feel it. The event had left something lingering behind, warmth, knowledge, an awareness. The light that emitted the impossible note was flickering inside him and had found a place within him that had never existed before and settled there. It was a broadcast, a calling card, a beacon?

It was God.

The rain began to batter down on the tin roof above in torrents. Jacob closed his eyes.

Sun 20 Sept 1959 *7:15am*
Jacob, Earlier that day

'...an ominous low pressure system forming, with strong south westerly winds expected to appear, intensifying into a potentially troublesome storm by noon...'

Today was just another day, probably tediously similar to yesterday but with worse weather, according to the newsreader on the wireless. Jacob stretched out an arm, turned off the alarm clock that had already ruined his morning and slowly opened his eyes. Streams of sunlight had found their way through the ineffective venetian blinds at his window and were dancing into the room. The thought fleetingly crossed his mind that it would have been quite a beautiful scene if only it didn't signify that his day and all that it would entail was about to unfold.

He observed a sea of dust particles trailing lazily in the sunlit air reminding him that his room was not as clean as it should be, and that was because it was now solely his responsibility to care after the whole house. Shutting that particular thought out of his head before it could snowball into something melancholy, he focused on more pleasing matters.

With a slight smile Jacob climbed out of bed. He already knew exactly who his first sentence of the day would be spoken to, and what those words would be.

Sadly, there weren't too many moments of interest in Jacob's life these days. He himself imagined that if he was a colour he would be grey, and a particularly drab shade at that. He was going through the motions of life, feeling no more real than a mechanical wind-up toy, barely wound up, the mechanism geared to operate confined within a limited range of movements.

Jacob commenced his morning routine and it was a routine of such precision and exactness that he was sure that each day every day the order of tasks he undertook to prepare himself for work was identical, and the length of time taken from getting out of bed to leaving the house could be timed to the minute. He was not particularly proud of this, nor was this something he aimed to achieve every day, it was just an observation of fact and a reflection of how stationary his life had become.

He had long since optimised his movements in the morning, refining the minutiae of his routine such as turning the kettle on before he went to the bathroom so it would be boiled by the time he came out. Most people wouldn't even think of that attention to detail and would fill the kettle all the way up to the top when they are only making a single cup, and then wait around aimlessly while it takes forever to boil. Jacob did realise, however, that even with all his efficiencies he really achieved nothing with all that extra time that he created for himself and coveted so much.

Sitting at the table, pouring a coffee with his pre-boiled kettle and savouring some toast generously coated with butter, his favourite breakfast, Jacob became annoyed. Maybe he was still dreaming at the time but he was quite sure that he heard the weather reporter on the radio say that there was some unpleasant weather on the way, and yet the sky he could see out of his kitchen window with his own eyes was of the deepest blue. *They really never get it completely right do they*, Jacob thought to himself.

Weather reporters, with all their access to sophisticated meteorological instruments still more often than not missed the mark. It was the only job on the planet as far as Jacob knew where you can be consistently incorrect and not appear to be accountable to anybody, least of all the thousands of members of the public who rely on the information. How has there not been some sort of protest about this blatant swindle?

He looked out through a small stained glass window that occupied a place above his front door and looked at the sky. This looked like one of those days again where the reporter got it wrong. Jacob picked up his briefcase and left for work, where he knew he would be accountable for all he did there "Unlike weather presenters," he mumbled to himself. This morning he didn't bother to take his umbrella.

Hastily walking down his grimy street on his way to the office, he put his irritable mood behind him as much as he could and rehearsed his first sentence of the day. He got it all mixed up once and he felt so embarrassed that he had never forgiven himself for messing up such a simple thing. Hence the rehearsals now became an important prelude to the performance.

His pace quickened, his lips moved inaudibly, practicing the words over and over. He strolled past a familiar brown unpainted picket fence that was missing some pickets and leaning over at an unnatural gravity-defying angle, then strode confidently alongside a well-kept hedge and eventually rounded a corner and turned into a narrow laneway.

Jacob looked up from his feet, which he often stared at whilst concentrating, and saw an imposing man walking towards him with a purposeful stride, wearing a smart trilby and a brown plaid suit, slightly too big to be a perfect fit, but close. A surly, bearded face accompanied the hat and suit, and a pipe emerged from somewhere amongst the beard. It seemed as if the world had become silent. The birds stopped singing and the sound of traffic reduced to a muted silence.

The distance between them closed, and when they were about fifteen seconds away from passing each other, Jacob stopped whispering his phrase to himself and the grip on his briefcase tightened a little. Closer, closer, the pair were only a few seconds apart. Jacob took a deep breath.

And spoke.

"I-I once was quite the poet, my written word could express my thoughts with an eloquence that my clumsy mouth never could." The words came out adequately.

The man in the suit, still walking, removed the pipe from his mouth and replied "I'm learning to fly a whirligig, one of those spinny helicopters, you know."

And that being that, the two passed each other and proceeded to keep on their way as if this interaction happened on a daily basis, which it in fact did.

Jacob had lived in the same house with his wife for many years, worked in the same office, and walked the same route to work every day at virtually precisely the same time with thanks to his honed routine. His neighbourhood had a happy feel to it and no matter what time of day it was there were children playing in the park, as ill-equipped as it was, with mothers looking on casually in between catching up on the latest gossip with each other, and laughter filled the air.

The grass was always way too long and in need of a mow, and in spring there were enough dandelions shedding their fluffy seeds that when the wind blew it was as if the winter snow had arrived. Jacob always had to walk around the park and once he tried to wade through the grass but ended up with green knees, just as if he was a boy again playing soccer after school.

After a few years of walking around this park and becoming very familiar with the neighbourhood and its inhabitants, one morning everything turned upside down.

A man he had never seen in the area before was walking the opposite way towards him. A stocky man with a carefully groomed beard was puffing a pipe, the thick smoke trailing behind and dissipating. The two approached each other. The speed of both men never faltered. Jacob veered slightly to the left, the other gentlemen to the right, and then the two passed each other.

This happened every working day at 8:45am for nearly a year before something curious happened. One morning the familiar and yet strange man said hello. His eyes glanced across at Jacob, who, purely out of reflex, replied with a startled hello. And so this was the new 8:45am standard for a couple of months.

The day that changed Jacob's mornings forever started when the mysterious man did not veer to the right, nor to the left, but instead stopped directly in front of Jacob's path preventing him from continuing on. Nervous and sensing trouble, but not having any idea what he could have done to provoke the man, a flustered Jacob was about to apologize for nothing and try to keep walking, though at a somewhat quicker pace but before he could execute that plan the man spoke.

"Excuse me my good man, I see you more often than my closest friends, and yet I know nothing absolutely about you."
His voice was deep, sure, and assertive. Not quite a booming voice, but very clear like it belonged to a presenter on the wireless and it had an air of good humour about it that relaxed Jacob and any nervousness he may have had was relieved. The man continued.

"To remedy this situation, I propose this-" The man stood himself tall and upright, folded his arms then gave a little double cough. "Ahem- I propose that every morning when we inevitably pass, we make a statement of fact about ourselves, about anything, whether interesting or not, and it won't be long before know each other quite thoroughly, don't you think? We won't even have to break our stride."

Jacob looked at him, and the extraordinariness of the situation got the better of him, and all he could reply with was a "Yes?" that emanated from his lips in a slightly higher pitch than he would have liked. He repeated the word in an unnaturally deep tone to compensate but it was clear that by trying to correct himself he had just done his masculinity even more of a disservice.

"So we are agreed? Well then, today my opening statement shall be - Good morning. My name is Mr Derby."

"And good morning to you, my name is Jacob."

Mr Derby doffed his well-worn trilby to Jacob, took a step to the right, and briskly marched off. And that was that.

Returning from his trip down memory lane, Jacob permitted himself a rare smile as he looked back at the day he met Mr Derby and how at 8:45am day by day, sentence by sentence, he could now count Mr Derby as one of his closest acquaintances, a man who knew as much about him as anyone ever had. And it didn't even strike him as odd that he didn't know his first name.

Continuing on his way to work, subconsciously talking to himself, he repeatedly uttered his sentence even though the performance was over. He drew looks from passers-by, both of derision and pity, before they quickly stared down at the ground avoiding eye contact.

Jacob had long since cared about making an effort on his outward appearance, his mostly grey curly hair was unkempt and seemed enthusiastically determined to take on a mad-professor type look, and this look was accentuated by a pair of faded brown pants and beige blazer which had a hole in the shoulder from where he carried his satchel on the same side every day.

He seemed enveloped in a fog of despair and hopelessness, and between this, his clothing and the muttering to himself, he resembled a vagrant more than he did a life insurance salesman. It even seemed as though the dogs were disappointed in him today, there was an unusual amount of barking on his way through the park that made his hair stand up on end.

Stop taking everything personally Jacob. The whole world isn't out to get you, only the people who know you. He sighed and with a grimace on his face that accentuated his worry lines, he had reached the point in the day that he feared and despised the most.

Carelessly banging the well-oiled door open to the office where he worked, Jacob cringed. He always tried to enter his building as hastily and silently as possible, keeping his head down and making sure to look at his feet, so as to go hopefully unnoticed by his less than friendly and less than intelligent colleagues, who, given their lowly intelligence, were actually surprisingly clever at finding new ways to belittle him and make him feel generally miserable whilst he was in the office. Fortunately he did not sit in the immediate vicinity of his colleagues, and so was not the pigeon among the cats of the office.

Sitting down on his adjustable chair which felt like it had a rusty spring ready to burst through the upholstery and administer a dose of tetanus, Jacob mentally began preparing himself to get into today's particularly undesirable workload. It was the part of his job which grated against everything he believed in doing, but which was essential for him to succeed- to go through pages and pages of phone numbers and cold call for new clients.

People who were at home trying to enjoy their day, cooking, working, whatever, had to stop doing what they were doing to answer their phones and listen to a complete stranger talking to them about what would happen should they die, and what would happen to their family's wellbeing. Were they insured? A depressing imposition upon the unsuspecting innocent.

He knew how he came across to these people that he telephoned- a heartless scavenger, preying upon insecurities to gain a commission. And that is what most people in the life insurance industry were, but Jacob actually really did care for the wellbeing of those families and was trying to help them, to make them realise that life didn't always go to plan, people in your life can and do get taken from you suddenly. He knew this because it had happened to him.

He reached under a pile of loose paper and pulled out a photo frame that he stared silently at for about five minutes, his mind in a different place, thinking of a time now long past when he was a very different person. He snapped back to reality when a shadow cast over him from an approaching figure and he hid the frame back under the mountain of paperwork.

Faraday approached Jacob's desk in much the same way an excited child approaches their favourite toy. His mind was visibly ticking over with thoughts of how he could have some fun with what was in front of him. He dug his thumbs with their well-manicured nails in underneath his braces and used them to pull up the expensive trousers of his new suit, revealing socks that were carefully matched to his paisley tie.

Jacob pretended not to notice his arrival. The number two salesman in the division, Faraday had a boisterous and aggressive nature which he spread to all corners of the office. His self-centredness knew no bounds, and his interfering made sure that everybody was forced to worry about him in one way or another.

His curiosity into his colleague's affairs was intrusive and on more than one occasion he had stolen clients from Jacob, but because he was drinking buddies with the manager he was able to continue to swan about the office as he pleased. If anybody was asked to describe him in three words they would answer "Selfish, selfish and selfish." Jacob braced himself for an interaction that could literally go in any direction.

"Jake, great to see you today. You look wonderful, new shirt? Just kidding, of course it's not. Look, I'll get right to the point, I've got a sale to close across town this morning which I need to leave for in a minute. So buddy, I hear your sales are down this month, well, we've all seen the leader board haven't we? Honestly, how do you survive on so few sales? Anyway, that's none of my business, but I just came by to tell you that Pete, I mean, Mr Higgs and I were talking last night at a bar about you and what we could do to help the business with this little problem you have with not being able to close any sales recently. And when I say recently, I mean since the dawn of time." He chuckled to himself. "You know what, after a few beers we found an answer! Jakey your problems have been solved. You can thank me later and you can also thank the power of beer. Higgs wants to see you in his office pronto," and with that he slyly backed away and in his place left a trail of question marks to keep Jacob wondering.

Jacob was about to tell Faraday that his name was not Jake or Jakey, it was Jacob, and that he was not interested in anything he had to say. He had long since formulated a standard response to anything anybody in the office had to say to him, especially

Faraday, and it was "Please leave me alone," but something Faraday said actually penetrated the walls he had put up around himself and he allowed himself to listen and process what was just said. He was living on the smell of an oily rag and he had such a confidence issue that he had not closed a sale in weeks, so he could not lie to himself any longer and pretend that everything was okay.

He stood up slowly and started to cross the floor of cubicles, making his way to the small office of Mr Higgs, the man who would solve his problem and make everything okay again.

Oblivious to everything around him, he did not notice that nearly the whole office had stood up and was watching his movements with interest. It was early enough in the morning that people were not fully engaged in their work as yet and could wait a few minutes to watch the proceedings before putting their heads down.

Approaching the office, he emerged from the zone he was in enough to notice a few muffled laughs and he thought he heard one person whispering bemusedly "He's actually going to do it!" but he wasn't sure. He shuffled onwards, all he was doing was going for a casual chat with the boss, and there was no fuss to be made over that.

What he did not notice was that behind those laughs was the sound of Carol, a newcomer to the business and maybe the only person in the office who had ever been truly kind to him. She was yelling angrily at Faraday for something, but Jacob didn't care, his eyes were fixed on that office door.

He realised he was seen as a no-hoper, he had no respect from anybody, he had lost virtually everything he cared about in his life and so if Mr Higgs could change his life for the better with some sort of solution to his workplace crisis then he needed to know.

All eyes on him, the office was electric with a contagious anticipation, and sensing this energy, Jacob nervously knocked on the office door.

And entered…

Sun 20 Sept 1959 **9:03am**
Faith

"Today was just another day, but Jessica knew that it was the day that she would finally make love to Juan for the first time." The piece of paper upon which that sentence had just been typed was pulled roughly from the typewriter, scrunched tightly and cast accurately into the wastepaper basket to join the five or so other rejected pages containing opening lines that had offended the standard of writing that Faith expected from herself.

She ran her hands through her less-than-carefully sculpted long sandy-blonde hair in frustration, her chipped fingernails covered in uneven strokes of multi-coloured nail polish giving away the fact that she was a slave to her job and not the type of mid-twenties girl who had the time to be immersing herself in the social scene with any vigour.

Her wardrobe of fun and colourful dresses had slowly given way to a more corporate style, pants and shirts in shades of black and white now all that she wore. She liked to think that deep inside she was still the fun, colourful girl and was writing her novel to try to externalise this, and though she did not realise it, behind her green eyes a glimmer of life still remained.

Her attempt at novel-writing was not going well. She did not really know what it would be about, or what the title was, or whether it would be a thriller, comedy, drama, or, as the previous opening line indicated, a steamy romance involving a cliché latino gardener.

Her strategy was simple. Centre her being, harness her spirituality, sit at a typewriter and type. Unplanned. Her subconscious would be the author, creativity spouting forth via her fingers through the keyboard and onto paper, weaving a masterful tale about… something. It seemed that her chakras were not aligned today and there was some blockage to her energy flows. She firmly believed that if she opened her mind and was receptive to the universe the words would come. She may need to try a different incense.

Why did her best work always happen when she was asleep! Emerging from deep sleep with the spark of an idea for a never-before-thought-of bestselling book idea seemed to happen often enough that she should have a substantial bibliography of award winning books by now.

Alas, whenever she sat upright in bed to reach for a pen and paper to capture the idea that excitedly brimmed forth, the idea drifted away from her mind like smoke from an extinguished candle. Upon reflection, she didn't actually keep a pen or paper next to her bed, so that was also a contributor to the issue.

Sometimes she imagined what the world would be like if all those lost moments of inspiration were actually captured and nurtured to fruition. She believed everybody had at least one inspirational idea hidden away inside themselves, a delicate seed that could either grow or die depending on the ever most subtle of factors. A glance in the right direction, a breath, an accidental insight could be all it took to tip the idea over from the realm of daydreams and into the world of reality.

Most of these moments, she knew, were lost. Luckily, there were people out there who found their idea and grasped it and shaped the world in some way, maybe in a way even more powerfully than they originally thought. Fortunately for the world there were people out there that *weren't* her.

Her mind drifted onto a surreal path, one that it had travelled along before. A familiar alternate world materialised, a world where the entire population was made up of... her. Not in the sense that she was a single lonely soul upon a planet, but that the entire race of humankind since the dawn of time had evolved as her, all with the same genetic code, the same skills, capabilities, values and beliefs that she possessed.

Faith wondered what the world would be like if every human, male and female, had her mind. Granted, there would never have been a Leonardo Da Vinci, or Newton, or Alexander Graham Bell et al, so this parallel world would have developed with no electricity, no strong grasp of science, no television, no aeroplanes, no wireless... In fact, Faith admitted to herself that right now she would probably be living in a straw hut, shabbily built at that, and eating raw potatoes because she wasn't sure if her or her ancestors would ever have learned to start a fire. But boy would she have a stunning collection of grass skirts and bark shoes.

On the positive side, in her world there would be no drainers. Faith gave this label to those members of the general population who in her opinion have no ambition, seemingly with a sole purpose in life to lie on their well-worn couches all day and idly collect cheques from the government for their cigarettes and booze, and just to milk a few more bucks, practice unrestrained breeding.

Why, at this stage of human evolution was there no intelligence test as a prerequisite to starting a family? She had studied hard at school and worked diligently to create a life that she could be proud of, and her reward was to pay a higher rate of tax so that her income could be distributed to that lazy boy who sat in the back of her class making paper planes and hindering her own intellectual pursuits.

She admitted that she may have extended her fantasy world slightly too far into the whimsical, but that's exactly what creative, successful novelists were supposed to do. She had the "creative" part mastered, now she just needed the "successful", and "novelist" tags to go along with it.

All in all, her mind reverting back to her surreal world of Faith clones, there would be no geniuses but conversely no dummies, and more importantly no drainers so this would average out, resulting in a world with a lot of bark shoe stores that would be a pretty nice place to be in. She was a nice person, after all!

Happy with what a wonderful imaginary planet she had created, Faith leaned back on her chair, ready to make another attempt at beginning her masterpiece. Inserting another piece of paper into the typewriter, she was full of confidence that this would be one lucky piece of paper that would not be joining the others in the wastepaper basket.

"Today wa.." was as far as she got, before a familiar yet terrifying voice whispered sternly in her ear. How did he sneak up like that?

"Where is the update on Khrushchev's visit you promised me by first thing this morning?"

Faith sat bolt upright in her chair, and then in a poor attempt to look unfazed, ran her hands through her hair, pulled off a pretty good fake yawn, and thanked her lucky stars that she had not left the previous opening line of her novel in the typewriter.

Looking at her watch, she realised with horror that it was close to 10am, and her output for the day thus far had been exactly six pieces of scrunched up paper that weren't even work related. A second wave of horror washed over her as she looked at the catastrophe that was her desk.

It looked like a deranged person had just tipped over a box of rubbish consisting only of chocolate wrappers, followed by another box containing paper, some soda cans and more wrappers. The last thing she needed was to suffer the paranoia that her boss was judging her on the state of her desk, or even worse, her diet.

"Oh, morning chief, sorry. I've had a lot on my mind this morning *like latino gardeners and alternate realities*. Here's the report. Its fifteen pages but I'll whittle it down to five for you if you give me half an hour." The frowning face that glared back at her told her that this was not acceptable.

"Well Faith, since you actually work for a newspaper and we write *ar-ti-cles*," he pronounced each syllable slowly and more than a little patronisingly. "I'd like it to be three hundred words maximum, just like every other *ar-ti-cle* that you write."

He was still whispering into Faith's ear, and she felt his warm breath on her neck, and knew that everybody in the office could see him leaning down and speaking softly to her. She was sure that it looked like something other than what it was, so her professionalism took over and she stood up to face him.

It upset her that she was the most talented journalist at the newspaper, and was able to command respect from everybody except for Maxwell, the editor-in-chief, a confident and intelligent leader who had the power of making her feel nervous and ramble incessantly whenever they conversed. She had lost count of the number of times that she had backtracked over their conversations in her head and cringed with horror at the recollection of spouting on about completely inane and irrelevant topics.

She could usually sense it was happening as it unfolded but her lips could never change their course, her gaze fixated on the symmetry of his face, her mind drawn in by the fact that he actually listened to her, a trait not common to most men she met.

Her journalistic talent was rewarded by Maxwell offering her the toughest assignments, stories she knew that very few other people in the office were able to handle. Only she could reduce complex subject matter to a level that the everyday layman could understand, surely a core skill for any writer? Standards were declining in the industry but not to fear, it made her look even better.

She leaned against the filing cabinet next to her desk and forced her words to come out casually, supressing the desire to get defensive and react to his unnecessary jab about not having the article polished.

"Sure thing chief, right on it," she smiled convincingly and sat back at her desk. "Great. I look forward to reading it. Have it on my desk in fifteen minutes." Their eyes met, and Faith could see that he believed he had sufficiently exercised his authority and put her in her place. She tried to tell her eyes to say "Okay I've let you do your boss thing, and you'll get your *ar-ti-cle*, but only because I want to have it published, not because you've ordered it of me."

Maxwell turned and slowly walked away, stopping at the desk of one of the sports journalists to have a laugh. She saw him glance her way and, not at all smoothly, she swivelled in her chair towards her typewriter then stared at the ceiling for a brief instant, centred her being, harnessed her spirituality and started typing.

Maxwell could wait for his article. She put a new piece of paper in her typewriter. Jessica, her novel's heroine was about to do…*something*.

Sat 19 Sept 1959 **4:15pm**
Mary

Today was just another day, but for Mary it meant a long Sunday of difficult but rewarding work. She was aware that most people spent their weekends enjoying their time with friends and family, watching sports, relaxing and taking the time out from their Monday to Friday personas. She used to be one of them.

The weekends were where your real life was lived, where you could do anything you liked, be whoever you really wanted to be without the obligation of conforming to the rules of a workplace in return for a pay cheque.

So, by forgoing weekends did this mean that Mary was never able to be her true self? She often wondered this, but decided that it was easier to accept that this was who she was now. Sure, maybe if she didn't have to work seven days a week she would be doing other things, but she had no alternative but to do what she did and would not have things any other way. Her life was once quite different though.

Doing the gardening was what she missed the most. Pushing the seeds from the packet into the carefully fertilised soil, soon to become green shoots rearing their heads towards the sunlight. They rarely made it past the infant stage however, and it was not often that their destinies were fulfilled. Once Mary's eager checking of the soil uncovered newly formed signs of life, something would possess her and within days most of the seedlings would be drowned, overwatered, over cared for. She knew she was doing it and yet could not stop it from happening.

Her husband Diah used to tease her about it lovingly, and say that if they ever had children she was not allowed to water them. Mary sighed. Yes she was a terrible gardener, but it didn't matter now anyway because she did not have the time to either plant or overwater anything. This was the reason why she was now at the grocery store, buying vegetables for dinner.

She was a simple cook, and quite often didn't really plan ahead, but Diah never complained though. He was as kind and loving a man as she had ever met, but even so, everybody has their limits and sometimes Mary felt like she let herself and other people down when it came to simple things like cooking. Simple things that should be easy to do competently.

Mary wandered along the aisles, picking the same can of this, the same bag of that as she always did. One of her eyes focused on the shelves, the other on her son Zach whom she had instructed to wait at the front counter. He would be all right there.

So far today, Mary had given all her time to other people. To make ends meet, she worked as a cleaner for a few of the wealthier families on her street, diligently scrubbing corners and windowsills, doing the laundry, dusting, polishing and performing any other duties that they demanded of her.

Her work ethic was impeccable, and needed to be. She knew that they knew she needed the work, and even though some of the families treated her as a friend, they were not afraid to work her hard because they knew they could. Most of them did not need her services and only hired her because they were aware of her situation and took pity on her, plus she was a very cheap source of labour which was very attractive. The wealthiest were quite often the most miserly.

After some polite gossip upon her arrival, and catching up on current neighbourhood events (Mary did after all, have her nose in a lot of the other families' homes and was a valuable source of inside information), they were quick to set her to task. Kindly though, they permitted her to bring her son Zach along to their houses knowing that he required her oversight, and without him present they could not have her and her inexpensive services. He was a very shy, quiet boy and a pleasure to have around, no trouble at all.

Half way down the sweets aisle, Mary heard trouble at the counter of the grocery store. The checkout operator had a raised voice and was clearly annoyed at something, or somebody. Conscious that this is where she had let Zach stand and play with some toys, she rushed to the end of the far-too-long aisle and hoped that what she thought was going on, was not actually going on.

"You know, you should answer somebody if somebody talks to you. What's wrong with you, kid? " The checkout operator was a girl around sixteen, chewing gum very ungracefully and was suffering from chronic acne. Her skirt was above the knee, exposing a couple of bruises, Mary did not even want to think about how she got them, and observed what was most definitely a love bite on her neck. This was a weekend job she clearly did not care about.

She was waving her hand in front of Zach's lightly freckled but emotionally blank face, trying to get a response but only succeeded in knocking his cap off, exposing a shock of dark hair. She picked the hat up, twirling it on her finger and turned to look up as Mary rounded the corner, and caught herself before she began her next tirade at the boy. She stopped chewing her gum.

"Hey lady that's your boy right? You should teach him some manners, what kind of mother are you? He won't even tell me his name when I asked, just trying to make conversation. Just stands there staring. Rude kid. Badly brought up I'd say, not like when I was growing up." She continued chewing and then proceeded to open and read a teen magazine at the counter. Zach was still just standing there, staring ahead, but trembling slightly.

The fury that Mary felt boil up inside her directed towards the young girl quickly turned to concern for her son. She ran towards Zach and smothered him in her arms, kissing him on the top of his head, walking him away from the checkout girl. "It's okay my beautiful boy, it's okay. Let's go. Let's go home baby."

Mary snatched Zach's hat out of the girl's hands and was halfway out the door but simply could not leave the grocery store without defending her mothering and justifying her son's behaviour. She walked over to the girl and grabbed the magazine from her grasp, slammed it closed on the counter and held the girl's head in between her hands so that their eyes met.

A frazzled woman with a look of fragility, behind Mary's timid façade was a woman who had suffered and developed an inner strength kept well hidden, so when it emerged it meant business. Her grey hair turned silver, her brown eyes burned red and her thin frame transformed into an imposing figure. A look of fear could be seen in the girl's eyes but she did not pull away. Mary saw this and very nearly didn't go ahead with what she had to say, alarmed that she had momentarily turned into a person she didn't know and had rarely become before. She took a breath and controlled herself before speaking.

"For your information -" she looked down at the girls name tag. "- Janelle, my beautiful son has autism and I know that somebody as young and ignorant as yourself probably doesn't even know what that is so I feel sorry for you, but the next time you go around accusing somebody of bad parenting or bad behaviour maybe you should shut your mouth until you know what you are talking about. Got me?"

Mary released the girl's head, turned around and quickly walked to her son who quietly remained where she had left him and departed the store without any groceries.

That night it was very quiet at the dinner table. Mary had a spare can of beans in the pantry that she heated up on the electric stove, burning them, her mind elsewhere, and separated them into two equal portions for herself and Zach. A single globe hovered above the dinner table, not even encased in a shade and uncomfortably bright but it hadn't even crossed Mary's mind to replace it.

Normally she would be continuously speaking to her son at the table, the many doctors they had visited all recommended as much subtle stimulation as possible for him, but tonight she just did not have the energy. The altercation at the grocery store was on her mind and she reflected it was just one of the many testing moments she faced daily from the public. She deserved these little punishments. She had made her son this way, she must now pay penance.

After the makeshift dinner was finished and the dishes were done it was time for her to put Zach to bed. They knelt by the side of his bed ready for nightly prayers, the same every night. Mary uttered the familiar prayers for their good health and that tomorrow will be a happy day, thanking the Lord and then performing the sign of the cross on herself and her son.

These were quite superficial gestures, her son was only eleven and did not understand the concept of a higher power, and to be honest she wasn't sure if any higher power out there would be able to connect with her son anyway. The impenetrable barriers that had developed and encased his mind, layer upon layer, were impervious, no matter to whom or what.

It was Diah who had brought up the idea of a family prayer before bed time. He was a good looking man, smartly cut brown hair, kind eyes that looked deep into Mary and could see her altruistic soul. Keeping up appearances meant a lot to him and she could see how Zach did not fit into this perfect picture he wanted to portray, so he worked on chipping away at his son with the hope of revealing a normal boy beneath what he saw as the imperfect exterior. He would insist that Zach be included and involved in as many activities as possible, even though without fail they would result in frustration and regret that the attempt was ever made.

Tucking her boy into bed and pulling the soft covers over him up to his chin, Mary stared down, bottom lip trembling. "He will be a good looking boy, such a waste," she had overheard one of her cleaning clients Mrs Curtin remark to Mr Curtin under her breath one afternoon, unaware that Mary could very easily hear the words echoing in the large and mostly empty house. A waste? Is that what people thought of her son?

A tear formed in the corner of her eye but was brushed away in an instant. She was used to hearing the comments, absorbing the pity, finding the strength to wear a smile. Mustn't dwell. She bent over to give her already sleeping son a kiss on his forehead and left the room. She knew he would remain in the same position until morning.

Closing his door gently, Mary continued her nightly ritual, and that was to walk from her son's room to her own, down the dark corridor on the worn carpet, and kneel next to her own bed and say her own personal prayers.

Praying for good health and a happy day were not on her lips here. Every night Mary pleaded to know what she had done to deserve this life, and though she loved her son with all her heart, he was the reason she was now alone and taking care of him singlehandedly. She prayed that one day he would respond, that he would look at her with recognition in his eyes, and that he would be able to utter his first word. Zach had never spoken in his entire life.

Time to climb into bed and do the same all over again tomorrow. Mary stretched out under her old blanket, scrunching her toes and enjoying the warmth it provided. Falling asleep was always a problem, a mind full of worry was always switched on and even when she slept her dreams were not pleasant. Consequently, waking up was never easy. She had bought a new alarm clock yesterday but it hadn't worked this morning, and made her late for arrival at the Newton residence.

Why couldn't things just work the way they were supposed to? How hard is it for an alarm to go off at the designated time that it is set for? How hard is it for somebody to keep some plants alive? How hard is it for somebody to just go to the grocery store and buy some groceries? Why is it so hard to have a child that can walk and talk and just be normal?

Mary sat bolt upright in bed and inhaled sharply, absolutely horrified at what had just crossed her mind. She became distressed with guilt and her heart pounded out of her chest. Had she just dozed off and her subconscious thoughts bubbled to the surface? She didn't think she was capable of such an inhumane thought about her own son. Mary was unable to get back to sleep and lay there as stiff as a board, afraid that the thoughts would come back.

Unmoving and silent, she could hear the nocturnal sounds of the house come alive. Ears straining, there was the slight creak of the side gate and the brushing of the neighbour's tree against her guttering. Hypnotised by the variety of sounds, she slowly began to drift off into the night and that was when she heard a voice come from her son's room. Indistinct, unintelligible, but a voice nonetheless.

Mary froze, afraid to breathe, every single part of her being on full alert with all senses focused on that small bedroom just down the corridor. Her heart thumped with an intensity that scared her and she slowly sat upright, head tilted at an angle as if that would enable her to capture the slightest whisper. The deep, muffled sound that came from her son's room this time made her wish that she had buried her head under the covers instead.

A long, slow shriek reached her ears from a closer source and, looking around, it took a moment for Mary to realise that it was coming from her.

Sun 20 Sept 1959 8:55am
Ira

Today was just another day, but Ira was up later than normal thanks to a nice sleep-in he had given himself because he only had one job on and that was going to be around lunchtime. Sitting at the dining table reading the paper and waiting for his wife Lucy to bring him breakfast, he flicked through the pages quickly. It seemed as if every paper was exactly the same every day, give or take. There was always at least a murder, an assault and a fatal car accident, guaranteed.

Oh, what fools people were to repeatedly read this relentless tirade of bad news and human atrocity, and at first thing in the morning before their day had even begun. It was no wonder the general consensus amongst the public was that the state of the world was deteriorating into another level of misery, suffering a daily barrage of depression like that.

Now in a bad mood, Ira barely grunted when his aproned wife brought out a very well presented omelette along with his favourite fruit chutney and a cup of tea. Berating himself for letting the newspaper get to him, he sang out "Thank you Lucy" appreciatively and made some noises of approval as he admired and then began to devour his lovingly constructed meal, his thin moustache capturing a portion until his strong calloused hands vigorously wiped his face down.

Lucy was the love of his life, a catch way too good for the likes of himself and he never became complacent within their relationship. She was an ex-model for used car advertisements in the local newspaper, taller than he and her long black hair and striking doe eyes caused many a head to turn, mostly to wonder what she was doing with a man like Ira.

Dex, the Staffordshire was as reliable as clockwork and trotted around the corner to lay at his feet, tongue lolled to one side, hoping for a stray morsel to somehow fall off of Ira's fork, miss the plate, miss the table entirely and land on the floor. Dex was often disappointed but never gave up hope.

Back to skimming the paper, he attempted to cultivate the bad mood he had developed because he would probably need to harness it at his job later. Ira turned to the political section. He remembered his father always used to read this section twice, and would state that it was the only type of news that someone of intelligence would consider worth reading.

"The political stories change, they matter, they are actually relevant to your life, kiddo. But don't you ever become a politician or you will bring the family name to shame. They are all crooks."

Ira turned to his left and looked at the photo of his father on the mantelpiece next to an icon of Jesus and made the sign of the cross. "If everybody followed the word of God, the world would be a better place, huh Pop. No crooks. But the paper would be a lot thinner."

He noticed how he was looking more and more like his father every day, a surly face more often than not presenting contradictory warm and caring hazel eyes to the world, dark sun-kissed latino skin contrasting against the wisps of grey hair forming at his temples, wrinkles forming at the creases of his eyes. Age was catching up on him and gifting him with a round belly that was harder to hide these days, courtesy of his wife's meals.

He licked his lips and turned back to his plate. "Damn this omelette is good. Lucy you are gifted, I will give you that!"

Scanning over the political articles, his eyes found the familiar face of a female journalist accompanying a lengthy piece on foreign aid. She was easy on the eye too. Not all journalists got to put their photo next to their articles, but he could sense what the criteria might be. It was quality, concise and informative and he read it to the end.

After reading the politics section twice he rolled the newspaper up, walked out the front door and threw the paper onto his neighbour Jim's porch. Jim wasn't doing so well financially and Ira helped him out whenever he really needed it, but for the most part he just acted as Jim's paper boy. The jobs section would at least keep him occupied for the morning, and then he could get back to lying on the couch.

"Hector!" Ira called for his son when he got back inside, and a four year old mini version of himself minus the belly and wrinkles sprinted into the room as fast as his little legs would propel him towards his father. Simultaneously, Dex bounded into the room to see what the yelling was about and before he could bowl Hector over, Ira scooped his son up with one hand. His son was already the little gentleman, with many adult traits.

A few months ago at a cousin's wedding, Ira had Hector dressed in a miniature tuxedo, and the little boy loved the bow tie so much that he now had a collection of six, which he wore on rotation and would not leave the house without wearing. People would point and stare, ladies would melt and men would nod their heads approvingly. Ira felt that his son was already heading on the right trajectory in life and as long as he didn't follow the footsteps of his father too closely he would do all right.

"Wanna come with me and grab some stuff from the hardware store for the job I have to do today? Daddy has been putting it off but this job can wait no longer. You can help him carry things. Can my big strong boy help his daddy?" Hector nodded enthusiastically. It filled Ira with an inner glow to know that his son would do anything to spend time and help out his father in much the same way that he used to enjoy feeling like an adult when his dad would take him along on errands.

He remembered once when he was maybe around five years old he helped his father repaint an old door. He was wearing a brand new pair of kids jeans, the type with an elasticated waist, and, being so proud of helping do a grown up's job he wanted everybody to know that he was grown up too, so he deliberately brushed his new jeans against the freshly painted door, resulting in a large white mark across his hip and thigh.

Later when they went back to the shops, Ira was beaming because everybody they walked past could see the paint mark, and now they knew that he had been painting just like a grown up. Looking back at that day, he now realised that nobody would have noticed, or cared. The spanking he received for ruining his new jeans was well deserved.

"Honey we're going to the hardware store, do you need anything?"

"Yeah, a wrench and some washers and please have a look in the husband section to see if there's one there that can help with the dishes every once in a while." The cheeky grin that Ira loved so much was all over her face. Her dimpled smile framed by that jet black wavy hair was contagious.

"Hilarious honey! So.. No wrench or washers??"

"What am I going to do with a wrench and washers you big dummy? I don't even know what a washer actually is."

"I love you baby."

"Love you too."

"Okay Mr Man, let's jump in the pickup." Ira picked up Hector and heaved him into the high passenger seat of the Chevy pickup.

Arriving at the local hardware store he grabbed a trolley, handed the job of pushing it over to his excited son who could barely reach the handle, and proceeded to walk through the aisles perusing his short shopping list.

"Shovel, concrete, rope, lime, tarpaulin." He wasn't sure if he would use all or none of the items today but it was best to be prepared for whatever the job had to offer. He was good at what he did and he had earned a reputation by being an immaculate planner and evaluating contingency scenarios.

They came across the concrete first, and after heaving it into the trolley it instantly became too heavy to push for the upset Hector who reluctantly accepted that maybe he was not as strong as a proper adult just yet. Ira stepped in to rescue his son from the situation.

"Hey kiddo, I can't push this big heavy trolley on my own, I need a strong man to help me. Do you know anybody who can help?"

"Me, Daddy, me!"

He could do this kind of thing forever. He knew that kids grow up so fast, he would only be experiencing this day, this moment once and once only, he needed to remind himself to take the time out to smell the roses and appreciate every second. He wouldn't be around forever and in his line of work there were plenty of accidents and occasions where fathers never made it home to their families at the end of the day.

He knew many friends who seemed happy to stick to one job and keep at it, progressing a little more each day until they had become extremely successful over time, forging reputations and growing their own businesses. Imagine where he would be now if he had finished school, started plumbing, locksmithing, it didn't matter what, but sticking with it was what would have made a difference.

The one thing Ira never wanted to do was live with regrets. He had historically made the decisions that he felt were right at the time, and now looking back he had lived a varied and interesting life while all his friends had been labouring away at the same craft for years. Some were happy, most were less than, whether they had a successful business or not.

It wasn't until he took on a labouring job for Aaban that everything changed. Ira had never looked for a mentor, and to be honest didn't really know what they were or did. Going about his business as per usual, not doing anything out of the ordinary, Aaban recognised something in Ira and helped him to focus and develop a new set of skills, and instead of becoming a jack of all trades he now had found a niche for himself and business was good.

He did not have to work too often, but when he did, the pay was good. In a short space of time he had accumulated a nice house, nice car, solid reputation equivalent to his friends that had been in business for years. It was nice to have found a path.

After loading the back of the pickup with the newly bought hardware, Ira and Hector drove back in silence. One of them was thinking about what the afternoon's job would bring, whether the preparation was sufficient and what degree of difficulty it might be, and whether contingency plans were necessary. The other was thinking about ice cream.

"Honey, your two favourite men are back!" Hector beamed at being called a man and he flexed his biceps at his father, who flexed his back in return.

"How are my two boys?" Lucy asked. Hector frowned at the sudden downgrade from man to boy, and flexed his muscles at his mother.

"I could not have lifted all my heavy equipment without this strong guy here. I'd be stuck in that shop forever!" He ruffled Hector's hair, who immediately brushed it back with well-practiced movements and then adjusted his bow tie.

"Okay honey I've gotta go and do a job, I should be back just after lunch time. Wouldn't it be amazing if there were toasted ham and cheese sandwiches ready to be eaten when I got back!" He winked at her boyishly and she smiled, then tilted her head and affected a puzzled look.

"What are you saying darling, I'm not quite sure I understand? If you want something, why don't you explain yourself clearly and make it known what you want! I'm not psychic you know. Jeez!"

They both burst out laughing.

"Okay I shouldn't be gone too long. See you a bit later."
He left via the back door and hopped back in the pickup. Lucy and Hector waved through the window, and he could hear Dex barking like crazy. Wow, the whole household really loved him, both human and non-human.

It was time to find Eddie and get today's job over and done with.

Sun 20 Sept 1959 8:00am
The Man Unknown

The rusty bell that was attached to the top of the door was virtually redundant thanks to the high pitched, irritating creak of the hinges, which did more than a good enough job at indicating that somebody was either coming or going from the tiny diner in which Doris worked. Doris was not the owner, however, her fifteen year tenure was as solid a foundation as any for her to assume a sense of ownership and pride, and she treated every loyal customer as graciously and with as much hospitality as if they were her own family.

The bell rang, the door creaked, and Doris's ears which were so attuned to the familiar sound did not even have to transmit a message to her brain, the automatic response came from the subconscious and the fifty one year old woman swivelled like somebody thirty years her junior, blue and white checked skirt billowing outwards and a smile appearing on her cheerful yet tired face.

"Welcome to Cassidy's! Best coffee in the state!" It wasn't technically a lie if you believed it was true.

The well-dressed older gentleman who had just entered was already making his way towards a long table in the dark back corner that would seat about six comfortably. He looked at his watch and then glanced at the loudly ticking clock on the wall of the diner, his weathered face curling at the edges into a smile as he sat down slowly with a degree of huffing and puffing as if his joints had not been exposed to such strenuous activity for a while.

He sank heavily into the chair and let out a sigh, as if pondering how he would inevitably go about having to stand himself back up again. He pulled a checked pocket square from his blazer and peculiarly rested it on his left leg, then took his hat off and placed it to his right.

Doris thought that the best words that would describe this gentleman were "well-to-do' and 'good-natured'. Probably well educated, aloof and dignified, very particular about how he liked things, possibly a military man who once, but no longer had a wife. Doris thought that she was quite astute at forming these profiles and would not be surprised if she were completely correct. Her eyebrows raised slightly and a semi-grin formed, pleasure showing at how smart she thought she was.

After being satisfied that he was now settled, Doris swanned over gracefully, notepad and pen in hand, and asked if she could get him some coffee.

"Black coffee please, I'm waiting for some friends to arrive, you see."

The order was taken, passed on to the appropriate staff member, and then the coffee arrived but was not touched until five minutes later. Preoccupied, the man's eyes scanned the front door, then to his watch, then to the clock. And repeat.

The bell rang, the door creaked, people came and went, drank and ate, chatted and laughed, but there was still no sign of the gentleman's friends. He was sitting bolt upright, looking very proud, dapper and formal, and yet with a sad look in his eye that would seem to ask why nobody would look his way, or compliment him on his outstanding appearance. He was the best dressed person in the diner, and sitting solo at this point in time surely it would be natural for somebody to approach him and admiringly ask why such a splendid man who should be very popular was sitting all alone? He sat.

It was sad for Doris to observe this clear longing for human acknowledgement and interaction. She walked over to the gentleman after his coffee was long finished and began to make conversation. She opened her mouth to speak, but was cut off when the man raised his finger in the air to cut her off.

"My friends will be here shortly, I'm expecting them any second now," he said. "I know it may be impolite, but you know, I'd love to have a coffee before they arrive."

"Of course. I'll get you that coffee sir, I'm sure your friends won't mind if you get one in ahead of them." The poor man, he probably doesn't have the mental acuity that he used to.

It was now 9:30am. The gentleman had been in the diner for an hour and a half, taking up the big table at the back. Doris didn't mind. She knew he would be here alone until 11:30am, and then leave cash on the table and exit without saying goodbye. Just like he had done every day without fail, for every year since Doris had worked at the diner.

Waiting for friends that would never come.

Sun 20 Sept 1959 *9:15am*
Jacob Disassembled

Jacob stepped hesitantly into the office of his manager and stood there. In all the time he had worked in the building, he had only been into this room twice. Once when he first interviewed for the job many years ago, and the second time was now. Several managers had come and gone in this time and never had the courtesy of a visit been extended to him.

It was a pristine office, not a huge space but it was cosy and shielded the hum of the office outside. Jacob's stride was cut off after only a single step as the room was taken up mostly by a large mahogany desk that was an obviously cheap piece of furniture posing as an expensive antique.

The current guardian of the desk was clearly so proud of it that they refused to hide it under any paperwork or signs of any work at all for that matter. All that was obscuring the view of the desktop was a phone, a typewriter and a pen. Jacob's mind immediately went to wondering exactly what Mr Higgs did in here. Next his mind went to the reason for what he was doing in there, and he spoke to the man sitting behind the desk.

"Mr Higgs, Faraday sent me in to see you."

Higgs looked at him for a second with a slightly puzzled look in his squinting eyes and then coughed, leaned back on his chair, arms behind his head. "O-kayyyy." Suddenly it seemed as if he remembered that he was the superior of the person in front of him and sharply sat forward, leaned his elbows on the desk and pointed to the chair in the corner of the room mustering an air of authority. "Okay. Sit."

Higgs had been manager for about a year now and was the friend of the son of someone who knew the owner of the business, or something like that as far as Jacob knew. A youngster in comparison to Jacob, he estimated there was about twenty years between them in Higgs' favour, though Higgs already was losing his blond wispy hair and was going to age quite badly. His white short-sleeved shirt had sweat marks at the underarms and his tie was poorly knotted. His appearance reflected his management style, a bit loose and lacking any serious care.

He normally didn't like to get amongst the troops, and preferred the ivory castle way of managing. Jacob imagined he used to be the bully in school, or was bullied because he took a visible joy in being superior to others and displaying that he was the top dog, even if in rank only.

Jacob sat. The two stared at each other for about a minute. Higgs was the first to speak. "Okay, talk to me," as if giving Jacob permission.

Jacob was a bit taken aback at this, he was expecting the manager to welcome him in and excitedly tell him about how he was going to solve Jacob's problem of not making the business any sales.

"Faraday mentioned that the two of you were out last night and were discussing my um, sales situation or lack thereof and how to remedy it. To help the business."

"Ah yes. Right. Ohhh that Faraday!" He smiled and shook a fist in the air as if to curse Faraday for something cheeky that he had done and caught him out on, but that he would get him back for later.

"Look, Jake, I wasn't going to tell you this until the end of the week, but it looks like now is the time. Yes, last night Faraday and I were discussing your performance and how it was affecting the business and how we could fix things. Your sales have been quite low for a while now, virtually zero, and you know what Jake, you are the best salesperson I have ever seen, you really actually care about the people you deal with and it's not like you are even actually selling to them, you genuinely are trying to help them, but what is the point of being the best salesperson if you can't close the deal at the end of all your hard work? You are too nice. You can't close. Do you realise that half of Faraday's sales are from families I send him around to re-visit after you have already seen them? They want to buy our product, Faraday makes sure that they end up with our product. Like I said, you are the best salesperson I have ever seen that isn't going to make it in this industry."

"Okay so what can I do about it then Mr Higgs?" Jacob found it difficult to call a man twenty years his junior 'Mister'. "What were you and Faraday discussing? Some closing techniques? I am keen to learn and find my form again. I used to be pretty good."

"Yes, I have heard from some of the longer serving staff members that you used to be a performer, but that was long ago, before your "incident". Now you are just a visitor to this industry. I'm sorry Jake, but last night Faraday and I were talking about you and how to help the business, and the only way to help the business is to let you go."

Blood pulsed through Jacob's ears, louder and louder until he thought he might pass out. His bottom lip trembled and the room spun as he processed this unexpected 'solution' to the business problem he faced.

Completely ignoring Jacob's stunned reaction, Higgs continued without empathy. "I was planning to keep you around until the end of the month before breaking the news but Faraday has obviously opened his big mouth and so now is the time. I'm sorry. You've been with us for a while, I've had a look at the package you will get and I think you will find it's quite generous. No gold watch or anything though, but there is a certificate of employment you can keep to remind yourself of us."

Higgs stood up and extended his hand which Jacob looked at it meekly before eventually shaking it. Higgs' hand was clammy, cold and inhuman. An insincere handshake, as if Higgs had just read that it is what you were supposed to do in this particular situation from some managerial textbook.

"Talk to the girl at the front desk and she will sort everything out for you. Enjoy, I'm almost jealous of you. It's for the best!"

Turning around slowly, not quite sure if what just happened actually had really occurred, Jacob exited the office for the second and last time. Everything seemed to be happening in fast motion. A million scenarios flickered and played out before his eyes, none of them optimistic for the future. How would he eat? Pay rent? Why was God doing this to him on top of everything else?

Failure. That was what he was successful at. Failing. What would everybody think? What would Ava think? How would she react? Ava... This and more flew through his mind before he had even shut the office door. It clicked behind him.

He was staring at a sea of faces, all focused on him with such a varying range of expressions he almost wanted to laugh except that he felt self-conscious at being the centre of attention. The office was silent until Faraday stepped forward and exclaimed cheerfully "Now, that look on your face is worth me being late for my across town appointment, even if it does cost me a sale!"

Carol stepped across the room and started yelling at Faraday again. Jacob did not hear what she was saying, he was too aware that he was the butt of a joke that the whole office was clearly in on and so just looked down at the ground and walked towards his desk, feeling eyes on him and all too aware now of the chuckles he could hear.

Arriving back at his desk and sinking into his chair, not even noticing the sharp spring dig into him, Jacob took stock of the situation and let everything settle. There was a time when he thought that he had reached rock bottom, everything he had cared for had been taken from him so his withdrawal into himself was his only form of protection against the cruel outside world.

He thought he had made himself impervious to all forms of hardship, whether imposed by people or circumstance, but now he had sunk even further into the swirling blackness enveloping him, and in full view of the entire office he began to cry.

Half an hour later Jacob was slowly walking home, retracing the steps that he had made only about an hour earlier, though this time carrying a small cardboard box containing his few belongings in it from the office. Not even looking to see if any cars were coming he crossed the road to his reach his home, well, it was his home for now as long as he could keep up with the rent.

The whole trip just a blur. In fact, the whole morning was a blur and seemed like some sort of surreal dream. His mind pictured Faraday laughing, and then his face faded away and became Higgs' face, then Carol's, then the whole office.

He remembered Carol coming over to him when he was in the middle of some deep, heaving sobs, putting her hand on his shoulder and just standing next to him. They never spoke to each other much on a deep level, but they had formed a bond in their short time together in the same building based on mutual disdain of the personalities they worked with. Embarrassment washed over Jacob but disappeared soon after he realised he would never see those people again.

Mr Derby! With no more morning walks to work he would never see his friendly accidental acquaintance again either. Jacob wondered if Mr Derby would even notice or care that their morning rendezvous would never happen again. This caused some pain. He didn't even know where Mr Derby lived, his phone number, not even his first name.

All these branches of his life were disappearing, being cut off, sawn away, cutting him down to what would eventually be just a stump, a man with nothing left but himself, no link to anybody else, or anything.

At least there will be nothing left to hurt me then, Jacob thought, just as the next door neighbour's dog snapped him out of his fugue state. Chloe didn't normally bark but was agitated at something right now.

He realised he had been standing at his front door for a long time, so he put the cardboard box down, found his keys, and let himself in. There was only one thing that could make his day any worse, and she was inside.

Sun 20 Sept 1959 *1:15am*
Mary Reflecting

Mary tore herself out from under her covers and ran down the corridor to Zach's room, cursing that she had never fixed his door which had a problem of sticking. Just another thing that she had not attended to in Diah's absence. Yanking it open on the second try, she entered the room and with a sigh observed that Zach was there, asleep in exactly the position she had left him.

Mary stopped and evaluated the situation. She had definitely heard a voice coming from her son's room, the only other person in the house. She had been asleep, or at least dozing, but there was no way her mind would just manifest an event that she had just been thinking about only moments before?

This thought brought the obvious to her attention and she felt foolish. Of course it was all in her head. Wanting Zach to speak was something that burned in her mind so brightly that it nearly engulfed all other thoughts with its intensity. The inability of Zach to partake in two way communication was what had hurt her marriage to Diah the most.

Mary and Diah had shared some classes in high school and had bonded over their stance on animal welfare. Mary's compassion for all living things saw her tirelessly standing up for the rights of those without a voice, and each weekend she would volunteer (or more accurately, just show up) at the animal shelter across town, nearly a two hour journey but the commute meant nothing to her.

On her way to the shelter Mary would look up across town and sadly visualise a dense black cloud of suffering hanging in the air, a marker, an indicator that the place she was heading towards contained innocent beings that had every right to carry out their existence as nature intended but were not able to. Instead they were either dumped or left for dead at the shelter because it was in the nature of men to act as God and decide that these animals who could not look after themselves were not going to be loved or looked after, and denied their right to exist in a nurturing environment.

Cruelty to a child is an atrocity that cannot be forgiven, but a child is human, and whether that child has an inner understanding of cruelty due to being human itself is unknown, but that child can surely comprehend cruelty better than an animal which is a truly innocent creature and could never know why it is being mistreated, in most cases by the human to whom it feels unconditional love for.

On her way home from the shelter she would decide that the black cloud hovering in the air was now a little smaller, a little lighter in colour. It was not long before herself and Diah were making the commute together hand in hand. Her enthusiasm for the cause was contagious and he was drawn into her world.

Every now and again they would each take home a cat or dog that needed special attention, and after they were eventually married and living together they continued to enjoy the patter of small paws around the house. It was not long before Zach became the new addition to the household.

Zach's diagnosis came at quite a late stage, Mary and Diah continually telling themselves in denial that he was just a late developer until there came a time when the situation could not be ignored any more. He avoided eye contact, suffered overreactions to certain moderate situations, and displayed a few obsessive behaviours.

At the age where Mary and Diah should have introduced him to the outside world, to other children, to their friends and family, they instead kept him sheltered inside and proceeded to do what they could to ensure he had a relatively normal life according to them, though Mary was sure that another reason for this was that Diah suffered a level of embarrassment of his son, which broke her heart.

The love shown to him was unequalled, and the caring hearts of his parents were just happy that they now had something to look after that had less than four legs. Diah could not stop commenting on how strange it was to have a little person in the house that looked a little bit like him, and a little bit like Mary. Mary would make fun of this, and tell Diah to stop staring at Zach because it would give him a complex, but inside agreed with Diah that to look at somebody that wasn't you, but to be able see yourself in them took some getting used to.

Life at home rolled on and Diah began to fulfil his fatherly dream and engage Zach in all the things that he himself had loved as a child: building model aeroplanes, soccer, learning the guitar, but none of these things attracted the interest of the child. Fun was still had, however, entirely by Diah who enjoyed the nostalgia of being able to indulge in long lost youthful pleasures in a totally legitimate manner now that he had a son, but he knew that the father-son factor was the most important element of this, and that element was missing.

One afternoon, Mary was inside baking a hummingbird cake, a popular choice of dessert for Diah who suffered from an extreme sweet tooth, when she heard his raised voice coming from the backyard. Ignoring it, she continued her work in the kitchen, until she heard the crying of the young boy. Sprinting out the back, she found Diah with his arms around Zach, cradling him and rocking him in his arms, a soccer ball lying nearby.

"What the hell is going on? Why were you yelling and why is he crying?" She snatched Zach away from Diah and proceeded to examine him thoroughly. "His face is red, did you hit him in the face?" Diah's face gave him away. "With the ball?"

"It was an accident sweetheart, I was kicking the ball to him and it just came off of my foot a little strong. Poor little guy." He ruffled Zach's hair playfully, hoping to avert the potentially explosive situation with his wife. They had rarely argued or had any form of disagreement during their marriage since confrontation was in neither of their personalities, but a mother's protective instincts could not be predicted.

"I heard you yelling beforehand, what was that about? To me it sounds like you were angry, probably because he wasn't kicking the ball back to you, and then all of a sudden he gets a ball in his face. Is that what happened?" The look she received told her that she was spot on with her recap.

"He never talks, he never does anything! I'm here kicking the ball to myself while he just stares. Hey buddy, it's not hard to kick a ball! Or talk!" He paced up and back, face showing extreme worry, and Mary could not tell if it was for their son or because he knew he was in trouble. A bit of both maybe. She didn't give him the benefit of the doubt, however, and her control over herself diminished further.

"He is right here, he can hear you! Poor baby." She squeezed him tightly, and carried him inside. The house was full of smoke. She lay Zach on the couch, pulled the now blackened cake out of the oven and threw it in the bin. She knew she would have thrown it in the bin anyway, rather than let Diah have the pleasure of eating it. Diah slept on the couch that night.

Looking back at this period, Mary realised this was where her happily married life began to unravel. She loved her son, of course she did, and she knew Diah did too but his expectations of Zach were higher than hers. She just wanted to be a mother, to feed, to cook, to look after him. Diah needed the interaction, to go and play ball at the park, to teach his son about girls, how to ride a bike, and he would never be able to have that.

She noticed the slow detachment of her husband, firstly from their son, and then from her. His coping mechanism was to make himself numb, and he learned that if he didn't interact with his son he couldn't be upset by him. He almost completely ignored Zach and then eventually Mary. She missed what they used to have together, a team, commuting to the animal shelter, fighting to help those without a voice, and now their very son was one of the voiceless, and her husband was giving up on him.

From the day she made Diah sleep on the couch, she could see that it was now their own house that had a black cloud hovering over it, and she knew it would not be getting smaller any time soon.

The day that Diah left Mary began like any other day. He silently got dressed and ready for work in the living room, the couch now his permanent bed. His clothes were draped carelessly over the furniture both clean and dirty, and once when Mary attempted to sort through them for a laundry run in an attempt to promote any form of interaction, Diah glared at her with a loathing in his eyes that made her physically shrink and cower away and back out of the room.

She had done nothing wrong. Why was he doing this to her? How could a person who was once filled with so much love now be so cruel? Their unspoken agreement was to stay out of each other's way, living like strangers, every second of it breaking Mary's heart a little more.

After Diah had readied himself for work, he closed the curtains once again and silently slipped out through the back door. Mary wept, as she did every morning when she knew there was nobody around to hear her except for her son, but the sound of the back door reopening for an unknown reason caused her to hold her breath and swallow her tears for a moment.

Diah must have forgotten to take something with him. She heard him open a drawer, then open another, and then his footsteps began up the corridor, where Mary was suddenly petrified. "He's coming into my room!" and she curled up underneath the covers. What did he want?

A curse word came from her husband as Zach's sticky door pulled open loudly. Mary's mind frame completely switched. Diah was not after her. Her adrenaline levels rose, her defensive instincts transformed into those of protection. Listening carefully, she heard speaking, it was soft but in the silent house she caught nearly every word.

"Hi buddy, how's it going? Sorry to wake you up," he whispered. "Wow, it's been a while since I've had a good look at you, you really are growing. And you need a haircut too, hey scruffy guy." He brushed Zach's hair away from his face and stared for a long while, then spoke again.

"Daddy's going away. I know you haven't seen him very much lately, I hope that makes things easier for you. Gosh you look like your mother." Another pause.

"I'm going away. Going back to live with my mummy and daddy for a while. You remember gran and pops? Christ, I don't even know if you can understand any of this. Can you hear me?? I have to go kiddo, but I want to give you a couple of things, you know, to have for when you are older and one day you can maybe think that your old man wasn't so bad. Diah carefully placed a book on the bedside table, then stood up and started to pace and talk.

"I just can't take it any longer, it really kills me to know that I have a son, but I don't actually *have a son*. Remember how we used to say prayers every night? This is my bible that my dad, your pops, gave me. Now it's yours and I wrote a little something inside it for you. I don't need it anymore because I know God ain't real or else he would never have put me through what I've been through with you." Diah sat there, then wiped his eyes and nose dry, and struggled to twist his wedding ring off of his finger, but succeeded and placed it next to the bible on the bedside table.

"You're the man of the house now buddy, I can't take this with me because your mom wouldn't want me to have it. I'm not sure if I deserve to wear it either. I don't know. Am I doing something wrong? Am I a bad man? Does any man think he is ever doing anything bad? I think all men think they are doing the right thing, it just depends on which side of the coin you are looking in on the situation from.

Your mom and probably all the neighbours will see me as a miserable runaway husband, escaping from a situation that he can't handle, doesn't want to handle, and leaving a poor woman alone with a massive burden. But the way I see it, it's the best way to stop your mom crying every morning. I hear her. I know I treat her bad but I don't mean to, she's a good woman and I love her. I think the only way I can ever allow her to be happy again is to leave. She needs to forget about me because I'm not good for her. And that's the side of the coin I'm coming from. I don't belong in the picture. I'm doing a good thing here…. a good thing." He blew his nose.

"I hope she puts the ring on a chain for you or something until your fingers are big enough to wear it. It's engraved on the inside, it's you and your mum versus the world now. So long son." And, after having a look around the room, and one last look at his boy's face, Diah turned and left them both.

Mary's eyes snapped open and she was drawn out of the horrible flashback, realising that she had been cradling Zach in her arms for maybe an hour now, re-living that morning when she became more alone than ever, for the thousandth time. The high pitched creaking of the house eerily reminded her why she was there in her son's room at that time of night.

The voice… could Zach have made that noise? Her mind sped frantically through scenario after scenario but could not come up with a meaningful or logical explanation. She must have been dreaming… but, imagine, if Zach began to start speaking.. she could find Diah and he would come home, surely? Surely he would. Her heart beat faster at the thought of a happy family once more, it had been so long. She was so tired.

"Don't be crazy, go to sleep," she told herself. Tucking Zach in, she trundled off to her bed, and fell asleep after her mind slowed down.

About two hours later in the dead of night, a dog barked in the distance and then all was silent again. Inside the bedroom with the door that stuck closed on occasion, Zach's lip twitched and his left eye flickered.

Three hours later, his eyes were wide open, his mouth opening and closing, gasping, mouthing words, the same words over and over. No voice, no sound except for the exhalation of air from his lungs.

"God is coming….."

Sun 20 Sept 1959 **11:35am**
Jacob's Revelation

Jacob trudged down the corridor and stopped after a few steps. The first thing that went through his mind was how different his house looked during the day. He noticed that the sun was at just the right angle so that it was streaming in through the small ornate stained glass window on his left, and projecting a glorious array of colours and patterns on the right hand side of the hall. That something so simple could create something so beautiful started to choke him up.

The realisation dawned upon Jacob that for most of his working life he had only seen the inside of his house when he was half asleep and performing his routine morning preparations for work, or after he had come home exhausted in the evening. Even on the weekends when he was not in the office, he was out on the road, paying house calls to potential clients and never home. To see something you are so familiar with but literally in a different light was a revelation to Jacob.

The shadows formed by the furniture were falling at angles strange to him, areas that were normally in darkness were now bathed in light and areas usually lit were now in darkness. It was like all rules had been turned on their head and everything you thought you knew was now wrong. One day you had a job the next you didn't.

Was this a temporary alternate reality, or would the world be like this forevermore? He didn't need the world to change any further. A voice echoed out down the corridor and disrupted his train of thought.

"What are you doing home!? I don't actually care so don't answer. Just make me some lunch, I'm starving." Ava, seemingly in a good mood today, kindly requested that Jacob prepare lunch for her. Jacob was well aware of the unpleasant repercussions of not complying with his seventeen year old daughter's demands, and so he hastened to the kitchen to prepare a meal for her.

A sandwich usually was satisfactory and so he pieced one together from foraging various mismatching elements. As he picked up the plate and then geared himself up to walk back down the corridor, open Ava's bedroom door and deliver her lunch, she yelled "And bring it here, I'm hardly going to come and get it myself now am I?" He tensed, knocked and entered.

Ava was outstretched on her bed, reading, and though it was around midday on a Monday she was still in her tattered pink teddy bear pyjamas that she refused to throw away. This was how Ava could usually be found. She did not get out as much as other teens, and had relatively few friends to go out with. Her room was littered with books, every single one of them read, and most read more than once.

If Jacob was concerned about the amount of dust in his own bedroom this morning, he did not react outwardly to the state of Ava's room. It had not been cleaned or tidied for weeks. He looked around to try to find a clean level surface upon which to place the plate.

"Put it on my desk. Why are you home anyway? I think I do want to know now." Jacob really did not feel like recounting the tale of his emotional morning again, it would be just too much for him to bear and he did not want his daughter to know that he had lost his job just on the off chance that she became worried or the more likely scenario that she would mock and belittle him. Thinking on his feet, not one of his strong points, he lied, also not one of his strong points.

"I managed to get most of my work done this morning and Mr Higgs said I could have the rest of the day to myself and do my paperwork at home. It doesn't have to be done in the office."

Ava sat up, flicked her long blond hair away from her face and her mysterious blue eyes stared straight at him. "You've been there at that job an awful long time, and this is the first time that's ever happened. Why are you lying to me? Look, just go away. Go away but come back with a soda. I'm thirsty." She lay back down on her pile of pillows and held her book in front of her face, making a statement. Conversation over.

Feeling like he had achieved the best possible outcome from what could have been an unpleasant situation, Jacob left and returned to her with a soda, then sank into his old recliner in the corner of the lounge where he may have stayed for five minutes or five hours, he did not know.

His mind was on Ava. He needed to do more for her, he needed to be a man, a father, a role model, but instead he was none of those things. Here was a person who in an instant had broken his family and taken it past the point of no return, six long years ago. Grateful that Ava could still bring herself to share the house with him, it provided him with an opportunity and the hope that he may redeem himself even if only partially, and he felt that day after day of trying he could melt away her icy stares and underneath find a warm loving daughter once again.

It's only been six years, Jacob told himself this, tried to fool himself into believing that the reappearance of the warm and loving daughter would eventually happen because it was the only flame he had left burning dimly inside himself now, though it threatened to flicker out. And if that flame extinguished, what then?

Slowly and reluctantly, the contents of the small cardboard box that he brought home from work were unpacked and examined. There was only one item of any value in there and Jacob gripped it and stared at it. The expensive silver photo frame containing a picture of himself, his dead wife and Ava stared back at him. Jacob began to cry for the second time that day.

Chloe was still barking next door and he hoped that the noise would hide the sound of two or three large sobs that he could not hold back. He placed the frame out of sight inside his leather briefcase, knowing that he would not be opening it again for a while.

As he was leaning forward to put the briefcase down, Jacob nearly vomited. A foreign sensation materialised inside him and caused him to lose balance. Thinking quickly he dropped to his knees and fell forward, lying face down on the floor where he could fall no further. It was as if there was an irritation inside him, in his belly, but it was not his belly, in fact, now that he thought about it maybe it was in his chest, his head. It did not seem to have a precise location that he could identify.

Was this a heart attack? He frowned, and concentrated on trying to determine what was going on. He was being filled up from the inside with something like a warm light, or a wavelength of a particular frequency that his body was absorbing. The sound of every dog in the neighbourhood barking echoed in his ears, every sense heightened.

His breathing seemed too loud and he tried to shallow his air intake. He must be hyperventilating. He tried to yell for Ava to get a paper bag for him to breathe into but no words came. The light or whatever it was inside him was slowly changing, increasing in warmth, and had somehow become audible.

How does light make a sound? Can it? This was no sound that he was listening to in the normal physical sense, it was a note he had never heard, an impossible sound but he understood it and knew what it was. It was a message. This was a communication straight from a source. And the source was? Jacob's eyes opened wide. The source was…

Gone. But it had left a residual behind, a mystery within Jacob.

Senses returning to normality, he looked around, eyes darting about from the face down position he had placed himself in on the floor. There was nothing to see, just the same old house he had always lived in but from a different angle. Saliva had formed in a puddle under his chin and it was then that Jacob realised he had had a stroke. How long had he been laying there? Which side of him would be paralysed? He couldn't afford rehabilitation now that he was out of a job. Maybe he was beyond rehabilitation.

He was quite sure he wasn't dead so there wouldn't even be a life insurance payout to Ava. One final joke the universe had left to play on him today. "Nice one, you really got me," he said, knowing he probably only had half a smile on his face. The words seemed to come out alright which surprised him, but maybe that was how having a stroke worked. You think you sound normal but really, nobody can understand you but you. He really didn't know much about the mechanics of a stroke.

He moved his left arm, which meant it was his right side that was paralysed. His good side. Brilliant. Concentrating on using his left arm and leg to manoeuvre himself into an upright position, he ended up sitting legs out straight with his back leaning against the corridor wall, and he was well aware that he had used both his left and right side to achieve this.

So not a stroke then. Probably just the day's events catching up with him and manifesting themselves in some weird physiological response. He was sure he had heard about this sort of thing.

At that moment, Jacob's attention was drawn to some loud banging and struggling noises came from Ava's room and from his seated position he heard her door being pulled open violently. A few seconds later she emerged from out of her room awkwardly, half on, half off of her wheelchair with a panicked look on her face.

"Dad, did you feel it? Can you feel it inside of you? Did it happen to you too?" she panted and adjusted herself in her chair, straightening her pink teddy bear pyjamas. "I thought I was having a heart attack, I dropped my book on my face, but it's not a heart attack," she spoke in hysterics.

Jacob could not understand her. His mind had been racing so quickly at the possibilities of what had just happened to him that he had not considered that it may have happened to others, and why should he? If somebody has a stroke, they don't expect everybody else to have one simultaneously.

Something foreign was now inside Jacob. He could feel it. The event had left something lingering behind, a warmth, knowledge, an awareness. The light that emitted the impossible note was flickering inside him and had found a place within him that had never existed before and settled there. It was a broadcast, a calling card, a beacon?

It was God.

The rain began to batter down on the tin roof above in torrents. The weather presenter from this morning was right after all. Jacob closed his eyes.

Sun 20 Sept 1959   *10:45am*
Ira's Revelation

Driving away from his house slowly, Ira inhaled and filled his lungs with fresh air, something taking him back to memories of summer holidays long past where he would sit squashed in the back of one of his friends cars on the way to some beach, hot vinyl seat burning his skin, windows rolled down, music turned up. He didn't care too much for loud music any more but nothing beat the feeling of wind in your hair, that would never change.

Feeling like he was on a road trip, he threw his cares aside and turned the dial of the stereo up just a fraction louder than was usually comfortable and permitted himself to hum along with the car radio. Leaning forward and looking up through his grimy windscreen to the overcast sky, he put his foot down on the pedal a little. Rain would made his work a little more messy and difficult than it needed to be, though on a positive note it would be nice to have nature wash his car and clean his windscreen.

Eddie only lived a couple of suburbs over from his place so the summer holiday-esque drive was over shortly and Ira got out of his car still humming the last tune on the car radio. He continued humming all the way up to the porch, had a quick look at the numerous empty bottles and cigarette packets clustering around the ashtray on a small round table and then knocked on the door that badly needed painting. No answer. A few louder knocks that could be heard to echo inside were next. Nothing.

"Well, he wasn't really expecting me I suppose," Ira mumbled to himself while checking around the back of the house to make sure. Nothing but more empty beer bottles. This guy either sure liked to drink, or was just really bad at throwing his empties in the trash.

Casually strolling back up to the front porch and looking around on the table, apart from noticing that most of the cigarettes there were not even butted out into the ashtray, they were all over the table and in bottles, Ira found a book of matches. "Aydies Bar and Tavern. I'll be seeing you soon Eddie," and he hopped back into the pickup.

Pulling up out the front of Aydies, Ira wondered what kind of person would frequent this place. Dilapidated, the front awnings were tattered and dirty, one of the windows looked like it had been kicked into a spiderweb of shards that were barely holding themselves together. A whisper of a breeze and they would splash into a million pieces on the pavement.

Ira tried the door. It was locked. He mentally kicked himself. It was still morning, of course it would be closed. Reluctantly, he pressed his hands up to the filthy glass and peered inside. There was somebody in there, a shadow was moving around and it looked like it could be a janitor mopping. Knocking, Ira could see the man inside making the hand gesture for what obviously meant "Sorry we're closed."

This guy was going to open the door whether he wanted to or not. Ira continuously knocked for about two minutes before the man gave in and came to the door with a clearly annoyed look on his face, but Ira did not even notice or care.

"Hey, thanks for that, I'm looking for a guy called Eddie that might drink here, do you know him? Five foot ten-ish, balding, seems to have a drinking problem? Smokes Tareytons?"

"How the hell should I know, I'm just the janitor and mister, I'm pretty sure nearly everybody that frequents here probably matches that description. Come back at five when we open and ask one of the bartenders. Now excuse me." And with that he stepped back, closed the door and locked it.

Annoyed, Ira walked back to the car. He had another address for Eddie which he probably should have gone to before stopping by Aydies although he thought that if he couldn't find Eddie at home, he would most likely be at a bar and not his own mother's house. Well, sometimes you just guess wrong.

Several minutes later Ira pulled up to the front of a quaint yellow and white house with a lovely white picket fence that was in surprisingly good condition with a garden that was painstakingly manicured by somebody with a lot of attention to detail.

It reminded him of when he was about eighteen or nineteen and he would visit his grandmother quite regularly after her husband passed away to keep her company for an afternoon here and there. Mostly she set him to task in her immaculate garden, pointing out the odd twig here or there that was barely even visible to the human eye that needed snipping but significant enough to her that she would lose sleep until it was removed. After fifty years of living in a house built by their own hands, every square inch was as familiar to them as they were with each other.

He could see the craving for human contact in his grandmother's eyes, and looking deeper knew there was a hole that could never be filled, caused by the departure of Ira's grandfather, her soulmate and companion for more than fifty years. She would cry whenever Ira came to visit, and cried whenever he left, thanking him and asking him already when he would be coming over next.

After standing to admire the garden in front of him for a minute, he swung the heavy ornate brass doorknocker and shuffling could be heard from the corridor approaching Ira's direction. There was no screen door, just the big wooden main door and it swung inwards, with Eddie and Ira finally face to face. A stocky man with a docile look on his face, more brawn than brain, looked Ira up and down before his eyes widened.

"Hi Eddie," Ira said quietly as he pulled the screwdriver out that was tucked into his belt at the back of his pants and stabbed Eddie neatly in the stomach with it through his white t-shirt, pulling it back out and watching a perfect red circle form around the hole. His job for the day was done.

The sun peeked through the northerly moving clouds, intensely bright at the fringes, virtually black in the thick billowy centres. Were the bright edges the silver linings that everybody spoke about? Ira was not too sure about where the saying originated though he felt that it was probably common knowledge and he should know.

It was strange that he did not know some very simple things and yet he could remember from high school that the sun's rays when radiating through the clouds were called crepuscular rays. He was not sure how his brain decided what information to keep and what to discard, sometimes he could not remember what he ate for breakfast and yet he could remember this random fact.

The sky darkened, the bright edges of the clouds diminished and the black centres became more prominent. It was going to rain. Was his own bright facade diminishing, just like the clouds? He knew he had darkness within him, but it was not close to taking control and overpowering the side of his personality that his family saw. That would always glow, he knew.

His wife and child would never see the blackness within. But it was indeed growing, and if it was growing, would it eventually take over? Had he now travelled too far down this path and could never return? He was unsure.

A groan and a bubbling sound snapped him out of pursuing this meandering thought. He hadn't killed Eddie. Yet.

"I'm sorry Eddie, but my boss provided me with strict orders to make this a slow process. Nothing personal, I hope you understand." He strolled casually toward his pickup truck at the front of the house, contemplating whether to use the tarp to wrap Eddie up in, or to use the shovel and have Eddie fertilise his mother's rosebushes.

Ira stood at the pickup truck, deciding which course of action to take. A weak voice trailed across the air to him. "Please, I don't want to die. I really…" the sentence trailed off into violent sobbing. "Please. Every bad man is capable of one good deed. I don't want to die. You can save me. Don't do this." A trail of blood oozed from his mouth.

"What did you say?" Ira spun around sharply.

"You can save me. Please save me. I've never done wrong to you."

"No. You said every bad man is capable of one good deed. My father said that once."

"So… you are going to help me?" Eddie was clutching his stomach and turned pale as if he were a chameleon attempting to hide against a white wall. He would not last much longer.

"Again, I'm sorry Eddie. No I won't. Not my decision." Ira grabbed the tarp out of the pickup. He didn't feel like digging holes today.

"Hey, have a think about this Eddie, it's a real blast, makes my head spin and might make you feel better. Do you know what the basic building blocks of matter that make up everything around us are? Atoms, consisting of smaller protons, neutrons, electrons, which are made up of other even smaller particles that I can't remember the name of. And so on, ad infinitum probably. If you look at a proton, a neutron, an electron, are they alive? No. When you combine them into an atom, are they alive? No. What do combinations of these atoms form?" He paused briefly for an answer that never came, then continued. "Correct Eddie, molecules. Now this is where things get interesting. Amino acids, proteins, what did we learn about these in biology? Well, the word biology itself gives away the answer, Eddie. They are found in the human body, in animals, are they not?" Ira had started pacing back and forth while Eddie had crawled his way down the front steps of the house and onto the stone path, pain and puzzlement etched on his grimacing face.

"So what I am getting at is that the human body is made up of non-living amino acids, non-living proteins and some other molecules, which are made up of non-living atoms, protons, neutrons and the other particles I mentioned earlier. The very same atoms and particles that make up rocks, air, water, just in different arrangements. Follow?" Eddie made no effort to respond but Ira was unfazed.

My question is: When does the human body, made up of all these dead building blocks, become alive? What defines it? We are all made from matter that has no life. It's like joining a whole bunch of stones together in just the right way and they eventually turn into a living being. Crazy isn't it! At what point is the line crossed where all the dead components combined are considered alive?"

He looked at his hand. "My hand is alive, isn't it? My heart is alive? I, as a whole, am alive. But if you had a microscope powerful enough and examined my hand, or my heart, you would just see non-living particles. It is something that I have wondered about since I was a boy." Ira was becoming frustrated at his unsolved puzzle.

"Eddie, you are going to die. But don't be afraid, you will still consist of exactly the same particle matter when you are dead as what you comprise of now, alive. There is just something that will be missing, something I can't comprehend, something indescribable. A soul? Is this what a soul is Eddie? I'm sorry for throwing all these questions at you, if only you could let me know the answer when you reach the other side." Ira gripped the screwdriver and stepped forward.

Eddie mumbled a choked up "No, no" and raised a limp hand into the air before some undefinable cosmic force washed through the men and they both buckled over with nausea.

The world changed.

It was raining, moderately. Ira did not know how long he had been out cold for or whether he had even been unconscious at all. Gradually his memory and bearings returned and he rolled himself over to come face to face with Eddie who was gasping for air like a dying fish, the rain washing away all the blood so it looked like he was simply waking up from a restful sleep on the path at the front of his mother's house.

"Impossible. It's just not possible. It's all… real?" Ira sat there for a few moments but still the realisation did not sink in. His mind could not comprehend what had just happened and refused to register, though somewhere deep inside himself there was now a glowing, divine light of knowledge that he could feel radiating throughout. Irrefutable evidence of what he now knew to be true.

He believed in a higher power so why did this new unquestionable knowledge and evidence that God truly existed seem so unbelievable to him? Surely he should just be nodding his head and experience joy that the day he hoped would one day come had actually arrived.

Since he was a little boy, prayer and worship were part of his life, both parents being devout churchgoers who contributed generously to the collection plate every Sunday. God was accepted as fact in his family and by Ira and yet was never front of mind. Ira had selfishly put his own life and desires before the rules and desires of God.

Thou Shalt Not Kill! Was it possible to believe in God and not follow the holy Commandments? Maybe deep down did he really not believe? Why would he act directly against a Commandment? He was a faithful believer and yet Ira could not explain his actions.

"Kill me." Snapping back to the situation at hand, he became aware of Eddie lying in front of him and was more than a little taken aback at this change of request from the dying man.

"I thought you wanted me to save you?'

"I am not afraid to die any more. Can you feel it? God inside you? It's all real." Blood trickled freely in great bubbles from his mouth. "Kill me, I want to be at peace. I am ready."

Ira still had the screwdriver in his hand and he remembered that before the world changed he was walking over to finish the job he had begun. But that was before the world changed. The screwdriver fell to the ground and Ira turned to walk back to his pickup truck.

Eddie became agitated and a whisper from his mouth accompanied by blood came from him. "Please. You were going to do it! You were going to. Do this one good deed. Put me out of my…" Exhaustion taking its toll, he rolled over onto his side and rested his head on the bottom step leading up to the house.

Standing there looking back at Eddie and absorbing the gravity of what had just happened, Ira knew he could not continue to live his life as he had been for any longer. Never again could he end another man's life. He had to leave this scene, in an instant this had become a reminder of a past life that he had already moved on from and could not face for a second longer.

"I cannot Eddie, I am a changed man."

"Practice mercy upon me then. You caused this. It will be looked upon favourably." Ira rolled up the tarp and strode to the pickup truck, Eddie's last words in his ears.

"You are the one who caused this Ira. You and you alone. So whether you walk away now or not, it is you who have killed me, regardless. You have killed me."

Ira slammed the door to the pickup and drove away from the white and yellow house with the dying man sprawled and sobbing out the front.

Sun 20 Sept 1959 *11:55am*
Faith's Revelation

A blurry light slowly came into focus, and took on a rectangular shape. Faith sat in her chair staring straight ahead at the window, her knuckles white from the exertion of gripping on tightly to the desk in front of her. She had been ill down the front of her shirt, however, ignoring this, the first thing she did was ease herself into a standing position and take stock of the situation around the office.

Although completely bewildered, her colleagues appeared to be conscious and she could see in their eyes that they had shared the same overpowering experience.

"What was that!? What happened?" Hal from Accounts' voice was high pitched and panicky.

"Unless I'm mistaken, we all know what just happened, am I right?" another voice replied shakily as a brown-haired head appeared from behind a desk and then lowered again.

"I don't believe it, I just….don't," Faith said to nobody in particular. The office filled with muttering, rising in volume and hysteria until a deep voice cut through and a silence allowed the voice to continue.

"People, people! Settle down. Something big has just happened so I think everybody should just stay still and relax for a few minutes, we don't know if it will happen again, or if there are any side effects. Now first of all, is everybody okay?" A general murmur responded positively to Maxwell's query.

"That Max..." Faith said with a sigh to nobody in particular, then realised that if anybody was listening it could appear a little odd and so she spoke up a bit louder to Mavis the receptionist and continued with a very unnatural sentence. "That Max sure knows how to take control of a situation, I certainly feel better about things, don't you Mavis?" Faith observed, feeling safer knowing he was there.

She caught herself. His name is Maxwell, not Max! Only his wife called him Max. She closed her eyes and tried to regain her bearings.

The office sat in an eerie silence for a couple of minutes, anxiety creeping in at the uncertainty of what was going to happen next, but also a level of processing and digesting new feelings of enlightenment and knowledge within. An almost soothing pattering of rain on the window made Faith relax, at least it didn't seem like the world was going to end. She hoped.

Even though a fondness for incense, spirituality, crystals and the like would seem to make her a prime candidate for being open to the idea of a higher power, Faith was a staunch atheist, never actually imagining this moment would ever happen, and if by chance she ever did picture a scenario of this nature, the event would happen accompanied by dramatic thunderclaps and lightning surrounding a man with a white beard.

Her imagination certainly did not foresee a pleasant medium-to-heavy rain shower and the discovery of some newly deposited information residing with her and permeating her body like being filled up with a warm bath from the inside.

When she was around thirteen, Faith picked up a bible out of curiosity, having learned from her school friends that it was the most published, most widely read and the most exciting book she would ever read, but what captured her attention and drove her desire to open it was that it was all supposed to be true.

With no belief in the afterlife, Faith was aware that her time in this world was limited to around seventy years, and then she would be no more than dust for the rest of eternity so in effect, she was able to experience the incredible universe for less than the blink of an eye in the big scheme of things, so why live an ordinary life in that time? Put the effort in, be the best you can be, learn all you can learn, and so she made the time to read.

The book was gripping from the beginning, however, as soon as she made as start on Genesis there was a paragraph where God looks for Adam in the Garden of Eden and calls out "Where are you?" Faith sensed something of a plot inconsistency.

The omnipotent, omnipresent, omniscient, omni-everything God needed to ask where the only man on the planet was? This didn't sit right. She read a little further but soon she felt that it became a little bit too far-fetched and interest was lost about a third of the way through. She put it aside and questioned how others could not only finish it, but read it many times over, believe it and allow it to form a basis for their lives.

A tale containing a storyline filled with so many glaring holes, how on earth could fools be gullible enough to believe in a higher being and impossible events that they had never seen or witnessed any evidence of whatsoever? "Facts" clouded by muddled storytelling and centuries of Chinese whispers describing alleged miracles of water turning into wine, which, if you asked Faith, was really a second rate kind of miracle anyway, indicating that whoever was present was probably intoxicated and unlikely to be completely reliable in their recount of the true happenings that day.

If something great yet seemingly impossible happened it was called a miracle, if something expected didn't happen then obviously God had a grander plan and worked in mysterious ways. All bases covered. Nowadays, a piece of toast with some burned bits that may slightly resemble a distorted version of the son of God's face was hailed as a miracle, with the foolish from all over the world embarking on a pilgrimage to see it first-hand.

Are these the straws religious people are clutching at now for validation that their beliefs have substance? A piece of toast? In Faith's humble opinion, the Almighty Lord was really scraping the bottom of the barrel with these petty miracles that seemed a bit beneath him and to be honest, really cheapened His reputation.

Why present these teasers solely to hillbillies and old Italian widows, why not pick a moment on national television, say during the Olympics when the whole world is watching and turn one of the swimming pools into wine in full view of millions of sane and rational witnesses?

In disbelief, the realisation was setting in that this was pretty much the equivalent of what had just happened and her atheism was not only questioned, it was obliterated. This is what it would feel like if she grew up believing that her name was Faith, but at some point it was pointed out by her parents that it was all a practical joke and her real name was Bob, and she now had no choice but to believe in something that shattered a foundation stone of knowledge that was ingrained deep inside.

It sat right alongside having to accept that the universe is infinite, an absolute impossibility, but with no other alternative than for it to be true. That first spark of life on earth, however improbable, actually did occur. So why not this?

She couldn't believe it, but she had to. It was real. The whole world now knew God was real. Most people would have expected just like her that if this historic event ever happened, it would be with the appearance of an old man with long grey hair and beard, but this made so much more sense now that she thought about it. This was real, no smoke, no lava, just the knowledge inside of her delivering the truth. There was nothing physical about God, God just…was.

"Maxwell, have you heard anything yet, from anybody? Did this happen everywhere? Did somebody decide to put a hallucinogen in our air-conditioning? One of the competing papers maybe?"

"No, I've not heard anything from anybody yet, I've been sitting right here in front of you while you have been staring into space with your mouth open for the last five minutes. All right people, we need to make a story out of this. Faith. Thanks for volunteering. This one is yours."

"But, is this even a worthwhile story if everybody in the entire world knows exactly what happened? It's not called news then."

"Okay Faith, you are right. Let's not bother to publish a story about the most significant event to ever happen in the history of the world for two thousand years. Hey Jo, tomorrow let's run with the article on the chimpanzee riding a bike for the front page. Or better still, about the chimpanzee writing articles for this newspaper." He looked over to Faith. She could not read the look he gave her, but she was sure it wasn't one that she would like to know the meaning of.

"People want answers Faith, there are plenty of questions, we need to piece it all together. Get in touch with all your contacts, see how widespread this phenomenon went. Find out and document everything everybody knows. Compare stories, see if there were any sightings of anything anywhere. And Faith-"

"Yes?"

"-You have my permission to exceed three hundred words this time. Whatever it takes."

"Okay boss. Thanks."

"I'll not be coming back till late, I trust you to prepare a story worthy of yourself and this paper. Right?"

"As always."

For an event that only lasted a moment, when she reached inside herself to extract data from the newly created source of information she had inside of her, it was a surprise to find how much she actually contained. She sat down grabbed a pen, and wrote for a good hour, amazed at what was pouring out of her. When she was done, she had about seventeen pages of solid notes that she felt covered everything held inside of her.

Next, she canvassed her fellow employees, either getting them to write down their recollections or allowed them to read hers to see whether their stories were consistent, and they appeared to be.

Still in shock at the turn of events the day had taken, her mind was nowhere near as focused as it needed to be to write a serious article on a topic as epic and important as this one, so going back to basics was what was required in the preparation of her report. She sat down and began to rearrange everything she had written, trying to find a logical order to the words that had flowed out of her like an unstoppable force.

Making some notes and jotting some numbers down on the pages she had already written, she began again, distracted somewhat by the noise of almost panicked chatter in the office, as well as the screech of sirens worryingly close. Her notes were very rough and casual in tone but she would have time to type them out once she had the general outline ready. Looking over them, she read:

1. Not responsible for setting events of the universe in motion, nor for creating the spark of life or intervening in the course of human history. Not responsible for animals, mankind, death, disease, famine etc like many think, Simply another conscious being in the universe, just like us.

2. Unaware of how own existence came about, or whether there are others. No physical form. Omnipresent and intelligent, yet only able to process a realistic single sphere of focus at any particular time, so the concept of simultaneously tuning in to the prayers of millions as religion teaches is, of course impossible.

3. No Heaven as we know it, no Hell, no other planes of existence either pre-this life of post-this life, at least, not any that this God has created or is aware of.

Her barely legible list continued, and it became evident to her that most concepts relating to religion that the world had assumed to be true since the dawn of time were human-made and used by men to wield influence and power over other men.

How all those religious crazies would be on their high horse now with an "I told you so" smugness she was sure they would have, though she was confident that this higher being was far more realistic and nowhere near similar to the all-powerful God that they had spruiked. All that had been correct thus far was the general concept of a higher entity, the facts and details around which now seemed to be far from accurate.

Enveloped within her own zone of concentration, she was unaware for some time that the office was practically empty. Was it that late? How long had she been working for? She looked at the clock. Only 2:30pm. She swivelled around, checked Maxwell's glass-windowed office to see if maybe he was holding a meeting, but the only person she could spot was Hal from Accounts, who never left his seat, even at lunch. Where was everybody?

"Excuse me Hal, hi, sorry. Where is everybody? Is there something going on that I should know about? Did Maxwell give everybody the rest of the day off because there are no other stories worth writing? Honestly, I can't carry a whole edition by myself you know. I'm sure there are still sports and finance-y things happening today?"

Hal responded less than enthusiastically. "Yes to the sports and finance things, and no, nobody has been given the day off. I didn't listen to what people around here were doing because I don't really care, plus nobody tells me anything around here anyway because all I really do is make sure that you all get paid. I've gathered that everybody has been called away to cover stories relating to todays' "incident". Oh, some guy was found dead out the front of a house, probably nothing to do with what's going on, but who knows. I wouldn't be surprised if things started getting a little weird, an event like this would have to have some repercussions throughout society. Just consider yourself lucky you get to stay here in the office is all I am saying."

She wrinkled up her nose and turned back to her typewriter, conscious of the unusual feeling of that new presence glowing inside of her, now that she had snapped out of her focused state and wasn't distracted by the buzz around the office.

She hoped she would be able to sleep tonight. The awareness of God was almost like a delicate feather caressing away at an unfamiliar place inside her, containing a warm and comforting sphere of knowledge that she wanted to tap into almost addictively so that she could push any trepidation out of her thoughts.

Considering herself to be in tune with the world and sensitive to its energies and the fluctuation of all its wonderful forces, she possessed the inner power to transform most situations into positive situations with feel-good outcomes, if not in reality, then at least in her own mind. Her mantra was "If you think it, then it shall be."

A useful technique that she had taught herself when she was younger and sensed that negativity, worry or melancholy was approaching and about to interfere with her wellbeing was to simply imagine a big pair of scissors and to snip the tether that bound the unwanted emotion to her and watch it float away from her body. An air of calm would come over her and allow her to move on unthreatened.

Her brief moment of inner peace was broken as another siren whizzed past the office, and this time it was a mantra of her mother that echoed inside her head. "Hope for the best, prepare for the worst." A sense of unease again grew and surrounded her. She did not even attempt to escape from the worrying feeling and snip it away.

Her story grew and took shape. Reading over it she knew that what was on those pieces of paper contradicted virtually everything that religion had historically preached and would certainly outrage some and make others look like fools and fraudsters. If this was released in another time, another place, under different circumstances, her statements would be reviled and dismissed by the entire religious community.

The kicker was that everybody on the planet had probably experienced this event, and by looking inside of themselves would accept the truth and learn that since the dawn of time a powerful segment of the community had been complicit in basically conning people and using religion to justify their own objectives. Hal's words echoed in her ears and now made began to make sense. Repercussions. Negative? Or positive? Shouldn't the world be rejoicing right now? She was not so sure.

She stayed until well into the night polishing her thoughts on paper and barely registered Maxwell arriving back at some unknown hour. When she was happy with her work he read over and approved the story with only a few minor changes before they recapped the inconceivable events of the day. She started yawning uncontrollably and, terribly embarrassed, made her excuses and caught a cab home, oblivious to the attempts at conversation by the driver, her mind miles away.

Sun 20 Sept 1959 **6:00am**
Mary's Revelation

As the glow of the morning sun slowly peeked in underneath her curtains and gradually revealed her immaculately sterile bedroom, Mary's eyes stared straight ahead at the ceiling, as they had for the past few hours. Her ears were the most engaged of her senses and she had laid stiffly in her bed all night, alert for the slightest sound in the house, secretly hoping and dreading to hear signs of activity from her son's room. Nothing.

She tiptoed silently down the dimly lit corridor to see Zach, and as she approached she could hear familiar rhythmic breathing, almost a gentle snore, the sound of a little boy asleep. Exhaling with relief, and glad that at least somebody in the house managed to have a restful night, Mary allowed Zach to remain at peace and continued on.

From within Zach's bedroom the sound of his mother's footsteps receded into the distance and the little boy lay in the half-light at the end of his bed, legs and arms rigid and straight, fingers and toes splayed wide, eyes open impossibly wide, almost as if there was a permanent bolt of lightning coursing through his body. And yet behind those staring eyes the boy's mind slept, though what dreams may have been unfolding would never be known.

After bringing in a pint of milk and the day's newspaper from the doorstep, Mary made a cup of tea and went over her schedule for the day. A carefully filled out diary that had seen better days was opened to a shabby page that had been ever so neatly written in, and then overrun with crossing out and scribble and words written over other words in bolder rough, dark scratches.

At 10am she would run some simple errands for Mrs Howlett, an elderly widow who was extraordinarily accomplished at painting and sculpting nudes, with a zest for showcasing all undesirable angles of the naked human body until sadly her arthritic hands started to fail her. Her lucid mind, however, remained passionately fixated on the subject matter yet could only suffer discontent now that her physical self was unable to provide the artistic release it needed.

To compensate for this, any of Mrs Howlett's exchanges within a social environment, no matter how formal, invariably contained double entendre, bawdy talk, cursing, or all three, depending on how lucky you were.

Mary's sheltered childhood and meek nature lead to her often standing across from Mrs Howlett with her mouth wide open and sometimes not even sure what she was talking about, although she could guess from the rhythm of the conversation what she was alluding to.

Upon arrival to her residence, one could not help being confused as to whether they were in a particularly flesh-coloured bawdy renaissance section of an art gallery or inside a to-scale frieze of a debaucherous party. It was all harmless though and Mary tried to see the experience as a bit of an education.

Further down the page on the diary there was a not so pleasant entry. The Rutherfords, 2pm. Best just think about that one at 2pm.

Onto her second cup of tea she was joined by Zach who sleepily stumbled across the kitchen and nuzzled himself into her. Her heart melted and she wrapped her non-teacup holding arm around him and held him close.

"Want to do the crossword with Mommy?" This was her little morning ritual that got her mind into gear and provided some brief enjoyment before the day really began. He would hold the pen, and with her hand guiding his they would fill out as many answers as they could. On a successful day, Mary would complete about three quarters of a regular puzzle and maybe get a few answers written into a cryptic crossword.

Today was not a good day and it wasn't long before Mary got annoyed that the answers she wanted to see weren't provided until the following day's paper, so she decided to give up and have a shower to get ready to go to work.

Zach remained at the table, pen in hand, doodling and scribbling on the paper as usual. This time, though, the random scrawls and lines were less random, and if anybody had taken a closer look they could see that the boy was writing words within the small boxes of the crossword.

Once Mary was washed and ready they ventured out for her first job of the day. Today's list from Mrs Howlett wasn't too long and didn't seem to contain any double entendre-type jokes or bawdy references as expected, however, it involved travelling around town to make a few pickups from a number of places, including the pharmacy, supermarket, and to Mary's dismay, a legitimate visit to the newsagent to purchase a certain magazine containing adults only content. For this transaction, Zach was made to wait out the front of the store whilst the shopkeeper had to endure yet another customer pleading their case that the publication that they were buying was "for a friend."

"Of course it is darling," the vendor said with a snigger.

With the cringeworthy publication now in her possession, the list was completely actioned and the journey back to the artist's house was made. Just in time, too, the clouds had become dark and rain was beginning to seriously patter down.

Mary rang the doorbell, which now to her seemed to resemble a breast though she had never really noticed before. "Mrs Howlett is corrupting my thoughts, that she-devil!" Mary chuckled to herself. And it was then that Zach started yelling.

"Oooouuu….." The little boy's high-pitched voice pierced the air, unfamiliar to Mary's ears even though he was her own flesh and blood. Mary dropped everything from her arms and the shopping hit the ground in slow motion. She felt the earth moving under her feet and she lunged towards Zach, so disorientated she was unsure whether she was even moving in the right direction. He was all that mattered.

Another voice now filled the air, that of a baritone man, curdling her blood and causing her to panic and look around trying to identify this new character in the picture and whether there was a threat she needed to deal with.

Satisfied that nobody else was present, she turned her attention back to Zach and realised the booming voice was coming from him. No, it seemed to be coming from behind him, around him? His voice became colours, every colour, emanating outwards from his form in powerful waves. Sheer terror gripped Mary. The scream became a siren of such a frequency and tone that her mind and body became completely detached from one another and she could sense that she was now lying down being ill.

The world simultaneously turned upside down, inside out, and contorted in a direction that there were no words to describe because it was a physical impossibility before everything faded to black and her world changed forever. The last image burned into Mary's mind was of Zach standing over her with a calm look on his face, then bending down.

Shadows flickered before her eyes and she yawned loudly. Was it morning already and time to get up? This didn't seem right. She wasn't in her bed for a start, she was out in the rain. The shadows solidified and she could make out Zach stroking her wet hair. This snapped her into full consciousness, although there was something different, something not quite right about him… or was it something that was very, very right? The reality of what had just happened washed over her and she recognised the significance of the new sensation forming deep within.

"Oh. God."

Steadying herself and managing to haul herself upright she hugged Zach, tears streaming down her face and getting lost in the rain.

"Oh baby, are you okay? I'm here, I'm here." She kissed his face and gave him a once over, although there was a new look in Zach's eyes that told her he was fine and that she was probably the one that needed reassurance, not him. Satisfied that everything was okay and neither herself nor her son was injured, Mary could now assess the situation and turn her mind to a bigger picture.

"Mrs Howlett!" Mary rang the doorbell and after a worrying long pause the door was opened by the grey-haired frail woman who had by all accounts only just put pants and a top on, the latter buttoned up incorrectly so that it tilted to one side, hanging awkwardly. There were more important things to be considered a priority now for her and the smile on her face was like she had just won a lottery.

"Mary! Isn't it just wonderful! Come in come in! I'm just about to put the news on and have a cup of tea. How are you dear? I'm lucky I was having a lie down when this all occurred, or else I can imagine there would be some people out there including myself with bumps and bruises! I'm assuming that you just had the same experience that I just did my dear? Amazing!"

Her enthusiasm was contagious and Mary began to worry somewhat less and was glad that there was somebody else that she could share this confusing but glorious time with.

Mary volunteered to make the cup of tea for them both while Mrs Howlett went to the linen cupboards and brought some towels to dry off with and then switched the television set on. The black and white picture took a second to form and as hoped, "Breaking News" appeared on screen, with any luck about to provide some further information as to the event that had unfolded.

A well-dressed man with slicked back hair parted at the side was fumbling around with some loose paper at a news desk, however, he seemed quite lost and discombobulated, meandering from topic to topic as he looked into the camera resembling a deer in the headlights given there had been little time to prepare any notes.

"…existence is confirmed. I'm currently waiting to uh see if anybody brings me any further information but at this stage it appears that this may be a world-wide event folks, so it's unlikely to be any sort of hallucinatory chemical attack by a hostile country against us." He pressed his finger to his earpiece. "I'm getting reports that London, Australia and most of Asia have confirmed identical events and I will make the assumption that more reports will come in confirming this event on a global scale. And to repeat, though I'm sure that if you all experienced the same thing that I just did, as in fact we all just did here at WJCS-TV you will know that the existence the being we call God has just now proven to be real, and in such a bizarre and ethereal way but when you think about it, it makes a lot more sense than the physical materialisation that we may have been brought up to expect. That's right folks and wow, if you can see inside of yourself now in the same way I can, uh, there's quite a bit that's different to what I as a religious man prior to this unprecedented event believed, compared to what I now know. What a day."

He closed his eyes and tried to generate something from deep within himself, finally emerging after finding the words he was searching for. "What we now know from this revelation, about Jesus, God's powers, heaven, angels, the Bible, other religions and other Gods, it's all different to what we thought we knew, to what we have been fed. More realistic if anything, that is if such an unfathomable event can even be separated into realistic impossibilities occurring versus unrealistic impossibilities."

He swallowed, wondering how much trouble dissecting religion could potentially get him into, but also aware that he had to fill an indefinite amount of time on-air without a script and was flying by the seat of his pants, so saying anything at all was better than saying nothing, which would get him into even more trouble. Besides, he was re-telling what everybody now knew anyway. Choosing the lesser of two evils, he continued.

"The problems started when religion cast aside the scientific theory of evolution which, based on the revelation of a few minutes ago is now a proven fact, and instead chose to believe the tale of the first humans Adam and Eve. Eating from the tree of knowledge which was forbidden, they lo and behold committed the first sin and as a punishment mankind is now subject to both a physical and spiritual death. Thanks Adam and Eve."

The reporter was on a roll now and in the absence of any further news rolling in through his earpiece he continued to adlib.

"So even though God created man in His own image and bestowed upon us the freedom to make decisions and choices of our own free will, He required blood to be shed should any of these free will decisions meet his arbitrary definition of sin. From this decree unfolded the chain reaction of events that eventually led to his own son Jesus dying on behalf of the sins committed by the human race, becoming the ultimate and final blood sacrifice, and for those of us who have faith and believe in Jesus, eternal spiritual life is now received in lieu."

Mary noticed the newsreader look repeatedly to the left of screen, like something was happening off camera in the studio.

The anchor then glanced towards the camera again with a steely look of determination to finish what he started.

"Don't we now feel a little bit silly that we believed such an obviously ridiculous story without question? It makes God look like a bloodthirsty barbarian with a very low tolerance threshold. And what kind of decision was it to provide His own son as the sacrificial lamb to atone for the entire sins of the human race as if there was no other way to deal with the situation? I acknowledge that his thoughts are not our thoughts and his ways are not our ways, but it just seems like a nonsensical thought process. I am glad I now know that the God that has appeared before us today is not the same son-slaughtering God that imposed those sanity-defying savage rules upon the human race. And how ludicrous that we as mankind still dutifully worshipped that barbaric God without question for so many years, without question at all!"

Bob Overton, the station's long time key news anchor now appeared on screen and sat down to take the lead with the aim of righting the treacherous path the broadcast had taken. This was not the news being broadcast, it had turned into a controversial opinion piece, and the particular television show where opinion pieces were aired was not due on for another half hour.

The previous newsreader was now off camera, however, before his microphone shut off he managed to get in one final sentence.

"It's all different….Viewers, this is going to change the world. This is going to change everything as we know it. Be prepared.."

Sun 20 Sept 1959 *2:15pm*
Jacob Adjusts

"Nothing has changed." Jacob took a cautious step out to the front porch of his house and surveyed the mostly obscured view across the city, courtesy of the rain and the several large trees across the road grown by his neighbours, almost deliberately attempting to spoil what little benefit he had by being on the high side of the street.

He did not know what he expected to happen after the divine event, however it seemed as if life in his quiet part of town rolled on uninterrupted. There were no signs of any explosions, no smoke, no people running around panicking and screaming.

A calm acceptance seemed to be how the human race chose to absorb this information, or had people just decided to conceal their hysteria within the confines of their own dwellings, succumbing to a state of shock and collectively trying to come to terms with next steps and contemplate what life would be like in a world where everybody now had belief?

Jacob felt a dull ache in his stomach, hunger surfacing and provoking feelings of inappropriateness within himself. Is this really a time to be getting hungry? Surely there are more important things going on right now that should be front of mind. He remembered making Ava a sandwich earlier, but yet again ignored his own needs. Deciding that his hunger outweighed his need to further contemplate the gravity of the day's events, he grabbed his car keys and headed down the corridor.

"Ava, I'm going to head to the shops to get some food. Want to come? Want anything?" She wheeled out with an all too familiar attitude resembling a child who was accustomed to getting everything and yet still insisted on being perpetually querulous.

86

"Urgh yes I'll come, there's no way I'm ever going to let you make me a sandwich ever again with whatever you put in that last one. You can't even get something simple like that right." She wheeled past him, and even with ample space in the corridor managed to violently bump him on her way to the front door. Jacob meekly apologised and moved to hold the door open for his daughter.

"And it's raining so you'd better cover me with your umbrella. I know, I know, it's so vain of me, not wanting to have both wet hair AND no functioning legs. I'm already such a hot catch."

Once outside, she painstakingly skidded inch by inch down the flimsy homemade ramp that her father had invested bottom dollar in and was more like a death-trap waterslide in the rain than a safety apparatus. With Jacob carefully chasing her on the way down and doing an inadequate job of protecting her with the umbrella, himself catching the brunt of the rain, they finally made it to the van sitting in the middle of the driveway.

"And when are you going to get a proper ramp. Do you want me to become quadriplegic? Jesus!"

"Hey, I'm not sure you are allowed to say the J-word now, you know.. since…well, you know. It seems a bit wrong, considering." He put one hand underneath her and helped her into the car, then folded up her wheelchair and put it into the back seat.

Ava considered this for a moment and then said "Jesus" again, this time to herself under her breath. So now, thanks to this holy event, cursing and saying the lord's name in vain, a great love of hers, was in jeopardy. One of the few things that brought joy and could make her smile was gone. Or was it?

"You know that God can't even hear everything we say, we now know it's impossible. Well, God's hearing isn't the problem, it's the comprehension. God can no more eavesdrop on mankind's collective thoughts on scale than you or I can. We have previously thought that God was always listening, omnipresent, but it's not true. Well, omnipresent, yes, but not infinitely conscious of the minute detail of every element of the universe. There is the capability for a singular focus, just like the rest of us, and that is all. So I can jolly well say Jesus if I like and I'm sure I won't get struck down by lightning."

"Ava! Ssssh! Regardless of who or what may or may not be listening, I'm listening, and I don't want you saying that."

"And that makes me care even less about what I say."

After several minutes Jacob slowed the van down. "Wait wait wait, what's going on up here, looks like a traffic jam. Must have been an accident or something up ahead."

A multi-coloured procession of vehicles made its way along the usually free flowing street in but a trickle, and the air was thick with seething from impatient drivers who were quick to use their horn and disrupt the peace of the normally tranquil part of the city.

It soon became apparent that there was no accident, and after suffering an eternity in the car with time seemingly at a standstill, the shopping centre loomed into view, the car park was the destination for the slowly moving motorcade. Never before had human behaviour resembled the activity of the ant in such a caricatural manner. From a distance there was no discernible pattern of motion, people were scurrying left and right, carrying food and beverages, wheeling trolleys, bumping into each other, yelling, arguing, self-preservation now the dominant instinct.

"What the…? What is going on here? It's absolutely crazy. I just want to buy some stuff for a sandwich and people here are stockpiling like there's a war going on?"

"I think they are just smarter than you dad and are probably scared a little bit of the unknown. You can't say that you feel entirely calm about this whole situation?" She surveyed the landscape and shook her head, not entirely happy with what she was seeing.

"Well, no. Not now I don't."

Finally pulling into the carpark, the car became part of the swirling school of fish, circling and looking, looking and circling, Jacob veered away from the pack, avoided an out of control overloaded trolley being pushed by somebody who bit off more than they could chew, and headed straight for the main entrance which is where he knew the handicapped parks were located. There were about four or five spots allocated, so his confidence levels were high that there would be one available for them to pull into.

Jacob shook his head and grabbed the steering wheel tighter. Out of the five available parks, three cars were parked at careless angles, leaving room for his car, but only if he also parked across two spaces. Honestly, Jacob wondered, how do these people get their licences? It's not that hard to park between some painted lines, or at least to face your car in the same general direction as the lines.

Exhaling deeply, and telling himself to let go of his resentment towards the human race's parking abilities, Jacob gritted his teeth and pulled in across two spaces at an angle that did not sit very well with him at all.

Helping an unthankful Ava out of the van, the two of them headed into the supermarket, sense of unease growing. Were people even paying for this stuff? Fully laden trolleys were being wheeled in every direction, collisions were frequent and tempers were overheating. Jacob surveyed the situation, and his rational mind dismantled the task at hand into manageable pieces, the process calming himself down somewhat.

"Okay Ava, we don't need much. Firstly I'll just grab a handbasket, then secondly we can go to the bread aisle, grab some water and other staples, and then last of all we can pay and get out of here. Simple."

Negotiating the in-store traffic was not too difficult once you were actually amongst it, and apart from a minor altercation over some special brand of biscuits that Ava insisted on, the shopping was over relatively painlessly, though it was apparent that bread and water stocks in the store were running own as fast as the staff could restock them. It was observed that everybody was actually paying for their groceries and Jacob was grateful for this because if looting was occurring then that was a sign that society is potentially at breaking point, with anarchy and panic only a short way away.

Being a religious man himself, Jacob could only feel hope and optimism within himself and was unsure why it was evident that others felt fear and uncertainty. The glow inside of him reassured and soothed, winning over the all too familiar emotions of melancholy and inadequacy that usually prevailed. Jacob felt strong, like he could face this world and charge at it head on.

They stopped back at their parked van, the neighbouring askew cars now gone, leaving his own exposed as being shamefully oblique. Jacob prepared to go through the familiar motions of onboarding Ava.

"Hey is this your car? Nice parking man. Are you handicapped as well as your daughter?"

A group of slick-haired teens who were all wearing black jeans, white shoes and white t-shirts laughed and high-fived at the disparaging comment made by their leader, a short stocky boy with long hair, cigarette hanging precariously from the side of his mouth and a nearly finished bottle of beer swinging in his hand.

He swaggered over and the rest of the gang followed a short distance behind. The feeling of strength that Jacob was embracing a moment earlier dissipated as quickly as the exhalation of smoke from the mouth of this unknown quantity.

"Uh-uh, actually I had to park like that because there were other…uh..cars.." his meek voice trailed off, reeking of intimidation.

Fearlessly, Ava stared down the thug with a brutal look in her eyes, pretty confident that even the most pathetic of human beings wouldn't initiate violence towards a paraplegic. With a hearty bravado that made Jacob feel more than a little ashamed, she growled.

"What are you looking at?" asked the unperturbed recipient of her stare, comfortable that his alpha male status would remain intact after a verbal conflict with a wheelchair-bound female.

"What do you mean?" Ava replied.

"I said, WHAT ARE YOU LOOKING AT?" He took a step closer. Jacob subconsciously took a step back, distancing himself from any danger.

Ava threw herself wholeheartedly into this altercation. "What do you think I'm looking at, you moron? Are you thick? Are you a bit slow?" Her momentum grew. "And also, genius, for you to notice that I was looking at you would imply that you must have been looking at me, thus making you guilty of exactly the same crime that you were just accusing me of! So what were YOU looking at, tough guy, picking on a girl in a wheelchair, and needing mates to back you up!?" She shook her head and muttered something else under her breath.

Requiring a moment to think about this comment briefly, another to decipher its exact meaning, followed by digesting exactly what level of humiliation he had just suffered, the boy finally came to his conclusion about what had just occurred.

Seething at having the mickey taken out of him in front of his friends by this slight girl in a wheelchair, the thug smashed his bottle into the ground and advanced towards Jacob, who was silently cursing his daughter whilst frantically trying to find the van key and remove them from this situation as quickly as possible.

"Come on old man. Let's go! No laws, we are all just animals now." A circle of white t-shirts gathered around Jacob and sheer terror flowed through his body. He covered his head with his arms and silently cursed his daughter while he waited for what was to come when an authoritative voice cut through the air.

"Hey you louts, get out of here, no trouble in my parking lot. Who smashed that bottle? Come on, own up." It was a security guard from the supermarket, alerted by the sound of a smashing bottle that something was amiss on his watch. He was no fighter, or even a large man, and he placed huge reliance that his uniform would communicate enough authority to get him out of any scrapes without incident.

The lead thug spat at a petrified Jacob, whose shaking hands had not yet managed to thread his car key into the keyhole.

"You okay sir?" the guard asked, without really sounding like he was concerned.

"Yes, thank you. You know I didn't actually w-want to park like this but there were other cars parked at angles and I had no choice really you see my daughter is in a wheelchair so I needed a handicapped spot and I found one and could only get in at an angle because of the other cars…"

Ava butted in, embarrassed. "You're rambling! Come on, let's go, this day actually can't get any worse. I just saw my own father cower in fear to a boy at a supermarket over a car park. Feel emasculated do you? You should."

The security guard had started to wander off, not wanting to have anything to do with anybody else's family issues since he already had enough of his own to worry about. Jacob got Ava into the car in record time, wanting to be on his way before the security guard disappeared altogether, opening up the risk for the gang to return and finish what they started.

The familiar weight of shame and humiliation pressed down upon Jacob's shoulders again, and he sighed. What kind of man was he? Was he even a man? No job, no backbone, no wife, hardly even a daughter, well, certainly not one that cared two hoots about him. Could things get any worse? Probably not, so at least that meant that things could only get better.

Things never used to be like this, the perfect storm of demoralizing events had broken him down and the residual was not a bitter man nor a resentful one, just a despondent and barren vessel. His similarly despondent and barren stomach rumbled its agreement with this evaluation.

Back in the sanctuary of his own home, and even after eating a substantial yet mediocre meal the empty feeling in his stomach didn't go away. His previous thoughts recurred and sat at the back of his mind. Things could only get better. If only he believed this.

Slumping into his armchair like a rag doll, he lay back and stared at the ceiling, brow furrowed. The anarchic scene at the supermarket concerned him on many levels, mostly at the irrationality of humans when faced with a new status quo, which in his opinion should breathe a sigh of relief into the species rather than initiate a panic.

Why, when confronted with a number of ways to perceive a scenario, do people always choose the context that begets the greatest amount of pain, angst, fear, negativity? The recent events could just as easily have unlocked unity and joy within the community, heralding an era of peace with everybody basking in the glory of a common God.

All it takes is one person to incite fear. When one person chooses to accept fear, when one person becomes scared, even wildfire does not spread as quickly among the population. And now fear had found Jacob.

Mon 21 Sept 1959 **6:08am**
Faith Investigates

Opening her eyes, Faith turned to look at her old alarm clock that she had owned and adored since she was fourteen and wondered if the mechanism had finally given up the ghost and refused to go off this morning. Seeing that it was only just after 6am, she raised her eyebrows and mentally scratched her head.

Contrary to her previous expectations of a dismal night's sleep, this was one of those occasions where she couldn't even remember waking up during the night, tossing and turning, or even needing to go to the bathroom. In fact, for the first time in a long time she felt rested.

"The best," she whispered to herself, and with the glee of a small child, promptly shut her eyes and drifted off again calmly until 6:30am when old faithful finally did go off.

"Darn it." The second sleep was always the best but the hardest to wake up from. Remembering how spritely she felt twenty two minutes ago she was surprised that in such a short time and with extra sleep, she could feel so groggy. *That's more like how I feel on a normal morning I suppose.*

Opening a fresh jar of instant coffee, she closed her eyes, stuck her nose right over the top and breathed in deeply. She didn't momentarily get transported to Brazil, but her caffeine addiction did learn that its fix was coming. Wonderful. Scooping three heaped teaspoons into an oversized mug that was stained from almost constant use, she realised she hadn't turned the kettle on, and then had an agonizing wait until it boiled. Ahhh, at last.

Opening her freshly delivered bottle of milk, pouring copious amounts into the mug didn't seem to change the colour of the dark sludgy liquid at all. She didn't even really want to add milk but felt that it was the only source of calcium in her diet.

Cramming into her mouth a piece of toast that she found still in the toaster from yesterday (she hoped), without any condiments, she chewed the dry lump with great difficulty and left her apartment, forgetting to lock the door behind her.

Annoyingly, outside it was still drizzling and she couldn't be bothered going back upstairs so she took her coat off and draped it over her head. It was unusually quiet out, she noticed. Must just be the gloomy weather.

By 7am she was the first person in the office except for a couple of guys from the printers who always came by to drop off a few copies of the day's paper. These were always swooped upon by whoever arrived first, and then fastidiously pored over to try to find any errors, although by this time it was always too late to correct since the papers were already in circulation.

"Did you come back and sleep here overnight or something? Your hair looks like you didn't do it this morning." Maxwell strode in and grabbed a paper, his opening line immediately deflating Faith.

"Thanks boss, you are too kind. It's a new style I'm trying, 'Cheveux en desordre.'"

"Is that how they are wearing it in France? Stick to what you know from now on. You aren't a fancy girl." Maxwell muttered while flicking through the paper, oblivious to her attempt at French-based humour.

Not expecting to hear silence in return, something inside him triggered an alert that warned he may have just made some sort of man mistake, the kind you don't get forgiven for easily. The alert also told him that it was time to dig his way out of the hole he realised he was now probably in. He looked her up and down approvingly, hoping she would notice. She did, and glared at him.

"But your makeup does look good today, do you do it yourself?" He shook his head at his own silly, panicked question. "Of course you do. You don't even need to wear so much you know. If you're a good looker, too much makeup can actually make you look cheap and worse." He continued. "And if you are ugly, then no amount of makeup is going to help you." For some reason, he chose to go on. "So it's really only a fine line of those middle of the road girls that makeup actually helps."

Phew, lucky he was a smooth talker. Man mistake successfully taken care of. Woman crisis averted.

"And which of those types of women am I, boss?" she said in a tone that made it very clear that he should think very carefully about his answer. The man alert went off again in his head. What now? He panicked, his mouth opened and words came out that he had no control over. The only thing that could save this situation was a quick subject change.

"Sometimes I think that maybe a hundred years or so ago they should have started some sort of breeding program where only attractive people were allowed to reproduce. What a wonderful world we would be living in today."

"Yes, but then you wouldn't be here right now, would you?"

They both burst out laughing, knowing that Maxwell had been let off the hook easy this time. He tried to redeem himself and attempted a fresh start at a sensible conversation.

"Okay, so I've got a surprise for you that I picked up on the way in."

"Ooh, you shouldn't have, boss. What is it?" Her mind whirled. Maxwell walked over to his desk and picked up his briefcase.

"Close your eyes."

Heart beating somewhat faster, she did as he bade. His footsteps came closer, then rounded behind her and she heard the briefcase clicking open, some ruffling and then it was put on the floor. The scent of his familiar cologne danced into her nostrils. She inhaled deeply, subtly. One large, warm, masculine hand suddenly reached around and covered her eyes, and she felt the other arm sweep around her other side and hold something in front of her. She felt encased by him and it felt comfortable.

"Okay, open!" And his hand pulled away from her face like a magician pulls his handkerchief away from the trick he has just performed.

Her eyes opened, and she came face to face with....The Chronicle? A print of the competitor's newspaper was staring her in the face, the top right corner leaning over lazily towards her. Inside herself she could feel disappointment and deflation, but tried not to let it show. She was wearing enough makeup on her face for this to be successful. What was she expecting, a diamond necklace? Divorce papers from his wife?

The half-page headline boldly read "God Descends!" which technically wasn't true. God did not occupy anywhere that could be descended from as there was no physical presence as we know it. There was no existence of what we have conceptualised as heaven or any other relatable similar ideal from where to descend. The most accurate representation of what had transpired was a materialisation into human consciousness. But that was just the fact-disseminating journalist-pedant in her coming out.

"Read the article, it's terrible compared to yours," Maxwell said with the excitement of a proud parent in his voice.

She found the story and gave it the attention it deserved, a quick glance. It was light and fluffy and did not convey the weight or the significance of the event it was covering.

"So you officially have written the most comprehensive and well-researched piece on this, probably in the country, in such a short timeframe. The printing presses ran hot last night, if this isn't the highest selling paper we have had to date then I'll eat my hat."

She swelled with pride. That was the most genuine compliment she had ever received from Maxwell and he had unknowingly just redeemed himself for his obliviously insulting comments earlier. She jolly well deserved a diamond necklace now. Her name and photo would be seen by more people than she could dare to dream.

Descending back to earth from her own idea of heaven, Faith became aware of the buzz around the office and the sound of typewriters typing, phones ringing and the usual hive of activity that signified the working day had begun in earnest. She strolled with swagger over to her desk and immediately heard ringing coming from beneath a messy pile of papers. First call of the day.

She sat down, got comfortable, and prepared to speak to either her mother or one of her friends for the next hour. Sweeping papers away from the phone, she answered.

"Talk to me Mavis."

"Hi Faith, some guy on the line for you about your article." Mavis from reception transferred the line. *Bah, let's hope this is short and swe*et, she thought, I've got follow up articles to write.

"Hi you've reached Faith, the Tribune."

"Hel-hello, is this the Faith who wrote the God story in today's paper?" a tentative voice with little confidence asked.

"Yes it is how can I help you?"

"I'd just like to say what a good news story it was, I thought it was written really well."

Blah blah yes yes I know it was, she thought to herself. "Why thank you, I really appreciate that. Now if you don't mind I have to get back to…"

"But you are missing ah.. some information is what I'm trying to tell you. I feel like you wanted to convey all things that everybody is now aware of about, err, you know what?"

"About God and the knowledge we were all imparted? Yes that's right, I believe I did a pretty comprehensive job of it and cross-referenced with many people as a good journalist should do. Everything should be there."

"Well I know you missed something. I know that God came to reset the truth. I can feel that information in me, but it was not mentioned in your article."

Faith frowned and raised her eyes to the ceiling. "What does that mean? All that we learned were facts, the who, the whats, the whens, the wheres, but there was nothing about the whys. Are you suggesting you know something about *intent*? I don't believe you."

This happened frequently when she broke a story, the loonies would call up to try to get in on a piece of what she called "razzamatazz". Over the years she had heard the most unbelievable claims from attention seekers. Best just to absorb it, play along, and then forget it ever happened.

"Okay that's really great, I have to leave the office right now for a story, can I get your name and number and I'll call you back I promise." She absentmindedly took his details down, and then scrunched the paper up into a ball and threw it at the bin, missing wildly.

"Who was that?" her colleague Christina asked. "Another crackpot?"

"Yeah, I sure do attract them."

"At least you don't have my problem. I end up dating them!" They both chuckled.

"He said that I was missing something from my article. He claimed to know at least partially why this is all happening."

"What, do you mean you are missing something from your article?" Maxwell had wandered past and heard a few key words that he never, ever wanted to hear.

"Don't worry, just some joker claiming he knew something I didn't. Nothing to worry about. All baloney."

Maxwell grunted "Better be," and moved on.

It wasn't long before her phone rang again. Mavis from reception. Here we go again. It was going to be one of those days. She felt sorry for Mavis already, that phone was going to be glued to her ear all day. After this call Faith would tell her to just leave it off the hook.

"Another gentleman for you, this is your lucky day, he sounds quite handsome!" Mavis was seventy years old and could barely hear at all, let alone deduce whether somebody sounded handsome or not, and hence most of Faiths' callers sounded handsome.

"Faith, Tribune." Already dispensing with the niceties.

The voice this time was, at a guess, a mid-forties man deep and not entirely unpleasant. Mavis may have been right.

"Hi Faith, I'm just calling up about your article in the paper this morning actually. I think it's really great.." At this point Faith zoned out and started thinking about how many more calls like this she would receive today if she didn't tell Mavis to ignore them. Probably a record number. Well, if she ever had a moment of low self-esteem during the day she could get Mavis to patch a few calls through for a quick pick-me-up.

Without even thinking, she intermittently interjected with "Yep, uh-huh, I know." She had mastered this technique, and was sure that she could keep it up for long periods and on occasion had to, whenever her mother called. The man's voice droned on. Handsome sounding or not, the subject matter was of no interest to her. Time to cut this off at the pass and get on with the day. And then a chill filled the air and her spine turned to ice.

"… and all that, but I also got that God came to reset the truth."

The whole room went quiet and Faith snapped to attention, blood pounding in her ears, her hands trembling so much that she nearly dropped the phone.

"Wh..what did you say?"

"Yeah so I was saying that your story missed a b-bit, you know where God came to reset the truth, that's why, you know, the appearance happened actually."

"Sorry sir, what was your name again?"

"Samuel ma'am."

"Samuel can I meet you as soon as possible? Where are you?"

"Uptown, yeah, I guess, i-if you want to. I can come to you if you want? I don't work you see, I'm…."

"Great Samuel, I will see you when you arrive. I'll be here, just ask for me at reception."

So it would seem that there were either two madmen who were hearing voices in their head that were communicating identical scenarios, or there were two conmen who had come up with a disturbing practical joke to play, or, option three which was that somehow, some people were getting more of the divine picture than others.

Faith decided that interviewing one crazy every now and again couldn't hurt if it got to the bottom of the story. Just to make sure that she herself wasn't going crazy, she asked once around the office whether anybody had heard or felt anything about "resetting the truth," however, as she suspected, blanks stares from around her desk provided her with the answer she needed.

Tapping idly on her desk with a dull pencil, leaning back on her chair and occasionally tipping over too far and startling herself into having to correct her balance, Faith immersed herself deep in thought about how to follow up her initial story, but her mind was blanker than when she was trying to come up with ideas for her romance novel.

Yesterday she knew that she had generated countless interesting angles from which she could approach the topic, but now her mind had been swept clean and was unable to think about anything other than this Samuel guy who she was expecting to come in any second now, she hoped. She turned and yelled to Hal, who was having a very heated conversation with his calculator and what appeared to be a folded piece of paper.

"Hey Hal, can you remember any of the story ideas I mentioned to you yesterday afternoon?"

"Sorry, I just make sure you all get paid, remember?" he said, quoting what seemed to be the only phrase in the English language that he seemed to know how to say to other humans. He continued his preferred discussion with his inanimate objects.

Faith rolled her eyes for the hundredth time and turned back to her desk where she promptly screamed. An unusual looking man had silently approached her desk and was standing a little too close within her personal space to be considered socially acceptable. Adjusting herself, slightly ashamed at being caught off-guard and looking foolish, she realised that looking like a fool should not bother her in this instance. This guy had her way beat in that department.

"F-Faith?"

"Samuel I presume."

An impossibly skinny man, completely dressed in charcoal grey with a shock of contrasting white billowing hair and who looked like he may have been made of dust, stood virtually on top of her and rocked from one bare foot to another. Faith's heart sank. Oh dear, he actually is crazy, she thought to herself, and braced herself for the next part of her day to amount to nothing. She mentally created a list of excuses for use to extricate herself from the situation.

Before she had a chance to back herself away from him a little, he commenced speaking, and so, with an odd man towering over her, Faith craned her neck, put on her "interested" face, and listened bemusedly to what Samuel had to say.

"I hypothesize that y-yesterday's hyperphysical promulgation of deistic existential certitude culminated in the unintentional divulgence of incongruous revelations. Actually."

Faith pointed to the door.

"Get out!"

Mon 21 Sept 1959 8:00am
The Man Discovered

"Well in all my years in this cafe I've never had such a slow day as this!" Doris shook her head and started to polish the glass cabinet at the front of the café for the third time that morning. The cherry pie on the top shelf within looked so darn inviting.

Freshly baked that morning, it was still warm enough to steam up the inside of the glass that was encasing it. Temptation had never been a word in Doris' vocabulary, however, the last twenty or so hours had caused Doris to reconsider her life and her work, and after dwelling upon the subsequent revelations she decided that she needed to pay more attention to her life and less to her work. And maybe just a little attention towards that cake right there.

"Ah to hell with it," she said as she threw the cloth onto the bench, pulled out the entire cherry pie and sat at a table on her own with a fork. Why oh why had she never done this before, it felt wonderful! Liberated, she even kicked off her shoes and slumped in to the back of the chair, the plate of pie resting on her lap.

Half way through her first piece of what was going to be many, the all-too familiar sound of the bell and the irritating squeak of the front door snapped her back to reality. She sat there quite sheepishly as, like clockwork, the elderly gentleman walked past her completely dressed in white from head to toe and sat at his usual spot at the table, first customer of the day. As usual he pulled a paisley pocket square from his blazer and rested it on his left leg, then took his hat off and placed it to his right.

What great timing. The pie would have to wait. Or would it?

Since Doris had already done one thing completely out of character this morning and with no degree of regret whatsoever, she decided that she may as well continue the charge and she stood right up, skipped over to the counter with the pie balanced in her hand, grabbed a spare fork out of the drawer, and then walked across and plonked herself down next to the man and placed it in front of him, carefully lowering the cake slowly in between them.

Shovelling the rest of her first piece into her mouth whilst trying to say "It's good," to the man, without any hint of recognition he said "Black coffee please, my friends will be here soon," and continued to stare out the front window.

Completely deflated and brought back down to earth, Doris slowly stood up and whilst still chewing, made her way barefoot to the coffee machine at the counter.

Looking at the gentleman today, there was something different about him, apart from the fact that he was wearing a suit and shoes so white that they almost looked blue. She couldn't quite put her finger on it, maybe he didn't seem quite so melancholy and desirous of attention? Instead of looking around for people to praise him and come to him, he had shrugged off the neediness and seemed confident in his own company.

"Anyway, I hope he doesn't spill this coffee on his nice white suit," Doris thought to herself as she delivered it to his table, wiping away remaining pie crumbs, evidence of her momentary lapse of work ethic.

Cherry pie back in its rightful home in the cabinet, she commenced polishing once again when the door creaked open slowly and the sound of footsteps crossed the floor. Hooray, another customer, it must have just been a slow start to the day!

She stood upright and saw a young man maybe aged twenty five, look around and then walk to the large communal table at the back and sit with the elderly gentleman, shaking hands as he did so.

Doris' eyes nearly popped out of her head. She stared for a good while, and then caught herself. The young man was speaking enthusiastically and peppering the elderly man with questions. Doris actually had the feeling that they had never met before, and her curiosity was piqued. Was this one of the friends the gentleman had been waiting for all this time? He was certainly not of the demographic that she expected.

After a good ten minutes of watching the conversation unfold in front of her, she got back to work and added a little pep to her stride, feeling like the answer to a big question had finally been revealed.

No sooner had she picked up her mop when the door opened again, this time an elderly woman and an asian teenager appeared. They too walked across to the communal table, the elderly woman being assisted by the younger, and sat down. A similar conversation to the one with the young man started, sounding exactly like old friends reacquainting themselves and catching up on lost time.

They were an unusual group, everybody completely different but all having the elderly gentleman in common, amidst it all and in his element that he was the central point of attention and had been discovered at last.

It wasn't long before more people arrived and the table was full of people laughing and patting each other on the back and talking over each other and having a roaring good time. The large table in the back of Cassidy's that usually remained depressingly empty except for one lonely regular customer was now a noisy congregation with barely enough seats for everybody, and soon people were standing around the table in a crowd.

Doris watched all this from her counter and observed divine happiness radiating from the communal table. Seeing the unusual man finally receiving recognition and acceptance when previously nobody acknowledged his existence, she forgot about all the new questions appearing in her head and tears welled up in her eyes.

Sun 20 Sept 1959   1:45pm
Mary Asserts

After expressing numerous concerns and repeated offers to stay and help, Mary was shooed out of the house by Mrs Howlett who insisted that she would be quite alright on her own, and in fact felt tremendous and newly injected with inspiration for her artistic pursuits.

"I'm going to take my artworks to the next level my dear!" she promised Mary who wondered what that could possibly mean, as she winked and pushed her out of the house with Zach trailing behind and receiving an affectionate pat on the head.

"Okay, okay I get the picture, no more procrastinating so I guess I have to go to the Rutherford's now anyway." That thought took the sparkle out of her step a little. Josephine Rutherford was a nasty piece of work who enjoyed belittling people in front of others and on quite a few occasions had inappropriately mentioned Zach and his special characteristics in a not so flattering way.

Nobody who was comfortable and secure in themselves as a human being would feel the need to bring somebody else down in an to attempt to prove to others that they were superior. If you were secure you wouldn't care what others thought, and Mary's mind had concocted some sort of rationale behind the behaviour that had to do with childhood and other influential events in Josephine's past, but that didn't mean she had to like her, and every weekly trip made to the large and extravagantly furnished house was reluctantly made.

Unfortunately it was that time of the week again and she was running late, so Mary buckled Zach into the car, climbed in herself and started it up. And then proceeded to drive straight home.

"Why should I have to do something I don't want to do?" Mary asked rhetorically, but partially including Zach into the one person conversation also. "I'm a grown adult, and if I don't want to do something I can simply say no, it's that easy! This isn't the dark ages, nobody can force me to clean a house, can they? I'm just going to say no!"

This newly-entered phase of enlightenment instantly relieved a huge burden from her. The internal awareness that God truly existed validated her existing beliefs and she felt as if she now had a powerful army on her side. It was like she had an advantage just by being on the team longer than other newcomers and had tenure.

All those times in her life that she had felt obliged to do one thing or another, she didn't actually have to do them! Why had she spent her life trying to make others happy at the expense of her own happiness? Just like Mrs Rutherford, Mary had her own type of insecurity but it wasn't the type that placed herself on a pedestal with the desire of appearing superior than others, hers was to win acknowledgement by placing others on pedestals and to make them feel superior to her.

At school when she was no older than seven or eight, her lunchtimes were usually spent sitting in solitude at the side of the oval, watching the other children form their friendship groups and play their games as children do. She didn't mind being on her own, and never really having had anybody close to her before, she didn't know things any other way.

She had company of a sort anyway, her tattered doll Esmerelda that was given to her by her grandmother was always within reach and was a reliable source of comfort. She stroked and brushed her blonde hair, participated in one sided conversations and at the end of lunch would tuck her away nice and snug in a special compartment in her schoolbag. Esmerelda reminded her of her grandma who wasn't around anymore. She missed her.

Seeing her on sit her own and not being warmed to by the other children, some of the more considerate teachers would try to speak with her, not appreciating that this would have an even further limiting effect on her popularity. Her grades did very well as a result of these closer relationships with her educators, however, and she soon became an exceptional student which finally attracted her some recognition from other children as a teacher's pet.

One day at lunch, a group of girls approached her at the oval and started to ask her why she was friends with the teachers but not the students. Mary didn't really have an answer for that, and felt a little uncomfortable at the way they were asking and had circled around her. She had Esmerelda in her lap and started to nervously brush her hair more vigorously.

"Hey that's a nice doll, what's her name?" one of the taller girls called Catherine asked.

"Esmerelda," she meekly replied.

Can I hold her?" The girl held out her hand and Mary felt like she wanted to say no but she didn't because she didn't really have a reason why not, and was unsure of what the girl's response would be. She gave her the doll to hold onto, but didn't take her eyes off it.

The rest of the lunch was spent talking and laughing with the girls, hearing their funny stories, learning about what their home lives and parents were like, and Mary came to understand what it was like to be around other people and part of a group, and to be acknowledged as an individual. The bell to signal the end of lunch rang, and the kids started to meander back to class.

"Do you mind if I take her home for the evening?" Catherine asked, stuffing Esmerelda into her bag.

"Uh, sure," Mary said to her newly found friend, but in reality was completely unsure about the idea.

"Cool!" And then they were off back to class.

A week later and Mary was sitting on the side of the oval in her usual position, confused and upset and lonely. Since that one lunch time last week, the girls had not said a further word to her or even looked in her direction, and Esmerelda had still not been returned. Every day she had wanted to approach Catherine but was too afraid of what she would say. She missed Esmerelda, and she missed her grandma. Timidly, she saw the girl after school and asked her about her doll.

"Oh yes of course! So sorry, I have her here with me but I really like her. Can I have her for just one more night please?" Catherine wrapped an arm around Mary.

Surprised at how easy it was to ask her and observing the good nature of the response, Mary was more than happy to agree to letting her keep Esmerelda another night, she could easily just ask her again tomorrow!

That night turned into weeks, and Mary kept agreeing to let Catherine keep Esmerelda for more extra nights. One day, Mary asked her if she could just see Esmerelda, as it had been such a long time.

"Look, I don't have your stupid doll okay! I lost it somewhere the first night you gave it to me, now stop bugging me!" and she pushed Mary away and walked off.

Mary collapsed to the ground hysterically, a poor figure sitting on the concrete more alone than ever, having had more than just a rag doll taken away from her. She couldn't comprehend what had just happened. She had been nice to somebody just like her parents told her, and doesn't that mean the person should like her and be nice back? Why was this not the case and where did it go wrong? Was she that unlikeable? And just like that, she had lost Esmerelda, the only real heirloom of her grandmother, and any remaining self-esteem.

How stupid had she been? She knew at the time and saw now this was no way to behave or earn respect. Her lack of assertiveness had seen her walked over in life and accepting of what was unacceptable behaviour. But enough was enough.

"I should probably call Josephine to tell her I'm not coming." She said to Zach, but after a split second of thought- "Well, that's one call from me that she won't be receiving. After all, God, THE actual God has been revealed to me, to the world. I think that cleaning some rude so and so's house is hardly on my list of priorities, pardon my French."

Arriving home and feeling very proud of her decision to only do things that were her choice to do, she turned her mind to all the other things that were causing her worry in her life and mentally geared herself up to separate herself from them too. "I don't have to do anything I don't want to do. I don't have to do anything I don't want to do." She repeated the mantra and with every sentence she mentally sliced another chore from her to-do list, feeling incrementally more in control of her life each time.

"Bye bye Rutherfords! Bye bye babysitting that little terror down the street! Bye bye pruning old man Bob's hedge down the road while he creepily watches me!"

Zach sat on the couch in the living room watching his mother pace up and down talking to herself with curiosity, he had never seen her like this before. The phone rang, snapping Mary out of her determined state of mind and, not thinking, she automatically answered, and as she did so she instantly made a face and kicked herself because she knew it could only be one person. A whiny voice carried over the line.

"Hi Mary, it's Josephine here, you do realise you are supposed to be over at my place this very minute cleaning? I don't know how busy your schedule is but I'm happy to overlook this slip up, this one time. We had a little soiree last night and the place is a complete mess so we really need you here I'm afraid. So I will see you soon?"

"Look, Jo, I am sorry that I didn't turn up today, and I appreciate all the work that you have given me but I think that with the extraordinary turn of events from this morning I just don't think it's right that I continue to work for you. You will have to find somebody else I'm afraid." There was a pause on the line, and Mary knew that Josephine was not expecting this response.

"So.. so you are quitting cleaning people's houses?"

Mary swallowed and forced out the truth. "No, not everyone's, just yours."

"Oh my. Is there any reason? I mean, I know it's a big house and there is a lot to do. Is it the pay? I can offer you more money? Not a lot mind, you, our cash is all tied up in assets, but I can give you a little more. You do a good job and we would prefer to keep you. It's hard to find new help." Her tone was so condescending that Mary slightly adjusted her response accordingly.

"No, it's not the size of the place or the pay, it's you. In the light of what has happened today I've made a few decisions that I should have made a long time ago and I'm choosing to prioritise myself. There are more important things going on now that means that worrying about the cleanliness of your house after a soiree is not high on my agenda."

"Look. You didn't even call to tell me you weren't coming and we had a prior agreement. That's a bit rude isn't it Mary, so how about I pay you double for this one and it can be your last time unless I can convince you to stay on. I mean, we all have to be nice to each other now that God exists don't we, so I will even come and pick you up now. See you soon!" and she hung up before Mary could say anything.

Josephine had a point and Mary dwelled on the fact that they did have a prior agreement which she had committed to. The right thing to do would be to just do this last one and then no more. And at double pay too, though she had seen the Rutherford residence after a party before and she wasn't sure that she was getting a good deal.

Her mind went back twenty something years and echoes of her old classmate Catherine pleading for Esmerelda rang in her ears: "Just one more day, just one more.." and Mary realised she was still that same little lonely school girl sitting by the side of the oval, willing to do anything for those that asked. Josephine could have her one more day more.

"Okay Zach, we are going to that mean old woman's house one last time. Don't feel the need to behave too well this time. I know you are a good boy but maybe you could accidentally break a vase or something while we are there. Mummy won't mind!" she said, knowing full well that Zach would sit in the Rutherford's big maroon velvet armchair and not move for the whole time she was cleaning.

Shortly, Josephine Rutherford arrived and impatiently knocked on the front door, expecting Mary to have been ready and waiting very apologetically to depart.

"Hi, come in, come in, I won't be long," Mary said as she opened the door and ushered her in, directing her to a seat. Josephine sat down and looked around the room, obviously not being used to setting foot in modest residences such as this and looked worried that the "condition" might be catching if she touched anything.

She pulled the collar of her jacket up higher and sunk herself into it up to her ears, hoping to shelter herself from whatever contaminants there were in the room. After looking around further, her assessment of the situation was that the place was adequately clean and so she sat back and relaxed somewhat.

After several minutes, feeling brave enough to stand up and walk around, she reached the kitchen and had a look around, opened the fridge, looked in some drawers, and generally stuck her nose in every area of interest to get some sort of glimpse into how people could make do without sterling silver cutlery or caviar in the fridge.

Moving across to the dining table and settling herself down there, she glanced at the newspaper in front of her and saw that the cryptic crossword had very nearly been completed in its entirety.

"Well, well, Mary, smarter than you look. You have the handwriting of a child, but nonetheless very impressive actually," she said, conceding on this rare occasion that there was somebody other than herself who was deserving of some praise.

She looked at some of the answers and tried unsuccessfully to figure out how they were deduced by looking at the almost nonsensical cryptic questions. "She probably had a chance to look at the answers somewhere. Who is she trying to fool, why bother with that little charade!?" She smirked at the thought that Mary had gone to such lengths to impress somebody.

"Okay Jo, come on and let's get this over and done with." Mary had appeared and was looking impatient even though Josephine observed to herself that Mary was the one who had been holding them up.

"Go and grab Zach and get him into the ca.." Josephine was nearly finished speaking when she saw Zach already up and waiting by the front door. "Oh, good boy you are learning to think for yourself that's so great!" she said with a large patronising smile.

"Oh Mary, that little boy has never been proactive at doing anything so it must be a refreshing change that he is finally starting to do things without being told!" Mary ignored her.

In the car on the way, the rain started pattering down again and Mary thought about how nice it would have been to stay inside and rug up all nice and cosy.

"So what do you make of everything that happened this morning? Can you believe it? I simply can't. I just can't! It feels so strange but comforting inside, to know there is something from God sitting there, just for me. Isn't it just a wonder of the world to know that it is all real?" Josephine trilled, making small talk.

She wasn't really interested in Mary's answer but knew that Mary was religious so expected her response would fill in the rest of the car trip which would otherwise remain deathly quiet between the two women who had nothing in common with each other.

Before Mary could answer, Josephine continued. "I saw on television some world leaders issuing statements saying that everything would be okay and not to worry. A lot of people are getting pretty worried you know, something like this doesn't happen every day and nobody knows what it really means. Is it good news? Why does everything feel so tense? Anyway, it was reassuring to hear all the important people of the world say that it's all fine."

"How the hell would they know?!" Mary snapped. "Every time some major event happens, the world leaders have to make some sort of statement and put their two cents in even though they have no idea what is going on and it has nothing to do with them. They can't guarantee anything or reassure us, they are made of flesh and blood like us and don't know any more than we do. They aren't privy to anything that we aren't. It's so insulting. But brainless people like you lap it up and believe that they have the situation under control but they don't! Just be honest that you don't know what is going on or what is going to happen next and at least I know you aren't blowing hot air at us. Don't feel obliged to ramble at us like we are all dumb sheep that need to have our mummies say nice words to us or else we will have nightmares."

Mary realised she had gotten worked up pretty quickly and made an effort to calm herself down. She did feel better after the vent though and knew how much she always bottled up. Venting was much more satisfying. She hoped Zach didn't get scared at her yelling and she turned around and grabbed his leg reassuringly as he sat behind her. She noticed he had a semi-smile on his face that she had never seen before. She gave his leg a quick squeeze and turned back around.

Arriving at Josephine's palatial mansion, they entered and tracked water into the house. "Sorry dear, one more thing for you to clean," Josephine observed. Her son Randwick, who was around Zach's age came into the room holding a wooden train which he was flying through the air like it was a plane, right in front of Zach's face. Zach walked across the room ignoring Randwick and sat in the big maroon velvet chair and stared dead ahead.

"He's so weird," Randwick said to his mother.

"I know Rand, just let him do what he needs to do while his mummy cleans our house for us."

Mary had already begun to clean, keen to get out of there as quickly as possible and with a handful of money. She started in the foyer, dusting the console table and made her way around the spacious room, planning to leave the area affected by the "soiree" until last, constantly reminding herself that this was the last time she would ever be inside this house, and that made the job a little easier to bear.

A loud crash came from the room that Zach and Randwick were in, and both Mary and Josephine ran in at the same moment from doors on opposite sides of the room. Surveying the situation, Zach was sitting in the maroon velvet chair, Randwick had his toy wooden train in his hand, and on the floor was a broken vase surrounded by a pool of water and exotic flowers.

"Randwick! You naughty boy, that vase cost a fortune!" Josephine screamed out, showing where her concerns lay. "Mary you will have to clean this up straight away before he cuts himself."

"Are you okay Randwick?" Mary asked. She wasn't a fan of the boy, but he was a child who was the product of his parents, so he wasn't really to blame for how he turned out, and he deserved to be asked whether he was all right.

"It wasn't me mummy it was Zach," the boy replied, pointing at Zach with his spare hand.

"Oh don't you lie to me young man, what did I tell you about fibbing?" his mother snarled angrily.

"It wasn't me mummy I promise!" the boy pleaded his case upon deaf ears. "I promise with a cherry on the top mummy!"

Mary looked across at Zach and noticed the smile on his face that she had also seen in the car. Was it him and not Randwick? She did tell him earlier that he should break a vase, but surely not? His face now had a look of awareness that she had never seen before. The last day had seen massive change in her son, something seemed to be awakening within him.

Wouldn't Diah love to hear about the development Zach seemed to be going through? If only she knew how to contact him. She felt a pang in her chest that she hadn't felt for a while.

"Okay Mary, if my boy says it wasn't him then it wasn't him. The cost of that vase is going to come out of your pay today, and what that means is that you owe me money for being here! That vase cost a tidy sum, a lot more than the cost of a few hours cleaning."

Mary snarled, protecting her son like a mother bear and only an inch away from laying a hand on Josephine, but aware that there were children in the room held herself back.

"Listen, you fool who has more money than sense! Both of us know that Zach is not capable of doing this."

That woman deserved a good slap, but it wouldn't come today. Still, her hand clenched tightly shut instinctively, and Josephine could see it.

"We are both leaving, and you can clean up after your stupid soiree yourself, and don't ever contact me again. And by the way, Norah Simmons' house is so much more tasteful than this monstrosity!" That felt good, Norah's son and Randwick were rivals for the tennis team captaincy, and the rivalry had spilled over into the parents' lives making everything a competition between the families.

Completely taken aback, never having been spoken to like this before, let alone by a single mother with barely two pennies to rub together who should know her place in society, Josephine watched Mary and her son leave in the rain, mortified mostly at the remark about Norah's house. Lies, surely!

"Now how on earth am I going to get this place clean? Where is the broom? Do I have a broom? I'm sure I've seen Mary use one. Randwick. Come help mummy clean this house. Yes I know it's beneath us but I fired our cleaner. Good boy."

The rain was still pattering down lightly and she could feel it running down her face but Mary had other things on her mind to worry about as she took off her coat and wrapped it around Zach's head as they started the trek home. The walk would take about an hour, and though it was not too cold, it was getting late and she wanted to be home before the sun disappeared.

The last time that she had walked in the rain was many years ago with Diah, holding hands and laughing as they got caught in a downpour one afternoon on the way home from getting off the bus after work, not a care in the world as they squelched in their shoes and got soaked through to their underwear. The fun began as they got in the door and removed their wet clothing, huddling together in front of the fireplace under the same blanket, shivering and clutching each other for warmth.

Mary smiled and pulled Zach closer. "If you can't enjoy a good old fashioned walk in the rain then I feel sorry for you," Mary said to nobody in particular, and ruffled her son's wet hair. The walk home was over quickly, and she dried Zach off, and they sat in front of the fire together, laughing at the eventful day that they had, in higher spirits than perhaps one may have expected.

Mary wanted to ask Zach about the vase at the Rutherford residence, but decided to let it go. The boy was going through some transformation, and she didn't want to draw his attention to it in case it made him self-conscious and close up again.

She went to bed that night without saying her prayers, for the first time since she had been taught how to by her parents as a little girl. She slept well, enjoying the warm feeling of holy awareness inside her.

Zach lay stretched out straight in bed, eyes wide open as per the previous night, seemingly on full alert but completely asleep. His lips curled up at the corners slightly, deep breaths passing through them rhythmically. In his left hand a small piece of porcelain belonging to a fractured vase was cradled gently before eventually slipping through his fingers and onto the floor.

Mon 21 Sept 1959 *10:00am*
Faith Interviews

"Get out!"

Faith scrunched up her face, held her face in her hands for a second or two, and shook her head in amazement. Surely there were no actual people like this in the world for real? Fleeting thoughts of what type of childhood Samuel must have had in order to turn out like this entered her mind and took her to places she did not want to be.

Surely, as a part of society where interaction was essential to some extent, one would try to assimilate at least one iota in order to lubricate that interaction by the slightest degree, no matter how unwanted that interaction might be. Samuel clearly disagreed with this theory and was truly his own man, presenting and conducting himself exactly as he desired with no regard for the opinion of others.

She looked around the office suspiciously, trying to catch whether anybody had an eye on her and the situation. She had experienced practical jokes in the office before, and if some members of staff put as much effort into their work as they did in generating genius ideas for pranks, the newspaper would double its circulation. To her dismay there appeared to be no sniggers, no subtle glances in her direction, no indication that somebody was particularly enjoying seeing their elaborate setup play out, which unfortunately led her to the conclusion that this man was the genuine article.

Samuel walked his bare feet to the door. Faith rolled her eyes again, thinking that if this guy leaves, she is just going to have to rummage amongst all the screwed up paper on the floor near her desk and find the details of the other weird guy who had called her earlier.

"Samuel! Okay, please come back. Sorry. I was just not expecting, well, somebody like you. I'm sure that sentence you just said was in English, however, as masterful with language as I am, I am no thesaurus."

The man turned slowly, white hair flicking around in a most inelegant way that would not make the final cut of a shampoo advertisement, and he strode meekly back towards Faith's desk.

"O-oh, actually, I'm used to that response from people actually. Hmm. Yes."

Faith had the impression that this may be the first time he had spoken to another human being in a while.

"Grab a seat Samuel and let's have a chat. Would you like a coffee or tea?"

"No, thank you. I have something to tell you, you see." His hands rubbed together in anticipation and he hopped from one foot to another.

"Yes, yes, I must say I am very curious to hear your story. If what you say is true, then you seem to know something that nobody, well, not many other people know about what happened yesterday. I mean, I think we can all recall everything, the information is inside of us, but you claim that inside you, amongst all the other information that was passed on, you know something more?"

"Yes, what I was trying to tell you earlier was my hypothesis that the information that was released, divulged, input or fed into us, or whatever you would like to call it, was not broadcast identically into all of us. I was delivered more from God than what your very comprehensive article described, actually."

"Yes, that the truth was being reset. That's right isn't it? Can you elaborate on that further?" Faith reached across to her desk and grabbed her notepad and pen, not entirely confident that what she was about to commence taking notes on she would be able to spell.

"O-okay, so, as you know, mankind has been around for a while now, and the recording of the history of man has chronicled past human behaviours which lead to significant events deemed worthy of being recorded for posterity. Are you understanding this so far, actually?"

"Yes, thank you for asking Samuel, I actually am. Sentence number two into proceedings and I'm still keeping up."

"Great. And since the dawn of consciousness, the belief in an all-powerful presence, a higher being, a God, whether just one or more, has influenced human behaviour and hence development and the entire direction of progress significantly. Religion, whilst being sold as an instrument of glory and greatness and salvation, has actually been responsible for more war, death and atrocity than I could ever be comfortable thinking about actually. From burning, stoning, sacrificing, to crucifying Jesus himself, Gods have been used to justify cruelty and killing for aeons, actually."

A melancholy washed over Samuel, and he shook his head at the human race with disappointment.

"And now, since we know that there is only one God, it becomes evident that every other one of the thousands of Gods, whether Roman, Greek, Incan, must have been created by the imagination of man, and created for a purpose, mind you. I can assure you that the purpose was never always altruistic either, actually."

"Imagine, many years ago, if you were a man or part of a group of men creating the concept of Zeus, or Shiva, Neptune, or one of the many other Gods. At the time you wouldn't have the foresight to think that the fictional characters that you were creating would develop into icons of massive cultural influence, with people dying for them, killing for them, for many hundreds of years after you had presented them as a concept, and for long after you were dead. The creator or creators knew that they were imagined, unreal characters, no different than if Superman or Batman were sketched in a studio and presented as real."

Faith pondered this and chimed in. "Of course, with wars and the defeating of foes and inhabiting of newly conquered territory, there was always some sort of revolving door of Gods over time, as the newly introduced Gods moved in and the defeated people were forced to convert or die. But imagine selling them to your own people for the first time. Did nobody ask where all of a sudden these new gods came from?"

"An uninformed, undereducated primitive population are easily led, actually."

"Okay so what you are saying is that this God is the only true God, and I feel that. But, maybe that's just what it wants us to think. How do we know that all we feel and know now is the truth? But then I suppose, if we aren't going to believe in the information that has been inserted within us, then what are we going to believe. Until another God comes along and contradicts this one, then I guess I'm going to have to board the single God theory that this one has presented." Faith was finding the conversation with the strange man extremely engaging.

"So over the millennia, through the creation of a myriad of deities and religions it is time to set the record straight, and reset the scales and the truth back to zero basically. A fresh slate, one God, and the truth about that one God being zapped straight into us. I'll be honest, I don't think it will be long before there are Chinese whispers over the years and that number creeps up again in some cultures actually, probably reinstating old familiar Gods even though it is now known they don't exist, or bestowing God with enhanced capabilities and powers. Can I have that cup of tea now please?" he licked his dry lips.

Faith yelled a junior over and demanded two cups of tea to be brought over.

"So that's pretty much it about the truth being reset? It's just a big recalibration by God. You know, it makes sense so I feel like I believe you. It makes me wonder if there is a reason for it all though, I mean, why now at this point in history? So was there anything in my article that you didn't get?"

"No I had all that, plus my little tidbit."

"I wonder, why you? I also wonder how many more there are like you in the world, you know, ones who received a bit extra and what the connection between you and those others might be. It will be interesting to see what unravels over the next few days, and whether more of you connectors reveal yourselves and any new information."

Automatically her mind went to the other person that called that morning with the same information, and the common link she had between that person and Samuel was that they both seemed, to put it in a polite way, odd.

"No idea. I was just a regular guy before all this." Faith spat out a mouthful of tea and coughed and spluttered. "Sorry Samuel, yes, you are just a regular guy."

"So Faith, what was your religious standing before all this happened?" he asked. She was surprised at the question from him. Usually as a journalist she asked the questions, and her interviewees rarely offered a two way conversation.

"I was an atheist."

"Oh really? How or why did you follow that path?"

"Because I'm educated."

"Oh."

"And as a journalist I need hard evidence before I can even think about writing a credible story, or else it's just speculation and hearsay. I think I just need facts before I am willing to jump on any old train without asking some questions, as any rational human being with common sense and a brain should. I wonder if the tooth fairy is going to show up next."

Samuel chuckled. "Actually, I happened to receive a message from the Easter Bunny the other day." He beamed, proud as punch at his attempt at hilarity and Faith laughed more at his reaction to himself rather than at his humour.

"I made a joke, actually! Other than that Faith, I don't have much else for you I'm afraid, so I hope I've been some help. I've told you all I know about that little extra parcel of knowledge."

"Yes, you've definitely raised some questions Samuel, questions that I sure hope that I can get to the bottom of. Do you mind if I keep in touch just in case I think of anything?"

"No, not at all." Samuel escorted himself through the hustle and bustle of the office, barely raising the attention of anybody on the way, indicative of how caught up in this moment each and every employee of the paper was.

Ordinarily a character such as Samuel would have been virtually running the gauntlet on the way out, and Faith would be dodging jibes, balls of paper being pelted, and have insinuations of alleged relations between herself and the very strange man thrown at her.

Faith sat in her chair, swivelling, deep in thought for a good fifteen minutes. She had taken ample notes, and was now not contemplating what the information was that Samuel had conveyed, but more *why* was he the recipient of that little extra portion.

Faith worked through until lunch, preparing her next story for Maxwell. This whole past twenty four hours seemed surreal, and if she wasn't so busy with her job reporting on the events, she didn't think she would be able to cope with how deeply she was having trouble realigning her entire belief system around this new information.

It really grinded her gears that she, with all her rational thought and intelligence, who so steadfastly and rightfully refused to believe in an obviously flawed and fraudulent fictional tale known as religion, was now proven wrong. What was worse was that she had ridiculed those gullible morons who did believe the not-so-cleverly fabricated story without question because they had faith and no evidence or any logical argument. But, they were the ones laughing now, right back in her face.

She reflected that if she could start over, she would still maintain the same beliefs if she was provided the same information and evidence.

The buzz of the office gradually died down as the day progressed, the number of typewriters being punched away at diminished, the ringing of phones and chatter lessened as journalists left to speak to sources, or chase their stories. Faith noticed none of this, deep in thought and working on a couple of other story ideas that she thought Maxwell would eventually be impressed by, but only after hopefully calling her into his office to discuss details and ask some further questions about her angle. Hopefully it wouldn't all be shop talk though, she really enjoyed their playful banter.

Her phone rang again snapping her out of her annoyance, and her first thought was that it was a bit late for a new crazy to call.

"A gentleman to talk to you. He sounds like one of those handsome latino fellows," Mavis said, then hung up.

Maybe inspiration for a character in her romance novel? She put on her pleasant voice. "Hi you've reached Faith, the Tribune."

A man with a strong Spanish accent and a noticeably anxious sounding tone of voice spoke.

"Faith. A priest is going to go missing from St Paul's on Aitken Street tonight."

Faith hastily grabbed her pen.

"Is GOING to go missing? Congratulations, you have my attention."

Mon 21 Sept 1959 *1:00pm*
Ira's Mission

A broken man sat alone in a room, attempting to locate the precise moment in time when the virtuous, light-filled path trodden beneath his feet had first begun to steer him towards decay and an impure darkness. Surrounded by shadows, mortality and despair, he had traversed the bridge of duplicity and become lost in a stifling forest, the concept of light and life banished to the unreachable part of his memories.

Ira had returned home yesterday after his meeting with Eddie, suddenly aware that he had become a man living within a body that had not been entirely under his control. His actions had not married up to his values for a while now, and the man he felt that he was on the inside was not reflected by the imposter on the outside.

Removing himself from his family under the pretence of illness, the true reason however, being self-exile into an abyss of shame, he needed to search inside himself to find remorse, not just for what he had done to Eddie but for all other previous positions of imposter that he had assumed.

Unmoving, and unaccepting of food and drink offers from his concerned wife, Ira immersed himself in a penitent state, one particular sentence of Eddie's repeating itself over and over in an infinite loop.

"Every bad man is capable of one good deed." Why did he say this to him? He was a good man, he was a God-fearing man who loved his wife and child. Eddie did not know him. Eddie was just a job. He had no right to call him a bad man. Angrily sitting up in his chair, he glanced towards the mantle, a black and white photo of himself and his father catching his eye. The frame and glass was dusty, so he picked it up and wiped it clean on his shirt.

He viciously cast away all thoughts of Eddie from his mind and stared at the picture before him, transported into the photo, warm summer wind in his glossy black hair as his father pushed him on that swing at the park near his old house while his mother held the family's Brownie camera which he still had in a cupboard somewhere, carefully snapping away.

The red and white checked picnic rug laid out on the fresh green grass displayed the remains of a well prepared lunch, carefully constructed sandwiches now nothing more than a sample of crumbs available for the benefit of any hungry ants in the vicinity. His father's voice echoed in his ears.

"So Ira, in life you are going to meet a lot of good people who will make you feel good inside, and you will want to be their friend. But also in life, you are going to meet a lot of bad people who will make you feel good inside, and you will want to be their friend too."

"But how will I know the good people from the bad people dad? If they are good to me, isn't that all that matters? Is it a trick? What if I make the wrong decision?"

"Good question son, and it's not one that is easily answered. If you want my advice, and this has been tried and tested mark my words, you put every damn person you meet into that bad category until they damn well prove to you that they deserve to be out of that box, and that takes time. Every man needs to earn your respect and trust."

He flicked his greying hair to the side in between pushes of the swing, muscular arms preparing for his son to reach the top of the arc, ready for a downwards push again. His rough hands, scarred and calloused from years of hard labour found Ira's back and propelled him with force.

"So are all men either good or bad dad? Can some be both?"

"Sometimes it's not all black and white, you are right son. And mostly it is all a matter of perspective in the end. You can only judge a man by what you yourself see before you, you see their actions with your own eyes, you judge their character, their integrity, and you may have to decide whether you think they will carry themselves with that same character and integrity even when you are not around. But don't get me wrong. Every good man is capable of a bad deed if the stakes are high enough. Sometimes a man needs to do something against his better judgement, especially if it means protecting his family and loved ones."

"But if a man does something bad, if it's protecting his family, then that would be considered to be good right? If somebody is threatening to hurt somebody's family, then that person should be the bad man, right? And if you do something bad to a bad man, then I say that should be good. God would agree with me I know it!"

Ira puffed his chest out proudly, enjoying talking to his father like how he heard grown-ups talk to other grown-ups, but it was exhausting for him. He asked his father to let him off the swing.

"Son, you are an amazing little man, I do believe he takes after me wouldn't you say?" He glanced across to his wife who was tidying up the picnic and waited to hear the positive response.

"He is just like his gorgeous father, a real thinker, a little smarty-pants!" his mother proudly replied.

"Okay, let's get this show on the road. What do you say little man, let's head home and grab an ice cream along the way, yeah?"

"Yeah!"

"Son if there is one thing I want you to learn today, apart from the fact that your mum makes the best damn Reuben sandwich in the country, it's that the devil comes disguised in many forms."

Ira's mother put her hand on her husband's shoulder. "Henry, don't talk to our son about the devil, he's only a boy. You will scare him."

Henry looked into his wife's eyes. "This is a scary world we are bringing him into. Scary people, scary times, I don't want to sugar coat things, he needs to know that the devil is out there."

Turning to Ira, he continued. "Like you just said, a good man can be capable of doing a bad deed. However, deep down in my heart I also do believe that every bad man is capable of one good deed. It's the devil at work, confusing your mind and you need to watch for this and still recognise disguised evil. One good deed does not a good man make."

"Every bad man is capable of one good deed." Ira spoke the words softly to himself.

Returning to the present, he dusted the photo frame off and placed it back on the mantle, his father's words echoing away, the voice now becoming dead Eddie's voice, dead Eddie's words. This disturbed him. Ira was the good man in this situation, doing a bad deed to a bad person, which in his eyes did not make him the devil. But what if he was wrong and he was actually the disguised evil his father told him about?

In all honesty, Ira wasn't sure that all the men that he had hurt were even bad men. His job was to carry out orders without asking any questions, so how was he even in a position to know that answer?

The rest of the day saw Ira lost in a cloud of self-judgment, undecided as to what side of the fence of morality he had been sitting on. Climbing into bed next to his wife that evening, he lay restlessly staring at the ceiling until at some late hour he finally drifted into an uneasy sleep.

The next morning he was still not any closer to resolving his internal struggle and he lay in bed staring at his angel of a wife, heart breaking at the thought that today she would see him for the man he truly was, his façade stripped away and revealing his true ugly form to her. He did not deserve her. She certainly did not deserve somebody like him.

Gently rolling out from under the covers he silently dressed himself and tiptoed out to the front porch to pick up the newspaper. Yesterday's rain had stopped, and it was going to be a gorgeous day. Ira would have preferred that it was still raining, which would have suited his mood.

The feeling of the higher power within him and the euphoria it carried was offset by the fact that now Ira knew he had become unmasked and there was one entity that he could not hide his true self from. Shame overwhelmed him once again and he quickly snatched the paper and closed the front door before anybody could see him for the undisguised devil that he was.

Brewing himself a strong coffee, even the glorious aroma could not drag him out of his slump. He sat down at the dining table and fanned the newspaper out, looking for the politics section as always, but put this to the side to read first the many articles about the events of yesterday. He hoped this would shed some new light and help him to come to terms with his new perspectives, however, the main article contained only information that he already knew.

A worrying thought crossed his mind. He was going to have to see his boss today and somehow tell him that he could no longer work for him. His was the type of industry that one could not just retire from and lead a normal life. Once you were in and caught up in the scene, caught up in the shady people, your face was known and never forgotten. He was working for the type who didn't ask for you to do something, they told you.

Under these unprecedented and unusual circumstances he was sure his boss would understand completely. He had to, and Ira wouldn't be surprised if his boss had opened his mind and seen the same things as Ira and come to the same conclusions.

Motivating himself to climb out of his slump, he emerged from his room of isolation and kissed his wife on the cheek, saying he felt a lot better now.

"You are so grumpy when you are sick, baby. For a big strong man you sure know how to act like a little infant. Waah wahhhh." She mocked. "Hey Hector, your daddy is a big cry baby. Are you tougher than your daddy Hector? Mummy thinks you are," she said with a mischievous grin directed at her husband.

"I don't know mummy, I think so? I am a big boy now so I think yes." Hector broke his gaze from the television to answer, then thought some more about this serious question, and then nodded to himself in agreement, returning focus to the screen.

Ira ribbed his wife. "Oh honey, if only you could experience the same suffering as us men do when we are sick. It's on a different level to what you lucky ladies go through, it's all magnified for us."

"Sure darling, probably because you men deserve it. Anyway, I am glad you are feeling better, you had us worried for a while there, you don't get sick very often. Are you heading out? Go sit and spend some time with your son first would you? Just five minutes, he has hardly seen you lately."

Ira had pressing matters on his mind, but decided that sitting with his son for a bit might calm him down somewhat. He planted himself down on the couch next to Hector and gave him a friendly elbow. "So what are you watching?"

"It's a show about animals. There were stick insects, an octopus, and some other ones that can change colours and hide from other animals that want to eat them."

"Oh that sounds really interesting!" Ira was happy that his son had taken an interest in the natural world. At his age there were many other less educational distractions that could be taking up his time. He turned to the television and listened to the narrator.

".. the Alcon Blue Butterfly lays its eggs on the ground and these larvae fool ants into thinking they are one of their own and are accepted into the colony, intruders in disguise. Not only are their chemical signatures aligned to the ants, but also the sounds made are identical to what the ants are used to hearing. It is only when the larvae pupate into a butterfly that the charade is up and the Alcon Blue butterfly must escape before the ants realise and attack…" A pretty, greyish blue butterfly spread its wings and flitted across the screen before the show cut to an ad break.

"Smart bugs huh, dad!" Hector grinned widely.

"Sure are son." Ira stood up and left his boy staring at the next animal being described on screen, and headed back into see his wife.

"Getting no love from him huh? He is finding animals more interesting than his own father today! Oh well, thanks for spending time with him."

"Thanks sweetheart, hanging with my boy is no chore! Anyway, today I just have to go to see Aaban about work. I think there may be a lot less jobs coming through in the future, so I may need to think of some alternative ways to bring us money, but don't be worried honey, everything will be fine. This will be my decision to make."

"Is everything okay? I thought everything was going well at work, you are always so busy. Is the business not doing well?"

"No it's nothing like that, I think I just need to re-evaluate if this is what I want to do for the rest of my life."

"Well don't make any rash decisions, okay, you have a child and a demanding wife to look after!"

"I know honey, love you, I'll be back later."

"Okay, mwah. Look after yourself, and if you start feeling sick again, come straight home."

Jumping into the pickup, Ira became increasingly nervous about his forthcoming conversation with Aaban, unsure of the direction it would take. The two had known each other for many years, however, that didn't count for anything in an industry where nobody was your friend.

Deep in thought, he drove on autopilot and arrived at his destination in the blink of an eye, with no memory of the journey he had just made. Even though no business was carried out at his property, Aaban had done his best to ensure that nobody had any reason to pay any form of attention to him or his house. Ira pulled up to such a non-descript house that it actually stood out conspicuously from its lavishly presented neighbours, delivering the opposite outcome to that which was intended.

Sitting and gathering his thoughts for a couple of minutes, Ira plucked up his courage and got out of the car, walking along the bland pavers on the driveway, towards the dull front door of the humdrum house.

An extremely well-dressed man opened the door as soon as Ira got out of the car. His dark middle-eastern skin contrasting against the white French-cuffed shirt he wore with opulent cufflinks, trousers held up with a black snakeskin belt and feet adorned with Italian loafers, Aaban was a man who enjoyed the finer things in life.

Once past the bleak façade of his house and through the dull front door, the interior somewhat resembled a museum combined with the penthouse of some luxury hotel. The residence was dripping with expensive pieces, fur rugs, and such a combination of tasteless decorations that it actually all worked as a whole, the eye of the beholder unable to take in every eclectic aspect of what was before them, the message to the brain being that what was being observed was nothing short of majestic.

"I was just in the kitchen preparing some lunch. You are interrupting. I was informed you were coming here." Aaban said, causing Ira instant paranoia about what types of observation or surveillance he might be under.

"Sorry for just showing up unannounced," Ira said, "but I have some important things to discuss about business and our future." He tried to read Aaban's face but just received a stare that Medusa would have been proud to possess. Ira's heart turned to stone.

"And I think I know what it may be about, and I believe that many people are probably thinking similar things at the moment after what happened yesterday. Ira, I don't like people rocking up to my house out of the blue. You can understand why, can't you? You are a smart man. Don't ever do this again. But come in, now that you are here."

He turned and walked inside, leaving the door open behind him. Ira stood there briefly, then quickly followed suit and closed the door behind him. A wave of doubt flooded him at the thought that the conversation was going to go a lot less smoothly than thought.

"But first, let me finish making my sandwich, do you want one? It's lobster, truffled mayo and lettuce, my favourite. You talk, and I'll sit and eat and listen, and then you can leave. How does that sound?"

"Ah, thank you for the offer but I'm not hungry. You eat, I'll talk." They both sat down at a large gleaming white French style marble table, candelabra occupying the centre, and Ira felt transported away to one of the palaces of Europe until he looked to his left and saw an American Indian totem sitting next to what seemed to be an African bow and some arrows. No consistency, but Ira respected the man for just buying whatever he liked without much of a consideration to any one theme. No rules.

Aaban picked up the sandwich in one hand and flicked through a newspaper in front of him with his other hand, alternating the turning of pages with the intermittent wiping of his mouth.

"Absolutely incredible, what has happened. The most momentous event in the history of humankind, the universe," he pointed at the paper, shaking his head side to side. "And we are here on this earth to experience it. How lucky we are. How are you feeling about it all? I personally think it is going to cause terrible problems, while I know some others think that this is going to solve all their problems. I guess only time will tell." So maybe Ira wasn't going to do all the talking after all. It was best if he just shut up and let his boss say whatever it was that he wanted to say without interruption.

Aaban tapped his fingers gently on the table. "So the Eddie job went okay I hear. I would expect nothing less. Just another day at the office for you, although..." He increased the speed and intensity of his tapping until it came to a crescendo before suddenly stopping, the following silence a deafening suspenseful wait.

"Although…. the body was left in the front yard of a house for everybody to stop and gawk at like it was a science exhibit! What the hell Ira! That better be a clean site, because if anybody finds anything and comes asking you for explanations as to why they find your prints or something there, you know you don't know nothing or nobody, right? Are you slipping in your old age? I don't need no liabilities."

A smouldering rage appeared behind his eyes but was being suppressed, for now. Hopefully it would remain suppressed. He sensed that Aaban had finished speaking and it was his turn now. Ira took a deep breath and very carefully delivered what was on his mind, moving on from the dangerous topic of Eddie to one that was potentially even more dangerous.

"Well I'll be honest boss, all this crazy stuff going on has made me look back at every sin, every bad thing I have done in my life, and you know what, there are a lot more than I would like. I'm questioning my whole behaviour from my teen years onwards, especially considering now that you know who has revealed their presence."

"You know who? You know who? What's wrong, are you afraid to mention Him, Her, It, whatever? The Lord is still a fearsome, imposing man to me no matter what the truth is, and He possibly may be listening to us but the chances are infinitesimally small. And yes, I'm sure we both have done things that we aren't proud of and hurt many people along the way but hey, we now know there is no hell so doesn't that make you the happiest man on earth? It sure makes me breathe a sigh of relief. No spiritual repercussions, no afterlife of suffering for eternity. Get out of jail, consequence free."

Ira disagreed. "Look Aaban, God is real and I have always believed that but I still committed horrific acts. Does that mean that there was a part of me that didn't truly believe, or just didn't care?"

"You don't need religion to tell you the difference between right and wrong, it's just a tool that has mostly been used to coerce people into doing right and avoiding wrong. Or the other way round too. What is more worrying are those people who only hold back from doing evil because they are religious and are afraid of God's wrath if they commit a sin. They are the truly scary people. Most people are innately good. You and I included."

"Yes, but are we? Really?"

"Absolutely, I believe that we choose to do the things we do, and have consciously chosen to step off of the path of good and deliberately taken steps in a questionable direction every now and again. We are not fixed on the dark path like some, we just detour onto it every so often."

Aaban finished his sandwich, brushed any crumbs away from his mouth and continued reading the paper, seemingly forgetting about Ira's presence.

The conversation seemed to be progressing and Ira felt that it was time to get back to the point of his visit now that the initial annoyance of his unannounced visit had faded.

"So boss, the reason why I'm here.." but he noticed Aaban was completely ignoring him, intently reading the paper. There was a look on his face that filled Ira with unease. He had seen this look before.

"Now this, this really makes me angry!" Aaban thrashed the paper onto the table and slammed his fist down with a loud thud, causing the plate in front of him to jump. A darkness filled the room and Ira recoiled. He knew his boss had a violent temper, a temper that sometimes was disproportionate to the source of the trouble, and this made him a very, very scary man. Ira had seen enough to know that being in the near vicinity of this man when he snapped was dangerous for all. Maybe this was not a great time to try to quit his job.

Aaban pointed to something in the paper. "This is absolute blasphemy. Idiots! They have interviewed a priest, some Christian church near here. Asked him his thoughts on all that has happened in the last day. Do you know what this Father Emmanuel says? He says that this revelation proves that his God is the one true God and always has been. The man is implying that other religions and their Gods have been false, nothing more than inferior replicas, calling MY God a replica. Listen to what the fool says."

"On behalf of St Paul's church and of the Christian faith around the world, we are overcome with joy that the one true God of Christianity was yesterday revealed to mankind." Aaban said, reading out the priest's words from the article.

Ira had read this article this morning and rolled his eyes at it but then moved on from it straight away. Obviously religions were going to try to capitalise on this and were positioning to claim this event as proof to followers who had placed their faith in them that they had done so for good reason and were now rewarded with the appearance of their Lord.

Aaban did not believe in eye rolling, he was the kind of man who took things very personally and felt compelled to respond with action, usually with an exaggerated aggression of a severity that was more than the situation actually called for, hence Ira's busy career.

"Christianity, Catholicism, in fact any predominantly western religion is fraudulent and disrespectful in the eyes of the true Lord. MY true Lord. Priests, bishops, committees of humans, allowing themselves to modify religious values over time to reflect the changing fashions of the modern follower in order to keep worshipper's numbers up and keep the collection plates full by winning back the favour of the people. Nobody can change the will of the Lord except for the Lord himself. No human, nobody! How can this priest claim that this God is his own? His God's image has been so distorted and twisted out of shape over the years by adapting to the changing needs of man that he no longer resembles anything like a God worthy of worship."

He continued, now venting about matters unrelated to the article and clearly releasing frustrations that had been building up for some time now.

"And when the Pope visits a city, everybody goes wild. The weak masses go crazy over him. They want to see him, want to love him, want to be in his presence. He visits underprivileged people, visits handicapped people, but what does he actually do? Nothing. When he leaves the city, the underprivileged are still underprivileged, the handicapped are still handicapped. The Pope is just a man, selected by other men to be the face of Catholicism on earth and completely useless. Once again, ineffective frauds!"

Aaban stood up now and was pacing up and down his hallway, pounding it with his fist.

"But my God, the Lord that I pray to, is ancient, unchanged, and merciless towards imposters. My Lord would never accept false claims from this priest and his false religion, and so I shall not accept it either. This man must pay for his lies to the world, for the lie he told yesterday and the lies he and his religion have been telling for centuries. I will make things right. We will show the people that they have been misled and they will be thankful." He looked to the sky.

"I shall make things right with this world. Ira, I have work for you. You will bring me this man. In fact, you will bring me religious leaders of many faiths. They will all claim that this God is their God. I will make them recant their lies and tell the world that the true God is not their diluted and modified God, but my unchanging God who does not adapt to the whim of mankind. That will make things right for me and my people."

Aaban nodded his head, agreeing within himself that this was a righteous solution that would be supported by his community and restore equilibrium. Long enough had he lived amongst a culture that glorified and revered false prophets, and followed unsanctioned paths leading to contravention of sacred ways.

"Ira, you will bring them to me, and they will be my lambs."

Ira's heart sank as he realised the gravity of what this meant.

"Lambs? Lambs means that you will slaughter them?"

"For their blasphemy and mass deception of their followers. It is the right thing to do. I want them. I want this Christian. I want a Catholic. A Jew. Everyone. They will admit their deception and then they will pay."

A cold shiver travelled down Ira's spine. He could not be part of this. Plucking up the courage, he swallowed and prepared to speak the most dangerous words of his life. But he had to. Aaban stared at him and spoke first, almost telepathically reading his thoughts.

"If you came to my house for the reason that I think you did, then let me just say, my old companion, that the quality of life of your wife and child would be put at great risk if the man of the house refused to fulfil his duties to his employer. Now bring to me those lambs." The meaning behind this message was clear. This was not a request.

Ira suspected that it would come to this. Caught between a rock and a hard place, he had to weigh upon the scales of his conscience the lives of his family and measure them up against the resolute value system he had newly committed to. And the scales balanced evenly.

Option one, to refuse to do his employer's bidding and place his family in undeniable and imminent risk, while option two, to comply, would place his soul and the very fabric of his morality in jeopardy, and would break him as a good man. If only there was a third option.

"I will herd the lambs." He spoke the words but could not look Aaban in the eye.

"Yes you will. Now go. I expect to hear stories about missing leaders of the flocks on the wireless and in the newspapers and on the television and I will know that you have obeyed."

Ira was awash with nausea, staggering out to his car as if in a dream, still trying to comprehend the tangled web he had found himself drawn into. There was no outcome that could provide him with inner peace, only pain. The pain of losing his loved ones, or the pain of losing himself.

Aaban watched him drive away, then went back inside to have a think about how much trouble this man could potentially cause him and what risk mitigation strategies he might need to employ, then calmed himself down. A man will always do everything for the welfare of his family. Ira was his obedient dog. He would round up the flock as demanded.

A few blocks away, the stone bench Ira was sitting on was starting to hurt his back. He had driven to a nearby park and spent the afternoon looking at the clouds, watching the wind blow them across the sky, feeling the warmth of the sun as it shone through the gaps, and the chill of the cold when it was once again obscured.

Usually if he cleared his mind of the problem at hand and soaked up the beauty of nature surrounding him, a solution would subconsciously present itself or at least an idea would germinate. Today though, nature was not the mother of inspiration that he was depending on to promulgate the answer to his impossible problem. It was as if he was staring through a lens that transformed everything beautiful into dying and infected mirror images of themselves. Every which way he looked there was disease and misfortune. Every future path he could travel upon led to a dead end. He had to accept that there was no option three.

After another hour of watching the world go by whilst hoping for the answer to appear before him, he realised that dusk was approaching quickly and he should get back home. Trying to stand up, he realised his left leg was suffering pins and needles from the uncomfortable position he had obliviously been sitting in and he nearly toppled over. Falling back onto the bench, he gave himself another few minutes to recover and it was then that he looked up into the sky and saw it approaching him, nearer and nearer until it landed next to his hand. It was a butterfly, and it was blue, just like that special one he saw on the show he was watching with his son. He tried to remember what was so special about it.

Shortly after, Ira found a payphone in a side street where every pane of glass in it was smashed, the smell of urine causing him to screw his face up and pull his t-shirt up over his nose to talk into the receiver through the material. "Operator. The Tribune newspaper please."

"Okay one second sir, putting you through." Ira waited for what was probably only a few seconds, but he was now being driven by desperation and so every second counted, every delay an eternity.

The voice on the phone that answered was that of an elderly lady. "Mavis, Tribune, how may I help?"

Ira's voice was laced with tension and he could not speak quickly enough.

"Hi. Hi...Is there a Faith there please? She is a journalist? I'd like to talk to her urgently please." He was eventually put through. A bored sounding voice answered.

"Hi you've reached Faith, the Tribune."

"Faith. A priest is going to go missing from St Paul's on Aitken Street tonight.'

He could hear the woman on the other end of the line rummaging around for something, probably a pen.

"Is GOING to go missing? Congratulations, you have my attention."

Ira's plan had begun.

Mon 21 Sept 1959 *1:00pm*
Jacob Congregates

A chill shuddered through Ava, and she pulled the tattered pink blanket tighter around herself, now so thin from wear that it offered little as far as protection from the cold, and yet it comforted her more on an emotional level rather than the physical ever could.

"Can you turn the heater on! I can see steam coming from my mouth. We aren't destitute you know, I don't have to live like this!"

"I'm right here, you don't need to yell." Jacob willed his creaky joints into action and crossed the room to flick the switch to the rusted heater. He and Ava had been sitting silently in the living area all morning, both lost amongst their own thoughts, mulling over the events of the previous day and Jacob's introspection had taught him how pathetically he had been participating in the game of life, as far as he was concerned he had not even come close to getting a score on the board.

The world had trapped him within his own sphere of low self-esteem, claustrophobically encaging him so that his soul was confined to a space as cramped as an elevator that was travelling down, down, only down, heading towards the terminal end, a receding speck of light above him signifying how far away he was from climbing out of this seemingly inescapable hole he was in.

Yesterday morning his livelihood had slipped from his grasp in humiliating fashion as he vaguely remembered sobbing in the office and being comforted by Carol in front of everybody, and to make a situation worse he did not even having the courage to tell his own daughter the news. In fact he was downright petrified of telling her.

He looked up, up towards that distant light so far away, that unreachable destination that was where he wanted to be, where he needed to be, the place where he was in control of his actions and the world around him, where he had not been for a long time since his wife had died. But, it was too difficult, there was no way he could change now, and no point. If he didn't even try then there would be no way he could fail. And that was when he heard it.

A voice, made up of echoes of echoes, like a thousand whispers caressing his mind, urged him to climb out of the darkness. It was his wife's voice, a voice he hadn't heard for many years that had travelled through an immeasurable distance of space and time to reach him, barely recognisable but unmistakeably hers. It spoke to him softly, words of wisdom, words of love. The echoes eventually receded and try as he might to grasp them, they left him wondering if they were ever there at all, but the message imparted remained behind.

He knew what to do. Every long journey starts with a single step and it was time for him to start his journey. He took that first step out of the darkness towards the light and resolved to speak to his daughter. Step number one. In a bold voice he said the words the echoes told him to say, the words he needed to say.

"Ava, this is difficult for me to tell you but I lost my job yesterday, and I know you want to yell at me but please don't yell at me because I don't think I can handle it right now. We will be okay I promise, I'll try to find another job first thing tomorrow but but we may have to tighten our belts a little bit." His shaky voice trailed off and he looked her in the eye, something he hadn't dared do for many years, aware that he was brimming over.

"What!? What did you do? Something stupid? I can't believe it, oh wait, yes I can! Now how on earth are we going to tighten our belts? They are already tight enough, everything in this house needs repair or updating, we survive on close to bread and water, how much tighter can we get?" She was livid and looked around for something to throw. Nothing being within reach, she wheeled out of the room in such a hurry that she didn't turn into the corridor quickly enough and her chair scraped a huge gouge into the wall.

Sitting back in his chair, Jacob reckoned the conversation went about as well as he expected it to go, and for the first time in a long time he actually felt a modicum of pride in himself. It's true, the first step is definitely the hardest, and he wasn't sure the second step would be much easier.

What now? Looking for work could wait until tomorrow. After losing his job and still trying to absorb the God revelation, some further reflection time was warranted. Thinking that some reading would provide him with peace, Jacob grabbed his dusty copy of the Bible of the shelf, flicked it open to a random page and tried to imagine now the circumstances under which it was written. He knew from his school days that around forty authors contributed over a period of fifteen hundred years or more to the content of the Bible, clearly nobody but men who claimed to relay the word of God. He was interested to take in the words now with his new perspective and see what his take would be.

Before he could find a page to begin reading he could hear Ava wheeling back down the corridor and he braced himself for another onslaught. She appeared, dressed in a red neat and tidy outfit that he knew was one of her favourites and was usually worn when she wanted to go somewhere nice.

"I want to go to church. Let's go."

"But, we haven't gone to church for six years, since…"

"I know, shut up, but I think that if there was ever a time that we needed to go to church it's now, right? So let's go! My friend Ishara is coming too so let's pick her up on the way."

Jacob meekly complied, but he had seen how chaotic the supermarket was so he could only imagine how church would be. Ishara had been a friend of Ava's since childhood, a beautiful Indian girl, and the two had been inseparable ever since they discovered a mutual love of hating boys. Their quick wits and mischievous nature had them well practiced at pulling pranks, and every boy at school who knew them knew of their reputation for finding novel ways to torment the opposite sex. This naughty streak had changed direction somewhat over time and now the girls were closer than ever, boys becoming a target of a different kind.

Jacob knew he was not going to dissuade her once her mind was made up and so he made himself as presentable as he could, and shortly they were on their way to St Paul's.

Driving along the familiar stretch of highway to the church, Jacob thought of the night six years ago, close to midnight on Christmas Eve. Ava was in the back seat, a young girl hugging her pink safety blanket. In the passenger seat was his wife.

Every Christmas they went to midnight mass, braving the cold and showing face to the community, not wanting to be the noticeable absentees that would be gossiped about in their social circle. Jacob was quite sure that was the main reason the majority of people attended such an inconvenient event. His wife's parents were devoutly religious and would not be happy should the entire family not attend the holy night.

Clutching the cold wheel and focusing on the road, Jacob wished that the heater of the car would be more effective and that he had worn an extra layer under his suit.

"Don't worry, it will all be over quickly enough and then we can jump back into our nice warm bed," his wife said. He could see Rose shivering more than he, the passing street lamps intermittently highlighting her discomfort and reflecting a glorious shade of blue off of her jet black hair.

He reached across and rubbed her slender thigh vigorously. "At least we will go to heaven for this. Well, we'd better!" Jacob chuckled and put his foot down a little more. It was a long straight road so it wouldn't hurt to get there a little quicker and get the whole affair done and dusted sooner rather than later.

The trees whizzed by the side of the car hypnotically, and soon all he could see was a blur as he concentrated on the headlights hitting the road, white lines in the middle of the road merging into a single white line. Line, line, line, line…

The white lines on the road disappeared and so had the trees, replaced by a view of his chest and legs. Why was he looking down there? He had nodded off and looked up just in time see a brightly lit tree approach the bonnet of the car at forty miles an hour, cutting off his wife's scream before all went dark…

Later when he woke up in hospital he would tell the police he swerved to avoid an animal, and that was the story he had stuck to telling himself and, shamefully, others for the last six years.

He lost his wife that night, and Ava lost the use of her legs. He emerged physically fine though, and remaining unscathed from the accident meant that he could now welcome the complete emotional suffering he deserved for the rest of his life, more so than if he had also succumbed to injury and paid some sort of penance.

And so to that very same church he now drove again, his unforgiving daughter with him, same pink blanket on her lap. His sweaty grip tightened on the wheel and he remained under the speed limit as he detoured to pick up Ishara.

Ishara lived in a house larger than most. Being the daughter of an investment banker and a lawyer, her path in life had diverged greatly from Ava's, however, they both didn't seem to notice and when they were together they were still the two little girls that used to play together for hours on end after school.

It had been many years since Jacob had visited the Singh residence and as he looked upon the sculpted garden blooming with exotic flowers bordered by the lush manicured hedges, he was reminded of what was possible if you just spent a little bit of time each day building something from nothing.

Ishara's parents worked hard on their careers and also their hobbies, one of which was gardening, their front yard displaying the rewards of their efforts and being their pride and joy. Over time the small repeat efforts add up and flourish into something grand, the discipline and tiny daily sacrifices becoming worthwhile.

Jacob imagined what he could have accomplished in life if he made little changes a year ago, two years ago. Where would he be now if twenty years ago he committed a little time each day contributing to the bigger picture. And as with all of Jacob's regrets, he knew that his lack of action was the reason. But he did not know what action to take, he was directionless with no goals and no dreams.

How do you build something if you don't know what you want? Some people just seem to know. Some lucky people just seem to know that one day they want to be lawyers, have wonderful gardens, drive nice cars and provide their family with the best support possible.

Jacob never wanted to be a life insurance salesman. He had never even heard of that career option when he was at school. He just fell into it, and not having any other better ideas, stuck with it and here he was years later, middle to lower class.

The Singh residence reminded him of what could have been, and what was possible. It reminded him of his failed potential and all the times he didn't study for tests at school. It stared at him and asked him why he didn't stand up to his boss and colleagues yesterday, or any previous day. It spoke and told him that this is what assertiveness and confidence brings, that if you have a sense of purpose then you too could have this. This reminder of things he had left undone was why he had not been to the Singh residence for many years.

Ishara had been sitting in the front room and heard the long shrill squeal of the old van's brakes as they arrived and bounded outside to greet her long-time friend and jumped in. Jacob quickly pulled away from the kerb, glad they had not been invited in. The parents were lovely people but Jacob always had the impression, wrongly, that they felt sorry for him and that was the reason for their polite manner.

"I'm so excited about this, I've never been to a church before!" Ishara beamed. "My family don't have many opportunities to go, in fact none, but hey, it seems like we are all the same religion now, right?"

Ava considered this. "I guess you are right, I hadn't really thought about that just yet. All religions must now admit they are the same religion, but what about all your Hindu Gods, there were hundreds weren't there? What's happened to all of them now, are you pushing them aside to start again?"

"Well, ignoramus, they were all just multiple facets that personified the same God anyway. One for this, one for that but really they were all the same entity and Hindus just created different characters so that we could apply them to different aspects of life easier. We are a very creative religion! It will be interesting to see what happens now actually, but I have a feeling that nothing will change and the same Gods and Goddesses will still remain part of Hinduism. I don't think the comfort provided by centuries of history will be so easily wiped clean, even if we do know better now about the true nature of God."

"But it's not up to man now is it? I mean, to decide whether or not they still want to continue with the old ways or not. It would be silly to go on worshipping hundreds of different or the same Gods if you know that they don't truly represent the reality? Anyway, we now know that worshipping is pointless and always has been. God doesn't need our worship. I mean it's actually quite laughable. Historically God has been seen as such a powerful, all seeing, all knowing figure, majestic creator and destroyer of worlds, and yet nobody questioned why such a magnificent being desperately relied on the worship and obedience of us mere humans to an extent that I would consider to be symptomatic of psychiatrically crazy levels of low self-esteem. The human race was worshipping a being so psychotically insecure that it paradoxically shouldn't really deserve our worship."

Jacob interjected. "So you acknowledge that worshipping is pointless but you still want to go to church?"

"Just shut up and drive would you?" Ava didn't really know why she wanted to go to church, but she thought that if there was ever a time to go again it was now. Just like Jacob, she too had indelible memories associated with her last life changing attempted church visit. She was not trying to overwrite them, but almost challenging herself to see if she could go through with it and how she would respond.

Jacob continued to drive as the girls caught up on their social lives in the back seat. He saw this trip as a pointless exercise and would rather have stayed at home until things resumed some semblance of normalcy.

St Paul's lay on the edge of town, a beautiful grey stone structure that was visible intermittently from a distance as long as you looked in the right direction between the rooftops of houses in the surrounding area. Quite often on a nice day, artists of all ages would find themselves a place to settle their easels and spend some time trying to replicate the classic architecture and calming feel of the church onto their canvas or sketchbook.

Today was not one of those days, however, because just as Jacob had feared, the entire road before the church was gridlocked with cars and people thronging, worshipping, chanting and screaming praise.

"It's 5pm for heaven's sake. Why can't people just stay home?" Jacob slowed down to a crawl and surveyed the hectic landscape before him.

"Same reason we can't stay home, now find a park and let's go," Ava impatiently ordered.

Jacob pulled over a fair distance away, aware that he may not be able to drive back out if he parked too closely. Already there were more cars passing them with the same intention of visiting the church.

Out of the van and with Ishara pushing Ava along, they looked left and right in wonder at the people around them. Some had covered themselves in strange markings and were wearing next to nothing. Others were sitting on the ground rocking, eyes towards the sky and humming repetitive rhythms whilst there were some that were literally screaming and crying, whether tears of joy or pain it was hard to tell.

"Honestly, I'm really, really happy that this has happened, I think it's going to be great for the world, but seriously, I do not feel the need to scream or paint all over myself because of it," Ishara said. "What is wrong with people?"

Using Ava's wheelchair as a makeshift battering ram, people were happy to move out of the way when they caught a glimpse of her stern face and the trio made their way into the crowded church.

The creaky old wooden pews in St Paul's normally provided service to twenty or thirty people regularly on a Sunday, though the seating capacity was closer to three hundred. Today there were close to five hundred people inside, standing and jostling for position, sounds of annoyance rebounding inside the acoustically brilliant structure.

Father Emmanuel was up the front trying to speak, though he wasn't the centre of focus today as per a normal Sunday service, and not everybody in the audience was listening intently. A few conversations seemed to be occurring simultaneously between people in the crowd who were directing comments toward the priest, who was for the most part ignoring the remarks and trying to maintain his course with the sermon, though fighting a losing battle.

Ava couldn't see a thing but could clearly hear a booming voice in the audience yell "There was supposed to be an afterlife. You said! You all said! The church has said this for years! Why were we doing all the praying and believing? Now we know you were lying to us, why? There's no heaven or hell. None!"

Nervously the priest kept on track, though the spectator seemed to be gaining the support of many other audience members who mumbled in agreement.

"Has it all been a con? It certainly seems to have been. What rubbish have you lot been feeding us?" a woman's high pitched voice cut through the air.

The priest, a young man no more than thirty five who was used to being in front of a silent audience less than a tenth of the size of this one, decided to try to address some of the questions being hurled at him since nobody seemed to care about the content of his sermon.

People were there in the quest for more answers, others to gain reassurance and to know that everything would be all right. The people wanting answers were being quite aggressively vocal about it, and the people there for reassurance remained quiet, glad to be among like-minded people and silently embraced the sense of community, though the tide in the room seemed to be turning and the threat of a witch hunt loomed as more people wanted to know what was really going on.

The priest was not a man who had the personality to control an unwieldy situation, and all of his years of study had not prepared him for this. He knew how to read passages from the Bible to an audience, whether willing recipients or not, and he also knew how to give Mrs Mills advice on whether or not her daughter would go to hell if she wore a dress above the knees, but there was no training for this.

He trailed off from what he was saying mid-sentence and stood there, taking in the crowd, more than a little afraid as he accepted that how he dealt with this situation could either appease the crowd or turn it against him.

It sounded a little cliché and asinine, but whenever he felt in a spot of bother, the question "What would Jesus do?" actually prevailed and would summon a strength and wisdom that directed his path of action. However, in this instance he couldn't fathom what the son of God would say to convince a mob that they had really been lied to in good faith, and so he had to rely on a hallelujah moment arriving with which he could find inspiration to get him out of this situation. And thankfully the hallelujah moment came.

Knowing no more than anybody else about what was going on, it struck him that the only tactic he had at his disposal was to take the side of the audience and plead a little ignorance himself.

A lit candle flew from left to right narrowly missing his face and hit a member of the audience. He had to speak now and with stern authority, even if the meaning behind his words was transparent and hesitant. The time is now. Both hands raised in the air, he spoke and the room hushed somewhat. An encouraging start. Now to make a grab for some empathy.

"My fellow parishioners, in all honesty, the comments from you are connecting with me and I admit I feel shame to learn that I have been preaching some untruths, albeit unintentionally, and that I have also been misled by the church. But who is to blame? The lies have been innocently carried along over the years by those who simply believed what they were told by the good book and members of the clergy. The source of these untruths are long gone, and all that myself and the church are guilty of is believing and perpetuating the lessons of the Lord that we had learned in good faith."

Looking across the crowd, all eyes were on him and the pressure to continue while he had built momentum caused his hands to start shaking. He must not lose them, they were in the palm of his trembling hands, for now.

"But how fortunate are we to be here, and to have learned the truth, to be set straight and to have the Lord choose us, us in our lifetimes to display a majestic presence to! I only know as much as you my good people, and it does disintegrate the very core of all I learned, to now know that the grace and beauty of our God is a lot simpler than what we were led to believe. But isn't simplicity also beautiful evidence of genius! Let's not dwell on the past and be angry that the framework of what we thought was the truth has been dismantled, let's rejoice that we have a new framework that is real and fact."

Turning his attention towards the man in the audience who yelled out earlier "We have learned, good sir, that the concept of heaven, hell, the afterlife were created by the minds of men, but to me personally, those concepts whether real or not, have guided my actions and sustained my desire to live the Lord's way, steering my blessed journey on this earth and I am thankful for it. No harm has been done, I have no regrets that I have lived life a good human being and I will continue to do so, and I hope you will too sir."

About half the crowd cheered him on in agreement, and the other half were still visibly disturbed that there was no ultimate reward for living the Lord's way. The church had now lost the major carrot that it had depended on for centuries to control the will of man, and in these times, there were no longer the sticks to enforce obeisance that were available in civilisations past.

"God is a being, a being that we now know needs no worship and hears no prayer. The comforting fabric of falsehoods that man has woven in layers around this being over time to reshape its true form has been stripped away, revealing the raw uncomfortable truth. To a reporter today I said that this being is our Lord, and always has been the Lord that this church has preached, so my good people, love, as I do, the fact that now we know our Lord better than at any other time in the history of mankind."

Father Emmanuel had come to the end of all he could manifest spontaneously, and he knew this was the most opportune time to draw the day to a close and disperse the crowd whilst the mood was relatively high and people had some food for thought.

For the first time in a while he felt like he really had been listened to. Reading to a group of disinterested folk once a week had not been bringing the satisfaction he longed for. He looked across the crowded church, breathing in the attention and could sense the people wanting more, but alas, he had no more to give, and so wearily he spoke.

"I am sorry but that is all I have for you on this day. Go to your homes with your loved ones, live in the wonder of the Lord, embrace the glory, spend time reflecting on the events of yesterday morning and most of all, enjoy this day and focus on that warm feeling of knowledge and awareness inside of you that was delivered generously." He decided that would be the note to finish on. "Enjoy these times everybody, and farewell."

The moderately appeased crowd dispersed more readily than he had anticipated, and soon he breathed a sigh of relief that it was all over. A few families loitered behind, in the vain hope that there may be some more to come, much like the inevitable encore at a music concert, but they soon filtered out.

Alone in the church, Father Emmanuel took a moment to sit down on a pew and take a breather. The collection plate was overflowing, normally five and ten dollar bills the most common denomination, but now there were fifties making up the majority of donations. The revelation of God was actually great from a business perspective.

Clearly people who regularly visited church believed in God previously, but now they *really* believed in God. Isn't belief an absolute concept? It's not as if there are varying levels of belief, you either do or you don't. So, to Father Emmanuel there should be no difference in behaviour of religious people before and after, and yet evidence states there clearly was.

The priest stood himself up and walked towards his chambers after doing a brief sweep of the church for lost property and to pick up any litter. He would sleep well tonight, but he suspected that tomorrow would start early and bring the same. He could hear voices outside, people probably still milling around after the service. At an uncertain time like this, people always found comfort in being with other people, whether friends or not, bonded by the common event that now connected all human beings.

Alone in his quarters, Father Emmanuel felt a longing for some human company of his own. His was a solitary life though it didn't have to be. Preferring his own company over that of others, his introversion sometimes had its drawbacks in that if he did for instance desire some company, he did not really have anybody that he could readily engage with and extend an invitation to.

Saddened by these thoughts but acknowledging that he had chosen to live this way and he could readily make connections with any of the parishioners if he wanted to, he climbed into bed early and grabbed the worn copy of The Bible on the bedside table, beginning to read but slightly distracted by the noise outside until eventually becoming engrossed and he settled in for a comfortable evening, making notes for tomorrow's sermon.

Meanwhile outside, Jacob and the girls had slowly left the church and looked at each other with an enquiring look as to what was next on the agenda for the group.

"Well looks like that's it for today," Jacob said, hinting that they should get back to the car and return to the comfort of home.

The emotional scars of the visit were opening again and he knew that God or not, religion or not, it would be the last time he would ever come back to this place.

Ava as usual disagreed with her father. "I'm not done yet. We only really just got here and I want to absorb the atmosphere, there is a real buzz about this place don't you find? Everybody is super excited and kind of one step away from holding hands and singing. I mean, those people we passed on the way in already were, and I almost feel like joining them."

"Well if you start screaming like them then I'm going to have to pretend that I don't know you," Ishara laughed.

"Singing? People are ready for a fight is the buzz I feel," Jacob shook his head but made no move to head to the van.

They milled around the area, listening in to other group conversations and discovered a mixed vibe, a bit like inside the church. Most people were still in disbelief and just trying to confirm that the events of the previous day had really happened and weren't a dream, whilst others seemed to feel a sense of impending doom.

A loud female voice boomed. "I mean, why now? The only reason this all happened is because the human race is so messed up that divine intervention is the only possible way to steer us away from self-destruction, but it is too late. It's the beginning of the end I'm telling you." The well-dressed but frantic woman was screeching to a group of people who were nodding in agreement with worried looks on their faces.

"She's got a point though," Ishara observed. "I mean, like she said, why now? You can't help but feel there is a reason behind all this, whether it's because the world is about to end, or God felt a need to reinvigorate belief again, or what if mankind actually reached some kind of checkpoint or passed a test that enabled us to collectively reach a next level or plane of existence and this is all a part of reaching that upper echelon? I don't know and I doubt we will ever know."

"Hey if you are all done hanging around and gasbagging, can we head off now? The crowd is thinning out and I think I can get the car out with no troubles now."

Jacob's tone now had an edge to it that the girls didn't question. It was getting dark and there were some fanatic people about who only yesterday would have been labelled as less than sane, but now they seemed to be recognised as visionary which didn't make them any more comfortable to be around.

Ava was glad to have visited the church, though she didn't really feel satisfied that the excursion delivered the experience or closure she was hoping for. Her thoughts turned to her mother and imagined an alternate ending to the tragic story as she had thousands of times already, the one where she was walking arm in arm with her parents just like any other regular family doing regular things.

What would she be doing now if she could walk, would she have a boyfriend, a job? Maybe, maybe not, but she knew she wouldn't be housebound and dependent on the man who put her in the chair in the first place. She could take the dog for walks, reach things off the top shelf without having to ask somebody, things that nobody thought twice about but she had to.

What hurt her most was the look of pity she saw in people's eyes before they quickly looked away, that flash of a look that was their first reaction before they realised that their guard was down and revealed their true thoughts. Ava knew she was an attractive girl and she had heard comments like "that's a shame," and resented that she would have been valued so much more as a person if only she had her legs. Her brain was still the same but how would anybody ever find that out?

She remembered a time she was out in a restaurant with Ishara and a boy actually approached the table and started hitting on her until he realised she was not sitting in a regular chair. He made excuses and ran back to his friends in a real hurry.

Anger and tears started to well and Ava wheeled herself ahead of the group so that her red eyes remained hidden from them. She rarely felt any emotion other than anger any more, mostly directed at one man.

Approaching the van first she saw the silhouette of a strange man sitting on the hood and resting his feet on the front bumper, looking at the sky, whistling to himself and she instantly slowed down to allow the others to catch up, cursing that it seemed too difficult for people to just be normal any more.

He was on his own, looked a little erratic and shabby with long hair and scruffy clothes, and personified that air of unpredictability they had been speaking about earlier so Ava thought it best to play it safe and let a grown adult sort this one out, not that she had any confidence in her father.

The others soon arrived and the three of them looked at him, simultaneously trying to think what kind of person just sits on somebody else's car, whistling. The two girls looked at Jacob, who emitted an audible sigh that expressed his awareness that there was no way out of this other than to ask the gentleman to get off of the vehicle and hopefully not suffer any consequences.

At least it was only one man this time, and not a gang like earlier at the supermarket. He stepped forward and braced himself.

"Excuse me, you happen to be sitting on our car, do you mind getting off because we would like to go home. Much appreciated, thank you," he said with zero authority in his voice.

It took a good few seconds to register with the man that he was being spoken to, and his gaze turned to them, piercing blue eyes focusing on Ava, then Ishara and finally upon Jacob, who felt as uneasy as he looked. The whistling continued, and his scattered tune picked up the pace and seemed to issue a challenge.

"Let's just get in the van and drive off, he can decide whether he wants to come along for the ride until he falls," Ava suggested and wheeled towards the van.

The whistling stopped. "You know…" said the man in a slow, strained voice. "It doesn't matter man. Nothing matters now at all. I can sit here.." a long pause as if he had no idea what to say next. "..I can sit over there…or over there… there too. I can sit anywhere. You can all sit anywhere you like. You can do anything you like because nothing is important now. God is real man. Doesn't that make anything we can possibly do just so insignificant? We are only people man. In the big scheme of things we are here for the blink of an eye. There is nothing a person can do that can make a ripple in the universe. Out of the infinite stars, planets and galaxies, we find ourselves here right now, and who are you to tell me that I can't pick this part of the universe to sit down. You don't own it. No human owns it. No human can tell another human not to do anything because we have no ownership, no jurisdiction over anything in this universe man. I could kill every human on this planet and the universe would not even notice man. I could kill you and who could stop me. It wouldn't even be wrong. Laws are only made by pencil pushing bureaucrats man, idiots pushing their own agenda. Some idiot called Frank was probably sitting in his office one day and said to his idiot boss "Hey, I don't think we should kill people. Can I make it a law?" and his boss said "Mm yeah sure why not?" but what do they know in their suits and ivory towers. They don't know how the universe works. I'm not going to change what I want to do just because Frank woke up one day with a stupid idea and wrote it down."

He leaned forward and jumped off the car, moving towards them whistling again and with a worked up look in his eye. All three noticed his left hand had reached around to his back pocket searching for an unknown object.

Jacob stepped forward and stood between the man and the two girls, shaking and unsure of what to do next.

"Okay girls, get out of here. Now!" Whether he liked it or not, he was committed to following through with taking care of whatever this threat presented. His eye firmly fixed on the man's left hand, he felt like he was going to faint first before any altercation occurred because he was so nervous, his heart beating wildly out of his chest.

"Man, why couldn't you just let me enjoy my own little place in the universe huh? Why would you want to come and bother a guy who was just minding his own business? You need to be taught a lesson to mind your own business!" The last few words were a shriek and he stepped towards Jacob.

Jacob froze and raised his arms up instinctively to protect himself but he knew he was as good as dead. His last thoughts were of how he deserved to join his wife and whether Ava would be okay without him. Thoughts of how much pain he was about to experience entered his mind, and then some more thoughts about his own death after that. Then thoughts of why nothing at all had happened yet caused him to slowly lower his arms, open his eyes and see what had happened.

About three meters away from Jacob he saw the man prostrate on the ground, arm twisted behind his back, grimace on his face while another quite well built man had him pinned and had placed his knee on the back of the man's neck. Despite his squirming, he was held down fast and there appeared to be a bit of a standoff because as soon as Jacob's rescuer released his pressure the other man would escape and do who knows what. But on the other hand, they couldn't just stay there like that all night. The stranger spoke to the man that he had restrained.

"Okay, so what is going to happen next is that I am going to slowly release you, and you are going to disappear without trying anything stupid or else I will damage you. Do you understand? I said do you understand?! You will never be able to use this arm again." And just to emphasise the point he twisted just that little bit harder.

"Arrh, get off me man, yes, just let my arm go man and I'll go away I promise. I was never gonna do anything to him. He was just ruining my vibe man and telling me to do stuff he had no right to. You should be fighting with him instead of me, man!"

Jacob saw the man give a final twist on the arm which was now in a very unnatural position and he was surprised he hadn't heard a snap of any kind. Even if the crazy guy did want to hurt them in some way there was no chance he was physically capable of doing so now. He was let up slowly and limped away into the night sobbing and muttering to himself, clutching his arm.

Straightening himself up and examining a fresh hole in his jeans with a frown on his face, the man dusted himself off, swept his fashionably messy black hair back and turned his attention to Jacob.

"Are you okay? That guy was just another weirdo, they are coming out of the woodwork at the moment. He probably doesn't even remember it ever happened. Lunatic." He stepped over towards Jacob and extended his hand.

"Hey, I'm Gabe, innocent passer-by who happened to be in the right place at the right time it seems. I live close by the church so I've seen the extreme fringes of society emerge this past day but this is the first time I've had to intervene in a situation with a nutcase. It's amazing the reactions I've seen to what's been going on and most of it is disturbing, trust me. Anyway, I'll keep on moving, have a good evening. Hope you are all alright." And with that, he turned and started to walk off.

"Wait!" Two wide eyed and nervously smiling girls emerged very quickly from the background to thank their saviour. Ava cut off Ishara in the race to get to Gabe first. He was tall, ruggedly handsome and had a presence about him that attracted double takes from most that crossed his path, but he also possessed that quality of being completely oblivious to the attention that he drew which made him even more appealing.

"I'm Ava, Jacob's my father, thanks for saving him! And us. Good job!" She said with a light-heartedness that did not reflect the gravity of the situation they were just in, eyeing off his physique without shame.

Jacob looked at Ava in astonishment. He could not remember the last time that she had acknowledged him in public, let alone as a relative and not inserted some sort of derogatory comment. His heart lightened.

They shook hands, Ava reluctant to let go until it became a little awkward. Still, she was happy. "Hi Ava, it's nice to meet you. And who might you be, other young lady?" he said, turning to Ishara.

"Oh, you know, I'm Ishara," she giggled flirtatiously and was not in the least bit embarrassed by it.

"A pleasure. So I assume you all came here as a result of the you know.."

"Yes, we thought it might be appropriate to drop by the church, as did about a thousand other people." Ishara laughed. "I'm glad we did though," she said, now putting on a shy act and looking at the ground.

He didn't pick up on the subtle message. "Hey look I really have to go, it was so lovely to meet you all but I have an important trip to make."

The girls pulled sad faces. "Awww!"

"Sorry, I don't want you to think I'm being rude, there's a good reason that's all. I can probably tell you, everybody will probably hear about it anyway." He looked around suspiciously like a spy trying to ensure he wasn't being followed. His voice lowered.

"This may sound crazy, but did you hear that there are whispers of events occurring around the world, like actual biblical miracles? Imagine it, water into wine and then some. I don't know much more than that, but I do know it's not just a case of a statue crying in a church, it's things like people healing, blind people being able to see..." he looked at Ava, "...people walking again too, probably..."

Jacob and Ava immediately looked at each other.

"So, events that could possibly make somebody walk who wasn't able to previously?" Jacob asked.

"Well, I would assume so, obviously I can't speak for the miracles or make any guarantees. It could just be idle rumours for all I know but I was actually on my way now to head outside of town and upstate with my little nephew who had polio to go check what it's all about. It's not something you can just ignore because it sounds too crazy, in the light of all that has happened. I have to know."

Ava interjected. "Wait wait wait, why upstate, what's there, are you saying that something is happening there? We don't have to go to another part of the world? One of those miracle places is here?" Ava's tone became demanding and she tugged on Jacob's sleeve.

"Dad, come on, we have to go, we have to. You owe this to me. What if it's real? God exists, so there could be miracles, right? It makes perfect sense! You can help right all your wrongs towards me. You put me in this chair, and now there is a chance I can get out of it? I want this."

"Ava, I don't think Gabe really knows what he is talking about, I mean it's impossible, surely. Gabe? You were really going to go with your nephew?"

"Apparently it is in the middle of nowhere, on a property owned by somebody so I can't say for sure if we are allowed on it or if we have to pay them extortionately or what. There might actually be millions of people there. I don't know much more than what I've told you, but that's all I need to know. If there is even a one percent chance this is true, I'm going to do everything I can to get there. I was going to make an early start tonight."

Ishara was the first to speak up. "I know we don't really know each other, but surely everybody here can see that we are all good people. We should go together, that has to be a good idea? Jacob, Ava, you can't miss an opportunity like this. How long will this place have its powers for? What if it's limited in some way, like only a certain number of miracles? Who knows? Because things seem to be getting a little on edge around here it's probably safer if we went with you Gabe? We can stick together, it will be fun. Do you mind if I come with you?" Ishara asked, fixated on him.

"Yes, do you mind if WE come with you?" Ava corrected.

Gabe looked at the two of them and knew there could only be one possible answer he could provide without seeing more needy faces pulled at him.

"I guess you have a point. It's a bit of a hike and things are seeming to spiral around here a bit so some safety in numbers might be wise, plus who else is going to keep me entertained with their hilarious senses of humour?"

Jacob had been observing the banter between the three of them with an air of dismissal, however, he now felt that he had to step in and provide a voice of reason about this plan.

"Girls, girls, and Gabe, I'm sorry but we aren't ready to go on a road trip right now. It's getting late and it takes preparation. Now I'm not saying you can't go, but I'm saying we can go in the morning. Gabe, would you consider going in the morning? The light of day would make the trip safer and easier."

Gabe didn't enjoy the thought of wasting any time but now looked back at the situation rationally and decided that Jacob might be right.

"Well I guess so, shall we make it for first thing tomorrow then? Like the very first thing, we can meet here at say 6am?"

"Deal. And we have a van so we can even scoop you up. 6am it is. Do you think your brother or sister will mind? Are they coming too? They are more than welcome."

"Ah, Simon is my sister's son, but unfortunately she passed away about a year ago so I am looking after him now." Looking up at the sky, he said "I actually think she would be happier if there was a group of us going so okay, I will catch you at 6am right in this very spot."

"I look forward to it," he said as he turned to cross the road and narrowly avoiding getting cleaned up by a pickup truck that appeared out of nowhere and was hurtling towards the church with its headlights off.

"Turn your lights on you idiot!" he yelled at the car that had already pulled up at the church in the distance. "Too late buddy, church is closed," he muttered. Looking both ways this time, he cautiously attempted to cross the road again and succeeded, disappearing into the darkness.

As soon as he was out of sight, Ava and Ishara looked at each other and mouthed the words "Oh my God" to each other and then laughed when Jacob berated them both for using the Lord's name in vain. In the car home they fought about who Gabe belonged to until Ishara was dropped off at her home.

That night Ava could not sleep. From the moment she first laid eyes on Gabe she felt like she was drowning, her body flooding her with sympathies that paralleled being lowered into a scalding bath feet first, until the unbearable heat rose and enveloped her entirely, melting away all rational thought, her heart abandoning her mind and body and forming its own detached and pained existence.

Every single tacky love song she had ever heard finally made sense, though she doubted that the superficial infatuation of the artists resembled anything as real as what she felt, and her feelings could not be captured or expressed by any combination of musical notes known on any scale.

Already every molecule in her body was singing out and making her aware that the muscular object of her desire was intolerably absent, and the only acceptable distance between them allowed was zero.

How can this feeling be what people searched for their whole lives? It kind of hurt. She prayed that night, a useless unheard prayer to a God that couldn't listen, that had never listened.

Tues 22 Sept 1959 *7:00am*
Faith Labours

Opening one eye slowly and unsuccessfully trying to focus on her surroundings in order to provide some sort of indication as to where she was and why her pillow was so uncomfortable, Faith slowly became aware that she was in the office and had fallen asleep face first on her typewriter. Another night in the office, this really had to stop. She had a perfectly good bed at home to sleep in and pillow to drool on.

Shielding her eyes from the brightness of the office, she sat upright slowly and received a round of applause from one or two co-workers who had arrived early and were there to witness her in all her dishevelled glory.

"Thanks you guys, it's called 'hard work', you should try it some time."

After her disturbing phone call the previous evening about the priest who was to go missing, she had set herself a deadline of two stories to be submitted in time for the print run to be in today's edition and she had made it. She vaguely remembered a whirlwind of typing, interrupting the overnight cleaner from vacuuming so that he could spellcheck the articles, and then arguing with Larry from the print department to find a position in the paper for the last-minute story about the abduction. She couldn't remember whose story got bumped, but she was sure that she would hear about it shortly.

"Does Max even know about that second story you wrote? You shouldn't have pushed that through you know." Alex was probably the youngest person working for the paper, fresh from college and was naïve enough and arrogant enough to act like the smartest person in the room on too many occasions for Faith's liking.

That pipsqueak thinks he can tell me what's right and what's wrong? He needed to be cut down to size. But that would have to wait until she had a coffee and could think of a retort. She started fuming because on this rare occasion, snivelling Alex was right.

Max would probably not be happy at all, so she had better come up with a really good reason for putting the priest story out unapproved, without actually revealing the true reason.

Blatant disregard for operational procedure did not go down well at the paper given that reputation was everything and a paper's credibility was the foundation of its success, hence very rigid rules and processes were set in place to protect this. She set her mind to work on an explanation but soon realised that she would soon be begging for forgiveness.

Two absolute gems of stories had been published before any other paper and as far as she was concerned the ends justified the means. Even if Maxwell was angry she knew it would just be feigned anger for the benefit of the other staff in the office who had to be shown that nobody was immune from disobeying policy. She was sure he would be secretly pleased at the outcome and hopefully pull her into his office with a stern face but congratulate her with a smile in private.

Pouring her second coffee, she started planning her day and thinking about how she could top her recent run of impressive submissions. She hoped that her article on strange Samuel 'the connector' might bring some other weirdos out of the woodwork who could share more information that could indicate why some people received a different communication than others.

She had a feeling deep down that there was some sort of jigsaw puzzle that had a few pieces missing and these connector people may hold some of them. And if her story could attract them to her like bees to honey then presto, another story of the century, as long as they had something more interesting to say other than rubbish about 'God resetting the truth.'

Sipping her coffee, Faith looked at the clock on the wall. 8am. The office seemed unusually quiet for this time of morning, and it wasn't because of journalists being out on the hunt for stories. Hal from Accounts was missing, and so were some of the other support staff.

"Hey where's Hal today? And everybody else, for that matter?" Heads were shaken, eyebrows were raised, and a general apathy around her was expressed towards the observation. Faith didn't mind that people were away, if they were sick they were sick. Maybe something was going around the office, it happened every so often though she never recalled hearing a single cough or anybody complaining about feeling poorly. From past evidence, if somebody was under the weather they were sure to let the whole office know.

She thought she might give Hal a call to see if he was okay. It was pay day tomorrow and there was no way that she was going to miss out on what she had well and truly earned just because the accounts team had caught a sniffle. Walking over to the wall outside Maxwell's office, she took a notepad and pen and jotted down Hal's number from the list of all employees details that were displayed there.

Dialling his number, it rang about fifteen times before she hung up. Trying again, it rang a further ten times before the phone picked up and a disgruntled sounding Hal answered.

"What."

"Hal its Faith, are you okay? Pretty much a quarter of the office is missing today, do you have a cold or something? The office is so quiet you should see it."

A long pause. "Mmm. I just didn't think I should bother coming in today. I mean, honestly Faith, my job is to look at numbers on a piece of paper, and make sure some add up, and then I make sure some numbers move from one bit of paper to another. Not exactly riveting stuff. After all that has happened recently, I just feel that there is more to life than that. I mean, the wonder, the majesty of what has just happened, don't you think that short of curing cancer, anything we do as humans is quite meaningless in the scheme of things? I think I am just going to stay home and watch TV because getting up and trying to do anything is just going to be pointless and insignificant, so I may as well do something pointless and insignificant from the comfort of my own couch. Working with numbers, watching TV, they both rank pretty much at the bottom of the list of important things in this universe. Don't worry, I'm sure you will still get paid. Bye."

"Wait! So what you are telling me is that unless you cure cancer, you aren't going to try to do anything with your life because there is no point, every action is too insignificant? That is the most ridiculous thing I have ever heard. A natural disaster hasn't occurred, life is going on as normally as possible you know. You can't watch TV forever. You have to eat, and you generally need money to buy food to do that." She actually couldn't believe what went through some people's minds.

"Look, I can maybe see from your perspective why you would think that, I mean, at least your job has a meaning and people rely on you for information and you contribute to society. Not all your stories are groundbreaking mind you, but in a way you still reach out and affect the population, you have no idea what kind of responsibility or privilege that is. Like I said, I just push numbers around paper. Only a handful of people count on me, and not in a meaningful way. I'm just the means for them to get paid for the work they do. Anyway, I'm going to get back to the TV until I figure out how to cure cancer or the world ends, whichever comes first."

Faith heard the receiver click down on his end and the line went dead. Did she really just have that conversation? Here she was, feeling alive and motivated and in awe of the possibilities now apparent in the universe, and there was somebody who was reduced to feeling so miniscule that they didn't want to even try at life anymore.

She could see what Hal was getting at, but the world was still turning, people still had to eat, and if this was going to be the new norm, life had to go on as per usual with the necessary adjustments made.

Turning back to her desk, she reread over the articles she had written the previous night, and set her mind to put together follow up stories for both, because there were still many questions left unanswered that would be demanding further explanation.

"Faith! Office. Now." The sound of Maxwell's furious voice echoed around the office and chilled her. She was expecting this and had mentally geared herself up for her explanation to him and gone over every possible scenario in her mind, so she wasn't too shaken. It wasn't the way she liked to be called into his office, but still, it was one on one time and she knew she would walk away with him eating out of the palm of her hand once she explained.

She put on her meek and mild face as she walked in and she already knew what he was going to do. Tell her to sit down and then throw this morning's paper in front of her and point to the unauthorised article and say…

"Can you explain what the hell this is!?" He yelled directly at her, less than a foot from her face and holding up the paper with his index finger pointing right at the article about the kidnapped priest. She had envisioned his reaction to that quite incorrectly. He seemed a little angrier than she expected. A lot angrier in fact.

"In case you were wondering why I was in a little late this morning it was because I have been talking to the police about why my paper had run a story about a missing priest, when nobody knew there was a missing priest until around about 7am this morning! Father Emmanuel teaches a before school class for underprivileged children at the church to help those that need assistance keeping up, and that's when it was discovered he was gone, and yet somehow you knew about it last night before the print run? I'm actually not bothered about the article, even though you disobeyed policy and submitted it without going through me, it's an exclusive story and nobody else will be able to print anything about it until tomorrow's run, but I need to know what you knew, when did you know it, and how did you know? And I need you to tell me now. Did you have anything to do with it? Who was your source?"

He reclined back in his chair and put his arms behind his head, waiting to hear one big revelation that would answer all of his questions adequately and satisfy the police who would eventually circle back to him.

Maxwell was not necessarily an alpha male, however his privileged and spoiled upbringing had led him to expect action whenever he demanded it. His parents had served him hand and foot and now that expectation of servitude had spilled over into the real world where he had never really politely asked for anything in years, he simply told people what he wanted in such a way that they felt compelled to give it to him, whether it be material objects or in this case, answers.

About fifteen minutes later, Faith left Maxwell's office with a semi-grin on her face, much to the surprise of her colleagues. She was astounded that they hadn't all gathered around the office door, listening in. He yelled out after her.

"Okay, we need to keep on top of this situation so keep me fully informed now because if something like this happens again I need to know. The motives behind this mean that it's more than just a missing person story now, so from what you've told me I'm tentatively happy to go along with it for the greater good until something comes up that tells me it was all a bad idea and we all go to jail. Got me?"

"Gotcha, boss."

"You're gonna be the death of me one day." Maxwell shook his head as she walked back to her desk. Whilst Faith knew she was going to leave his office in one piece, the conversation they just had reared up some things she would need to consider going forward that she hadn't planned for, like police involvement.

Sitting back at her desk, she found a message next to her phone informing her of a missed call from somebody called Saul. Scrawled next to the phone number was the word 'Connector?' She dialled the number straight away.

"Oh hello, this is Faith from the Tribune, is this Saul?"

Possibly the creepiest voice she had ever heard responded. The raspy voice sounded like a teenage boy who had lived in his parent's basement for too long and been deprived of any human contact, let alone contact with a female.

"Yes this is Saul, how are you on this fine day ma'am?" Faith wondered how he knew it was a fine day since he was probably in her imaginary basement scenario somewhere.

"I'm great, just great Saul. You left a call indicating that you know something about the connector people I mentioned in my story? What are you able to tell me?" She was sure she was going to like the answer, but not the delivery of it. It was most likely going to be an incredibly simple concept wrapped up in incomprehensible gibberish.

"I believe I am one of those connectors you speak of that seems to have received some information from God that has not been publicised yet. Something sad is going to happen."

"Sad?"

"Yes, sad for humanity."

"So, did you receive this information with all the other information that we received a couple of days ago? It just doesn't sound very specific. Sad for the entire human race? What could that possibly be, like a war or something?" She was slightly annoyed at the lack of detail once again delivered by these strange people.

"I know, it is just a feeling I have that I can't put my finger on or clarify any further. Something incredibly sad is going to happen and it is going to happen very soon. That's all I have. I'm sorry it doesn't mean a whole lot, but I am absolutely certain of this." His raspy voice continued. "Will my name be quoted in your next story? My surname is Glenlyon."

"Probably not Saul Glenlyon, I'm sorry. I do thank you for calling though, I just don't think it's enough to base an article on at this stage. But please, if you do recall anything else feel free to give me call here at the Tribune."

Saul started to speak again but she hung up the phone. Nothing useable but the disturbing meaning of his message had her a little worried.

"Hey Faith, a couple of us are going to grab a coffee at the diner around the corner, wanna join?" Margie asked, one of the Accounts team who now was the person everybody expecting to get paid would be relying on since Hal was not going to show up for a while until he figured himself out.

"Oh, thanks Margie but I'm just going to keep on working here for a bit until lunchtime."

"Such dedication to your job, I do love your work ethic." Margie looked left and right, and then stepped forward closer to Faith and said in a more hushed tone. "I sometimes do wonder if you sacrifice so much for your job that you will never have time for a family, or even a man! Me and my Johnny are so happy together you know, having little Georgie was the best thing I, well, we, have ever done."

She stepped back and spoke at regular volume again. "Anyway, we will leave you to it. If you change your mind, you know where we will be. See you soon." And with that, a group of them headed downstairs leaving Faith pretty much alone in the office. Just how she liked it.

Faith squeezed the pen she was holding so tightly that she felt it would nearly break. Margie was a lovely woman, one of those quiet girls who would always be in the background watching other girls get asked out on dates and fall in love, whilst putting on a brave smile and lying to herself saying that she was quite happy as she was and that she didn't need anybody.

She fell in love and married the first gentleman who showed interest in her, a plain but kind man, and within a year little Georgie was born. Margie was now the main distributor of life advice around the office, and a source of pity for all those who were unmarried and consequently had incomplete and meaningless lives.

Faith justified her own situation to herself. She was more than happy with her career and life balance at the moment. She loved the pressure of a deadline and the feeling of exhilaration when she read her own stories, saw her name mentioned and photo at the top of each article. It would take one hell of a man to make her feel that good.

What they don't realise is that I'm not sacrificing family life because of my work, I would be sacrificing my work if I had a family life. Some people just don't understand.

"Faith. FAITH!" Mavis had been yelling to her but she had been in her own little world of justifying her life situation.

"Sorry Mavis, what's up? Are you going to tell me that I need to get married too?"

"Well I don't know, maybe I don't need to, it's that handsome sounding latino gentleman on the phone asking for you again. Maybe he wants to ask you out on a date?"

Faith snapped to attention and all thoughts of marriage and dating were cast aside. "Transfer him through Mavis."

She picked up the phone with nervous excitement and before she could even get a word out she heard that familiar voice.

"Faith? I've got another story for you."

Tues 22 Sept 1959 *7:00am*
Mary's Breakthrough

Mary lay in bed for ten minutes longer than usual this morning, not only because she had a restless sleep with endless tossing and turning, but also because her guilt had caught up with her and she was holding an extended prayer session to compensate for her disrespectful neglect to do so the previous evening.

The lifelong habit was hard to break, and even though she knew prayer did not fall upon any ears as intended, her mind could not persuade her heart of this. She dared not think about seeing all those hours of her life, those incremental minutes every evening as time wasted, every Sunday morning at church, more time wasted.

She knew that she could still love the Lord and believe and worship without having to make the trek to church, and it was particularly tough on those cold and rainy days when she would much rather be warm in bed.

She knew the Lord would still love her even if she didn't make the trek. The church was merely a structure where like-minded people could congregate and embrace the comradery, much like supporters at a sports match who all barracked for the same team.

So had she wasted a large portion of her life praying? Maybe, now that she knew that the mechanisms of communication between herself and the Lord were virtually null. But on the other hand she felt better, cleansed in mind and spirit, and prayer was her time to reflect also on what was important to her and her life.

She always felt better afterwards and a little closer to feeling in touch with her inner self. In the end, she decided that it had done her no harm and had been almost an unintentional form of meditation.

Deciding to indulge in another form of meditation to her, Mary sat at the table and stared at the freshly delivered newspaper. Flicking though it to see if anything caught her eye she found a story about a dog that had become separated from its owner and travelled half way across the country using some kind of animal-radar to finally be reunited several months later.

Mary's first reaction was to get angry at the irresponsible dog owner, heaven knows from her experience with Diah at the dog shelter that the gorgeous animals suffered the same spectrum of emotions as humans do. Her second reaction was to feel the pangs of hurt inside as the memories of her own separation from a loved one emerged, her distance from Diah still as painful as it was the day he left.

She wondered if he had moved on and found somebody else. She had the means at her disposal to find out through a variety of connections, but she was not brave enough to go down this path.

It would kill her to know.

It killed her to not know.

She didn't know why after all this time her love for him had never diminished. Wasn't love just a series of chemical reactions within the human body? Reactions which are initiated when pheromones and some other factors establish that there is a genetic compatibility that would result in a high probability of a couple producing healthy offspring? Then why hadn't these chemical reactions stopped yet? The scientific test tubes and the beakers weren't only empty of chemicals and back in the cupboard, they were in completely different laboratories!

"Love" is a series of events that occur on a physiological level, but Mary knew there was also some indefinable constituent that defied chemistry and all laws of the known universe. True love, as society knows it, however, is almost a completely separate entity to that of chemical love.

It is a concept created by man which has a set of rules that are superimposed over the urges and natural instincts of man as an animal. It defines a set of feelings and behaviours that you must feel and obey before you can meet the prerequisites of calling something love.

Movies show us what it is. The romance, the chivalry, the selflessness and the support, all quite removed from genetic compatibility and procreation. The rules of love are none other than those we have created for ourselves, and society imposes and enforces these rules. Love comes from the heart.

"And the heart is really just a muscle that pumps blood around the body, isn't it darling? Come here my gorgeous boy."

Zach had made an entrance, rubbing his eyes sleepily, and as her heart melted, all thoughts of Diah did too.

She grabbed him, sat him on her lap even though he was almost getting to big to do so now and continued to read the paper. She read with interest the article suggesting that some people seemed to be aware of more information inside themselves from the communication from the Lord than others.

She closed her eyes and felt the glow inside, and allowed the feeling to wash over her almost as if she was tapping into the heart of God directly. Was it fading a little?

So some people had different versions of this? Some more, some less? These connectors, why were they chosen, were they special in some way?

"Maybe they are the new priests of the future, huh Zach? If they have privileged access to the intentions of God I would imagine they will be highly sought after by the church, though

from the description in the article of the person interviewed he didn't really sound like a people person."
Zach jumped off her lap and sat on the other dining chair opposite her. "Is mummy not comfortable enough for you any more sweetie?" Mary said lightheartedly.

"It must be a lonely existence for God, a bit like mummy's although she has her wonderful boy to keep her company."

She stopped because Zach was sitting there staring at her and tilting his head from side to side. She could sense that he really wanted to communicate something with her and she scolded herself for thinking it but he reminded her of when a dog looked like it wanted to tell you something with great urgency but frustration showed in its eyes that it was doing its best but the message wasn't getting across.

"What are you thinking, my boy? What's going on in that head of yours, huh? I wish I could just hold your hand and everything you are thinking and feeling could zap across to me like magic. Wouldn't that be good?" she asked, feeling the same frustration that had pushed Diah over the edge welling up within her.

And then the word came out.

"God." It came from Zach feebly, faintly but in the surrounding silence of the morning it could have been as loud as an aeroplane or a clap of thunder to Mary's ears. His lips continued to move, as if trying to continue on with a sentence, or was he just trying to recreate with his mouth the word he had just struggled to get out? He struggled on but eventually his lips stopped moving as if exhausted from the effort and he stared ahead.

Mary became weak in her chair and had to grab onto the table as she began to see stars. She felt as if a heart attack was coming on, her chest was beating so violently. His voice was everything she imagined it would be, soft, innocent, and the most beautiful sound she had ever heard. She knew he seemed different the last couple of days, and this was why! Sobbing hysterically, her blouse becoming saturated and nose running like a tap, she hugged Zach close and then grabbed him by the arms, frantically shaking him.

"Zach! Zach! Speak to me baby, speak to mummy again like you just did!" Her eyes were wide and pleading with him. "You can talk! Oh this is wonderful! So wonderful!"

She looked around and then realising she was in her kitchen where nobody could see her, she punched the air and her voice took on a higher pitch. "Yes! Yes!" She picked Zach up off his chair and thrust him into the air, then made a face and calmed down a little when she narrowly missed banging his head against the ceiling.

Who could she tell? She had to tell somebody. It was too early in the morning. Dr Eunice! She looked at the clock. Dr Eunice was Zach's specialist and Mary had paid good money over the years for little result and she could darn well open her front door at 8am for this turn of events and maybe help explain what just happened. Had it just happened? Second guessing herself already, she wondered if it was her imagination.

"Did that just happen baby? Was mummy imagining things?" Then checking her composure and seeing the mess she was in, she knew the answer.

"Yes, that definitely happened, you would not be covered in my tears right now if it hadn't." She laughed to herself at her tragic appearance. "Let's go see Dr Eunice."

As much as she just wanted to pick Zach up and run, she knew the right thing to do would be to at least warn Dr Eunice that they were coming. She picked up the phone and dialled. No answer.

She tried again. On about the fifth ring an unimpressed voice answered. "What is it?"

"It's Mary and Zach. There's wonderful news and a big development. We are coming right over. Right now!"

"Wait, wait, what development, what news?" The doctor had no appetite for guessing games.

"No time to talk, I'll tell you soon, see you at your house!"

Dr Eunice resigned herself to the fact that this was happening whether she liked it or not, but she did have to admit she was intrigued. She had never heard Mary's voice raised above a whisper before so this must be quite some news that she had.

"Just go to my practice, I'll meet you there and you can tell me whatever it is that you have to say. And it's on the clock. Weekend rates because of the early hour."

Like a flash, the mother and son were out the door. Then two seconds later they were back in the door while Mary dressed Zach and put shoes on him. "Dr Eunice doesn't need to think I am a negligent mum! That won't do at all." And then they were back out the door and on their way.

Tues 22 Sept 1959 *8:35am*
Mr Derby

Reaching for his second favourite trilby off the hatstand by the front door, Mr Derby simultaneously popped the loaded pipe into his mouth and made his way out of the grand entrance to his house, pulling the large, ornate mahogany door closed behind him and walked down the path of white pebbles to the front gate, puffing away.

Latching the gate, he turned and strolled down the road, waving at the boy riding past him on his red shiny bicycle who lived two houses down. After living in the prestigious street for over fifty years, there wasn't a person in the area that Mr Derby didn't know. On the rare occasion that a family decided to move out of the neighbourhood, he was always the first person knocking on the door of the new family moving in, welcoming them and handing the man of the house a bottle of fine cognac.

Call it intelligence gathering or what you may, it was never long before he had imposed a barrage of questions upon the newcomers to establish a background history and form an impression of them to be recalled at a future date for any number of reasons.

He successfully managed to deflect all enquiries as to his own state of affairs, though he was not an overly private man, but was adamant that if anybody should want to know more about him then they should knock on *his* door with a bottle of cognac in hand.

It was one of those annoyingly windy days, not ideal for those who smoked from a pipe or wore a hat, and both of Mr Derby's hands were constantly occupied ensuring all items remained where they were and functioned as intended. Eventually he gave up on smoking and with a grumble, tapped out the remaining tobacco which was soon to have blown out anyway and commenced inhaling on the empty vessel instead.

"Time to think of my sentence to say to Jacob I suppose," he said to himself and set his mind to selecting something of interest for his 8:45am rendezvous. He never planned ahead for this, and quite often just waited to see what came out of his mouth at the moment. Quite often he had so many competing ideas that he thought at times that he really should stop engaging in so many activities to relax and stay home and read a book every once in a while. Just like his friend Jacob clearly did.

The poor man seemed to have such an uneventful life that Mr Derby was surprised that he didn't use his imagination to at least make up more interesting things to tell him each morning. It must be embarrassing for the poor fellow to tell me he is thinking of buying a tie that is either of two shades of the same colour and I am telling him that I have been invited to the governor's house for lunch, or have raced the newest sports car on the track outside of town. Still, maybe it brightens his day up rather than depresses him, or maybe it does nothing for him at all.

After walking up the slight grassy incline that led to the alley, he turned in and proceeded to keep an eye out for his old friend. He usually finished puffing and panting from the walk up the hill just in time for his sentence to be spoken clearly and without any wheezing.

Proceeding along, he furrowed his eyebrows and squinted ahead. There was nobody in sight. Continuing to walk ahead slowly, he pulled out his pocket watch and checked the time. It was dead on 8:45am, the same time as every other morning that he reached the alley. Very unusual. This was most unlike Jacob, whether rain, hail or shine, whether sick or healthy, he had never known him to miss a day.

Mr Derby stood in the centre of the alley for perhaps two minutes, looking around in a puzzled manner. Then, remembering that he himself had a place to be, he shrugged, proclaimed his sentence to the world, bowed with a flourish to nobody in particular and continued on his way.

And then he saw them.

Tues 22 Sept 1959 **5:38am**
Jacob and Company

"I need a coffee. Strong. Now." Jacob moaned to himself as his alarm went off and the events of the previous night outside the church flooded back and filled him with trepidation. A situation had presented itself that offered outcomes of such polarity it could deliver his only remaining family back to him again and relieve the burden of his guilt, or it could see hopes dashed from such elevation there would be no chance of recovery.

There was no choice. He had stepped out onto the ledge and once he jumped he would either fly towards redemption or fall, and he had no influence on which of the two would happen. He had to roll the dice and sacrifice all or nothing.

The place where the miracles were allegedly occurring was surely a fraud. Knowing the worst of human nature, somebody was capitalising on the recent events for a quick buck and would clean up a tidy sum until word spread that the phenomenon was an example of profiteering.

People with hope always ignored warning signs and their better judgment, seemingly able to believe absolutely anything no matter how irrational, if it meant that there was a potential solution to their pain and yet here was Jacob, a rational man agreeing to go many miles upstate for the sake of his daughter even though the only possible result would be disappointment and then more resentment with a renewed enthusiasm.

To make the trip and fail would not have the same consequences as not making the trip at all. As was discussed the previous evening, even if the odds of success were close to zero and yet infinitesimally greater than zero, they had to go.

Grabbing a handful of various things from the pantry as snacks for the trip, Jacob packed a bag and was about to knock on Ava's door when she appeared in the kitchen with such verve and vim that he hadn't seen for a very long time. She had a bag on her lap, and her familiar pink pyjamas were sitting on top within easy grasping reach for her piece of mind.

He also noticed that she had a lot of makeup on and wondered at what hour she had started getting ready for the trip. Jacob estimated her energy was sourced about fifty percent from the hope offered by the miracle place, and fifty percent around seeing the young man from last night again.

He tried to start the day off on a positive note and anticipated that this road trip could be the most time that he and Ava would have spent together in a long time.

"Hey sweetie, looking good! I'm super excited about today, aren't you? Should be fun, a bunch of us in a van, hitting the open road."

"Yeah, I bet you are real keen to get me back on my feet again so you don't have to push me around everywhere. Must be so inconvenient for you," was the reply.

Although he suffered these barbs every day, they remained just as sharp and pierced him just as deeply as they always had from the first day that Ava had emerged from hospital after the accident. He put his brave face on as he always did. It was not good for a daughter to see her father hurting, even if that was her intention.

"Let me put your things in the van and we can go and collect Ishara. Are there any other snacks you want me to bring? We don't know how far away this place is or what the traffic will be like. I would rather be prepared for anything."

"Let's just go shall we, Gabe will be waiting and probably go without us."

Still dark outside, there was a creepy feeling in the air as they pulled out of the driveway and headed towards the Singh residence. Everything was quiet, there were no other cars on the road, no signs of life. It felt like they were on a stealth mission of some sort, and they did not want to be caught or have to explain their motives as to why they were moving under the cover of darkness.

Of course Jacob knew this was just silly, but travelling before dawn always made him think of spy movies and he used to play a game with himself that he was trying to get somewhere undetected by some villains, although now he felt that he had scared himself somewhat. Considering the strange behaviours he had seen in others the last couple of days it probably was best not to bump into anybody in a dark street in the early hours of the morning.

Ishara was ready and waiting for the van to arrive and also bounded in with much enthusiasm and copious lipstick applied. Jacob was oblivious to the split second where the two girls eyed each other off imperceptibly in only the way that women can, and then they snapped to best-friend mode once again and greeted each other with a hug of such authenticity that almost masked any underlying feelings of rivalry that may have been present.

After an uneventful drive to the place where they had met Gabe the previous evening just up from the church, the passengers in the van did not have to wait long before a tap on the window startled them.

"Gabe!" the two girls exclaimed in unison, Ishara jumping out of the van and giving him a hug that might be seen as a little too familiar for somebody who had only been briefly introduced the evening before. Ava watched the embrace from inside the van, her face now emotionless.

Their eyes met and Gabe waved hello to her before his face contorted into an incredibly wide yawn, offending Ava greatly. Composing himself, he greeted his travel companions.

"Hello everybody, how are we all? I would like to introduce you to the one, the only, my amazing nephew Simon that I told you about yesterday. Such a little champion, aren't you?"

He raised up a young blonde boy of around nine years above his head, crutches and all and bounced him up and down while the boy maintained a look on his pale face of grim acceptance as if this sort of thing happened often. After not too long, he was placed carefully back on the ground and his hair mussed up by Gabe affectionately.

"Can you do that to me?" Ishara asked playfully.

"Ha ha maybe a little later, Simon is becoming a big boy and his uncle's arms are tired now aren't they?" He deflected the forward comment and mussed Simon's hair again, who once again resigned himself to the fact that it was always a bad hair day when his uncle was around.

"Hi Jacob, are you ready to go? I've got a tonne of food and drink and some rough directions. I have a feeling we will be able to find the spot pretty easily, I think it could be a popular destination but I hope word hasn't spread far. It's about one hundred and fifty miles so it shouldn't take too long if we take it sensibly and have a few rest breaks. I'm actually pretty glad we are going as a group even though it is not what I planned. It will be nice to be able to share such a positive experience with others. I'm already looking forward to the trip home when we have done whatever it is we need to do to and all is made right." He looked at Ava and Simon.

"Jeez are you okay? You sound insanely optimistic and happier than a Mormon. It's off-putting," Ava said, poking fun.

"Well, we are all Mormons now aren't we? Might as well act like one." Gabe replied, bursting into laughter as he saw Ava's face.

"Just kidding, you are so gullible. I'm not a Mormon, just super keen and excited to get this show on the road. Can I say a little prayer on behalf of Ava and Simon?"

"That's a great idea!" Ishara said sycophantically.

"Are you kidding again?" Ava asked seriously.

"No I'm serious, I think it feels right. This trip actually means a lot to all of us for our own reasons."

"Well, if you want to, I suppose, sure. For whatever it's worth. Still weird though," Ava said.

"Okay I've never said a prayer before and I know they have always been completely useless, and evidence now shows them to be totally ineffective but I am going to anyway."

"Wow this is off to a good start." Ava said.

"I want to thank the Lord for bringing us all together and providing Simon and I with like-minded company with the same goals who know what it is like to confront demons, and to seize the opportunity to defeat them for the opportunity to live long and happy lives. To our health. To our improved health!"

Once again he looked at Simon and Ava who now felt a little self-conscious and a bit like a charity case. She spoke up to cover her slight embarrassment. She did not need Gabe to think of her as an item that needed fixing.

"That just sounds like a toast. You need to say Amen." Ava reminded Gabe.

"Oh yes, Amen," they yelled in chorus.

"Now let's get the hell out of here," Ava said.

"Ava!" Jacob reprimanded her for her semi-blasphemy, but eased off from using the severe tone that would normally accompany such a reprimand if there were not others present.

He took the wheel and Simon claimed the front seat of the van as he was most comfortable with his legs outstretched. Ishara and Gabe were immediately behind, and Ava with her wheelchair station at the back.

"Easy over the bumps would you, idiot!" She yelled at her father, forgetting that there was external company and became annoyed at herself when she saw the bemused way Gabe looked at her.

"Sorry. Just nervous about the trip!" She laughed off her comment.

Her natural instincts were to hurt the man that hurt her, at every opportunity that she could. It had become part of her, and she could not remember the last time she was even civil to her father. She did not know if she could consciously bite her tongue for the whole journey, it was such an automated response to his presence that she felt she could never turn it off. But he did not deserve for her to turn it off. So maybe she might just have to turn it down a notch temporarily.

Gabe leaned forward and whispered to Ishara.

"Wow, is she always like that? Her dad seems really cool, and is driving her across country. You'd think she might be a bit nicer to him? What's the bee in her bonnet?"

"No, Ava is really lovely! I have a lot of time for her. Must just be that she is not a morning person." She looked over at Ava and saw her staring dreamily at Gabe. Ishara frowned, and decided to reveal just a little of her true thoughts.

"Well actually, she kinda has been really mean to him for years now but I never say anything about it, I really do feel sorry for him, he tries to give her everything and she throws it back in his face. He is really a lovely man, always been great to me and is like my second dad. But as a second daughter, I am a lot nicer than his first one as you can see!"

It was Gabe's turn to frown. "Why would she treat her own dad like that? Family is everything to me, I would do anything for Simon, I treat him as if her were my own."

"I know right? Me too. I think she is a little harsh on him. She has been like that ever since the accident though. I can see why she harbours some resentment."

"Accident?"

"Well, I suppose on this trip you were going to find out eventually so I might as well tell you. A while back her dad was driving one night and he swerved off the road to avoid an animal and killed her mother and put her in the wheelchair that you see before you. In twenty five words or less that is the sad tale, it's just the most devastating thing."

"Oh my God. That is terrible, that poor girl, and poor Jacob! He must be carrying so much guilt inside. I can completely understand how Ava can be like this now, it must be so hard to let go when the man that killed your mum is your own father and living with you. That is the most painful situation I could ever imagine. Poor Ava." Ishara saw him glance over to Ava with hurt and pity in his eyes.

"What are you two talking about over there?' Ava asked, conscious of the whispering and dying to know but not wanting to appear nosey. She started fidgeting with her pink pyjamas on her lap.

"Nothing interesting. I never talk about anything interesting," Gabe said with a forced smirk, trying to make light of the moment. Changing the subject he joked "What's with the little girl pink pyjamas you are playing with? You gonna try them on for me? They look cute!" Ava's eyes widened.

Ishara shrunk into her chair mortified and whispered to Gabe.

"They are what she was wearing in the car accident. They are like a security blanket for her, she takes them everywhere."

Gabe mentally kicked himself. "Uh. I'm an idiot, always putting my foot in my mouth. I wasn't to know! Poor Ava. I know exactly what she is going through, with losing my sister and now I'm looking after Simon. The death of a family member is like having a piece of your heart torn out and never replaced again. I know that for my whole life I will miss my sister. In fifty years' time I know this pain will still be as intense. We fought tooth and nail, but family is family and maybe we only fought so much because we were so close with each other. No matter what the topic or situation we could just say straight out whatever it was that we were thinking. Now that I think about it, that's probably love. That's a brother and sister who didn't hide anything, not feelings, not thoughts, nothing. Even if it caused a fight we would say it. With everybody else you have to hold back and be polite and appropriate and try not to hurt their feelings. That's basically telling somebody you aren't going to let them in, keep them at arm's length and tell them only what they want to hear so that you don't have to have the difficult conversations which makes life easier for everybody."

"Would you two honestly stop whispering! I'm becoming paranoid it's about me!" Ava couldn't stand it any longer and was more worried they were whispering something resembling sweet nothings to each other.

Gabe looked over with pity and admiration in his eyes. "We weren't discussing anything interesting. Just a dull old conversation." Oblivious to Ishara's incredulous face at this comment he continued. "And how are you, are you excited about the trip?"

"Yes of course I am! Best case scenario is that I don't have to wheel this hunk of junk around my house any more. I'm surprised I'm still alive with all the rickety ramps my dad has made out of toothpicks and dental floss around the place. It's such an un-wheelchair-friendly dump. You should ask Ishara about her house! A way more interesting tale."

"Oh? Something I should know?"

"Yeah, ask her how many bathrooms she has, or servants!"

Ishara shook her head and tried to play down the conversation. She hated it when friends made a big deal about her family situation. She was not responsible for how successful her parents were. If anybody else had the chance to be in her circumstances she knew they would take it. She was an innocent bystander, why did she always feel punished because her parents had done well at their chosen vocation? People should be rewarded for doing well, shouldn't they? But instead she had always been teased and her parents spoken about as if they had somehow cheated at life. She addressed this topic with her standard approach.

"Yes, yes, well I would tell you how many bathrooms we have except every time I have a spare week to count them all I get a different number. I'm sure it's because our pesky east wing seems to just be growing of its own accord! Still, you've got to put an indoor golf course somewhere am I right, I mean, we aren't barbarians." Gabe erupted with laughter much to Ishara's relief.

Driving through the town as it was coming to life for the day, heralded by a brilliant purple sunrise that peeked over the rooftops and revealed just how much had changed since the event of a couple of days ago. Jacob noticed that some store fronts had been boarded up whilst others had windows smashed with signs of looting, and a convenience store already had a line-up out the front of people impatiently waiting for some item or foodstuff that must be in short supply.

It was naïve to think that human behaviour wouldn't change after the most significant event in history had transpired, however, from what he could see there was a similarity to one of his favourite books, Lord of the Flies being played out. In that novel, however, the deterioration from civilised people to savages occurred due to the removal of higher powers, not the affirmation of one.

Jacob hoped that for whatever the reason was that the dark side of human nature had been engaged, there were also extreme acts of kindness and altruism being acted out by those who felt compelled to immerse themselves in their acceptance of the divine.

"So why is this all happening in such an out of the way place, does it just limit the number of clientele so that there isn't a complete inundation of miracle-seekers? Almost like a test so that only those who have the drive and determination to undertake the pilgrimage are in with a chance." Gabe asked.

"I know. I am racking my brain to think why God doesn't just perform a full sweep of miracles across the earth? Why a little backwater place here and there? This all suggests to me that for God there is the desire to help, to make people happy and healthy and put things right. So if you have the power and the desire then why not just abolish all pain, suffering and disease worldwide?" Ava became frustrated. "And save us all the trouble of a quest to the middle of nowhere!"

Gabe looked at her. "Maybe all suffering can't be abolished by God because God isn't responsible for creating famine, death, disease as we once thought. That all just occurred organically, if that's a good way to put it. This was all in the paper yesterday, didn't you read it and can't you feel it inside you? If they aren't of God's creation then it might be difficult to abolish totally. The sphere of influence here could be very small with only capacity for small influential efforts. Anyway, that's just a guess, who will ever know. Let's see if these extraordinary events are even real first before we try to solve their reason for being."

"No I never read the paper, dad generally just gets tabloid trash." Ava shook her head and then took a long pause as if listening for something. "Hey, that feeling inside me is still there, but all the information is becoming a little like a distant memory though. Are you guys getting that too, it feels like it is dissipating? I wonder if it is because I am getting used to it. And why does God care about us or what happens anyway? It's like a human being interested in a bug or something."

Jacob had been listening from the front seat and now felt inclined to input his two cents. "Yes, but some people ARE interested in bugs. And some are interested in even less significant animals. But on a side note you have actually made a good suggestion Gabe, we should get today's paper and see if there are any updates on anything."

He soon pulled over to the side of the road, jumped out of the van to pop a coin in a fully stocked newspaper vending machine, quickly yanked out a paper and was back in and driving within thirty seconds. He threw the paper into the back of the van and let them fight over who got to read it first. "Anything happen yesterday that can beat the appearance of God?"

Ishara was the lucky one who had managed to commandeer the paper. She rifled through it quickly and landed back at the front page to something that had caught her attention.

"Uh, only that the priest we saw at the church yesterday has gone missing! I knew some people weren't too happy in that church but what the.."

Jacob slammed on the brakes and screeched to an abrupt halt. Ava reprimanded her father for this, holding back somewhat from her normal tone of voice with him this time.

"It's disturbing that we saw him yesterday but you don't have to slam your brakes on like that! I nearly tipped my chair over."

"No, it's not that. Look!" Jacob pointed ahead and they all craned their neck to peer through the front windscreen. They had reached the outskirts of the city and just turned onto the road which would take them to the freeway. There were cars backed up as far as the eye could see, which was some distance since they were in the van and quite high above the other cars which simply weren't moving.

"I'm sure they will move along soon," Ishara offered up some positivity.

"It's a quarter past six in the morning, where on earth could everybody be going? Oh." She realised that the cars had not been there from only this morning. Looking more closely, the cars were empty and were packed four cars across in a three lane street. It was just chaos, and Jacob imagined most of the cars ahead had been abandoned, indeed it looked like one had even been set fire to.

The excited mood of the van instantly shifted to disbelief and all sentiments hit rock bottom. Ava started crying hysterically even though it was the last thing that she wanted to do in front of Gabe. He reached forward and grabbed her knee, saying something reassuring but at this stage she didn't care and didn't listen, the words only a blur to her ears.

For about five minutes they all sat in the van, silent and staring at their feet. Not even a half hour into their quest and they had the rug pulled out from underneath them.

"Can it be that damned hard just to drive somewhere on the freeway!? I never ask for much, in fact I never ask for anything, and the one time I just want to simply travel from A to B oh no, can't let you do something as simple as that, the universe says to me. Can't possibly make anything easy for you." Jacob snapped, realising what it meant for him and for all of them if their hopes were truly dashed. There was no other way out of the city, except for on foot or…

He slammed the car into reverse and actually managed to make the van burn rubber, tyres spinning on the asphalt. Everybody was jolted around inside like a rag doll and arms were thrown out to assume brace positions.

"Are you crazy? What are you doing? That's it. It's over. We can't go, the freeway is stuck solid. There's no other way you know. We are all going to stay like this forever and ever and ever." Ava became hysterical.

Jacob's eyes opened impossibly wide and he looked exceptionally pleased with himself. "Well guess what guys, Uncle Jacob knows how to get us there, but first, I have to know what time it is. Well? What's the time?" The occupants of the van looked at him like he was crazy.

"Urgh, about 6:50am" said Gabe, looking at his watch and hoping that his answer would draw out an explanation as to why the time was important right now.

"Okay, we have exactly one hour fifty five minutes, should be easy, but who knows. Hold on!"

Tues 22 Sept 1959 **7:08am**
Ira Obeys

Lying in bed and knowing that he was about to experience another tumultuous day, Ira reflected upon the long and eventful evening he had endured. He had silently climbed into bed next to his wife well after midnight and admired her beauty, running his fingers gently through her hair, aware of the precipice that he was now edging ever so close to. Hoping that he did not draw his family nearer as well, it would be a very, very long fall for them all if he did not tread carefully.

The first step of Aaban's plan had been executed, the first of the lambs now herded. Ira was caught in a game of chess, and had been forked by a player who was not necessarily more skilful, but had the underhanded power to be able to manipulate the rules to their own favour.

Ira had his own risky game plan but in order to walk away with a checkmate every single move had to be perfectly executed and a lot of luck had to come into play. Could it be done? For the sake of his family, he hoped so.

He rolled out from under the covers and plodded out to the kitchen bleary eyed and hunched over. Dex sidled up and gave him a quick sniff before turning his attention back to the squeaky toy he was attempting to tear apart in order to find out where the noise was coming from. Ira managed to give him a quick pat on the head.

Lucy welcomed him with a smile. "Breakfast in your pyjamas today, honey? I hope you aren't hungover, you were in late last night I suspect?" She turned the hotplate on, preparing to make her husband breakfast.

"Not too late," Ira lied. "The boss and I had a bit of a catch up at the bar, talked some boring business and then I came home, nothing major."

The smell of pancakes filled the air. Just what the doctor ordered. Ira was sure that if there was some sort of pancake award, his wife would win it by a landslide. His eyes turned to the newspaper at the table, already unwrapped from its plastic and ready to be perused.

The front page caught his eye, in large bold font he read "Local Priest Abducted." followed by a short paragraph discussing possible motive, police investigation and a lack of leads at this stage. Good girl Faith. Ira knew his boss would read the article and confirm that his wishes were being carried out, making any upcoming conversation with him easier and involving no threats to his family with any luck.

His internal conflict was getting the better of him. For now he had chosen the welfare of his family to be a priority over his own newly defined value system. He had done many things in his life before the eyes of God that he would be seeking forgiveness for, and if it meant protecting his loved ones against a great evil then he was prepared to continue to those actions temporarily, since the damage was already done in his mind.

"Gee honey, are you going to chew those before you swallow them? Maybe I should just pour the batter straight down your throat?" Lucy laughed. Ira had absentmindedly rolled up a pancake and stuck the whole thing onto the end of his fork and was gulping it down in much the same way that an anaconda would detach its lower jaw in able to be able to eat its prey whole.

"Mm. Hungry. Is good," he replied, glad to be momentarily taken away from his thoughts.

The back door swung open and Hector ran in, puffing and panting. "Dad, dad, look what mum helped me make!" He held up a tray with some children's plastic cups and saucers on it that had seen better days. Grass and dirt was floating onto the floor from ones that had evidently been dropped on the lawn many times as he waved the tray around. Ira stepped in.

"Not inside little man! Your mother spends a lot of time to keep this house clean! Don't you have something better to do? Watch a documentary, learn something? Don't play with cups of tea. It's time wasted." Then, looking at Lucy, "Honey why are you teaching him things that are nothing but a pointless waste of time? Serving invisible tea and muffins isn't going to activate his mind or help him get a good job when he is older. It's a competition these days out there. Maybe he can do that nonsense stuff after he reads a book or something."

"Honey, he is four years old. Firstly, he can't read yet, and you know that. Secondly, what's wrong with letting a kid be a kid? He should be having fun. What are you expecting from him, to be reading books about law or construction, or medicine? Thirdly, what's your problem?"

Ira wished he had closed his mouth, He had spoken without thinking, the pressure he was under making him already concerned about his son's future job, whatever that may be. Realising he was in for a debate, he braced himself.

"You think it is wrong for somebody to do something that may potentially be pointless? I learned the piano when I was younger but I never use it for anything. Is that pointless? I enjoyed it, and isn't that what life is about? You are in the construction industry. When you were a kid, did you only play with trucks and plastic tools? Well?"

Ira knew he was beat. "No honey. I did a bunch of other stuff too," he admitted begrudgingly.

"Being a kid is all about experiences, discovery, discovering your talents and finding out what you do and don't like. Who knows what they want to do when they are four, and then only focus on doing that for their whole lives. Honestly honey, sometimes I really do wonder where your head is at sometimes. You don't have a problem with him playing soccer now, do you?"

"Sorry dear. You are right." He hoped the conversation had been put to rest.

"So can he play with his plastic tray and cups and invisible cakes?"

"Yes dear, as long as this silly grown up can play with some more real pancakes and coffee?" He tried to steer the conversation away and back onto things less contentious. She was right of course, as usual. This time though, he was not so lucky and Lucy had really latched on to the topic.

"So you want him to watch a documentary. Using your argument, if he is probably never going to use the information for anything, what was the point of watching it? If that was the case, then anybody who ever watched documentaries or read anything would only do so with the intention of appearing on a trivia or quiz show or becoming a zoologist. Sometimes people just like doing things for no reason, or just liked to do it for themselves and to expand their horizons. It's not just all rattling around in your brain taking up space. There is plenty of space in there. You never know what might sit with you and change your perspective on the world."

Lucy suggested they cancel their newspaper subscription since there was absolutely no point in reading it. He didn't know why he opened his big stupid mouth sometimes, he didn't need his own wife questioning why she married him, even though he gave her good reason.

"Well, I'd better get out of here before I say anything else stupid," he said, rolling up the newspaper and tucking it under his arm. "But first, Hector how about you give daddy a cup of tea and a muffin before he leaves? He is going to get hungry out there on the road."

"Daddy, I would but they aren't real, they were only make believe. I thought even you would be smart enough to see that." Hector replied with such an innocent and unexpected statement that both Ira and Lucy burst out laughing. Ira picked him up and gave him a squeeze, and then his wife.

"I'll be back later, I've got a job on and then I have to catch up with Aaban again, so I'm not entirely sure when I'll be back, but I'll call if I'm going to be late. Love you."

"Bye!"

Closing the front door, Ira walked out to the car, but first took the paper out from under his arm and threw it across to Jim's yard. Now, time for business.

Climbing into his pickup and grimacing for no other reason than feeling his age, Ira thought about his difficult day ahead. There was a time when he would just plough through tasks without too much thought, one after another, whether they were criminal in nature or as simple as doing some light grocery shopping. Now the burden of right and wrong lay over him like a blanket, threatening to pin him down and render him immobile.

Shaking his head as if that would help shake off the blanket, he started the car and backed out of his driveway, drove around the corner for about thirty seconds and stopped. Getting out of the car he slowly walked to a telephone booth that he often used when he did not want Lucy to hear his work calls. The next minute of his life would potentially decide the fate of him and his family.

Dropping a coin into the slot, he dialled some familiar digits and waited for Aaban to answer. A painfully long wait.

"Hello." A relaxed voice answered.

"Boss it's me. Have you read the paper this morning?" Ira heard paper rustling in the background as if Aaban was just flicking through it only now, but he knew he had read it.

"Yes I have, so it looks like the first lamb has been shepherded and the powers that be have decided it worthy of front page news. You must be careful. They are safe?"

"Of course, they are in my care and will soon be joined by more."

"Good, a good start. There are many more imposters claiming untruths and I must send a message to them all. And now, did you also read about these liars who claim that they know more than the rest of us, more than even I, a true follower and believer. Preposterous."

"Yes, yes, the connectors." Ira could see where this was heading.

"Are they real, are they charlatans? Who knows? The problem is that nobody can substantiate their claims that God is here to reset the truth. What is that? What does this nonsense mean? If they were really accessing the mind of God they would have more profound statements to make! I want you to find one and add them to the flock. Anybody who is making false claims against God must face judgement and that puts these connectors in the same basket as the others. We will not be disrespected like this, not by anybody." His tone carried pure hatred across the phone lines.

"Aaban I think this will be a big ask. I can't just go to a church or synagogue to find them like I can with the others you want me to steal and take them away. How do I find one of these connectors?"

"You are a resourceful man, you will find a way. You know what will happen if you don't, so I have faith in you. I expect to read more interesting stories in the paper tomorrow, hear more news on the radio and see people talking on the streets about my plan unfolding! Goodbye." Ira was left listening to the hum of the dial tone.

What did he do to deserve this? He had made the ultimate decision to become a good man and perform good deeds, and this is how God repays him? By allowing his family to be used as leverage and extort him to act in completely the opposite way to that which he had committed himself?

On the positive side, the conversation had proceeded relatively smoothly, and also he had an idea on how to locate a connector, he was sure his new friend at the newspaper could provide him with some useful information there. He must remember to call her later about that and another matter.

It was time to make the drive across town to check on the welfare of his captured lamb and then set his mind towards how to ensnare the next. He still had no idea who his next captive would be or what unacceptable religion they belonged to, but this was more because there were almost too many options to choose from. Ira didn't know how many religions and Gods were worshipped in the world but it must be hundreds, thousands even and he could not hope to gather somebody from all of them for Aaban.

Religions came and went, merged and divided, an ongoing rotation and evolution that shaped and steered humanity. How did so many different beliefs evolve, and how were people foolish enough to believe that out of the hundreds or thousands of gods, theirs was the one true One?

In many cases, Ira knew that there were subsets of beliefs relating to the same God, different areas of focus, some on love, some on fear, some on more extremist aspects, and Ira couldn't help but wonder why certain groups focussed on one thing and others on another, it would seem to make sense that if you truly loved and believed in God, then one would want to engage with every aspect simultaneously, not just a select few.

It was man who created the offshoots, the splits and separations, dividing one original God and one source of power for a church or sect into many sources of power for many churches and sects. What better way to create power where previously no power existed than to create a new church preaching a new and different facet of religion and attract new devotees? Man was always gullible enough to follow anything if persuaded in the right way.

Lost in thought, something brought his mind back to reality, instantly. Slamming on his brakes much to the annoyance of a bus close behind him, Ira screeched to a halt on the side of the road. Checking his rear view mirror, he backed up about fifty metres until he was in front of a large stone building which must have been hundreds of years old, gorgeously covered in moss and lichen and a few sinister crows perched on top for added effect.

It was quite early in the morning but the broody temple beside him could potentially solve his problem of where to acquire his next lamb from, if there were indeed any lambs on the premises. Nodding his head at his luck and appreciating how convenient it was that this synagogue was on his way to the warehouse, Ira had just freed up some time in his day and would hopefully see that he made it home in time for dinner with his family.

Grinding his gear stick into reverse, he backed his truck right into the yard and pulled the handbrake up, leaving the engine running. Getting out, he walked to the side of the truck, rummaged around in the back with practiced hands and found a length of rope which he slung over his shoulder and then proceeded to the large wooden door.

Knock knock.

Tues 22 Sept 1959 *7:45am*
Mary's Loss

Mary's hands trembled as she tried to hold the steering wheel straight and her mind willed the car to go faster as it hurtled down the road, twisting and dodging the odd stray car abandoned in the middle of the road for reasons only known to the owner. Her heart was still beating out of her chest and she didn't realise it but she was screaming at Zach, imploring him to repeat what he had done earlier.

"Honey, say it again. Honey! Say it again baby. Say anything so mama knows she isn't crazy." On and on she begged, as Zach remained as passive as ever, glazed over and staring straight ahead as if nothing ever happened and had no idea what his mother was in such a flap about.

Mary knew that most children with autism will have the disorder for life, however, there were a growing number of records where many seem to outgrow it or even overcome it if provided the proper attention and appropriate clinical stimuli.

There was even a young girl that attended some group socialising sessions with Zach that Mary clearly observed shedding her inhibited behaviours and then was never seen again, presumably a successful conversion into a person better able to cope better with the stresses and anxieties of the world.

With all her heart Mary hoped that life ahead for Zach was to be one of improvement, communication, and connecting with the world. One word was a small step, but when previously there was not a single word ever uttered, a single word was as significant as if Zach had read the entire Bible out loud.

The drive seemed to take forever, even though Mary, who considered herself to be such a model citizen was obliviously travelling at nearly twice the legal speed limit and, should there have been any onlookers they would have been impressed at the screeching tyres and her deft weaving in and around cars.

The practice she was driving to was located amongst a small row of shops including a convenience store, cafe and a hairdresser, all run down and so much so that at first glance they would appear abandoned to unfamiliar eyes. The neighbourhood was not great, but the rent for the location was cheap and Dr Eunice was extremely careful with where she spent her hard earned money.

There were a few people around, a van of travellers who were loitering around and stopping for refreshments at the convenience store. There was good old Ed, the kind homeless person who frequented the area and was waiting for the café to open because they were kind enough to provide him with a free coffee every morning in return for him washing their windows, though the windows typically ended up looking worse off than before he cleaned them.

A few other cars came and went, busy for the time of day with people grabbing cans of food, bread and water from the store to replenish their emergency stocks at home that had been eaten and drunk during their lengthening wait for the world to end.

Dr Eunice was waiting out the front of her practice when they arrived, immaculately dressed in black pants and crisp white blouse, makeup perfect, and Mary wondered how she had managed to squeeze at least an hour's worth of beautifying work into what must have been ten or so minutes. "Probably sleeps like that" she thought to herself.

"Maryyy, good morning to you," Doctor Eunice delivered an extremely fake greeting and was clearly not happy to be there at that time of day, wondering to herself if she could bill Mary more than her weekend rates for working outside of regularly scheduled hours. She would decide on that later but suspected the answer would be yes.

"So tell me what is going on? What has you so riled up and dragged us all here this morning? Is Zach okay?"

A bell rang and the squeaky café door opened. A middle aged woman propped it so that it wouldn't close, and began to heave tables and chairs from the inside to the outside and set up an alfresco dining area, nice and close to the car park for those who would like some vehicle fumes with their sandwiches. Mary immediately thought that this task should probably be left to a man, however this lady was really swinging them around with ease, suggesting that it wasn't the first time she had attended to this.

Turning her attention back to Dr Eunice, Mary proceeded to tell her about the events of the last few days and the words just poured out.

"Well you know it's just the darnedest thing. The other night when I put Zach to bed, I also went to bed but then swore that I heard a voice come from his room! And then the next day I cleaned a dreadful woman's house and flippantly told Zach that he should break a vase and then wouldn't you know it, a vase got broken! I still can't prove that it was him but when you bundle it all up into all the other odd things then you know I think it might have been him! And then guess what Dr Eunice. He spoke. He tooting well spoke, pardon my French. He said 'God'! I couldn't get him to say any more but he spoke! Something is happening and he spoke!"

Dr Eunice was listening to Mary with one ear, and yearning to find a break in her monologue to suggest that they go into her practice where the general public could not hear every single personal detail. Plus, she just wanted to sit down.

"Okay Mary that is indeed incredible news. Now..ugh, we are doing this right here are we?" To the doctor's annoyance, Mary had sat down at one of the café tables with Zach and continued talking.

"So tell me what you think is going on? I think it could be a couple of things.." The café door squeaked open and the waitress bounded out with great enthusiasm, apparently watching like a hawk for the opportunity to serve a customer to the best of her ability.

"Drinks ladies? Best coffee in the state! And we can do an iced choc for your lovely boy?"

Dr Eunice rolled her eyes. They ordered two coffees, and Zach had an orange juice. Dr Eunice wondered whether there were any legal ramifications for somebody exaggerating about the quality of their coffee.

"So, as I was saying Mary, that is really, really great news! Now let's talk about the hows and whys of this. It's not such an uncommon occurrence, but remember that even if Zach is improving I would still like to see him regularly so that I am able to track his progress. We need to take all the learnings we can from this fortunate event." *And I don't want to lose a stream of income just yet* she thought to herself.

"You know, I was actually thinking that he could either be growing out of it or it could be the treatment, but then in the car I had a thought about Zach reciting the Bible and I connected a few dots, thinking whether this whole thing could be related to God's self-revelation? His whole change of behaviour occurred right around the time of the incident and he definitely has had a light in his gorgeous eyes ever since then. I mean, we all feel something on the inside, so why wouldn't Zach? Maybe it opened up something within him. I mean, out of all the words he could have said, like 'mama', he chose to say 'God' and then it really looked like he wanted to say more."

"Don't get ahead of yourself there Mary! I think that my treatment is the most likely catalyst for what triggered all this. I really know what I am doing you know, don't forget about what I did for little Christie, Charlotte's daughter. She is now living a happy normal life." *A happy normal life means that now she doesn't have to pay me for treatment any more,* she bemoaned to herself.

"You know, I read an article in the paper this morning about some people who seem to have reacted differently to the revelation and seemed to take away more from it than the rest of us. It got me thinking, maybe Zach is one of those 'connector' people? Imagine if that were true! My baby boy would be like some sort of chosen one. We always were very strongly religious in our household and it would not surprise me if he was smiled upon in some way, and that's why he has been a bit different to others."

Dr Eunice had just about had enough of this and wanted to get into her client's stubborn head that if there was any reason for her son's change in behaviour it was due to her treatment, couldn't she see that?

"Look, I'm not sure what you read or where you read it but I can guarantee that it was just some journalist making up a story to sell papers. There is absolutely no reason why your son should be one of those connectors that you talk about."

"I have a feeling though that he is!"

"Well has he said anything other than one word? Didn't you yourself say that connectors took away more than the rest of us? I see no evidence of that having happened from what you have described and can assure you that you are suffering from what is known as delusional wishful thinking."

"My little boy is a connector, you shyster!" Mary lost her temper, self-conscious that her voice had risen above a whisper in a public place, but frustrated that the arrogance of the doctor had blinded her to the seemingly obvious truth that her boy was special.

"Look, I'm leav.." was all that the doctor managed to say when from out of nowhere a short man in a checkered shirt and smelling pungently of sweat made a bee-line for their table, the sound of loose change rattling in his pocket as he snatched up Zach with one arm and slung him over his shoulder as if he were a small rolled up rug, then walked at a solid pace straight ahead and disappeared around the corner of the strip of shops. The odour of his sweat remained behind.

Mary looked at the doctor with her mouth wide open, looked at the corner where the two had disappeared, then looked back at the doctor, trying to compute what had just transpired. It was not long after that her open mouth emitted a frantic scream and the two women remained frozen in their chairs with shock and panic. Did that just happen?

"Zach! Zach!" She stood up and knocked her chair over, but all she was physically able to do was scream and point.

None of the other groups of people at the shops had noticed the event, it had happened so swiftly and subtly. Their faces seemed to question why this lady was making a commotion and spoiling their morning.

A young man and woman rushed over from the parked van to try to calm her down and find out the details of why she was in distress, whilst another older gentleman seemed to piece together what had happened and sensed that whatever the lady's issue was, it had disappeared around the corner of the shops and so he went running off in that direction.

It all became a blur for Mary, she recalled hearing somebody yell out 'Fire' from behind the café, and then silence.

Tues 22 Sept 1959 **7:48am**
Ira's Warehouse

The air inside of the warehouse was humid and smelled of mould, rotting wood and what were most likely animals that had perished in the floors, ceiling and walls. The combination of these unpleasant factors led Ira to spend as little time there as possible, the space only utilised when somewhere was required that was away from a residential area and utmost privacy for Aaban's

217

business to be conducted. In fact, Aaban didn't even know about this place.

A constant drip, drip, echoed from somewhere in the building threatening to drive somebody mad should they remain on site long enough. Rusted bars protected all windows to dissuade any temporary residents from attempting to leave in search of more luxurious accommodation. Currently inhabiting the building were a priest and a rabbi, the latter being newly introduced to the facility and who was yet to acclimatise to the modest surroundings.

"Why am I here? Are you going to kill me?" the man pleaded to Ira who was used to hearing those exact words being delivered in a petrified tone.

Usually the people brought there knew why they were there, they belonged to some group or faction that Aaban considered an enemy, or they had either failed or crossed him. This time it was the former of the reasons, though it did sit uneasily with Ira that the two captives did not know Aaban or why he would consider them an enemy.

"Quiet," Ira replied. He did not owe these people an explanation, he was just doing his job as always and had nothing to say. He was itching to get out of there, with every breath he could feel his lungs filling with the putrid air but he did need to go to the shops to pick up some food for the prisoners and drop it off before he could leave the warehouse behind and get on with the rest of his day.

"Please sir, I am a good man and I have done no wrong to you. Why am I here? Release us. Let us be." The rabbi, a tall, lean man with a sickly pallour had backed himself up to a corner and crouched down, looking up at Ira with fear in his eyes. As soon as he saw Ira recognise the fear, he closed his eyes and started muttering to himself.

Ira was ready to leave and head back out into the clean air but his conscience was gnawing away at him and it was a new feeling he had little experience with. He acknowledged he did not want to be going through with this task and bore no grudge to the men, but his family were being used as leverage to ensure he delivered and this was the only reason he was here. He spoke.

"You are both arrogant enough to think that the God that is inside us belongs to each of you. Don't worry, you are not the only ones and more like you shall soon fill this room. You are safe for now. This is for your own good." This seemed to calm the priest down a little, and an audible sigh escaped his lips.

The rabbi stood up in the corner and angrily gesticulated towards the priest, sidelocks swinging wildly. "It IS my God that is inside us all. I am here for no good reason!"

"So why did this priest standing right there tell the newspapers that it was his God? You know that is why you are both here right now. How do you know his version of God isn't the one, and you, rabbi, how do you know this priest's isn't the true one? What makes you so sure? It is this thinking that has caused the world to go mad over the last couple of days. You would think that something like this would bring harmony but instead it has brought nothing but more problems, problems caused by man who will never agree on anything and never admit that they are wrong about something, even when the answer to the biggest question in the history of the world has materialised inside them!"

Ira was getting angry at the topic of conversation already, knowing that this issue was the cause of conflict between men for centuries, an unprovable, unwinnable argument that would never end, even with the materialisation of God into the hearts of men on earth.

"Shut up, the both of you and calm down! Please listen to me. Look, I have always believed in God, whichever God it is that is out there. Will this God allow me to redeem myself for the terrible things I have done in my life? I have committed many sinful acts and thrust them upon many, many people, but my heart now is true. Is it too late for me? I do not want to live the rest of my life with wife and child knowing that I carry a shadow with me for eternity. I must find my way to the side of light."

The priest meekly spoke up. "Well keeping us trapped here in this dungeon for some unknown reason is not going to shed any light on your shadow. Just let us go and I'm sure you will have nothing to worry about."

"Ah my good lamb, if only you knew what is in store for you and the role I am playing, you would prefer to stay here than be out there, trust me. There are wolves about, and I am but an honest shepherd. And a good shepherd protects his flock so I will go and fetch you some refreshments then return shortly. And I am wondering, you two will not harm each other while I am gone? I cannot allow that to happen, under sufferance of great pain to whoever casts the first stone."

"We are both servants of God. What kind of question is that?"

"I have learned that it is the servants of God who need to be worried about the most. Do not misbehave, mark my words you will regret it."

Ira was ready to leave. He could feel his lungs become heavy and he longed for some cool, dry air. The two captives remained silent as he left, resigned to their fate for now as he locked and bolted the door behind him. Walking down some creaky stairs and treading carefully on a rotten landing, he finally emerged in sunlight and swore that he had never seen clouds so beautiful. He saw some movement out of the corner of his eye but shook it off and accepted it as his eyes adjusting to the light.

Walking amongst the weeds growing through the asphalt surrounding the warehouse, he arrived at his pickup and climbed in. His stomach growled and he was surprised that the huge portion of pancakes that his wife made him for breakfast had already moved on and he was hungry for lunch, though it was barely 8am. It looked like he would have to pick up food for three at the store a few blocks away. From memory there was also a phone booth there where he would call his reporter friend and inform her about the rabbi.

A sickening feeling churned his stomach as he remembered the wellbeing of his family was at stake here. He did not like what he was doing but he had no other choice, and he was treading such a fine line it would take a hell of a lot of luck, chance, whatever you like to call it, to pull off something as big as this. The Alcon Blue butterfly was flying close to the sun but the integrity of its disguise still remained sound.

Driving along, he tried to momentarily forget where he was driving to and why, and attempted to live in the moment and enjoy the day. Easier said than done, he turned up the music and just concentrated on the words. He very rarely listened to lyrics, he more absorbed songs as a whole. There were favourite songs of his that he had listened to hundreds of times and yet still didn't know much more than the chorus to sing along to. He wasn't much of a listener, but if you showed him those lyrics on a piece of paper he would read them and remember them forever. It was funny how the brain worked.

Pulling up to the shops, he observed they were quite busy for that time of morning, but nothing that would keep him waiting for too long. Parking his pickup at the end of the carpark, he jumped out and spotted the payphone. Grabbing a handful of change from the ashtray in his car, he jumped out.

After speaking to the elderly Tribune receptionist, he was finally placed through to his reporter. "I've got another story for you," and proceeded to inform her about the events of the morning, commencing the next step in his plan.

He was impressed at how much he had already accomplished for the day. Aaban would not be disappointed when the paper was delivered to his front door the following morning.

Satisfied that he had set the ball rolling, he headed to the store, thinking that he would pick up a selection of snacks and drinks for the two captives to fight it out over, and a sneaky chocolate bar and sugar-laden soft drink for himself.

In a world of his own he vacantly strode along, coins jangling in his pocket to a steady rhythm which he hummed to. He would have sung a song if only he could remember the words to one but before he could reach into his mind for the right selection he was distracted by a commotion in front of him.

An unflatteringly dressed woman sitting at the café up ahead yelled directly at the sour-faced woman only a metre away from her, whilst a young boy sat in his seat and stared straight ahead, oblivious to the fact that his right eardrum should be ringing right now.

"My little boy is a connector you shyster!"

Snapping out of his daydream, Ira looked toward the angry woman, then looked at the shocked recipient of the abuse whose mouth was now hanging wide open, assessed the situation, continued to march right up to the table and without even breaking a stride grabbed the boy and hurled him over his shoulder. The first thoughts that struck him were that the boy was so light, much like his son Hector and that he did not resist in any way, shape or form. Ira took long quick strides and aimed to disappear with Aaban's connector around the side of the café.

Heart beating fast, Ira knew he had taken a huge risk to do what he had just done in public and broad daylight. He acknowledged to himself that he hadn't completely thought this through and now he just had to cross his fingers and rely on the cowardliness and apathy of humanity to allow him to make an unimpeded getaway.

He knew the mother wasn't capable of chasing him down, she had probably barely registered that the event had happened or most likely was in shock. There were several other people around, however, he had taken the connector boy so silently and seamlessly that he doubted that anybody other than the two women at the table knew it had even happened.

"Zaaach! Zaaach!" Ira cursed at the woman's scream, brain not thinking quickly enough in the search for solutions on how to evade this potential catastrophe now that everybody had been alerted. He had to somehow circle around the shops with the boy on his shoulder and make it back to his car before any angry locals took it upon themselves to confront him.

Soldiering on, he managed to walk another twenty or so metres when he heard a man yell behind him. What was shouted was so unexpected and nonsensical that Ira stopped where he was on the spot and turned around, expecting to see five or six saviours of the day come to bring him to justice.

"Fiiire!!!"

Ira could not run away with the boy over his shoulder, but a far better option was to put him down and fight his way out of the situation, it was what he was good at and he had great experience. It was but one man, and an elderly, lonely, sad-looking example at that. He looked like he already had had the life beaten out of him and Ira felt a hint of pity that he would have to hurt him. The man took a step back and looked side to side for help that would never arrive.

"What fire? Are you okay in the head man? Are you using that trick where you yell 'Fire' because people are more likely to come help than if you yell 'Kidnapping!?' You think I care if some scared nobodies come running around the corner? Go. Just go. I don't want to hurt you, and I think we both know that I can."

Ira thought that saying that would do the trick and make the man come to his senses and realise the battle was over before it had even started. Surprisingly, the man took a step forward and slowly raised his fists uncertainly.

"Ohh, it's like that is it?" Ira put the boy down gently and clenched his own fists.

"I..I don't want to fight you," said the man. "Just let the boy come with me. His mother wants him back. Why are you doing this? Are you the father and this a custody thing? Is he even yours? I can tell you as a father myself that you don't want to do wrong by your own child, they will never forget it. I'm speaking from experience. So, come on, do the right thing. Give him to me, I will return him to his mother and I promise I will forget this ever happened and you can be on your way."

"I can't do that. I'm sorry. This is bigger than you or me. It's my family at stake here. I'm not a bad man. I'm not. This is for my family."

"I'm sure you aren't a bad man, I can tell you must be a loving father, really. But right now you are being a bad man. But let me tell you, every bad man is capable of doing one good deed. So please, do a good deed and give up the boy."

The words uttered by Ira's father many years ago now echoed in his ears again for the second time in as many days, firstly by Eddie and this time spoken by a stranger.

The boy was still standing where he had left him, such a purity and innocence in his eyes that Ira nearly choked with emotion just looking at him.

The stranger spoke again, with such a calmness in his voice that Ira almost felt hypnotised. "Come on now. Is this really who you are? A child abductor?"

Ira winced as the reality of what he was doing and who he had become solidified, and he dropped to the ground in tears, face in his hands, apologizing to nobody but at the same time apologizing to everybody he had ever wronged.

"I-I-I'm sorry---, I'm sorry Eddie, it's not who I am any more, it's not me. I only did this to protect my family---. I want my father to be proud of me, I'm not a child abductor." The words came out as a single long cry. He took a sharp intake of breath and let himself sob deeply, face buried into the litter-covered ground behind the shops.

The stranger looked around, puzzled at the unexpected development and unsure of what to do next, eyes filled with pity seeming to want to console the man on the ground, but checking himself, instead took the hand of the boy and walked him away slowly around the building to reunite him with the woman he had been taken from.

Ira rolled over but remained on the ground, and through the blurriness of his stinging eyes watched the silhouette of the man walk away holding the boy's hand, but now what he saw was the man walking away with his own son.

"Hector, Hector don't go.." he managed to whisper to himself before closing his eyes. When Ira opened them again, the man and the boy were gone.

Tues 22 Sept 1959   *8:00am*
Jacob's Idea

"So why are we just here and hanging around doing nothing?" Ava glared at her father who for some reason had a smug look on his face that she hadn't seen in a long time and she found quite disturbing. She noticed the worry lines around his eyes and it struck her how much he had aged since the accident. She had never really paid much attention to him except for when she needed something, and it had been a while since she had actually looked AT him, and not through him.

As far as she was concerned they should be spending their time trying to find a way north as quickly as possible because as Gabe had warned, who knows how many people were also trying to make the long journey?

She didn't think that she could harbour any more feelings of resentment to her father, but if something happened and she missed out on the opportunity to regain her legs she would never forgive him, even more than she could already never forgive him.

The electric feeling of excitement at the thought of being able to walk again coursed through her and the anticipation nearly overwhelmed her, although counterbalancing that feeling was an intense anxiety should it all fall through and the existence of the place be nothing more than a myth that had fatefully made its way to her.

Overcome with impatience, she reached down and grabbed a packet of crisps from the bag of snacks which she then threw at the back of her father's head. "Hey! Idiot, you know you have driven us all the way back near our very own house? Wrong direction!" She was about to continue but caught herself before she could give Gabe another reason to think she was an aggressive ungrateful child. She grunted instead.

Instead of being on the road and looking for a way out of the city, Jacob had pulled the van over to the side of some non-descript suburban shops and had been staring at his watch for fifteen minutes now, lazily glancing behind him every now and again at his impatient passengers with a knowing smile that puzzled everybody and more than slightly aggravated them. He felt the need to break the heavy silence.

"Not too long now. We can head off soon, there is just a little bit of time to kill. I just thought that if anybody needs the bathroom they can go over the public ones over there. I don't know how clean they are but I'm sure they do the job."

Gabe had been keeping his eye on Simon in the front seat and could see that he was becoming a bit restless. The poor boy couldn't get out of the van and run around, but like any youngster the opportunity to get outside and explore was beckoning.

Unable to get any useful information from Jacob was quite frustrating and so he thought it might be a good idea for everybody to get out of the stuffy confines of the van and wait until whatever it was that Jacob was waiting for arrived. He jumped out and opened the front door of the van, ready to haul Simon out but wanted to make his feelings clear to Jacob first.

"Look, I would have thought that we would be well on our way there by now, I hope you know what you are doing," he said with an annoyed tone that hinted at how unhappy he would be if whatever plan Jacob had didn't successfully come to fruition.

Gabe loved his nephew Simon more than anything in the world, especially because he could see his sister reflected in him, but the responsibility of being a guardian that had been thrust upon him had started taking its toll. He had always been a free and easy character who didn't live life to a routine, flitting from one circle of friends to another and never knowing when he would arrive home each day.

That had been turned on its head, and his lifestyle was now as regimented as a clockwork army and it was fair to say that now bestowed with the task of watching over Simon he guiltily felt like a wild animal trapped within a cage of rules and schedules.

None of his friends even considered asking him out any more as they continued to live their lives untamed, able to fulfil their every desired experience as he put Simon to bed every night at 7pm and climbed into his own soon after.

He happened to hear about the place where the miracles allegedly occurred very soon after the God revelation. Although his social life had quietened down significantly, he still had a large number of acquaintances and after the event he was quite touched at the number of phone calls he received from people concerned about his and Simon's welfare, even if the motive of some of the callers was the pure obligation to become nicer to others now that they were aware there was a higher power.

On the evening of the twentieth, Gabe was getting ready for bed when the phone rang for the umpteenth time and although touched by the calls he was receiving, he now just wanted to be left alone and go to bed to digest the events of the strange day.

"Hello?" he said in what was not one of his more pleasant tones.

"Gabe? Oh, hi, it's Martine. How are you? It's been a while.."

"Uh, uh, hi. Yeah it has," wow, this was one call he did not expect and was caught completely off-guard.

Martine was a kind, fun French-Canadian girl that he dated briefly about a year ago and had left a tiny hole of regret behind in his heart that was still lingering. He had ended it with her for some reasons that seemed so trivial now and he thought of her regularly, considering her with a pang to be the one who got away. She had clearly retained his phone number and Gabe hoped that it was for the same reason that he still kept hers. Unlike him though, she had been brave enough to be the first to call.

After she enquired as to his wellbeing and struggled through some awkward small talk, they spoke through the night and Gabe remembered just how easy everything was with her and how they naturally fell on the same page when it came to almost every topic.

Around midnight and long after his usual bedtime, Gabe couldn't stifle any more yawns and it came time to acknowledge that the end of the call was near, leading to a somewhat uncomfortable moment when they knew that goodbyes were approaching although there was the elephant in the room that was on both of their minds. Neither had the courage to come forward first and broach the topic of whether meeting up again would be welcome idea.

"Oh, oh, I nearly forgot the reason I called, silly me!" Martine was happy that she had subverted the awkwardness and then proceeded to tell him what she had heard about a friend of a friend of hers who owned a property up north where some strange things had started happening there. She couldn't give many details but suggested that there might be a chance that if Gabe brought Simon to the property then there might be the possibility of something amazing happening to him.

Gabe hated to admit it but instantly he was awash with thoughts of being able to leave the house on his own and catch up with buddies again and, hopefully, Martine. On the off chance that there was some truth to all this, Simon would still need his guardianship, but not the full time care that he currently required.

He wrote down all the details about the property that were on offer and hung up the phone on Martine after a small but awkward thank you accompanied by a promise to get in touch again. He lay awake all night in bed, imagining a new future for himself. And for Simon of course.

And now, Jacob, the bedraggled man in the front seat of the van he was travelling in was jeopardising his future way of life by parking them by the side of some shops instead of driving them at a hundred miles an hour towards the destination that would change all of their lives. He picked Simon up and walked him off towards the restrooms.

Remaining in the car and now with a little privacy, Ava took the opportunity to talk to Ishara. "Hey Ishara, you don't need to come on this trip you know, just to keep me company. You can see how tedious it already is and I'm in pretty good hands here. Want me to get dad to drop you off home?" Ava said as nonchalantly as possible.

"Oh, you are in pretty good hands are you? Well, I know a pair of pretty good hands that I want to be in too," Ishara replied, her eyes following Gabe as he walked Simon away from the van.

It took all the control Ava could muster not to lose her temper, but she held it in and simply smiled and laughed. There was no way that girl was going to win this battle and so she delivered a lighthearted comment with a deadly sharp edge to it.

"Well it's too bad your parents would never give their blessing and allow yourself to date outside your religion, so I'm going to have to have him all to myself!"

"Ah Ava, such a bad memory, don't you remember our discussion from yesterday where I said that we are all the same religion now! That is my get out of jail free card!"

"But are we really the same religion? I love how you question my memory but your own selective memory seems to forget the bit where you said that you don't think that centuries of tradition will be instantly wiped clean, and I am thinking that your parents will not simply be convinced by the emergence of some new facts enough to change their minds in a split second on this one. This particular discovery has long term cultural ramifications that will linger for a long time to come and change may come, but only slowly. Looks like the burden of Gabe deciding which of us he wants is now moot, sorry! I'll take good care of him, don't worry."

Ishara's smile disappeared from her face as fast as if somebody had wiped it off, and she spoke with a low, solemn tone to Ava.

"Look, Ava, I love you to pieces and you know that, but I have to tell you something that might upset you. Gabe said that he really did like you but he could never go out with somebody in a wheelchair. I'm so, so sorry to have to tell you. He is not the nice guy you seem to think he is. He would hurt you. " She looked at the ground.

"He did not say that, he did NOT! Don't lie to me!" Ava felt the anger inside her boil up like lava and erupt, tears welling in her eyes. She gripped the side of her wheelchair as tightly as she could, worried that if she let go her hands might consider the person sitting in front of her as the new target to grab. She hated to think that what Ishara had said was true, but her rational mind kicked in and deep down she actually believed it. Why would a guy like him be interested in a dead weight like her? She was nothing but a helpless pile of flesh and bones that had to be lugged around by everybody. She knew that she wasn't even a nice person, broken and flawed in body and mind.

"I'm sorry babe, I didn't want you to get your hopes up, best friends tell each other everything, even the bad stuff. I'm so sorry."

Ava sniffled "That's okay, I know I'm unlovable, I just haven't felt rejection like that before, usually I only receive pity from people. It just all makes me want to get to this miracle place all the more." She diverted her attention away from Ishara. "Come on what are we waiting for let's move!" she yelled to Jacob.

Ishara moved to get out of the van. "Look, even though he said those terrible things, I still want to come on this journey with you because you are my best friend okay?" Ava nodded, though hesitant. "Okay that's decided then. Right, I'm going to grab Gabe and Simon and bring them back so we can head off to wherever it is that your dad is taking us. Enough is enough."

Ishara climbed out of the van and walked off towards the shops. Ava was dreaming if she thought that she could attract a guy like Gabe. The sooner she stopped worrying about guys and more about her improving her personality, the better off she will be. Ishara had known her for years but the friendship was only just hanging in there, she didn't know how much more of her bitterness and negativity she could handle.

It was a real test for her, she admitted that her life was a bit of a storybook fairytale and she was quite removed from all things bad, from the neighbourhood that she lived in to the people she associated with. Except for Ava.

At some level deep down she still knew the real Ava from when they were children, though that girl was long gone and the only thing keeping the relationship together was the memory of that little girl Ava with pigtails who she was inseparable from all the way through school.

Her thoughts were interrupted when she spotted Gabe approaching the other way with Simon on his shoulders, and Ishara loved the fact that that he was great with kids.

"Hey you two, ready to get back on the road again? I think we are nearly good to go. I just had to get out of that van for a minute, Ava is not in a great mood. What's new though, huh? It's hard to be around her when she is always yelling at her dad. Imagine dating her, it would be a nightmare," Ishara said.

"Poor girl, I actually think dating somebody would be the best thing for her right now, I really hope she is happy one day."

Ishara smiled flirtingly and batted her lashes "Well, aren't you just mister tolerant guy! Honestly you are so nice, is there any dark side to you at all? I would be so surprised. Maybe you should date her?" she enquired, hoping to hear the words come from his own mouth that would let her know once and for all if she really had any competition in this two-girl race. She was disappointed somewhat with his non-committal response.

"Well maybe I should, maybe I shouldn't! I need to get to know a girl a little better first than just sitting in a van with her for a few minutes." The answer could have been addressing both Ava and herself. She humphed.

Arriving back at the van, Simon was carefully placed back in the passenger seat. Jacob, content that the other adult male was back at the van now and able to stand guard, decided that it was the opportune time for him to take a bathroom break.

"Hey Gabe, I'll be back shortly and then we can make a move. Happy?" Gabe nodded as Jacob walked away from the van toward the shops.

Jacob knew that the decision that he had made not to drive in search for another way onto the freeway was met with disapproval from the others, especially since he had refused to provide a meaningful answer as to why. A lot was riding on this trip and to disappoint not only his daughter yet again but some strangers as well would be a severe blow to his already floundering self-esteem. Still, he was gripping to the iota of confidence that he had in his plan which was an extreme long shot and had a small percentage chance of actually succeeding.

Half way to the bathroom, a high-pitched scream hit his ears like a lightning bolt and he looked around for the source, his heart racing with panic that he and everybody else were in danger. He spotted Gabe and Ishara running towards a pair of ladies lady sitting at a café, one of whom was the source of the disturbance.

He couldn't make out what she was screaming, but he could see where she was looking, though there was nothing there. Something must have happened and whatever it was had disappeared behind the shops.

This was the third time in three days that his courage was to be tested, and he had failed on those previous attempts to protect and provide security to those around him. He was determined that this time was going to be different. He knew he could simply just walk back to the van and drive away, but he had to prove to himself and his daughter that he was a man, and a man who would not cower in fear any more at the first sign of any trouble.

And how bad could this trouble be? The lady probably just realised she left the oven on or something. Better take a look behind the building anyway, just in case there was something there.

Making haste over the rough ground towards the edge of the row of shops, he slowed down once at the corner and slowly peered around the bricks, trying not to make a sound. He could see a smallish man with a child over his shoulders who was walking in no great hurry around the back of the building. Even though the man was of small stature, Jacob questioned how dangerous he might be since he had gone to the desperate lengths of presumably abducting the child belonging to the woman sitting at the café.

He was about to scream for help in the hope that Gabe or some other good Samaritan might rush around the corner and provide some back up but he remembered reading in a book or magazine somewhere that to yell for help can actually scare people away who don't want to get involved and provide the opposite response to what you intended.

The thing to do in circumstances such as this would be to yell fire, since it provides a more accurate picture of what the threat might be to potential helpers, and a fire is more likely to bring people to the scene rather than just yelling for help or for a frightening kidnapping. And so Jacob yelled.

"Fiiire!!!" The man with the child stopped and turned around with a puzzled look on his face. He looked like he was of latino descent, a friendly face though his eyes betrayed a darkness lying underneath, warning not to be provoked. Jacob tensed up, sensing that this was going to be more of a dangerous situation than the group of kids or the drugged out guy sitting on his van from yesterday.

The man said a few words to him but the blood was pounding so hard in Jacob's ears that he was deaf to them. The man hadn't run away as planned and so Jacob knew he had now committed to the situation. He raised his fists, cursing that his hands were shaking.

The man put the boy down, who just stood on the spot unmoving and Jacob wondered why he did not run away or seem frightened in the slightest. Was he the boy's father? Jacob knew his best option was to talk to the man.

"I..I don't want to fight you," he said. "Just let the boy come with me. His mother wants him back. Why are you doing this? Are you the father and this a custody thing? Is he even yours? I can tell you as a father myself that you don't want to do wrong by your own child, they will never forget it. I'm speaking from experience. So, come on, do the right thing. Give him to me, I will return him to his mother and I promise I will forget this ever happened and you can be on your way."

He knew there was no reasoning with these people. The man mentioned his family several times, and when it came to family, a real man did what they believed was the right thing to do and nothing could stop them or talk sense into them.

In a dream-like state, words came out of Jacob's mouth even though he knew that words were useless. He vaguely recalled telling the man not to be a bad man and that he wouldn't want to live his life knowing that he had abducted a child, or words to that effect.

Jacob didn't know what it was that he said but something worked and the man collapsed on the ground crying, apologising to somebody called Eddie who Jacob assumed was the name of the boy, and he could barely make out the man sobbing that he wanted his father to be proud of him.

Jacob did not know what to do. Clearly the man was messed up, maybe on drugs or something and needed help, but Jacob felt that he had succeeded in subduing the moment, and the best and safest thing to do would be to walk the boy who was still standing in the same position back around the corner to his mother and get out of there quick smart.

Adrenalin still pumping, he grabbed the hand of the boy and escorted him away from the man on the ground and then once around the corner, picked the boy up and ran as fast as he could towards the café where he could see the two women still sitting and accompanied by Gabe and Ishara.

The older looking of the two women wiped tears away from her eyes, looked over and saw Jacob with the boy emerging from behind the building. She squealed and stood up, tipping over her chair and rushed full speed towards the two, grabbing the boy out of Jacob's grasp and set him on the ground, stroking his hair and telling him that everything would be alright. The boy just stood there and Jacob thought it strange that he didn't even put his arms around the mother for a hug.

"Are you the mother of this boy?" Jacob thought he had better check this minor detail just in case, and was hoping it would lead to an explanation from the woman about what had just happened. She continued to cuddle him, and pressed him what looked uncomfortably closely into her and said "Yes, yes, he is my beautiful little boy. Sorry, I haven't thanked you yet. Thank you, thank you for getting him back from that man."

"Was that man the father? Are you fighting over custody?"

"No, he isn't the father, his real father is… out of the picture. I have no idea who the man just now was. He appeared out of the blue and took…" She broke down and hugged the poor boy so hard that everybody wondered if he would turn purple.

"Is he okay? He seems to be in shock or something, he hasn't moved or said anything or even hugged you since this all happened." Jacob went to ruffle the boy's hair but the woman pulled him away and protected him with her body.

"The boy is autistic, I am treating him and he is improving thanks to me," chimed in the other woman much to the evident dismay of the mother. She held out her hand formally and sternly spoke.

"Doctor Eunice, pleased to meet you. Here is my card. And this is Mary with her son Zach. And you are?"

Jacob extended his still shaking hand. "Jacob. And this is Gabe and Ishara. My daughter Ava is in the van. We were trying to get out of the city on a road trip but with all the crazy stuff happening, the way out of town is totally jammed so we are waiting here for a bit because I have another idea on how to get out." He stopped when he realised he was rambling about something they would clearly have no interest in. He continued, more on topic.

"Now I want to make sure you two are okay? I don't know what happened to the guy, I just left him there, he could be anywhere now. But I don't think he will trouble you again now that there are a bunch of us here. There are all kinds of creeps around at the moment."

They all looked around just to make sure that there were no signs of danger, or strange people lurking about. Jacob was about to suggest that Gabe and Ishara head back with him to the van now that everything seemed to be sorted, when Dr Eunice spoke.

"You know Mary, before that all happened, I was facing behind you and past your shoulder I could see that man walking. And that man was not walking towards us, I can recall it as clear as day. But when you shouted out that Zach was a connector he changed path so distinctly and came at Zach in a bee-line. There is something to that, I am certain of it. But why on earth would a random man want a little autistic boy? It makes no sense."

Jacob's eyes grew wide. "Wait! Your boy is a connector? Amazing! I never thought I would cross paths with one ever. What has he said? What does he know? I'm dying to hear!"

"Aren't we all, Jacob" Dr Eunice said dryly. "The boy says his first word and now he is apparently God's best friend. Mary, you have to let that idea go, it's crazy, and they all think it's crazy too."

Mary looked at the group of people surveying her, judging her and she instantly jumped into a defensive mode. "He is one, I am sure of it. I'm his mother and who would know best! His behaviour has been really different since the event a couple of days ago. There is something going on inside him. I'm sure only a matter of time will tell." Her eyes pleaded for the audience to believe her.

Something about the woman told Jacob that this was somebody who was used to constantly feeling the need to win the approval of others and was always apologising, even when she had done nothing wrong. Just like himself. He knew how difficult it was to have every action and decision questioned, and the constant justification of everything you do to yourself and others was heartbreaking. He did not want to leave this woman in this state. He wanted to help her, and he thought he knew a way.

"Look, I know it's none of my business, but the road trip that I mentioned I am going on with my companions, well, it's actually to a place that may be able to assist you and your son. It's crazy to believe, but I think after God's appearance the other day I think it could possibly be one of the more sane things that have happened, but there is supposed to be a place north of the city where events resembling miracles are supposedly happening. My daughter is in a wheelchair, Gabe has a nephew who can't walk without crutches and I think that you could maybe come along with us and see what might happen with your boy, especially if your son is a connector? I obviously can't guarantee anything, in fact we have almost talked ourselves out of going a number of times because it just seems too absurd, but if there is the smallest chance that it could be true and we can help the ones we love then I think it's worth a day of driving. I promise we aren't lunatics. I can tell you have had a challenging life, and in fact you remind me of somebody and I just want to help. That's all." He put on his best 'I'm not a serial killer' smile.

Gabe and Ishara were about to protest toward the increased liability but were sure that the woman was about to say no, after all, she had already had one run in with a random stranger, she surely didn't want to climb into a van with some others for an unknown length of time on the off chance a miracle could occur. It was some time before she responded, her eyes had welled up and she was lost in a distant place.

Mary looked at the man making the offer to her, and whilst she got the point of what he was saying, her mind was already looking into the future as it had countless times before, picturing Zach speaking, playing, reading and writing and all the normal things a normal child should be doing. And then she pictured herself contacting Diah and telling him the good news. 'Honey, our son is back. He is okay. You can come home now.' And Diah would move back in and the happy family would resume, the painful past long forgotten. She had played it over in her head so many times that she was sure it was real, the future that was going to be. And here was the chance to make it happen.

"Yes, yes I will come.' She sobbed happily.

"Think about what you are saying Mary!" Dr Eunice interjected. "I'm sure these people are lovely, but are you really going to traipse off into the unknown out of town on the chance there is some ridiculous place that may make your son normal? Its lunacy!"

"Yes, yes I am. Okay Mr Jacob, I am willing to put myself and my boy in your hands and see where this trip may lead, I have no job that I need to be at. I am trusting you. Doctor Eunice has seen you all and can report you to the police should I not come back. Now this place is just out of town. Do you want me to follow you in my car?" She tapped at her handbag and the noise of carkeys jangling within jolted Jacob back to the present and he looked at his watch.

"It's eight forty! We have five minutes! We have five minutes! Hurry hurry hurry! Come on, we must go! You don't need your car Mary, the roads are out of action and we have another means of getting there, just jump in my van but we must leave now!" He flailed his arms around wildly in an effort to spur everybody into action.

"I think this may all be a bit sudden you know."

"It's now or never. We have snacks, we have seats, you just have to climb in and come along for the ride." Jacob seemed disturbingly frantic and was worrying Gabe and Ishara, as well as Mary.

Gabe spoke up. "Mary, we actually do have something time critical that we needed to attend to, and this little incident has crept us right up to the time where we need to be somewhere. Please come, I can vouch for everything. Your Zach can sit with my Simon, I am sure they will be great buddies together." He held out his hand.

"Okay, okay, but what is the time critical place we need to be at?"

"I don't actually know," Gabe said, casting a sharp look at Jacob. They all piled into the van, and Jacob apologised to Ava for the delay.

"What on earth is going on? I have been sitting here for what seems like hours now. And who are these people? And why are they here?"

"Ava, meet Mary and Zach, they are coming with us." He wanted to impress her by telling her about his courageous act but thought it better to wait until another time. Ava rolled her eyes as if to just give in to the whole ridiculous situation.

Making sure that everybody was in and buckled up, Jacob flew away from the shops, passengers heads flying side to side and shoulders bumping together.

"We're gonna make it!" Jacob yelled excitedly as he careened around corner after corner. The ride took about three minutes, and then Jacob screamed up the side of the road, and parked with two wheels on the nature strip. Just up ahead and to the right was a laneway.

"All right, everybody out! We are here!" He climbed out and opened the back door of the van where everybody proceeded to tumble out as if climbing out of a rollercoaster.

"And now what?" Ava asked once Jacob had wheeled her out of the van and to the footpath.

"And now we wait. Sixty seconds." Jacob said eagerly. He was eyeing the top of the laneway and tapping his foot excitedly.

"Forty seconds." "Twenty", "Ten", "Aaaand… now."
Nothing.

"Aaaand.. NOW!" Jacob tapped his watch.

"Look, what is it that we are supposed to be seeing, doing or hearing right now?" Mary asked nervously.

"Welcome to my dad, Mary," Ava said. "Always finding ways to disappoint."

Jacob couldn't believe it. "What on earth? He's like clockwork. Always." He sighed.

And then they heard footsteps approaching, louder, louder, until an eccentric looking man wearing a trilby and smoking a pipe popped around the corner from the laneway.

"Jacob, there you are my good man!"

"Mr Derby!"

Tues 22 Sept 1959* *2:45pm
Faith Muses

Blinking rapidly in an effort to focus on the piece of paper in front of her, Faith realised she had been typing away for a few hours straight now and her fingers as well as her eyes were aching and deserved some respite. She was well immersed in what they call 'the zone' and could very easily have propelled herself on for a lot longer but was conscious that she didn't want to burn out.

A rest and if possible a nap at her desk would do her a world of good and enable her to face what was most likely going to be a very productive day with a clear mind. She had learned her lesson many times that writing continuously for hours upon end resulted in some very embarrassing and strange work being handed in to Maxwell, and she didn't like the feeling of Maxwell questioning her capabilities or, worse still, her mental state.

She cast her mind back to the particularly busy time last spring when she had been typing away at several articles over a period to eight hours or so (she had lost track of time), and submitted what she thought was one of her more thought provoking pieces very proudly at the end of the day.

She had strangely found it back on her desk the next morning with a handwritten note attached to it that said "Please read this and tell me what you think." Maxwell had never done something like this before so she picked up the submission.

"Strange," she thought, "it's my own article, I know what it's about and I know what I think. I think it's splendidly amazing of course."

Nevertheless, she impatiently proceeded to read it, patting herself on the back as she did so and then her mouth opened wide, as did her eyes, and she read the same paragraphs over and over again as the realisation dawned on her that half way through the piece she had mixed herself up and started writing about another story. The beginning was great, the ending was great, it was just that the first half had absolutely nothing to do with the second half. She wanted to go to Antarctica, find a little ice cave, crawl in there and die of embarrassment surrounded by penguins.

"And thus, nap time it shall be," she said, convincing herself that another muddled article would be a bad idea. Hauling her typewriter to the side, she swept away all the dust and crumbs that had been accumulating underneath, leaned forward and rested her head in her arms. It felt good to have her eyes closed. Now without the distractions of the everyday world around her, her mind started to tick over and project all the subconscious thoughts that had been swirling around in her head but had been put to the side temporarily.

This mysterious latino guy who had called her twice now. Who was he, and why did she feel it was important to believe to his crazy story and write about it. He had convinced her to think that the upside to listening to him and reporting on the story as he told it was a lot larger than the downside. After all, if the story had turned out to be false, then the worst that could happen was the news that there wasn't anybody that had gone missing, and it should be possible to come up with a follow up story to explain the misunderstanding, leaving her reputation intact.

She had made a judgement call and as it turns out, what he had said was true. The priest had indeed gone missing. She didn't know how he knew or whether it was he himself that perpetrated the act, but he emphatically persuaded her that it was in the best interest for society that it happened and the news was made public.

Was the man good, was the man bad, was the man insane? She was sure that she would find out one way or another. This morning's phone call would not be the second and last time she would hear from the man, she was certain of it.

Starting to doze now, her mind started to loop through real and unreal scenarios and hypothetical situations, pose further problems and generate implausible dreamlike solutions.

Was she dealing with a madman, and if so, was he dangerous? Should she continue to take his calls? And if she didn't, what would happen, to her or to the victims?

It can be argued that the standard default way that humans are wired is to do good, to commit acts of kindness and generosity, to help one another and promulgate a benevolent society. Any action committed by a person that is not furthering society in this direction surely cannot be considered to be a rational, normal behaviour by definition. And so does it stand to reason that if a human commits any act that is not normal and doesn't conform to rational ways of thinking, then they should be defined as insane?

By this definition then there would be more insane than sane people, so are there any qualifying factors?

Humans are complex creatures, and the nature of insanity gets clouded by confounding factors such as emotions. Can somebody who commits murder be considered insane if jealousy is driving their actions, or if they themselves have suffered abuse at the hands of somebody and commit an act of revenge, the emotion of anger temporarily diverting them away from rational thought.

And as for her latino informer, whom she was quite sure was responsible for the abductions, what was his motive, was there something underlying that would qualify his insane act and reclassify it as the good deed that he claimed? Who in their sane mind would want to take a human being against their will, and then claim that what they are doing is a good thing? A good thing in their eyes maybe, but Faith was sure that the abducted priest would have other thoughts on the matter.

Stirring from her uneasy slumber, she came to the conclusion that she should hang in there, play along and entertain the man, insane or not, and at least stay in the loop of what he was up to. She could pull the pin at any time she started feeling really uncomfortable. Plus, he was giving her some real scoops.

She felt two strong hands gripping her shoulders in a not unpleasant manner, though she was unsure of who the hands belonged to or why they had chosen to grip her. She sat upright and spun around, only to come face to face with a grinning Maxwell. *Oh no, I probably have drool running down my chin,* she thought before he spoke and became lost in his deep voice.

"Good morning Faith, sorry to wake you," he said sarcastically. "Actually, no I'm not, it's four in the afternoon. How are your submissions looking for tonight's print run? All done I assume? Any unapproved stories today?"

She flushed at this last question. He walked around beside her and then sat on her desk. Lucky she had cleaned all the crumbs and rubbish away.

"Yep, they are coming along great, one small story about a snippet from some real oddball called Saul who is a connector, plus a couple of other pieces." She left out the detail that she might be running another unauthorised abduction story. He didn't need to know about that just yet.

Maxwell sighed and shook his head, seemingly troubled by something. Faith was about to ask him what was wrong but didn't have to. She was delighted that he might consider her to be some sort of confidante and could definitely be there for him if he needed somebody to talk to.

Her mind drifted, imagination picturing her arms around his strong form, her head nodding as he released his innermost thoughts unto her, unburdening himself and feeling very fortunate to have somebody like Faith close to him.

"So Faith, I get to see nearly every single story this paper prints, and I'm talking sports, politics, world news, local news, the lot. After all these years I am not surprised by much, but do you know what is puzzling me right now and I can't get my head around it?"

Faith just shook her head, both as a response to his question and because her imagination was so far off the mark around what this conversation was going to be about.

"Two days ago, the most significant event in the history of mankind occurred, an event that should bring humanity together, bind us as one, grant us all a common icon to look towards, and finally bring an end to the scourge of humanity that is religious confusion and competition. In these two days I have not seen one, not one single story about a good news event resulting from this."

He rose from Faith's desk and found a seat a bit further away much to her dismay, sitting with a sigh of contentment. He went on.

"Whilst everybody is affected individually and most people seem to be in a state of shock, re-evaluating their lives, like Hal for example, oh and by the way remind me to put his job in the want ads.. anyway maybe it's still early days but, I don't know, I naïvely thought that society would undergo an instantaneous substantial behavioural change. No more homeless people, no more petty crime, some sort of utopia would form because people would do the right thing by one another. Instead there is looting, general disarray, more fighting than ever, people trying to evacuate the city and get to the country in case the apocalypse is coming. After all I have seen, I thought I would have a pretty good insight into human behaviour, but no, people always manage to surprise and find some way to disappoint." He leaned forward and took a close look at Faith with a frown that caused her some self-consciousness.

"Want a coffee? You look a bit bleary eyed from your nap." Faith nodded and Maxwell walked over to the pot and poured a couple of mugs, handing one to her. She took a sip and it was lukewarm but she didn't care, she only cared about the words coming out of his mouth.

"Imagine last week if we knew this event was going to happen we would have treated it with the same disregard and humour as if we knew we were about to prove the existence of the Tooth Fairy. A fictional character coming to life," he chuckled to himself and continued.

"We learned a lot two days ago. We learned that God is just an entity, an entity like each of us but on a grand and ethereal scale. Don't you find it strange that according to our knowledge of the universe, there are microbes, plants, animals, then mankind and then God. But nothing lies between ourselves and the one God? There is such a vast gulf between us I find it hard to believe there is nothing that even remotely fits between. I was hoping that these connectors could shed some more light on all the remaining questions but from what you say there wasn't much there other than cryptic messaging."

Faith nodded, listening intently to every word, she liked the way he thought about things, and even though it seemed like he was actually only talking to himself right now, she smiled and nodded with complete enthusiasm as if her were dreamily reciting French poetry to her.

"We have learned that it has been mankind of old who has bestowed upon this entity all the omniscience, omnipotence, supernatural powers, and even created the surrounding fictional religious universe containing angels, heaven and hell. How amused God must be at all the embellishment! And the fact that mankind actually believed that a single being was capable of all those ridiculous impossibilities, shame on us. No wonder more and more of us were becoming atheists, we were finally developing some sense to question things. We were close though, we were right that a lot of those qualities were impossible, we just completely missed the fact that there could still actually be a God of sorts, though a more passive, realistic version. Just another being along for the ride in this universe."

Faith felt that she should try and join in this one-sided conversation with some of the things that were on her mind, and hopefully impress Maxwell with her insight.

She sat upright in her chair and in a very contemplative voice asked "Why did this God only appear now? Now, in the whole history of humanity? Did we reach a certain point in our civilisation? We are at the right stage of evolution or something?"

"Or devolution maybe. God could have appeared not because we have progressed technologically, but because we have regressed spiritually. We are now further away from being a religious race than ever. Like I just said, our common sense has started to prevail as we have started to question things where faith previously sufficed. But you could be right, maybe it's just time. We mastered fire, created the wheel, developed cities and machines. We could have hit the right level as far as progress goes."

Faith blushed at how connected she felt to Maxwell right now. Had they been talking for three minutes, two hours? She didn't know. She wanted to show him that she could think on the same level and hopefully promote further non-work related conversations with him in the future.

"You know, I always thought how funny it was that there is that natural evolution of discovery, like you just mentioned. Fire, then the wheel and whatnot. Have you ever thought about what would happen if cavemen accidentally played around with just the right materials somewhere someday and discovered the secret of teleportation or time travel? Like, they didn't even have the wheel yet, and then Ig and Og are playing around in a ditch and then all of a sudden they are on the other side of the world or on the moon. I mean, it's not set in order what discoveries must be made before what. In fact, I'm sure that most inventions come about by accident. We totally could have bypassed the steam engine, and even the internal combustion engine and just jumped straight to interstellar travel!"

She trailed off as she saw the amused look on Maxwell's face. "What?" She felt extremely self-conscious and worried she came across as a fool. "Well, I guess I'm about to find out how stupid I really am." She felt embarrassment flush her cheeks.

"Oh my, Faith, Faith, Faith. I have never met anybody with a mind like yours. Amazing, I love it. Such creativity, you should write a book or something. What's next in line for mankind to achieve? Maybe one day man will even make it to the moon! Only a couple of weeks ago the Russians crashed Luna 2 onto its surface, so anything can happen."

I AM trying to write a book, dumdum, she thought to herself. Out loud she said "I wonder how far the human race will go. I mean, we can only learn so much in one lifetime. Asides from living longer and maybe incremental improvements in our brain, there must be a finite amount of knowledge that one can learn. If you studied from age three until death, all day every day, how much could somebody learn? And even then, you wouldn't have time to do anything with that knowledge. So can you see, we will hit a wall eventually!"

"Not a bad point there actually, but I think mankind will progress enough so that maybe we won't have to store everything in our brain, and make use of machines or something. Who knows?" He looked at his watch and judging by the surprised look on his face, Faith guessed that it was getting late.

"You out of here?" She asked, with a wistful look.

"Yeah, it's past dinner time, and you should get out of here too, it's dark out."

"Okay, okay, I'll be out in ten or fifteen, just going to finish everything off first and sort myself out for the morning."

"Don't stay long. Catch you tomorrow." He stood up and walked casually to the door. Faith could smell his cologne lingering and breathed in deeply as subtly as possible.

Disappointed at losing her handsome company, she was now alone in the office and pottered around for a while, using the time to catch up on some reading and she even had a go at beginning her novel again but failing miserably. After she couldn't procrastinate any more, she decided to head home.

Outside of the office, she briskly walked her familiar route absentmindedly and was taken completely by surprise as the dark van that had been following her from the moment she had stepped onto the street pulled over just behind her. The side door slid open and two masked men clothed head to toe in black emerged and ran towards Faith.

Hearing footsteps approaching her from behind, she only had time to emit the slightest high pitch shriek as a cloth bag was pulled over her head. She was lifted off the ground and bundled into the van, kicking and screaming. She heard a man yell "Shut her up!" Then she felt a sharp pain on her forehead and her consciousness departed.

Tues 22 Sept 1959 8:47am
Jacob & Company Assembles

"Well, well, well old chap, I was wondering where you might have gotten to, I had to deliver my morning sentence to nobody but myself! And that wasn't very interesting, because unfortunately I happen to know everything about myself already!" Mr Derby rolled his eyes and took a puff from his pipe.

He did not seem in the least bit phased or curious about the entourage that had appeared alongside Jacob, and Jacob attributed this to the fact that from what he had learned over the years was that Mr Derby lived a life which consisted of a sequence of spontaneous events and random occurrences, the frequency of which was so regular that this unusual event would be blurred into one of many others that would probably take place this day.

"Morning, yes, I'm very sorry if I kept you waiting or wondering but it has actually been a very unusual day for me and us all, so far. How are you?" The question came out sounding as insincere as it actually was, and Mr Derby easily picked up that Jacob had dished out the question without really caring for the answer, as there was obviously something else on his mind that he wanted to broach. Jacob had always found it very difficult to ask others for their time or assistance and this occasion was no different.

"What can I do for you old chap? As you know I am always briskly on my way every morning and I can sense that you want to ask me something, perhaps on behalf of this group of people you are with, am I right? Be out with it Jacob, I am more than happy to listen but am pressed. I shall have to make this time up by proceeding to rush onwards and possibly forgoing my second pipe of the morning. I will admit that I am curious as to what this is all about though. Interest me Jacob, interest me."

His broad chest was still heaving in and out from his brisk morning walk. Fleetingly, Jacob wondered yet again where he went every morning and how far he had to go. Judging by his puffing and panting, hopefully not too much further.

Jacob was aware that only he knew why they were all there at that particular spot at 8:45am, and his accompanying party were staring at him, as eager for an answer to hearing the plan he was hoping to execute as was Mr Derby.

"I understand you have time pressures Mr Derby and believe me, I hope you can grasp what a difficult decision this was for me to make to ask you for your assistance, but I can assure you that it is because there is absolutely no other way for us to be able to do what it is that we want to do without you." He was unaware that he was doing it, but he was wringing his hands in a pleading manner, and the rest of the party thought that he might be about to get down on one knee and beg for whatever it was that he was wanting.

"Well out with it man, we have known each other long enough to be able to deliver a single line to each other each day. Now what is the single line that you want to deliver to me right now?"

Jacob felt immense pressure to just ask Mr Derby immediately, however, against all his instincts, knew that the best hope for success was to place some context around his question.

"Look, I have a group of people with me as you can see. There is myself, there is Gabe there with his nephew Simon who has suffered from polio, this over here is Mary with her dear son and over here is my daughter Ava."

Mr Derby looked at the girl in the wheelchair, a broad smile suddenly appearing on his face and he walked over to her, gave her a hearty kiss on the cheek and shook her hand firmly. Ava noted that asides from the pipe smoke he smelled impeccably clean and his hands were soft and moisturised. She almost blushed, finding his confidence and charming manner intoxicating.

"My dear! Ava, I feel as if I know you already, very pleased to meet you. I am having one of those moments where you finally meet somebody you have only heard about and can put a face to a name, and now can put another piece of the puzzle together that is your father's life."

Ava looked at him with a raised eyebrow, wondering who this man was that seemed to know all about her, and yet her father had never once mentioned him. She had to ask the question.

"Dad, do you have a…friend?"

"Everybody, please meet Mr Derby, one of my close acquaintances.' He nervously looked at Mr Derby to judge his reaction to that comment. For all he knew, Mr Derby didn't consider him to be anything at all.

"Why are we here dad?" Ava asked impatiently. Her question brought up murmurs from the others wanting to know the same. Jacob nervously spoke and revealed to all the reason why this meeting was happening.

"Mr Derby has a helicopter… a whirligig, a spinny thing, as you put it a couple of days ago?"

Excitement filled the eyes of the party and the disappointment they carried that their journey might have been thwarted was instantly wiped out and replaced with hope.

"Wait, wait, everybody, before you get carried away. Mr Derby, we have somewhere to be that is very far away and we cannot get there by car as the roads out of town are inaccessible. You are the absolutely last and only chance that we have to get to this place, it's about a hundred and fifty miles north of here. Please, can you fly us there? It is so important to us."

Mr Derby had a look on his face that suggested he was asked to do "small" favours, help people, lend things out "just this once" all the time, and it was making him weary.

"Jacob, Jacob, I am on my way somewhere, you know this. I would love to help. But actually your whole premise is mistaken. I don't own a helicopter." Ava emitted the loudest sigh of disappointment, and she was not the only one out of the group to do so.

"But you are learning to fly one right? And you have access to a helicopter?" Jacob didn't want to give up so easily. If he didn't find a way to get them all into a helicopter he would be hated by five people, not just the one that currently hated him. Actually, make that six others. Mr Derby would probably hate him too.

"Yes, yes, that is true. I would love to help, but my hands are tied. The helicopter has room for six so there are far too many of you."

Mary piped up. "So you are saying that you would do it but the problem is the helicopter is too small?'

"Yes, I think so. Eight people is far too many. I'm so sorry."

"But Mr Derby, two of the people are small children, we can put them on our laps very easily and hold them. Please, we can all fit, I guarantee you. This would mean so much to us." Jacob was glad that Mary was buying into the idea and trying her best. It was the first time in a while that he felt he had somebody on his side. She continued.

"We can pay you and we can fit. Before you know it you can be back and doing what you were doing, but having the satisfaction of knowing you did the right thing and making some people very happy, potentially changing their lives."

"Well, at least tell me what on earth you need to travel a hundred and fifty miles north of the city for. What is there that is so important?" Mr Derby felt torn. He actually did really want to help these people for whatever insubstantial reason they provided, but the one thing he was really quite averse to was being interrupted from his schedule. He was never late and never liked to deviate from arrangements. It would have to be a most significant reason.

Jacob felt he must speak again. He was the one who knew Mr Derby, he had brought them here, he should do the talking.

"There is a place north of here where, believe it or not, miracles *may* be occurring, as crazy as that sounds. We don't know much more than that, although, in the light of the events of two days ago we feel that it is a journey that we should make whether the rumours are true or false, to see what may happen. The benefits of undertaking this fantastical adventure far outweigh the costs should it be nothing more than a red herring." He looked at Simon, Zach and Ava. Mr Derby followed his eyes and understood.

"I see what you are getting at and I completely understand my good man. Each of you adults has a child that you consider needs repairing, and you want to make things right by going against what nature intended. I needn't say it now, but it's unnatural. I'm undecided as to whether or not I approve because Jacob my good man, things always happen for a reason, the universe is the way that it is and I believe that when the dice have been rolled, what's done is done and shouldn't be tampered with."

Jacob was floored by this turn of events. The last person he expected resistance to this idea was Mr Derby, whom he imagined would take on the situation guns blazing and be excited to pursue the unknown. He did not expect to hear from somebody concerned with altering nature's course, even if it meant that three young human beings could have a better life.

"Look Jacob, nature can be cruel, nature can be kind, and I do believe that we should suffer the hands that we are dealt."

"But nature didn't deal this hand to Ava, I did!" Jacob was desperately generating arguments to convince Mr Derby that his reluctance was unfounded.

"That may be so Jacob, and I do know all about the tragedy that befell you that night but still, I feel like the universe has spoken. I am reluctant to help here."

"The universe may have spoken that night, but then tell me why now are miracles occurring, why would we be granted that hope? If nature dealt us these hands then it appears that nature or the universe or God is dealing out new hands. It is a sign that nature is okay with being changed." Jacob's voice was becoming desperate.

Mr Derby was wavering on his opinion, thinking that there might not necessarily be a right or a wrong clearly defined, but that helping six people could not be a bad thing.

"Look, I am just a single mother that wants her son to happy and healthy, are you really the type of man who would be against that? You are in a position to help us, so please do." Mary spoke up again, impatient to end the debate.

Gabe put forward his argument. "And I am just a man looking after his sister's son out of love, nothing more, nothing less, just living day to day and seeing him struggle to walk and move, it's difficult. Would helping to make that right for him be so terrible?"

"And I see three adults who seem to be burdened by their children and might just want their own lives to be a little easier."

"Yes, Mr Derby, I'll admit it. You are right, our lives would be a lot easier, but I can assure you that we are not doing this selfishly for ourselves, we are doing it for the right reasons. Please help us."

"Whether it's an offer from nature or God, or if it's an act against nature or God, that is a debate that could never be resolved, the point is that these miracles seem to be occurring as you suggest, and I think all six of you will benefit, and there is nothing wrong with you all wanting to make your lives a little easier. I am fortunate enough to have avoided the sufferings of the common man and I feel blessed for that, so who am I to say no to relieving the suffering of you lot. Let's fuel up a helicopter, squash in and get you to wherever these darned miracles are."

The group swarmed around Mr Derby in a group hug that he found a little claustrophobic, but at the same time he could not stop grinning as he saw how happy he had made them. He reflected that even with the variety of people he crossed paths with day to day, he never really had the chance to make a difference in their lives to a great extent other than sharing with them his grand personality, and this was an experience that made him glow on the inside, just like the tobacco inside of his pipe during a puff.

"Actually, don't mind if I do," he said to himself as he reached into his pocket for his matches and lit up his pipe.

The trip to the airport saw Mr Derby sitting in the front seat of the van with Simon on his lap, and in the back was a group of beaming passengers.

"Well if we can all fit in here then the helicopter will not be an issue," Mr Derby commented, looking around at the cramped environment. He turned to Jacob and said in a more hushed tone. "Look Jacob, I will do everything in my power to get you to this place but I have to warn you, the helicopter is not mine. I am only learning to fly, it may or may not even be there, and there may or may not be fuel in it. These are strange times and in matters such as these nothing can be certain, but if fate smiles upon us then I will do my utmost to help you reach your destination."

Jacob nodded his head indicating he understood, and continued driving. After maybe twenty minutes the van pulled up to the rusty rear boom gate of a small private airport where Mr Derby eased himself out of the vehicle to talk to a burly man in some sort of civil aviation uniform who raised the gate so that they could drive in. Jacob was directed to proceed slowly between a few Cessnas that were scattered around in front of two large hangars, dodging high tufts of grass that were growing between cracks in the asphalt.

"Haha, I hope this swerving around doesn't make anybody queasy, it's going to be a lot worse up in the air you know, especially the way I fly," Mr Derby warned everybody light-heartedly. He continued. "Just up here. Ah splendid, the babies are still there."

Just ahead, two helicopters sat neatly side by side in what appeared to be pristine condition, rotors drooping earthward, waiting to spin into action. Jacob raised his eyebrows and breathed a sigh of relief, nodding his head in approval at finding them apparently operational.

The van slowed to a halt and all passengers made their way out, none of them having seen a helicopter up close before. Simon was the most excited, and couldn't move his crutches fast enough to propel him to the closest bird. "Wowww," was all he could say over and over, circling the vehicle examining every angle.

"Neither of us have ever flown before, it has been too expensive for us, not that we have anywhere to go to anyway," Mary told the group as she walked Zach over to stand next to Simon. Zach seemed to be more interested in the airfield's wind sock which was gently flitting about, puffed out but curiously spinning around the pole it was attached to in a circular direction rather than the normal single direction as dictated by the wind.

After proudly watching the joy his passengers-to-be were having inspecting the whirligigs, Mr Derby looked at his watch and announced to the group, "My good people, I must make a phone call, I nearly forgot that I have a place I should be at right now and I need to let somebody know as a courtesy that I will be unable to be somewhere as arranged. I will be back shortly and do all the necessary pre-flight checks so that we can leave here safely and be on our way." He walked off hurriedly towards one of the hangars.

"This is it sweetheart!" Jacob grabbed Ava and looked into her eyes with a big smile, and the glare he received in return did nothing to dampen his enthusiasm. The outcome of this journey would change the relationship between him and his daughter forever, one way or another. It was close now. He had come through with the logistics of getting there, now it was all up to the miracles. He looked up at the sky out of habit and uttered a thank you.

"Baby! Baby!" Coming from the direction of the helicopters, Jacob heard the same high-pitched yell come from Mary that he heard from her back at the shops when Zach was abducted. He turned toward the sound and he saw Mary frantically trying to deal with something that made him turn pale.

Zach lay on the ground convulsing unnaturally, blood oozing from a cut on his forehead and eyes rolling to the back of his head, the whites showing and transforming the little boy into a twisted, petrifying form almost resembling an insect in its death throes. His writhing and twitching was so rapid it created the illusion that he was hovering above the ground.

Jacob ran over as quickly as he could, took off his jumper and tried to place it under the boy's head for protection, but Zach's movement was so violent that this was impossible. Nothing could be done except to try to restrain the boy for his own safety. He hurled himself onto the ground next to Zach and tried to grip onto whatever body part he could to start with and then made his way along the body to eventually be able to comfort Zach's head and hold him close. All he could do now was hope that it would be over soon. He looked around and saw the worry and fear in Mary's eyes and realised he did not feel anything except the determination to see this boy through the situation safely to the end.

After maybe twenty long seconds, the mysterious seizure subsided slowly and Jacob found himself face to face with Zach who appeared exhausted at the physical toll the episode had taken. He looked into the eyes of a calm, aware boy who seemed unafraid at the events that had just transpired and his tight grip loosened.

Almost defying gravity, Zach sat upright, his straight torso at a perfect ninety degree angle to his legs and Jacob had to lean back to get out of the way, still keeping a steadying hand on the boy's back. Zach turned his head towards Jacob and blinked, but what Jacob saw looking at him now were not the eyes of a young boy. In those eyes he saw the past, the infinite future, the impossible, life, death, pain and ecstasy. He saw and felt everything that had ever happened since time began.

Though his lips did not move, a voice came from the boy, but it was not the voice that should belong to a young child, it was the voice that belonged to those eyes, ageless, deep, multilayered, complex, not so much heard as felt.

"God is dying."

And with another blink the eleven year old boy was back.

Tues 22 Sept 1959 10:15pm
Ira's Warehouse Discovered

Bump, bump, bump. A splitting headache and a bizarre nightmare where she found herself trapped on the inside of a tumble-dryer brought Faith back to consciousness and when she opened her eyes to find herself still immersed in darkness, the horrifying events that had transpired when she had left work returned to her memory.

She was lying down in a van and travelling over what seemed to be a road with an inordinate amount of potholes. She supressed the urge to cry out, thinking it may make things easier on her if she just continued to play possum for a while longer and not alert her captors that she had woken up. She listened for voices that may give some clues away as to where she was going or why. Nothing.

"Stupid." She criticised herself for getting into a predicament that she should have seen coming, but her lust for a breaking story clouded her judgment and she knew the only reason that she was where she was right now was something to do with the kidnapping story that she had run.

But why had she been abducted? Surely she was part of the latino man's agenda and it was still in his best interests that she continue to publish stories for him? What benefit could there be for him to have her in person, unable to write stories anymore.

Unless it wasn't he who was responsible, which then led to more sinister questions. She hoped the answers would reveal themselves soon and that she could get out of this mess safely. She didn't know anything, couldn't identify anybody, she was not a threat.

She didn't know how long she had been out for, and so didn't bother keeping track of time as an estimate of the distance she had travelled thus far. It could have been a mile, maybe fifty. The vehicle slowed down noticeably and continued for a while, eventually stopping with a squeal of brakes. Her heart raced as she knew she was closer to finding out her fate.

The door slid open and rough hands grabbed at her and hauled her out onto her feet. She considered just collapsing to the ground and forcing them to carry her but she knew that struggling wouldn't endear them to her and she would end up wherever they intended anyway, so she reluctantly allowed them to push her along.

Tripping up a flight of stairs, Faith could smell through her hood the odour of sickness and decay as her feet crunched on objects she dared not think about, and she knew that when her sight was restored to her she would wish that it hadn't been. She could sense that this was not a place where nice things happened.

At the top of the stairs there was the sound of a key turning and a bolt being slid across, followed by a heavy door opening. Faith held her breath, the air in this room was thick, putrid and never meant to be inhaled by a human being. Marched forward, she heard something being slid behind her and she was pushed backwards into a small, uncomfortable wooden chair.

A sound like duct tape tearing cut through the still atmosphere, and after her arms were roughly bound to the chair she was now completely restrained. Her hood was torn off and when her eyes adjusted she could see herself in a damp, rotting large room accompanied by about fifteen men, ten of them bound just like her and five armed men standing guard.

All eyes were on her, and plucking up the courage to look around at the bound men and the guards, she noticed one scared face that stood out. Father Emmanuel from St Paul's cathedral, the missing priest from her article the previous day. He saw her staring at him and she realised that he had no idea who she was or why she could possibly have singled him out of everybody to focus on. She looked away and surveyed the rest of the captives. Most men were aged around sixty five or older, and judging from some of the clothing they wore, she guessed they were also various religious figures.

Why had she been brought here? She was a nobody, certainly not religious, and as far as she knew, could not contribute in any way to whatever it was that was going on.

The bolt of the door slid open again from the outside and echoed around the room. A very well dressed man of middle-eastern appearance strode confidently into the room, flanked by two more men trying their best to look nonchalant but their nervousness could not be disguised.

To Faith, it seemed like there was only one person in this room who knew what was about to happen, and it was this man. If he told the armed men to jump, they would jump. And Faith knew that if he told them to shoot, they would probably shoot. She sunk into her chair as far as her restraints allowed.

"It seems like my flock has been gathered, so welcome to you all, though there are not as many of you present as I would have liked." The man shrugged his shoulders as he spoke slowly and loudly to the group, however, to Faith this did not help make any sense of what he was saying.

"My lambs, I know you are all wondering why you have been brought here and I can assure you that it is for a good cause, my cause, worthy of being recorded as a historical event although you may not like what will be written about you in your chapters." He looked around the room and enjoyed seeing the frightened faces as well as the feeling that his plan was coming to fruition. After walking the length of the room and back in silence, the suspense of needing to know what he was about to say nearly overwhelmed Faith. He continued.

"You are all guilty of worshipping false Gods and claiming them as true. In your chapters you will all be remembered as infidels and tomorrow I will be the one bringing justice unto you as you renounce your imposters and pledge yourself to my Lord, and through your sacrifices will you be redeemed."

The group of bound men reacted to this with horror, some emitting loud involuntary screams, others frantically trying to free themselves from their bonds.

"We have done nothing wrong, let us be free!" A man dressed all in white who had not succumbed to panic like the others pleaded, "We are men of God, just as you claim to be. We are the same!"

The well-dressed man walked over and slapped the captive, who keeled over in his chair and was mortified at the sensation of blood coming from his nose. It ran down his chin and was absorbed into his robes, spreading into a type of scarlet Rorschach ink blot and nevertheless he continued. "As a man of God you should be a man of peace!"

"Aaban, these men have not wronged you or anybody else, they have just followed what they have been taught to be true. Do as the man in white says and leave them be."

A badly beaten man sitting on the other side of the room to Faith seemed to know who the captor was and his voice was very familiar although his facial injuries clearly made it difficult for him to speak. His latino accent was unmistakeably that of the man who had been calling her with the news of the kidnappings. Why was he here and imprisoned with the rest of them? He didn't seem to be a religious type and in fact Faith had thought that he was most likely the one responsible for the abductions.

The man called Aaban walked over to the man, gently put his hand on his shoulder and spoke in a soft but chilling tone. "Ira, Ira, Ira. Who would have thought that my most faithful shepherd, a man loyal to me for many years would decide to betray his master and hide the sacrificial lambs from him out of his sight?

And what kind of master would be stupid enough to be unaware that this was happening?"

He walked over towards Faith, smiling. She started shaking with fear, sweat beading on her brow and an involuntary whimpering sound came from within her as he walked up to her so closely that their toes were touching. He spoke directly at her, his tone chilling and accusatory.

"So my dear, I found it more than a little strange when I read in the paper this morning that a priest from St Paul's church was taken, which now seems like such a long, long time ago, and my good shepherd Ira calls me to ask if I have read the story. And what is wrong with this you may ask? Maybe nothing. But I ask myself. When did this abduction take place? Either late the previous evening, or the early hours of this morning. Now, I do not claim to be an expert on how newspapers operate, but it did strike me as odd that the story came out so quickly after the event. There should be a day's delay at the least, no, as they are printed nightly? How it could it be that the article had been written and printed the night the lamb was taken? Either the journalist with incredible clairvoyant investigative skills uncovered the story almost before it happened, impossible, or else, curiously and slightly less impossibly, there must have been a tipoff? And the only person who had this information and could provide this tipoff is my shepherd. And the reason? I admit I did not know, unless it was because some trickery was afoot. Something did not smell right. And so, being a cautious and intelligent man, I had my shepherd Ira put under watch as well as the reporter who wrote the article. Imagine how shocked I was to find out the collusion between the two of you." Aaban paced to and fro now, in much the style of a lawyer questioning a witness.

"Lo and behold, one of my men followed Ira and discovered this wonderful little hideout, completely unknown to me. Instead of reeling in my sneaky friend, I simply kept an eye on him whilst he accumulated more lambs, bringing them here for their safety and protection out of my reach. I thank you Ira, in a way you did what I asked of you." Aaban looked at Ira mockingly, who reacted with an emotional outburst.

"They are all innocent men! There was a time when I happily did your bidding, but things have changed now, I am a different man to then, I am a good man! I must learn to live with my past, and the only thing that I can change now is my future. I saw the opportunity to help these men and save their lives, and the only way I could do that was to disguise myself as the man I used to be, the trusted man who did your bidding and remain undetected as a camouflaged intruder so that I could manoeuvre safely within your environment. I became the Alcon Blue Butterfly. The news stories protected my new identity and tricked you into thinking I was still one of your kind and doing your bidding." He puffed his chest up, proud of himself and his idea even though it had not succeeded.

"I do not know what this butterfly is, but your tiny wings have flown you into my trap and I am now the one who will decide if you even have a future," Aaban said menacingly, "or will I squash you like an insect tomorrow with the others?" his hands clapping together and grinding the life out of an imaginary bug, emotions finally flaring.

"And the future of your wife and boy, Lucy and Hector? I wonder if they want to hear what a bad employee their father is."

"You leave them alone! They are good people, better than I deserve. I did you wrong, so punish me and me only." Ira realised the gravity of his situation. Aaban was not a man to make idle threats and he knew his family were in danger, most likely captive already somewhere.

Ira looked across the room and focused his eyes on Faith. She cast her eyes to the ground, afraid to have any attention shed on her in case she drew Aaban's wrath also. Her fears were realised. Ira called her out.

"And why is the reporter here? She had nothing to do with anything except to help me broadcast my deceit to you. Let her go, she is not part of this."

Aaban enjoyed seeing Ira squirm and decided to deliver a little piece of news to him that would make his stomach churn and regret that he ever tried to doublecross him. He considered himself to be a reasonable man but always relished the opportunity to demonstrate to others that he was the most powerful person in the room and in control.

"Ah but Ira, thanks to you, I can see the benefit in having a reporter around to document events for posterity, and so I have decided to take a leaf out of your book by using this young lady to participate in her final news piece on the proceedings of what will happen tomorrow. You didn't think I was going to simply put right the wrongdoings of all these infidels within the solitude of this lovely warehouse? The world must hear of these men renouncing their blasphemous belief in phony idols. Think of the power I wield as they admit their deception to their followers and how they led them to believe that fictitious gods existed. They have executed the biggest scam in history and for that in turn they shall be executed." He raised his fist and punched the air in punctuation to his final statement and the room erupted in cries, men trying to wriggle their way out of their bonds, pleading, begging to be released.

Hysteria broke out, but through it all Faith remained passive and deep in thought in her chair. She had not heard anything that Aaban had said after a certain ambiguous sentence had caught her ear and she was beginning to shake involuntarily. Needing to know, she broke her silence.

"Hey, what do you mean I will participate in my final news piece? What do you mean by that? Hey!" Her initially wavering gentle voice was not heard by Aaban and so she yelled over the sound of the other men in the room to get his attention.

"Hey! Tell me what you meant!"

Aaban heard her voice, distinguishable from the other exclusively male voices in the room, and turned towards her.

"Yes, my dear?"

"When you said that I will participate in my final news piece on the happenings of tomorrow, what did you mean? She lowered her voice somewhat and prayed that this would not be the intended meaning, "Did you mean this would be my final news piece, as in final news piece…ever?" She went cold. As she said it she knew the answer.

"My dear girl!" Aaban said cheerily. Such astute attention to detail, I think you must be very good at your job and I am glad you are here. Let me ask you one question. These fellow captives here with you, they all believe in a God that is not the true God, and will admit to me and the world that they were wrong. Now, what could possibly be more powerful and meaningful than this gesture?" He paced to and fro, shaking his finger at her.

"Somebody who never believed in a God at all, this is the most heinous of blasphemies. Yes, I know about you. You have never believed in a higher power and yet now you must. I can only imagine how that feels for you, your universe must feel turned upside down. You do not know it, but you are actually my greatest prize out of all the men here.."

Faith's heart beat so fast that she did not think she could remain conscious. Tears ran down her face and combined with her dripping sweat as she realised the inescapable situation that she was in. There was actually no way out of this, there were armed men everywhere so even if she could work her way to freedom she could never hope to slip past all of them.

Through her teary eyes she could see Aaban slowly walking up to her, footsteps as loud as thunderbolts, and she pulled back in her chair as far as she could as he leaned over and brought his face next to hers. She could smell his cologne and it was almost a welcome smell in this dank, rancid dungeon. He whispered in her ear.

"But to answer your earlier question my dear, sorry to keep a lady waiting for a response though I think you already know the answer, let me tell you that this news piece tomorrow will be your final news piece....ever."

Tues 22 Sept 1959 11:15am
Jacob & Company Departs

The morning sun streamed in through the plexiglass bubble of the helicopter's cockpit and a spectrum of colours made it seem as if the excited travellers had painted themselves in the colours of the rainbow.

Jacob leaned over to see if he could see the ground and observed far below them the traffic that had banked up around the outskirts of the city like a mess of tiny toy cars, and then hastily sat back upright in his chair as a wave of vertigo washed over him.

He could quickly open the door and jump out right now before anybody could stop him and fall, fall, fall. Would that be considered a quick way to end it all? The part where the earth did its job would be instantaneous, but the trip down would take a minute, maybe two. He didn't think that he could bring himself to do it, not that it was on his mind. Were these types of thoughts normal?

An air of trepidation filled the cabin like an elephant in a room. Nobody dared talk about what Zach said earlier before the flight, everybody unsuccessfully put on a positive air and trying not to consider the implications if what he had said was true. Was God dying? Was death even possible? If so, when? In a minute, an hour, a year? Would they have a chance to make it to their destination in time and realise their desires?

Jacob shifted uncomfortably on the bench he was sitting on, Mary on one side of him with Zach on her lap, Gabe on the other with Simon on his lap, all facing Ishara and Ava. The silence was not awkward because the helicopter was quite loud and it was probably easier not to talk than to talk, but he took it upon himself to relax the mood by attempting conversation. He said the first thing that came to mind.

"So Mary, how long have you and Zach been living alone?" he yelled.

"Dad! What kind of personal question is that!? You have only just met the poor woman, so rude." Ava shook her head at her father's lack of tact and looked apologetically at Mary.

"It's okay Ava, I don't mind. My husband left about six years ago Jacob, when Zach was five and it has been the two of us ever since." She spoke vacantly, appearing not too disturbed by the dredging up of memories past, however, on the inside her stomach was wretching with anxiety. This whole trip was an attempt to get Diah back, and not to have to live life as a lone parent any more. The possibility that God and all things miraculous may not still exist when they got to their destination was eating away at her. Jacob interjected and brought her mind back to the present.

"It's funny, my wife left us about six years ago also," he said in an attempt to find common ground in the worst possible way.

"Are you serious right now?" Ava jumped in angrily. "Mom did not leave us in the way Mary's husband did. Why don't you tell her what you did? Go on, or I will!" She folded her arms in disgust and shook her head, completely gobsmacked at her father's attempts at conversation.

"I'm sorry Mary, I didn't mean to pick such a poor choice of topic. I've never been the great conversationalist. I'm just an insurance salesman, and not even a good one. I actually lost my job a couple of days ago and now somehow have to support myself and my own daughter who I put in a wheelchair. This trip is all I have to make things right in my life. If it doesn't come through I don't know what I will do." He started welling up. Ava rolled her eyes, but Mary reached across and held his hand gently.

"Look Jacob, we are all in it together, whatever happens. I know we have just met, but I can sense you are a kind man, and that is rare these days and your daughter is lucky to have you." She removed her hand and Jacob left his open hand out staring at it, very conscious of the rare touch of a woman.

Mary continued. "It's so hard, you try and you try so hard for them and you don't even know if they appreciate you, you just have to trust that they do, deep down on some imperceptible level. They are our children after all. And even if there is no conscious appreciation, as parents our behaviours still won't change, we will continue to give them our all no matter what and even though we ask for nothing in return, we hope for a sign, some glimpse of acknowledgement and that will make it all worthwhile." She sighed, and hugged Zach tightly as he stared unblinking out the window.

"Yes, yes! You are right. Couldn't have said that better myself," Jacob agreed excitedly, happy that there was at least one person in the world he could connect with.

The helicopter suffered a heavy bump in mid-air which threw them upwards and then sharply downwards, and this was followed by a faint apology from Mr Derby up front.

They continued to talk and laugh intently for the remainder of the trip as the helicopter sped along, and in the meanwhile Ava had tuned out, not interested in the slightest at watching somebody converse engagingly with her father, though she did observe he was doing a lot better now that he had moved on from his nervous opening topics and she was now going to make her mission to focus on finding out more about Gabe.

Leaning forward to speak to Gabe who was sitting opposite her, Ava crowded out Ishara and made sure she was obstructing her line of sight of him. It was the little things that brought her the greatest satisfaction. In her nicest voice she questioned the muscle-bound man, in particular to find out whether he had a brain as impressive as his body but she suspected she knew the answer and prepared herself for disappointment. She knew she was risking him losing his shiny new glow, but also wanted to give him the chance to shine.

"So Gabe, what do you think the long term repercussions of the confirmation of God's existence will be on society?" And she left it at that, her silence leaving a void waiting for the ambushed Gabe to fill.

"Huh? Tough question for one that is completely out of the blue. I haven't really thought about the future too much just yet, still trying to deal with the new reality of today. It can only be a positive thing though right because I've always associated religion with bringing the worst out in man on a larger scale, but thinking about it on an individual level, you know, the mums and the dads and the churchgoers, they all seem to be good people, but whether that is because of religion or whether it's because being good and kind is just how you are supposed to be is another story. I mean there are plenty of really nice atheists too, right? I think in theory nothing should change, any religious people should keep on trucking in the same way. It's probably the atheists who would be impacted the most and have to come to terms with a fundamental change in beliefs and I have no idea what the scale repercussions of a large section of society having their belief systems crushed might result in." He seemed satisfied with his answer and Ava was secretly impressed that he managed to produce one that wasn't neanderthal. But still, it wasn't quite homo sapiens either.

She felt a hand grab her shoulder roughly and pull her back. Ishara now leaned forward and made herself known, much to Ava's annoyance. Commandeering the conversation she extended the line of questioning to a more self-centred one.

"So Gabe, how do you feel now that you can marry girls that you wouldn't have been allowed to before? Fancy putting any ex-Hindus on your to-do list? I was discussing with Ava earlier that my parents can't object to an inter-religion wedding now since there is technically only one religion! You should take this chance while I'm still single." She winked playfully at Gabe and Ava's face showed visible disgust at her forward behaviour and ditzy subject matter. Gabe seemed oblivious to the battle for his attention and happily answered the new and easier question that had been thrust upon him this time.

"You know, it never really sat right with me that somebody could convert religions in order to get married to somebody. I found the whole thing such a phony gesture and a hoop that needed to be jumped through but surely the outcome couldn't fool anybody could it? I compare it to living your whole life committing to the belief that one plus one equals two, and then, to satisfy somebody else's marriage prerequisites you say 'Hey, you know I used to believe one plus one equalled two, but now, just for you, I will live my life believing that one plus one equals three.' You just know that person isn't truly converting their belief and you know that nobody else believes they believe it, it's a token gesture that helps the paperwork get approved and gets the rest of the family on board. Surely if you truly believe in something, a conversion to a new belief is impossible."

To Ava's joy, Ishara seemed deflated that Gabe had not taken to the playful tone in her question and submitted a serious essay as an answer, maintaining the tone after Ava's serious question. The poor man felt like he was being probed and tested, which was actually the case.

They sat in silence for a while, the outside sound of the engine whirring above them making it easier to focus their own thoughts and contemplate what may lie ahead in wait for them that day. Never in a million years would any of them have guessed that today they would be hurtling in a helicopter towards a remote location that could alter their fates. Their very normal lives had taken an unlikely turn for the curious.

Mr Derby's voice boomed back to them from the front. "Okay everybody, I'm going to have to put her down soon, the trees are starting to get too dense so I can't see that I can land any further on, plus I'm quite close to hitting the range of this helicopter and I need to have the fuel to be able to get back. Taking her down." The chopper started to descend and the excitement built once again among the passengers.

"I wonder how far away we are?" Ava asked, peering out the window but seeing nothing except unspoilt land which was the nemesis of her wheelchair and sign of a difficult journey for her ahead. She hoped they were close. Her father and Mary were still in close conversation and it was her natural instinct to interrupt and break up the proceedings for her father, however, on this occasion she decided to ease up on him.

The helicopter landed with a savage thump uncomfortably close to a tree, and as the party grimaced at the thought that some damage had been done, they were surprised to hear a cheer of success come from Mr Derby. "Best landing to date!" he shouted back to them ecstatically. Nervous eyes shot around the cabin as they wondered what his previous landings had been like.

Their vehicle had touched down with one of the struts firmly landing on a log, causing a severe tilt to the left side. Once the rotors had come to a halt, everybody climbed out and stretched their cramped muscles.

After being assisted out and helped into her chair, Ava looked around at the landscape and was able to see at close range the difficulty she was going to have in travelling any type of distance. There was barely an inch of ground that wasn't covered by a rock, a bush or some other impediment which would emphasise her disability. She mentally geared herself up for a challenge which in truth was no bigger than what she faced on a regular day to day basis in the city. Motivating herself was a daily habit.

Just think Ava, at the end of today, you will probably be able to simply step over all those rocks and obstacles, so quit your whining and get this bunch of people moving! The sooner you get to this place the sooner you walk. And quite possibly, the sooner you walk the sooner you get a date. She glanced over at Gabe who had picked Simon up and put him on his shoulders again. Time to round up the troops. She wheeled herself to the centre of them all.

"Okay you lot. I don't know what you are all thinking, but we all heard what Zach said before we flew out here and to be honest, whether or not there is truth to it I would rather proceed with a sense of urgency around this because I will be damned if we get there and it is too late. I think we all agree this could be the most important thing in our lives right now and so I say let's get moving. If it's all true and there is something out there beyond those trees that can help us, then I want that help as soon as possible. If it turns out, God forbid, that it is not true then I would also rather find that out sooner rather than later." Speech finished, she glanced over at her father and saw a beam of pride. She wheeled away in the opposite direction.

Jacob walked over to Mr Derby who had eventually unbuckled himself and eased himself out of the pilot's seat, now pacing to and fro waving his arms about to get the blood flowing. He spoke sincerely.

"You know, I can't thank you enough for this. There was no upfront notice from me, I mean, until today all we had really shared was a few seconds in passing each morning. For you to be confronted with a large group of unknown people and coerced into giving up your own important schedule to fly them to the middle of nowhere in your helicopter, well, that's about the nicest thing that anybody has ever done for me or anybody I know. So thank you. I can't possibly imagine what I could offer you that you may want, but if there is anything I can ever do for you in

278

return, please let me know." The profound gratitude emanated from his voice and touched Mr Derby who appreciated that he had done a lot for this broken man who had so little.

"Look old chap, we may only see each other for a few seconds each morning, but it has been each morning for years now. Imagine how awkward it would be between us in passing every morning in the future if I had said no to helping you today! And what's one day out of a lifetime for a friend?" And with that word he stuck out his hand and Jacob grabbed it with both of his and shook it. Turning to walk back to the helicopter, Mr Derby stopped for a final word.

"Oh, and by the way Jacob, you just mentioned how I flew you all to the middle of nowhere in my helicopter. I know that you know it's not mine and that I borrowed it, but in fact I stole it ha ha! I will probably have a stern letter of complaint written about me back at the aerodrome!" His beaming smile almost convinced Jacob that this was some minor thing. Jacob's face comically expressing shock was exactly the outcome that Mr Derby was looking for.

"Well, let's just say I borrowed it without permission then shall we if that makes you feel better about it? For goodness sake, God has appeared to us all on this earth, surely a little thing like taking a flying whirligig for a spin is as insignificant as a mere speck of dust in this universe. Oh and one last thing, from up in the sky I saw the north-south road you probably want over in that direction, not far at all. Good luck Jacob!" He walked off towards the helicopter, left hand nonchalantly pointing off into the distance in the direction of where he thought the road lay.

Jacob bid farewell to the mysterious man and headed back to the group who had all found makeshift seats. Gabe was sitting on a log while Mary had found a gnarled trunk of a tree that had leaned over at just the right height and angle to lean on. He noticed that Ishara had sat a little outside of the rest of them, and seemed to be contemplating something serious. He strode over to find out what was on her mind.

"Hey. Why so serious? Out of everybody here you probably have the least on your mind to worry about." She looked up at him with a frown. Catching himself, he said "Sorry, I'm not downplaying your feelings or your role in this, I know Ava is one of your closest friends and I am sure it would mean the world to you for her to be able to walk again. You have as much right to be concerned as everybody else." He squatted down next to her. "If you have something on your mind you know you can tell me."

"Yeah I know, it's just that I have been thinking that if God does die before we get there, then this will all have been for nothing. The same as what Ava said back in the van, I think I can also feel that glow of awareness inside me fading and I don't know if it's because I am getting used to it or because it really is fading, maybe away to nothing. I actually really believe Mary when she says that Zach is a connector and has insight into what is going on. I mean, from what she says, the kid has never spoken in his entire life and then he comes out with that gem of a phrase, out of all the possible things he could say. There has to be a reason for that." She shifted around on the rock she was sitting on, her face scrunching up and giving away her comfort levels.

"I know it will be a slow trek to our destination, and we don't know what we will find when we get there and whether it will be worth it. I want to go ahead of everybody and do some sort of reconnaissance mission. Scout around, find the place and check it out. I can travel pretty quickly, probably triple the speed the group will be travelling. It makes sense doesn't it? I can make it there and come back to find you guys with some news in no time.

And I know I don't need your permission for this but I would like you to just let me do this. For Ava." She looked at Jacob pleadingly.

"Mmm I don't know Ishara, It could be dangerous out there. It's a good idea in theory though but I would be worried for you." He turned to the group to float the idea.

"Hey everybody, since we might be a bit pressed for time, Ishara was thinking of running ahead and scouting out the path for us and seeing if the destination really is what we are hoping it to be. Mr Derby pointed out that the road that should take us there isn't too far away. It seems quite deserted around here so I am happy for her to go, but.." He didn't have a chance to finish.

"Maybe Gabe can come with me?" Ishara asked hopefully. "I would feel a lot safer just in case anything happened, and all you guys will be okay on your own." She looked at Gabe with raised eyebrows, evaluating his levels of enthusiasm for her idea.

Ava was about to voice her opinion but didn't have a chance to get her words out before Gabe replied.

"I'd love to and I think it's actually a pretty good idea but there is no way I am going to leave Simon and the group. I think you would be okay on your own, there doesn't seem to be anybody around apart from us. Take a bunch of snacks, find the road, and at a guess from me I don't think it should be more than a couple of hours away at most. We are definitely keen to hear what you find though, make sure you come back with good news!" He turned away to indicate the matter was decided, and continued playing with Simon.

Ava could see that Ishara had been brewing a scheme that had not paid off and now she had to commit to her idea and leave the group, probably for the rest of the day in order to go on her mission.

"Have a safe journey, and thanks for doing this!" Ava said to a visibly frustrated Ishara, the phoniness of the sentiment not lost on her friend.

Ishara moodily stuffed a bag with some water and enough food for the afternoon, then had a small chat with Jacob and Gabe who ensured that she found the road okay and knew which direction to travel.

"Just keep going north, and look, we won't be too far behind you so if you just come back down the road we will bump into each other. Good luck. I hope you find the place and come back with some news that might cheer us up. Take care and see you soon."

Ishara departed the company with a few waves and well wishes, then headed off into the terrain over a hill and disappeared on her mission.

Mary was over at the pile of bags, fastidiously moving things from one to another, lifting each and testing their weight and, finally satisfied according to her own criteria, stood up and beckoned Jacob over.

"So I have made each bag weigh roughly the same and each contains about the same ratio of food and water," she said proudly. "Sorry I didn't contribute anything, as you know I really had no idea this would be how my day would pan out."

"Nice work Mary, that is exactly the type of thing that I would have done! It's all about fairness, though I am more than happy to carry more than the others. And Ava can actually carry quite a heavy bag on her lap too, she won't mind. I think we definitely brought enough supplies don't you, so there is no need for you to contribute! I really used to enjoy hiking, before Ava was born my wife and I would regularly take a trip out to the country, do a bit of camping and seeing nature. It was just so nice to be able to see the horizon for a change instead of a bunch of city buildings blocking the view."

He sighed at the memory of good times long past, but for some reason with Mary around the sharp pain that usually accompanied thoughts of time spent with his wife was not present. Was it because she had experienced a similar pain of loss to him? Perhaps her pain was worse if you think about it. Her husband had made a conscious decision to voluntarily leave her. Knowing that your partner would rather leave you and your son than stay with you must be an excruciating feeling.

Forgetting that they were still relative strangers he put his hand on her shoulder and said "Come on, let me help you with those shall I?" He felt close to her and could sense the aura of sadness surrounding her and hoped that he could ease that hurt even a little. Realising his hand was lingering on her for slightly longer than appropriate he removed it, blood rushing to his head as he wondered how long she would have been happy for him to leave it there without saying anything.

Another shout from Ava quickly snapped everybody into order and once loaded up with supplies, the company made their way towards the road. The crystal clear skies lifted spirits, and slowly but steadily the team picked out the easiest path onwards, moving logs and stones so that Ava's wheelchair would be as unimpeded as possible. A couple of times Gabe and Jacob had to either haul her up or lower her down more difficult terrain and do the same for Simon. It was maybe half an hour before they could see a clearing in the trees ahead and with relief, the road had been located.

"This should make our lives a lot easier now," Jacob said breathlessly, already worn out from the exertion of the minimal physical activity he had just undertaken. He was not a fit man, and now learned just how unfit he actually was. Hiding his deep puffing and panting as much as possible, he was ready for a break. "Let's get to the top of this hill and stop for maybe five minutes, what does everybody think?" he suggested.

The going was a lot more simple now although the length of the incline they were walking made Jacob's calves burn as he pushed Ava along closer and closer to their agreed upon rest spot.

"Nearly there. Nearly there. Boy, I can't wait for some water. It's like a desert here."

With only fifty yards or so until the top of the hill, Jacob held his hand up into the air and shooshed the party, head cocked to one side, listening. He could hear some clattering ahead, accompanied by voices. As they continued and cautiously progressed over the rise, the road flattened out and there on the side of the road a man and elderly woman were having a cup of tea out of a thermos. Upon seeing the large group approaching, comical surprise showed on their faces and once a quick scan of the members of the party had been completed, the surprised looks were shortly followed by smiles and a friendly greeting.

The lady, who Jacob guessed at a glance was around seventy years old, had beautifully long silver hair tied in a loose ponytail, a kindly face and a flowing red dress on that seemed more appropriate for a ballroom than to be perched on the side of the road in the middle of nowhere. Her whole fascinating persona seemed young at heart and confident, age only betrayed by the veined and wrinkled hands holding the plastic mug.

"Well I never!" she exclaimed. "Here we are thinking there was nobody around for miles and having a soothing cup of tea to make us forget our aches and pains, and then peekaboo, here y'all are coming up over this here hill and simply surprising the life out of me and my boy!"

Putting them all at ease with her easy-going demeanour, they all laughed and Jacob asked for permission to join them as they took a well-deserved break.

"Be my guest! The only company I have had is my boy Earnest here and he is running out of interesting conversation for his mother, isn't he?" She looked at her son, and rubbed the fifty-ish year old man on the head who rolled his eyes and withdrew embarrassed. Jacob noticed a trickle of saliva running down his chin.

"And my name is Rosalind, pleased to meet you. Pull up some ground and join us," she curtsied with a flourish and resumed her position.

Jacob and the crew were extremely curious as to why such an unlikely couple were in reasonably inhospitable surroundings, and were sure that the same was being wondered about them.

After a polite enough length of time where drinks and food were consumed in peace, conversation began and the two groups began to exchange information.

Rosalind was the first to open the line of questioning, and after screwing on the top of her thermos and placing it carefully back into her bag she set her attention to Jacob and cleared her throat with a small cough.

"So Jacob, your collective don't seem like a regular group of hikers, what brings you all out here, though the countryside is indeed lovely and scenic? Getting back to nature?" Her eyes looked across the group and lingered a little too long on Ava and Simon, revealing to Jacob that she had probably guessed their intentions but only if she herself had knowledge of the rumours about their intended destination.

His suspicions about the condition of Rosalind's son lead him to believe that they too were also not out here just for a simple hiking expedition. He thought he might as well mention it, they seemed harmless enough and might be good travelling companions should they wish to accompany the group.

"So Rosalind, would I, er, be correct in assuming that we might all be heading towards the same, er, miraculous destination, if you know what I mean?" He whispered the word "miraculous" and glanced down at the ground, missing the fleeting frown that appeared on her face before her sparkling blue eyes flickered up towards him and she responded.

"Ah, so my intuition about your little group was correct. Well young man, it wasn't hard to guess where you were all going, I do indeed know about your miraculous destination, but I'm sorry to say that Earnest and I won't be accompanying you."

"Oh, why is that? It could be fun to travel as a bigger group, I promise you that we are great company." Jacob could not hide his surprise at her response and he frankly felt a bit embarrassed that his invitation had been declined in front of the group he was travelling with and he couldn't fathom the reason why.

"Oh, I can see the disappointment on your face. Don't be like that, it's not that we don't want to go with you to you know where. It's just that we have already been there, you see and are coming back the other way now. The place is a sham."

Tues 22 Sept 1959 *7:20am*
The Man in Decline

Cassidy's café was open for business a full ten minutes earlier than the sign on the door indicated, bright lights inside switched on to entice those looking to indulge in a morning coffee not to search elsewhere. Inside, Doris kept one ear engaged, listening for the sound of the rusty bell and squeaky hinges to bear news of entering customers, while the rest of her senses were engaged on the cherry pie slowly disappearing in front of her.

"Well I probably appreciate you more than the customers do," she said, talking to the cake and chewing with her mouth open, wearing a smear of cream that had somehow found its way to her cheek. "I know what goes into you, I know the time and effort involved, I mean you are basically my baby. My big, delicious baby." She stroked the cake with her fork, scarring lines across every piece. "Oops, silly me. Can't sell you now."

She walked over to the coffee machine barefoot and poured herself her second for the morning. Slurping it on the way back to her table, she thought of all the years that she had given herself to the business for minimum wage and never thought to appreciate the little things that were probably owing to her. Like cake.

The owners were fair and kind people, however, never went above and beyond as far as reward and recognition went, and Doris knew that she was the face of the business and its foundation.

"Though if I ate cherry pie at this rate every day for the last fifteen years there is no way I would even fit behind this table right now, and the cafe would most likely be out of business," she mused.

Aware of her out of character behaviour, she contemplated the drivers and decided that it must somehow be connected to the elderly man that came in every morning and the unusual turn of events that his visits had undergone lately. She did not have many people in her life, certainly none who would impact her behaviour, in fact she felt a gnaw of regret at just how mundane things were for her outside of the café. And the fact that the café was the most interesting aspect of her life festered a sliver of resentment towards herself and her complacency towards her own growth and development.

"Well not everybody can be a rocket scientist or doctor and make a difference to the world," she said to herself. "I'll make a difference to one person at a time, one coffee at a time."

If she had noticed a change in herself and the only other thing that had altered in any way was the elderly man and the arrival of his friends, logic dictated that the two were related. When she saw him and witnessed the arrival of his friends she had in some way felt a joy inside her come alive and grow just like the first rays of light peeking over the horizon, becoming brighter as the sun emerged from behind the darkness. She realised that some things in life were meant to be more fun that what she had permitted them to be. What a mystery had unfurled, but so satisfying and happy to witness.

She saw a shadow move across the front of the store, momentarily interrupting the outside brightness from streaming into the café and the door squeaked ajar, simultaneously setting off the bell. The noise was unnecessarily irritating, and instead of jumping up with a greeting to the elderly man who had entered, Doris made a mental note to oil the door hinges and remove the bell that she had been a slave to for her entire career. Excited to see him she observed that he was alone for now but was sure that that would change. Glancing him up and down she noticed that he was a slightly different man to yesterday, although she could not really pinpoint what the differences were that she sensed.

Was his suit a little shabbier and not quite the bluish-white that it was yesterday? Was that stubble there before? The eyes were a little red, there may have been signs of a faint limp and he seemed to painfully ease himself into his regular seat. Just little things, but the combination of them let slip that something was not quite right. Maybe it was just the darker corner where he was sitting, but his skin seemed to have a ghostly, grey pallor, almost sickly.

Within a few minutes though, similar scenes to the previous day unfolded and a variety of characters of differing ages and races had entered the café and surrounded him, seemingly oblivious to the deterioration from his previously heavenly presentation that Doris could now clearly notice.

The man maintained conversation and engaged energetically with this different group of people to those who visited yesterday and Doris simply assumed that the man may have had a big night and was a little under the weather but keeping it together quite well considering.

Doris served a couple of ladies and their child out the front of the cafe,and then continued to observe the busy back table, delivering coffee and tea when requested. It was quite boisterous and Doris wondered how the conversation could progress when everybody at the table seemed to be talking simultaneously and nobody was doing the listening.

The man coughed a few times and pulled a handkerchief out of his pocket and pressed it to his mouth. Tucking it away again he continued talking to the young gentleman next to him who laughed and appeared to have been the recipient of a very amusing joke.

Doris heard a high pitch noise coming from outside, maybe somebody yelling, probably somebody stealing somebody else's parking spot again, it happened regularly here in this small strip of shops. It was drowned out by the hubbub inside and soon stopped.

The table at the back of the café seemed to be right for now and so Doris went back to the original task at hand, being the disposal of the 'damaged' cherry pie, via the use of a fork and her eager mouth. "Where have you been all my life....now come here, you!"

Tues 22 Sept 1959 5:18pm
Jacob & Company Onwards

"What do you mean you've been there? It's really a sham?" The group collectively gasped and surrounded Rosalind, pawing at her, shaking her, demanding to know more. Even Ava wheeled her chair intimidatingly close to the elderly woman who stood up and backed away defensively, hands in the air telling them to calm down.

"Whoa there kiddies! Just leave me be and don't be stampeding me down now, you hear? I'll tell you all you need to know, but I'm telling y'all you ain't gonna like it I'm afraid." She eased herself back down again, eyes looking to the sky as if hoping for a sign on how to break some bad news in the best possible way. The group surrounded her again but remained respectfully quiet in anticipation of her story.

"As you may be able to tell, my boy Earnest here ain't quite right." She shook her head sadly and patted him on the leg and then squeezed his hand. Earnest smiled and nodded his head in agreement, then stared ahead with a far off look in his eye. "He was born that way, just one of the unlucky ones I guess. No explanation. My husband was quite successful so the dear boy's upbringing was about as privileged as it could be, we loved him as much as we would have loved a more regular boy. Anyway, my husband passed on a while back but I remained in contact with a lot of his many caring acquaintances, one of who got in touch a day back and informed me of a place out in the middle of nowhere where strange things were happening. Strange but good things, as I am sure you have also heard." She was playing with the hem of her dress, examining it and brushing dust off it. Jacob noticed she did not make eye contact.

"So anyway we make it to the place and there are hundreds of people there, fighting, praying, begging, it's a real scene do you understand, and then we gets told that the miracles have all dried up. And so, we pack up our disappointments and left. So I'm sorry to say, there is no point in y'all continuing any further. It ain't real. Well, it was real but it ain't no more."

A solemn hush fell over the group, complete and utter deflation enveloping them before disbelief and anger set in. Gabe kicked the ground and swore loudly, grabbing Simon tightly and giving him a long hug accompanied by reassurance through gritted teeth. He was aware that he had been the one responsible for instigating this wild goose chase, and bore the brunt of guilt imposed upon him by the crushed hopes of all.

Mary sat through the revelation with quiet acceptance, acknowledging to herself that it had all sounded too good to be true anyway, she probably didn't deserve Diah back and was perfectly fine making do with her life as it already was. She was not unhappy, just incomplete and lonely without her husband to share her life with. It was all about Zach anyway, and he was most likely oblivious to the whole journey and this turn of events and how close he had potentially been to some sort of salvation.

Jacob's heart sank into the ground, tunnelled through miles of the earth's crust and rock and was incinerated violently as it approached the intense heat of the core where it could not sink any lower. He had invested every ounce of his emotional self into this expedition for the purposes of making things right by his daughter, it was the first, last and only opportunity to redeem himself and that carpet had now been pulled out from under him with such force that he was left reeling on the ground, injured and unsure whether he was able to get back up again. It would be so much easier just to stay down, battered and defeated, grinding time down until the end came.

Whether he was delusional with disappointment or whether his mind entered self-preservation mode because it was dangerously close to imploding, for the second time he heard a thousand familiar whispers echo in his ears once again. Softly, softly, the voice of his wife reverberated within his subconscious, incomprehensible at first, until the phasing of the sounds aligned and as clear as a bell the perfect tone of his wife delivered him a spoken message from a dark and faraway place telling him to complete what he had started, over and over, again and again with an insistence that could not be ignored until the lingering voice faded gently out of reach and into the atmosphere, once again leaving Jacob wondering whether or not he had really heard anything at all.

He concentrated and strained to catch just a second more of the voice but it was gone. Whatever the source was, the message was clear and he knew what to do now but Ava's voice snapped him out of the limbo his mind had fallen into and brought him back to the reality of the situation at hand and the repercussions of this new revelation.

"Great, just great! So here we are stranded in a location that might as well be the surface of the moon, I'm going to be stuck with my idiot father pushing me around forever and never get a boyfriend and never get married and be miserable for the rest of my.."

"Shut up, just shut up would you!" Jacob could take it no more and his anger exploded. He had just come from a faraway place of such peace and now had been unwillingly wrenched back into the world of guilt and aggression inflicted by his daughter. His face reddened and he became oblivious to the group around him as he focused on the girl and the dam that had held strong for years now broke.

"I've had enough of you taking out everything on me and treating me worse than you would treat an enemy. I know you despise me and wish that I had died in the accident instead of your mother and you know what, sometimes I do too, but the fact is that I didn't, and how do you think I feel having to live with what I live with on my conscience every single day, and on top of that to have the only person left in my family treat me with such disdain even when I do everything I can for her, every minute of the day! When is it going to stop? Nothing can bring her back, nothing! And nothing can bring your legs back! I made a horrible mistake but I am your father damn it, so start acting like a daughter and not a spoiled entitled brat because I have been punished by you enough and am not going to put up with it anymore!"

His chest heaved with the exertion of yelling, and as the red faded from his vision, the others came into view and he became embarrassed at the scene he made and backed out of the circle. Ava was quiet and stared at the ground, face flushed and ashamed at his behaviour but also at hers.

After a few long minutes of awkward silence, Jacob decided that the best thing to do would be to clear the air and try to get a move on after seeing who would still like to continue on and who wanted to back out.

"I'm really sorry you had to see that folks, you all know my story, and I think that the news that our destination is not what we hoped just got to me as I am sure that it has also gotten to you all." He shuffled his feet and made an effort to look at everybody in the eye. "We have all come this far, and I am just going to say that I want to continue on, at least see things with my own eyes, talk to any people who are there and hear what they have to say. We are nearly there, it would feel wrong just to pull out now."

Rosalind spoke, maybe a little too quickly. "No, you really shouldn't bother, I can assure you there is nothing there, don't waste your time, you should just turn back now. Don't expose these people to more disappointment."

Jacob frowned and spoke over her. "Regardless of what she says, I'm still going, who's with me?"

Gabe and Mary raised their hands, and shortly after, Ava raised hers.

"Okay it looks like we are going to finish what we started. Rosalind, Earnest, it's been a pleasure but we will be hitting the road now, whatever the outcome. We just want to see the place for ourselves and never regret wondering."

Rosalind chimed in again. "Jacob you are making a mistake, I assure you. Let my story save you from facing the disappointment in person. We have done the scouting for you."

This reminded Jacob of something. "And actually before I forget, I don't suppose you were passed by a young Indian girl travelling alone not too long ago?"

"No, you are the first people we have seen. Why?"

Jacob frowned but shrugged his shoulders. "No reason. Okay everybody, time to pack up and move on." He looked over towards the group, eyes resting on Mary and he saw a look of pride in her eyes directed at him and for the second time she caused a torrent of blood to rush to his head, and he was sure he must be blushing as red as a beetroot right about now. He was not used to receiving glances of the flattering type and felt very unsure of himself and felt compelled to make an excuse to leave.

"Err.. umm… I'll be back. Nature calls," he stuttered and walked behind a tree out of sight of the company. Whilst he was there he tucked his shirt in and made a few other adjustments to himself.

Once done, he headed back and rounded everybody up. "Okay, let's go now shall we? I reckon we can walk a bit longer and then try to figure out the best way to make a camp for the night."
He noticed that the group was looking at him strangely and he instantly felt self-conscious and sounded off at them.

"What are you looking at? Is everything packed? Goodbye Rosalind, goodbye Earnest, I wish you all the best."

Rosalind just shook her head, but managed to look up and issue a generic smile.

Ava looked at her father suspiciously.

"Um dad, have you just done your hair? Impressing someone?"

"No. What? Shut up. Let's go."

Tues 22 Sept 1959 *3:45pm*
Ishara Conspires

Ishara bade a sulky farewell to the company and wandered off alone in the direction of the road that Jacob had pointed out, cursing that her gamble had not paid off. Kicking herself that she didn't have the foresight to think the situation through properly first, she accepted the position she was in and wanted to use this solo time that she now had to see if there were alternative means by which she could shift the Gabe and Ava tussle in her favour.

She had hoped to be promenading with Gabe right now, laughing and sharing moments but instead she was tripping over stones and scraping her knees jumping over logs with no company but her own and the God residing inside of her.

Of course Gabe would never have left Simon with the group to come join her on her scouting mission. Any idiot could see that except for her apparently, and now she was stuck with the dire consequences of having to follow through with her pointless trek whilst Ava was no doubt taking full advantage of the abundance of one on one time that she had been kindly donated.

Ishara had a little laugh to herself. She didn't even think she was that besotted with Gabe and could sense that Ava wasn't either, he had come like a bolt out of the blue that evening, a knight in shining armour to rescue them from the man sitting on their car by the church, but he was not the typical man she was drawn to. This was more competitive behaviour on her part to keep the status quo between herself and Ava static, with herself firmly grasping the upper hand. She did love her friend to bits, but secretly needed somebody that she could feel superior to in some way.

In Ishara's mind, Ava had always been a little prettier and consequently received more attention from the boys, but if she possessed the modesty to be a little more introspective she would see that that wasn't the case at all, as appearance had little do with it.

Before the tragic accident Ava was a more vivacious and outgoing person than she was, making friends and followers very easily whereas Ishara was a bit more hard work to become close to. This was driven mostly by nurture over nature. Jacob and his wife provided Ava with a lot of freedom to engage in the pursuits of her desire, socialising with many new groups and associations as one interest flowed into another.

Ishara, on the other hand was bound by her firm but fair parents to study long hours every evening in the attempt to attain the highest grades and make schooling the priority over other avenues of life.

The accident completely changed the dynamic between the pair. Ishara regained some lost ground when her friend withdrew into herself and developed a hatred for her father and the world. Ishara did not gain any more friends and popularity, however, Ava did lose hers.

And now, thanks to unprecedented events, the possibility that Ava could regain her old life back and disrupt the equilibrium that now favoured Ishara utterly petrified her, and as much as she loved her childhood friend, her resolve was steadfast that she must not reach the place where the miracles were allegedly occurring. Ishara always got her way, and this was no different.

Having found the road and travelling a lot quicker and easier now, she headed up a rise and saw two figures ahead. One was clearly a woman, age indeterminate as yet, but wearing a flowing red dress, blustering in the breeze. Her companion was a stocky and tall male. They seemed to be travelling in the same direction as she, and Ishara increased her pace in an attempt to catch up with the pair. The slow pace at which they were meandering meant she was upon them in next to no time.

She yelled out and the woman turned with surprise, eventually followed by the lumbering brute of a man, fathoming how and why on earth an unaccompanied girl would be traipsing along this lonely stretch of road.

"Hey! Hey!" she caught up to them and was met with a beaming smile by the lady, who was a lot older than her dress and long hair revealed when spied from a distance.

"Hi little lady! Fancy meeting you here. Now why in tarnations are you to be found in these parts? It's too out of the way for you to be lost on your way to somewhere. Are you going somewhere…. specific?" She winked at Ishara and then extended herself into a curtsey and stuck out her hand. Ishara took it, and poorly imitated the curtsey in return. She felt like she was meeting the Queen of England, excluding the palace and any sort of royal surroundings.

"Hello my lady, or ma'am, sorry I'm not sure what to call you. I'm Ishara. I'm trying to head to some sort of farm or property near here where there are supposed to be strange phenomena occurring, have you heard about it?" She could tell by the twinkle in the woman's eye and slightly turned up corners of her mouth that she knew what she was talking about.

"Well, well it seems like word did spread didn't it? I wonder how many people may be there already. We are on our way my child. You can call me Rosa, short for Rosalind, and this is my boy Earnest. We are going for his benefit."

Ishara could see the man was quite old, but behind his eyes there resided a child. A sweet and innocent soul lived within him, however the body which it inhabited was ill fitting.

"Ah I see. Hello Earnest, pleased to meet you." The man didn't respond, but smiled broadly.

The trio continued together for a stretch, chatting away and Ishara found the woman to be charming company. Her son never said a word, however, his presence made Ishara feel safe and content in some indefinable way. Eventually, the conversation turned from trivial small talk to more pointed questioning.

"So my dear, what on earth brings you out here? After speaking to you for some time now I can see absolutely no reason for you to be travelling in the direction you are travelling? Is there something about you I cannot see that you feel needs to be seen to by a miracle? Enlighten me dear."

Ishara was brought back to earth with a thud by this reminder of her scouting mission.

"Oh yes, I am sorry I very nearly forgot. I'm with some people actually and I have gone on ahead to see if I can find the place quickly, and then get back to them with some information on how it is and whether the rumours are actually true or not. We all jolly well hope so after coming all this way."

Rosalind shuffled a little uncomfortably. "So you are saying that there are more people heading there too? I do hope there aren't too many people, something precious and special shouldn't just be allowed to be accessed by everybody. What if there are thousands of people there now? What if we miss out? I'm not sure I like this at all. Not at all." She shook her head worriedly.

"I know Rosa, imagine, the more people that are there, there is probably bickering about who was there first and what if, just what if Earnest misses out? I would think that you wouldn't want more people to be heading there at all. Let me tell you something Rosa. The people that I am with, well, I don't know how to say this but they aren't nice like you. I think it won't be long before they catch you and pass you, and get to the place first! I have an idea if you would care to hear it that might ensure Earnest gets a fair chance."

"Yes, I am all ears my dear?" Rosalind was listening intently.

"Well, I imagine they will be upon you soon. I might rush ahead, perhaps you could persuade them that there is no point in proceeding? You could pretend that you have been there already and the whole thing is a hoax, make them think it would be in their best interests just to turn around and go back to where they came from. Then yourself and Earnest would have no more competition beating you there."

"I don't know dear, I'm not a good liar, and not sure if I want to lie, even if it is potentially in the best interests of Earnest here."

Ishara got out her purse. "How about I give you fifty dollars, and you never saw me?"
Rosalind stuck out her hand and grabbed the notes.

"They won't proceed a step past us, honey."

Ishara continued on north up the road, gritting her teeth and still annoyed at the situation she had committed herself to. She would travel on, find the place she was looking for as a token gesture so that she could say to the group when she returned that she had seen it and it wasn't for real, crush Ava's hopes and get back to having some quality Gabe time.

Surrounded by a bleak landscape, the sound of her own footsteps all that she could hear, Ishara had no real distractions to confound her thoughts and this offered her the rare chance to look within herself. The awareness that God existed was still within her, but what she had said to Jacob earlier was true, she was either becoming accustomed to the awareness or else it was indeed fading somewhat, with quite the amount of concentration required to locate the fragment inside her.

The last few days had been such a whirlwind, not only for herself but for the entire world, she was certain. The varied range of responses from the human race to the events that had transpired demonstrated how, even though every person belongs to exactly the same species, the differences within the species are as varied as colours in the spectrum.

Some chose to panic, others resigned themselves to the new status quo, others celebrated, some had still not come to terms with the state of affairs yet. Ishara was somewhere in the middle, still trying to find within herself what it all meant to her.

She had a religious upbringing and had always believed in a higher power but ashamedly, as she grew up and became older and wiser and consequently started asking more questions of the world she lived in, she came to the realisation that she no longer had the faith to blindly believe in something that lacked any sort of evidence whatsoever.

There was literally not even a fragment of undisputable proof that any God existed, and so she did what she needed to do and put her belief to the side, resurrecting elements of it to appease her parents when at certain times of the year they required it of her. This seemed to work well and she was proud that she was mature enough to adapt to circumstances in order to keep the peace and maintain a happy family relationship.

Up ahead, a bird circled lazily in the air, content with not attempting to travel anywhere in particular, simply happy to observe whatever it was that it found interesting below. Ishara wished that she had majestic wings that could propel her into the air instead of the sore blistered feet that she currently possessed and were doing a poor job of propelling her anywhere.

After half an hour of slow progress there was a slight veer up ahead and once she negotiated the slow long turn, her eyes opened wide and that little bit of God inside of her worked its way out of her mouth.

"Holy…"

Wed 23 Sept 1959 *6:15am*
Ira's Warehouse Deadline

The faces of the men in the room slowly became recognisable as the ominous glow of dawn of a new day appeared through the rusty bars that protected any entry or exit via the solitary window. A few of them had somehow managed to fall asleep during the night even though tightly bound and upright in a seated position, their snores causing Faith to question how anybody in the room could have cast aside the fears of what was to come and managed to doze off. She wondered if their slumber was peaceful, or whether their dreams were of darkness and the terror that they were experiencing.

Only yesterday she was happily chatting to Maxwell in the office, and now she was caught in the middle of a religious altercation started by a disturbed man with some bizarre point to prove and it didn't seem real.

"I'm sorry." A soft voice reached her ears from across the room. The voice was a whisper but from the direction it came from she knew that it was the latino man.

"I'm sorry. He has my family hostage you know. I used you to try to make it look like I was doing his bidding by taking all these men and hiding them here where they would be safe from him, but I didn't think things through completely and now you are here too. I'm sorry."

The room was still dark but she could see the light falling on tears upon his cheek. She sniffed and realised that she too was crying. Shrugging her shoulders as much as her restraints would allow, she told him there was nothing that could be done about it now.

So this was to be her last day on earth. Not quite how she imagined she would go out. This was somewhat more eventful than dying peacefully in her bed one night of old age. And how about the irony of living as an atheist and knowing that when death came there was no afterlife, yet now that the absolute verification of God had transpired, one of the accompanying truths was that still there was no afterlife.

"Do you have a family?" the man asked. Faith shook her head.

"No, I let my work get in the way," and it was then that she had a moment of revelation and honesty with herself. Funny how only now she could see everything so clearly. Margie from the office was right about her after all.

"I have a wife and a son." Faith could tell that the man had some last minute burdens that he wanted to get off his chest and fortunately for him she was a captive audience. "I have lied to them my whole life. They think I work in construction." He gritted his teeth. "I am a bad man. I AM a bad man. I am not a good man. Well, I was bad but now I am good, though it is too late now. I have lost everything and now I am losing my family. They have done nothing wrong, their only crime is to know me."

Faith had nothing to say, no words of reassurance, no kind thoughts to offer, nothing. She did not know this man, what he was or what he had been through. He probably didn't even need or expect a response, he just needed a listening ear for his final words.

At that moment a car could be heard pulling up outside, gravel crunching under tyres. Extreme panic set into the room and Faith had never experienced pure terror like this before, feeling like an animal in an abattoir and hearing the slaughterman arriving for work in the morning. Her fellow captives pointlessly struggled, yelled and attempted to free themselves from their chairs as if now their bonds may yield and break when they had not yielded or broken during their previous attempts.

This was not a dream, this was not a nightmare, this was actually happening. She was going to die. Footsteps and voices were heard coming up the stairs outside. Faith wet herself and broke down as the door opened.

Aaban strode in, each footstep as loud as a bomb until he reached the centre where he stood and surveyed the room. Three other large men entered the room and took up position by the window, casting shadows inwards, faces emotionless. Aaban carried a large smile of anticipation as if he had just entered an amusement park and was trying to decide which treat to excitedly indulge in first. He rubbed his hands together.

"Good morning my sheep, are we ready to tell the world today of your mistakes and untruths? Who wants to begin? Allow us to get the equipment set up and then you can be recorded speaking about how you have lived your lives imposing your false beliefs onto others. Shame on you all. And I, I shall be seen as God's righteous hero, communicating the truth and cleansing the liars and tricksters from the world." His face transformed into a sneer. "On a personal note, I am disgusted by your arrogant beliefs and assumptions. It is my God that you can feel inside you. Mine. I bet you feel like fools now that I have shown you the error of your convictions."

A weak voice reached out from one of the circle of captives. Father Emmanuel, the first to be captured and more worse for wear than the others, came forth with a final attempt at negotiation.

"No matter what we believed before, none of us can deny that now we all must share the same higher power now, am I right? So.. if it is your God that we can feel inside of us, then it must be our God now too." He shifted nervously in his chair, uncertain of how his shaky outburst might be taken.

Aaban smiled and raised his hands in the air as if about to give an invisible being a hug. He walked over to the man who dared speak and slowly put his hands around his neck. The young man turned his head to the side and began hyperventilating, chest puffing in and out so rapidly that Faith thought that he may suffer a heart attack then and there.

And then Aaban kissed the man on the cheek and released his grip, returning to the centre of the room leaving the man gasping for breath.

"My friend you are correct, correct indeed! I am glad you can see the truth now. This feeling, this feeling of joy and wonder, warmth and piety that you now have had within you for some days now has been bestowed upon each and every one of you by the same ancient being that I have devoted myself to for my entire life."

He closed his eyes and lookup at the sky. The sun was now up and casting a warm golden aura around him and he was revelling in the sensation of actually channelling the words and thoughts of God. At this moment, he *was* God. The sensation was abruptly broken and the moment spoiled by the same young man.

"So you are in a room of men who share the same God as you, and yet you still want to kill them? Surely that does not make sense to you?" He was pleading for Aaban to see reason and understand. "We are one of you and you are one of us. You cannot kill a man in the name of your God when that man lives in the name of your same God."

The words were spoken meekly and pleadingly, but with them they carried the weight of a thousand worlds and from the reaction in the room it seemed to the captives that those few words with infallible logic could be their salvation. Aaban nodded his head in agreement, as if acknowledging the point was a fair one.

"Yes, yes, what you say is true, but I am not concerned with the current state of affairs, I am teaching you a lesson for your previous unforgivable wrongdoings. We may have the same God at this present moment, but only a few days ago we did not. And even yesterday you considered the Lord now inside all of us to be your own modified and watered down Gods and were lying to your followers about this. This is the reason why you are here."

"But how do you think God will feel about what you are doing to us, God's own people? There is no way this could be endorsed. Admit it, you just want to kill us, you are a monster that cannot even see logic and reason. Nothing could change your mind. You are acting with no rationality and are the least pious one of us in this room."

"Enough! My mind is made up. You, untie the talkative one and bring him here. He has volunteered to be first." He spoke his directions angrily to one of the large men by the window who slowly lurched over to the petrified Father Emmanuel and after several attempts managed to loosen his restraints and dragged him to a corner of the room in front of the camera perched on a tripod.

"And bring the journalist here too. I have a script for her to read to the camera, do you think you can do that? I suggest you say you can. I also have a script for you, my talkative man, but I bet you don't feel so talkative now do you?"

Faith was roughly untied and she rubbed her aching bruised and bleeding wrists. "Why can't you just be happy that this has taken place? A world-shaping event like this happens and you react like a savage fanatic? You are not my judge and jury."
Aaban ignored her words. "Let us begin."

Wed 23 Sept 1959 **6:15am**
Jacob & Company Arrives

It was as cold as an eskimo's refrigerator and her nose was absolutely freezing but Mary could sense a warm presence on either side of her providing a comforting source of heat, one of which also flamed an internal fire of a different kind. She had fallen asleep last night on a large toasty rock that had absorbed the energy of the day's sun and conveniently had natural contours that her body fit snugly into. On either side of her were huddled Zach and Jacob who must have been terribly uncomfortable in comparison but seemed to still be sleeping soundly.

Sleeping arrangements had been awkwardly made the previous night and she was nervously uncertain about the suggestion of staying close together to share body heat out in the open air and when it came to the crunch it took her a long time to eventually relax and succumb to slumber.

This morning however, she felt extremely comfortable and the presence of a man next to her offered a sense of protection and fulfilled a basic human need that she thought she may never have experienced again.

She liked it, and instead of getting up and readying herself for the day now that dawn had broken, she decided to close her eyes again and nestled a little more snugly into the man next to her.

Never in a million years would she have taken up such a random offer from a group of strange people to go on such a fantastic adventure with a medium to low probability of success at best, but there was something so innocent and kind about this man Jacob, she knew he genuinely only had her best interests at heart.

The poor man carried such a burden of guilt that Mary didn't know how he had not broken. He appeared to be held together by the need to win approval from his daughter, which as a mother she could completely understand, even though from what she could see as an outsider, Ava was unfairly still punishing her father and for some reason he was still allowing her to, although his retaliatory outburst yesterday at her seemed to break new ground.

Hearing a yawn coming from next to her, Zach had awoken and finding himself in unfamiliar surroundings had gripped onto her with panic. She turned and reassured him, stroking his hair until he calmed down.

Getting up, it wasn't long before the others were also up and stretching out their stiff necks and putting their shoes on, then rummaging through the bags of supplies looking for the best meal to start the day.

"Morning!" Jacob's smile seemed warmer than the morning sun and Mary smiled back, more of a secret smile to herself as she wondered what Jacob would think if he was aware of her thoughts earlier on while he was still sleeping.

It wasn't long before everybody had eaten and was ready for the walk ahead, uncertain of just how far that might be. Everything was a bit up in the air but the end game spurred them on and provided them with the energy to continue the march, even with the unwelcome information provided by Rosalind the previous day.

Mary sidled up to Jacob, whom she noticed walked a little taller as he noticed her pull up alongside, and subtly swept his hair away from his face. She noticed he had some sleep creases on his cheek and her first instinct was to make fun of it, but she was not sure he possessed the self-esteem to accept that type of joke with good humour.

"This is quite the spontaneous holiday isn't it?" she started the conversation on a positive note, somewhat trying to convince herself that this was an elective voyage of pleasure. "Nothing like a good hiking adventure to make you feel at one with nature," she said, trying to while away the time.

"Well it's not the streets of Paris, but yes, I never thought of it as a mini-vacation. In my mind it's been more of a mission that needs to be accomplished than anything." Jacob said, reflecting the thoughts she was attempting to steer away from.

"Oh, have you been to Paris then? I imagine this would not be quite the same. I guess I can imagine that this is just the French countryside, although there would be more vineyards than this and some Frenchies hovering about. How about I tie a string of onions around your neck and you grow a quick twirly moustache just to make the illusion a little more real?" They both laughed as she finished her sentence with a terrible French accent.

"And don't forget ze beret and accordion," Jacob said in an equally bad accent. He sighed and looked dreamily into the sky. "But to answer your question, no, I have not been to Paris. In fact, this is about as far away from home that I have ever been. Sad isn't it? Anyhow, I wonder if they call French Onion Soup just plain Onion Soup over there, what do you think?"

She laughed. "I think I shall have to go and find out for myself! The food, the wine, those mysteriously attractive French men.." She noticed Jacob's smile disappeared at this comment and she regretted the words even though she had not said anything wrong. "Well, there you go, another thing in common, we've both never been to Paris."

"Never been to Paris, cheers to that. How do they say cheers?" He frowned, trying to remember words that may or may not be inside his head somewhere.

"I think they say 'Cheers o-haw-hee-haw'," she said once again in a terrible accent. They both cracked up laughing in a way that they both hadn't for a long time and then continued on with content smiles on their faces until a voice rang out over the sound of footsteps.

"Well hello there!" A familiar female voice shouted out from ahead of them. Mary turned and squinted to see what was going on in the distance. "Who's ..?" but as soon as she opened her mouth she knew who the owner of the voice was and her eyes widened with excitement. A puffing and panting Indian girl appeared.

"Ishara, you're back! What the..." Gabe ran over to welcome the returned scout first, and soon everybody crowded around her eagerly to hear the news.

"Did you find the place?" "Is it close?" "What IS there, come on!" Mary even grabbed Ishara's arms and shook her a little bit with a sense of urgency, frustrated that she wasn't immediately forthcoming with any news within the first three seconds of her arrival.

The rowdy group calmed down quite quickly as they noticed that Ishara did not have the smiling, excited demeanour that they expected and Mary sensed that something was wrong and some bad news was about to break. It had been wishful thinking of course, and Mary was secretly disappointed in herself for allowing herself to believe and to invest hope in this wild goose chase. She felt sick inside.

They provided Ishara with some space and she backed away slowly, looking at the ground and trying to piece together some words in as kind a way as possible to inform them of the outcome of her travels. Stepping up onto a rock, she wavered a little as she lost her balance, righted herself and began to relate her tale down to the group in dot point form to satisfy their impatience.

"Hi everyone, good to see you all again. So yes, I am back, and yes I found the place that Gabe told us about. Yes, I believe there are extraordinary events happening there that may be attributed to some sort of divine power. No I don't think we will have any chance of being able to get access to use these powers. We may as well just turn around and head back and forget this ever happened. It will just be easier, physically and emotionally so please trust me." And with that, she stepped down from the rock and walked past the group in the direction that they came.

"What? No explanation? You better tell us what happened to you and why you think this. Don't you dare go anywhere until you darn well give us the full story, okay?" Mary stepped forward and her tone meant business. "We already had one person telling us that the place wasn't worth visiting and it didn't deter us one bit. So now we hear it from somebody else that it's not what we thought and we shouldn't go, but you are also saying that it seems there most likely are miracles happening, whereas the last lot told us the miracles were exhausted. Now I want to know what you saw. Out with it." Mary had a face on that clearly indicated that she would not stand for any more dilly-dallying.

"Fine, fine. I arrived at the place yesterday, and how did I know it was the place? Because there were about two hundred people waiting impatiently there, and let me tell you it was not a pleasant or miraculous environment. These people were desperate, anxious, greedy, pushy, literally the worst of the worst that human beings have to offer. One perfectly healthy woman I spoke to said she was there because she wanted help to win the lottery. Seriously? Also, there are people camping there, which makes me think that they have been there a while, and why is that? I thought to myself, are they not being allowed in to wherever it is to be exposed to the miracles, or do the miracles just plain not exist? There really was no indication as to how it all worked, what you had to do, whose property it was, anything. But then after a bit more walking about, I see a couple of characters who are spruiking that they have been healed or fixed in some amazing way and they have like twenty people surrounding them like they are cult leaders, so it all COULD potentially be real but there must be a wait or an invisible queue of some sort, and trust me it feels like everybody is everybody else's competition for a spot, it feels dangerous. Dog eat dog. It's raw. It's survival." Ishara took a breath, and the crowd gathered in close once again, still left in the dark as to whether or not there was hope for them.

"Well I'm still taking Simon, whether you lot come with me or not," Gabe said, grabbing his nephew by the hand. "The girl that told me about this, Martine, would never have lied to me or tried to send me on a wild goose chase, no way, not when it comes to Simon. I trust her one hundred percent. So who is with me?"

He shot a quick, worried glance towards Zach before leading Simon down the road, his worry that time may be running out quite visible. The others followed, having too much to gain and not that much to lose.

Ishara hopped down off the rock and followed behind the group begrudgingly, a heavy frown on her face and her blood boiling, but not because her companions were still committed to seeking answers and hope, it was something else creeping up on her that felt wrong.

At first she acknowledged that her initial attraction to Gabe and unspoken competition for his affections with Ava was one of the juvenile reasons she wanted to sabotage any chance Ava had of accomplishing her personal mission. What kind of friend thinks those things about another friend, and their best friend at that? She despised herself for letting superficial feelings get the better of her. But the guilt that was affecting her at the moment was also of another type.

Dreams were possibly about to come true. Jacob and his daughter. Mary and her son. Gabe and his nephew. All with a heavier weight on their shoulders than most, and an opportunity to shrug that weight off. Ishara had no dreams, because when she thought about it, all of her dreams were true already. She had nothing to desire, needed nothing fixed. She had everything, always did and most likely always would.

Looking at Jacob's love for Ava, Mary's love for Zach, Gabe's love for Simon, how fair was it that they all suffered and struggled day by day? It wasn't fair at all, and Ishara felt ashamed that she had been trying to hold back these people who had it tough and truly deserved something better in life.

Who was she, somebody who had been gifted with everything, to stop others from achieving their dreams too, especially dreams that were significantly more meaningful than hers ever could be.

"Hey guys, wait for me!" Ishara shuffled quickly up the road, eventually caught up to Ava and gave her a big kiss before pushing her along playfully in her wheelchair. "We are really close now, beautiful girl," she whispered in her best friend's ear.

It wasn't long before they could hear a commotion, a high pitched tangle of voices rising up over the trees hitting them with brutal force. Argumentative tones were drowned out by crying, which were in turn drowned out by yelling. Some sort of conflict was escalating and they were about to walk straight into the middle of it.

The group walked for about half a minute more and were met with an uncomfortable scene resembling that from a war documentary. Scattered wide across the front yard of a large wooden house that had been badly neglected and in desperate need of some paint as a bare minimum, a sea of ineffective makeshift tents had been constructed and occupied by a swarm of cold, hungry people with desperation branded on their faces.

There were those who seemed to be content to lie there and wait for something to happen, while others who maybe had just arrived and had a little more energy and enthusiasm were calling out and knocking tentatively upon the house in the attempt to persuade whoever was inside to let them in.

The dilapidated house appeared as perfectly normal as a run down and isolated place could be in every way except for the fact that all the windows were boarded up and barbed wire had been painstakingly curled around the structure such that it looked like a huge metallic thornbush or even worse, a house of horrors where unspeakable inhuman activities might occur, certainly not miracles. It was almost as if the house had the ability to suck the will right out of a soul just by an observer standing close to it. This was no holy place.

"What on earth…." Mary's words reflected the group's thoughts as a whole. "This.. isn't right. We shouldn't have come." Her voice sounded panicked, and given what they were witnessing around them, the panic was catching on with the others very quickly.

"No, no. This is the place, and there have to be miracles. Martine told me and I believe her." Gabe kept his voice under control as much as he could but he couldn't hide a slight waver that indicated he was less certain than the words coming out of his mouth suggested.

As a group they found a place to sit down, as far away from the others as they could. Being able to take the load off their feet was welcome, and for the next half an hour they ate and replenished themselves. None of them had any idea how long they might stay there for before there was any sign that they were not there in vain.

Mary had sat uncomfortably cross-legged opposite Jacob and as she passed him a box of biscuits she noticed that he had the look in his eyes of somebody who had seen a ghost. He was staring back over her shoulder with his mouth agape and so Mary turned around to witness a flowing red dress entering the camp. She looked back at Jacob who looked back at her with a confused look on his face that would have been more comical if she too didn't have the same look on her face.

Rosalind in her distinctive red dress strutted forward between the makeshift tents with her eyes darting about, absorbing the camp and taking in everything around her until they inevitably rested on the group she had encountered earlier, causing her to stop in her tracks. Her lumbering son trundled into her and snapped out of his daze. Questioning why his mother had stopped walking, he spied Ishara and ran towards her, stepping over a couple of people and knocking a tent or two down along the way.

"Ishara! Ishara! Hi! Hi! Ishara! Hi!" He waved like a child at her as she shrank back into herself with horror, scrunching her face up as she knew what was about to unfold.

"Wait, what the hell is going on? How do you know each other?" Ava asked Ishara suspiciously who couldn't bring herself to look at her friend.

"And why are you here Rosalind, if you had already been here and the miracles had dried up?" Jacob snarled. The atmosphere was as tense as a thunderstorm about to hit.

Rosalind sported a sheepish look on her face as if she had just been caught shoplifting, but then she quickly realised that she had no accountability to these people and in any case wouldn't be the one who was about to be put on trial. She addressed her recently acquired acquaintances.

"Well, well, well, it looks like the cat has truly jumped right out of the bag," she drawled. "Well uh, I ain't got nothing to hide from y'all, plus I already got my fifty dollars here from the young lady there so I'm still up on the situation." She plucked a note out of her purse and stretched it out in her fingers in front for all to see before sliding it back inside and then winked at the mortified Ishara.

"What did you give her money for? And why did neither of you tell us you had met? This is the second time today I am demanding answers from you Ishara and let me tell you I am raging right now." Mary looked like she was having trouble keeping her small frame back from tearing Ishara apart. Rosalind answered on Ishara's behalf.

"Well this exotic one here paid me fifty dollars to dissuade y'all from coming here. Sounds like you ain't the nicest of people from what she says. Anyhow, all the best sorting out your little differences, I'm off to get myself a miracle for my boy here," Rosalind replied before casually walking off with her son in tow, a streak of red fading into the distance.

Ishara was absolutely horrified at being caught out at doing something for reasons that now seemed to belong to another time, another place. "Look, I'm not going to explain to you why I did what I did, yes there were reasons I didn't want you to make it here but let me say I regret it and I am truly sorry and will make it up to you any way I can." Her tone was that of genuine regret but Ava wasn't buying it. She was not in the mood to be betrayed by her best friend, especially if they were for the reasons she suspected they might be.

"We don't care about your 'sorry'. You are now dead to us, dead to me and you can go away, I don't care how long you think we have been friends for. Unforgivable. I never want to see you again, got it?" Ava spat out her piece and then spun her wheelchair around violently so that her back was to Ishara.

"I completely understand, and I don't blame you. Look, I'm going to stay close even though I know I'm not wanted, I don't know anybody here and don't feel safe. Please don't begrudge me that. Once again, I'm sorry and I hope you can forgive me." She sat down a few metres away from the group who instantly ignored her and turned to each other to attempt to figure out what their options were now.

"Okay, so let's think," Jacob said, already trying to figure out next steps. He was so close to redemption in his daughter's eyes, Ishara was already forgotten.

"What's there to think about?" Ava shouted out, contributing to the already aggressive atmosphere the place was oozing. "I bet that 'thinking' is what everybody else here is doing, and where is that getting them? We will be a pile of skeletons sitting here soon, but oh, at least we are thinking."

"Well, I was thinking, everybody here is either just sitting around or circling that place. What is it that we have that the others don't have, that we can use?" He looked around the group as if the answer should be obvious. He stood up tall to declare his idea. "We have.. a name."

"Okay genius. Tell us more," Ava said sarcastically.

"No wait, I think he may have something there," Gabe said, catching on.

Jacob continued to expand on his idea. "There is a person or people inside that house, right? And if you were in there, would you dare open your door to a group of desperate aggressive maniacs? No way. You would probably be petrified. So what would you want to hear if you were surrounded by a pretty scary bunch of people who wanted to invade your house?" He waited for an answer, then gave up waiting as he stared at blank faces.

"You want to hear the voice of somebody out there who you know is normal and is not a threat. At the very least, you would want to know that there was somebody out there who knew somebody that you know. A safe, common connection." The group took a moment to compute the sentence just spoken and it eventually clicked.

"Martine." Gabe finished off the thought process.

"It might sound crazy but I think we should go and mention Martine's name around the windows of the house, quietly, so that the others don't hear and catch on, and hope that whoever is inside puts two and two together and realises we aren't one of the regular crazies out here and lets us in. If anybody has a better idea please let me know, because that's all I have."

"I think it is as close to a good idea that we could come up with," Mary said, a look of admiration once again in her eyes directed at Jacob, and once again he blushed and stared at the ground.

"Well I think that I should be the one to go around," Gabe said. They might ask questions or something and I at least know Martine. But stay close."

The group's response was to push him towards the house, and they closely followed, excitement levels once again reinstated to maximum. They did not notice, but Ishara followed closely behind.

Gabe tiptoed towards the house, then realised that there was absolutely no point in doing so and walked up to the first boarded up window to the left of the front door. The pieces of wood had been nailed to the frame of the house by somebody who really did not want anybody to get in. There were hundreds of nails hastily hammered in, some all the way, others with an inch to go or so, rusted and bent. Barbed wire had been coiled in one long spiky garnish around the house. Nobody was getting in. Or out.

"Please, we know Martine. We know Martine." Gabe half-whispered into a gap between two rotting pieces of wood and rapped gently. Nothing.

"They have a gun inside you know, so I would be pretty careful about hovering around them windows like that, why else do you think all these folk are mostly staying away? My particular recommendation is to not go near the front door if you want to keep your head, if you know what I mean," a dishevelled woman with grass in her blonde hair and no shoes on said before continuing to knock pointlessly on one of the poles holding up a small verandah.

Gabe moved on to the next window, around the left side of the house, more out of view this time with nobody else around except for his companions who still kept a bit of distance. "Please, we know Martine, you know, Martine? She told us about this place." Still nothing.

"Hello, we know somebody is in there and can hear us. I know somebody you know. Martine. French-Canadian girl. She told us to come here. We are sane and not looking for trouble, just looking for help that's all." Silence.

Listening carefully for any signs of life inside, Gabe faintly heard something like the sound of a chair being moved out of the way and he pushed on, rapping a little louder.

"Hello, my name is Gabe and I am a friend of Martine. You have nothing to fear from me or my friends. We just heard about your house from her and thought it could help us. Please let us in."

A deep, gruff voice emerged from behind the wooden boards, barely audible. "Go to the front door."

Gabe's eyes opened wide and he turned to the others, who instantly saw from the look on his face that he had met with success. He half-whispered, half gesticulated, "I have to go to the front door," and walked back around to the front of the house, resuming his tip-toeing. He gave the door a single knock, and said "Hi, it's me here. We just spoke."

The unmistakeable click of a shotgun being cocked echoed as loud as an actual gunshot itself through the air, accompanied by an even louder voice carrying a terrifying message.

"Get the hell away from my property or I will fill you so full of lead you will be using your fingers as pencils for the rest of your short life! Beat it! I will give you to the count of five and then I'm unloading one round right through this door."

Every single person in the vicinity who had made the trek to the property with an ounce of hope in their veins about having any sort of miracle granted now accepted that any hope there may have been was dead after hearing the threatening outburst. All eyes were fixed on Gabe at the front door, wondering morbidly if they were about to witness somebody being shot, whilst the man himself had frozen to the spot as the countdown began.

"One.." was shouted loudly and clearly through the door for all to hear. And then, just as Gabe was about to turn tail and flee he heard the voice again, hushed.

"Meet me at the back door in one minute after I finish counting. Now run."

Gabe did not need to be told again. He fled as if the devil were on his heels and bolted through the camp, jumping over numerous reclining bodies who were keenly watching the scene unfold as the voice behind the door continued to count. People began to stand up and run in all directions, fearing that they may potentially be in the line of fire.

"Two…."

"Three…"

"Four….."

Bang.

A small metal flap set in the door for the purpose of slipping mail inside lifted and the end of a shotgun barrel peeked out and pointed upwards as it sounded off, shooting its deadly payload into the air with a deafening roar before the count was up.

"Five.."

Gabe continued to sprint around behind the camp out of sight and back to the side of the house where the others were still gathered. "Boo!" he wheezed, scaring the skin out of every one of them who couldn't see whether he had been standing in the wrong place at the wrong time just now as the shot rang out. Ava wheeled over and leaned out to give him as big a hug as she could without falling out of her chair. "How? What? We heard.." she struggled to get words out.

"Quick, we have to get the back door, now while everybody is distracted." Gabe's voice communicated the urgency of whatever situation it was that they were now in and they made haste to the rear of the strange fortress.

He made his way to the back door and knocked again with trepidation, hoping that no more shotguns would threaten to make an example of him.

"How can we even get in? There is barbed wire wrapped around this whole house?" Gabe quickly surveyed the whole back of the house before being convinced there could only be a secret tunnel to allow entry and exit from the building.

There was a haunting silence washing over them that wasn't natural. The shotgun blast had scared all the birds away and the loudest sound to be heard was that of their hearts beating inside their chest. The dull thud of footsteps approached the door.

"Did the gunshot scare everybody away? Are you alone? I still have my gun you know, and enough ammo to blast away hundreds of you crazies," the voice asked through the door. Gabe looked around to double check there were no unfamiliar faces with them and reassured the faceless voice that it was safe to do whatever it was that was about to take place.

The back door creaked inwards, the coiled barbed wire detaching as if by magic and bending inwards with the door. A fifty year old or so short man with long greying hair and more than a few days' worth of stubble greeted them with a grubby index finger on his shotgun trigger. He smelled like he had not had a bath or shower for days, and it appeared that he had overcompensated for this by finding the time and forethought to indulge in too much cheap cologne before meeting with his guests.

"You see, I wrapped this whole place in that there wire to stop that lot out there trying to get into my bathroom, and then cut each line of wire right carefully at the door so you can barely notice it, and it opens right up, easy."

He looked pleased as punch with himself and had a large welcoming smile on his face which the very next second turned as black as night, and even though of shorter stature he seemed to loom over them as everybody made steps to enter the house. He outstretched his arm and pushed Gabe in the chest, shoving him back outside the doorway. He eyed the group suspiciously.

"Now let's talk business, which of you has got food for me, and money?" He pointed the gun at each of their faces one by one and they all threw their hands up in the air in turn. More than happy to comply with whatever demands the man may make, Mary and Jacob offered forward the bags of supplies that they had brought and handed them over to the man who greedily snatched them away.

"I'm hungry enough to eat my own arm, we don't have much food left in here so I'll kindly take all you got."

Keeping his finger on the trigger and gun pointed at them, he clumsily put the bags on the ground in front of him, rummaged through them with his other hand and pulled out an apple which he stuffed into his mouth with a crunch. Chewing loudly, he half-finished the apple and threw the core into the bushes behind them.

"Right, now give me your money. Money!" This was said with substantial menace and after a few seconds without a reply he spoke again. "No money? Martine or no Martine, you get no miracles today my friends." He pulled the bags of food inside and made as if to close the door in their faces.

"Wait!" A female voice behind them pleaded. Gabe was bumped out of the way as Ishara stepped forward through them all and fronted up to the man, putting her foot in the doorway confidently and attracting a gun to her face for her trouble.

"I have money. Lots of it. My family is very wealthy and I can get you whatever you need. Just let us in." Ishara made eye contact with Ava and in that split second the girls' friendship from day one flashed between them and once again they were two little girls who would do anything for each other. For a second, all was close to being forgiven between the two before Ava put on her scowl once more, though Ishara could see thanks in her eyes and in response she threw a wink over to her old friend before confronting the man.

"How much do you have on you?" The man asked curiously, mulling over in his head how these negotiations should go. He had never had much money, never had it easy, and never had he possessed anything of quality or luxury. Once, just once in his life he would like to know what that feeling was that other people seemed to enjoy so much.

"How much do you want? Just name it and I am sure it can be done. I don't have much on me now but I can get it." Ishara smiled nervously, bracing to hear the extortionate figure proposed to her.

The man seemed taken aback at how easy this was going to be, and had not finished mulling over in his head what might be an acceptable number so he began to talk out loud to himself.

"So there be a lot of you wanting something from me, and uh, it's gonna cost you. Some uh, some hundreds, yep, some uh, hundreds." He looked up in the air as if doing some maths, trying to decide what number might be too high for them such that they walked away and he received nothing, and what was too low, so much so that his kind nature was being taken advantage of.

"Some hundreds, being seven of you, so seven hundred dollars. Cash." That was the perfect number and should squeeze them enough but not too much. What was the first thing he would buy with the money? He got excited and subconsciously began to hop on the spot with anticipation.

"So seven miracles, seven hundred dollars?" Ishara confirmed. "One hundred dollars per miracle, if they even exist here?" She raised a single eyebrow towards the man.

The man once again looked up in the sky to do some calculations. "Yes indeedy, I can assure you that they do exist and that makes one hundred per miracle. Cash. Now."

"Hang on, hang on, hold up there. Only three of us are wanting miracles, so that will only make it three hundred dollars, according to your pricing that we both just agreed upon, right?" Ishara was cunning and grew up in a family that was always wheeling and bargaining for a better deal. She had the seven hundred dollars covered easily, that number was about ten times less than what she was expecting, but why pay that when you can pay less than half as much?

The man crumbled, all excitement drained from his body instantly as he realised his own words had been used against him. He instantly capitulated without even a counteroffer and agreed, a defeated man.

"Okay, I suppose a deal is a deal. Mom won't be happy though," he said dejectedly.

Ishara rifled through her purse and much to everybody's surprise pulled out some crisp notes to hand to the man whose heart broke when he saw that there were many more notes still remaining in there, realising that his list of future luxury purchases could have been a lot longer. He snatched the notes disappointedly but admired their crispness as he stuffed them into his back pocket, then opened the door wide and ushered them inside, latching a series of bolts and clicking locks shut behind them.

The single light in the living room cast an insufficient glow which flickered around the interior, highlighting many dusty surfaces and an assortment of strange ornaments, ranging from the taxidermy of various unidentifiable creatures to a bell collection consisting of around thirty bells perched on a mantelpiece. The man noticed Zach examining the collection, and as if slightly embarrassed by them, he qualified their existence with "Those bells are my moms, they aren't mine no way."

The place was a hoarder's delight and the company spread throughout the living room, picking up objects and examining them, putting them back whilst the man quickly followed behind them as best he could and moved everything back to their exact place.

"My-my mom doesn't like her treasures to be touched. Just look only please," he said as he gently nudged Simon away from a particularly delicate looking lamp in the shape of a dog. After everybody had finished with their own personal investigation of the plethora of curiosities, they gathered once again to discuss the elephant in the strange room.

"So we really are in…" Jacob began before being cut off.
"My name is 'Thew," he began in a low deep voice. "I live here with my mom, she is in the bedroom at the moment. I had to keep her there. She calls me 'Thew. She says all the time 'Hey, my 'Thew.' You know, so I'm her 'little 'Thew." He spoke as if recollecting happy times past that no longer existed.

"So 'Thew, we really are in.." Jacob tried to get the conversation back on track, mentally noting that they had really met some unique characters in the last couple of days.

"Why are you all here anyway? Do you want to be fixed too? Three of you only. Which three?" He pointed at each one of them as if playing a guessing game. He put his shotgun down in a dark corner of the room and pointed his index finger at Ava. "You are one aren't you? Oh yes you in the chair certainly are. And you are number two." He turned towards Simon who was half leaning on his crutches, half leaning on Gabe. "And who is the third one of you? Is it you?" He looked at Ishara accusingly who threw her hands up in the air as if removing herself from any accusations and she said "Nope, you got the wrong person. I'm fine. It's the little guy over there," nodding over in Zach's direction.

"Oh so it's all the littler ones. That makes me happy. The minds of adults are tainted, corrupted, greedy and impure, they don't want honourable innocent things, only things that serve their own self-interest. Don't you?" he said staring in turn at the adults in the room.

He walked over towards an uncomfortable looking sofa and plonked himself down on the armrest, half squatting, half standing, but still it looked more accommodating than the couch itself.

"Things started getting a little strange a few days ago, you know when we all blacked out and got that little injection inside of us with all this information we never really knew for sure about before. It really blew us away because you know, God and everything. So I wake up from being passed out and I can smell I've got sick on me and so I go to take a shower. I do all the usual things you know, I get undressed, jump in, turn the water on, you don't need all the details, but anyway, I clean myself and I get out again, reach for the towel and then there it is. Strange symbol on my mirror made out of steam or something, just staring at me. And I'm pretty sure it weren't there before." He scratched his chin as if trying to reconfirm in his mind the details as if they were a complex physics formula.

"Wait, how is it that you are not sure that the symbol on your mirror wasn't there before. I mean, had you ever seen it before when you had a shower or not? Surely a simple thing to notice?" Jacob had had enough of 'Thew's questionable story. At least it was more original than seeing the face of Jesus in a piece of toast. "Well?" He probed for a simple, sensible rational answer from the confused man.

"Well I'm just not sure about that. Was it there before? I just don't know. Before that shower, I had no idea what the mirror was like. I've been blind since the age of seven."

Wed 23 Sept 1959   7:45am
Ira's Warehouse Escalates

Faith typed away frantically, not wanting to awaken the wrath of Maxwell by delivering the most important story of her career post the deadline he had set. She thrived on the adrenaline, gathering her thoughts and notes into a logical order to ensure she was communicating the key pieces she wanted to inform the readers about. The hardest part of what she did was breaking down complex concepts into easy to digest language for the layman. Why couldn't the general population just be a little bit more intelligent? It would make her job so much easier, but alas.

The office was now nearly completely empty and any attempt to guess the time would be a guess in vain although she didn't really care about working late. She felt that it was very rare that people ended up in careers that they truly loved and utilised their strengths. To her, working late was simply an opportunity to do more of what she enjoyed.

Take Hal from accounts for example. The first reason he could find to detach himself from the responsibility of employment and he was fleeing the scene, whereas Faith felt that wild horses would have to drag her away from her typewriter. And she told herself that no matter where she worked, Maxwell or no Maxwell, as long as she was writing meaningful articles she was in her element.

She heard footsteps approaching from behind her and she felt warm breath on the back of her neck that gave her goosebumps. Was the scenario with her boss that she had always imagined in her mind about to happen? What should she do?

"My darling, it is your turn now." A hot flush overcame her and she shuddered. After so much skipping around the issue it seemed like there was no ambiguity now. She sighed and waited for nature to take its course, tilting her head back and exposing her neck as a sign that she was not going to resist whatever came next.

Suddenly her hair was yanked with force and with a yelp of pain she was transported from her happy place and rematerialized back into the putrid warehouse, where the evil reality of all that was happening solidified.

"My darling, it is your turn now. You have much to say for me." Aaban whispered the words again in her ear before walking away and two burly men stood her up and walked her over to the window.

Looking around her, aside from the lurking cronies belonging to Aaban who remained as relaxed as if they were having a picnic at the park, the remainder had elevated to an echelon of fear that exceeded any scale previously attained in any story that Faith had ever covered, no matter how sickening.

Atrocity upon horrific atrocity would soon be committed with a quiet calm and captured on camera with Faith acting as the conduit between the television screen and the reality of what was taking place. Like a procession, each and every one of the bound men in the room would be led to the window, read a prepared statement, their final words. The first man that Aaban selected began to read the script placed in front of him.

"There comes a time when the devout, there comes a time when the pious, there comes a time when the faithful realise that they have been deceived by the false shepherds of their flock. This deception is only revealed to the misguided followers upon their death, when the promises of light and glory that they wait to embrace do not come to bear, and it is too late to atone and turn to the true Lord. Aaban has torn off the blindfold of lies that prevented me from seeing that I have taken the incorrect path and accepted and shared a false truth, and now that my vision has been restored I can see the imposters and I turn my back on them. Aaban has shown me the way. He has shown me the true Lord and I thank him, though it is too late for me. Today is my day of confession as a shepherd of falsehoods. Today is my day of trial. And today is my day of punishment." After barely being able to enunciate the final sentence the man fell to his knees, knowing that now there was nothing more to be done before his final moment arrived, unnaturally and cruelly.

Faith could barely keep it together as she was stood in front of the camera by the window and a microphone forced into one hand, and a piece of paper in the other containing the few words that she had been commanded to speak.

"Faith from the Tribune here." Her voice wavered and broke when she read the script, her survival instincts on full alert and barely allowing her to perform an act as simple as reading, each word spoken a word closer to being her last. The paper shook like she was suffering from hypothermia but she managed to issue the words.

"Faith from the Tribune here. You have just heard Father Emmanuel of St. Paul's admission of guilt for the unforgivable crime of deceiving his followers and claiming his false God as being the true God. Aaban will act as the hand of the true Lord and dispense justice as a faithful servant, restoring order and demonstrating the foolishness and fate of any man who spreads the word of false idols." The words were simple, brief, and after the recital Faith turned away and crouched to the ground, blocking her ears before the individual prayers being murmured by the men stopped and the choked, stifled cries would soon begin.

Aaban stood before Faith and stared into her eyes, relishing the fear he saw and the feeling of power to grant life or death that he possessed. This time he would not be granting life.

Wed 23 Sept 1959 *7:45am*
Jacob & Company, The House

The room remained silent for an insufferable period. It is difficult to speak when you have a thousand things that you want to say. So it was all true, every word, every rumour. The risks, the helicopter flight, the difficult cross country trek, it was all worth it. Everything would be made right. Today, six lives would change forever.

"So my mom goes and tells a bunch of people about what happened here to me and as you can see, word spread pretty quickly which is why I have locked her in her bedroom. Soon we had some pretty pushy people trying to barge the door down and we had to take some drastic measures to protect ourselves. We don't have a fence or anything so I wrapped this whole house from top to bottom with wire and boarded everything shut. Do you know how bright the sunlight is for somebody who has not seen it for forty something years? And it's ironic that with my new eyes working I'm now trapped inside this dark, boarded up house with nothing to see except for my mom's treasure. And my mom. Boy she looks older than when I saw her last. Funny how the world works huh. To be re-gifted something and then denied the opportunity to really use it. You lot are actually a relief, something new for my eyes to look at." He waved his hands in front of his eyes and shrugged his shoulders with resignation.

"Um, my take away from what you just said is that your mom is locked in her bedroom? I don't think that is okay and I am not sure how worried I should be right now," Ishara said, standing up. "I think we should get her out shouldn't we? I mean, it seems like a lot of people know about this place now, the damage is done so there is no need to prevent her from spreading the word to others by locking her up. Plus, it's very creepy. Reminds me of this book I just read about a deranged guy and his mom who run a motel off a disused highway and bad things happen. It disturbed me and it feels like I'm in that book right now," she shuddered at the thought of the demented work of fiction playing out in reality.

Jacob decided it was time to get things moving along. They were all so close now. He was so close to having his daughter back, the pain of the past written over, memories eventually to be lost in time. Also, he sensed he felt a little different inside but couldn't put his finger on what or why, but he felt a twinge of anxiety gnawing at him and he couldn't shake it.

"Ishara, I'm sure his mom is fine, she is just in the bedroom." Turning to the haggard man who harboured the means to transform all of their lives, "Hey 'Thew can you tell us how the miracle happened in the bathroom? I'm very curious to know what to do, how to activate it. Is it as simple as just having a shower? Is just entering the bathroom enough? Was it the towel? Did you have to wash your eyes with water or something for your eyes to regain their function? So for example would Ava have to clean her legs? What?"

"Man, man, I don't know, I just had a regular old time in there. It's up to each of you all to figure it out for yourselves I guess. Or maybe one of you go in and then tell the others when you have worked it out. I don't know any details man, why me, why this house, it all just happened. Just go and hope that it all just happens for you too."

The group were led down a narrow corridor in a single file procession as if being marched towards some ancient ritual, the solemn atmosphere dissolved after being warned by 'Thew not to knock any picture frames off the wall along the way or his mom would be very angry. Ava's chair only barely fit and her swearing was audible as her fingers were mashed against the wall every so often as she pushed the chair along and it deviated slightly in direction.

There was a skylight about two thirds of the way down which allowed some light into the shadowy area, and as Mary passed under it she looked up to notice that there was a proliferation of dead spiders spread across the glass. She shuddered and kept walking with an uneasy sense of what the inside of the room they were about to visit might be like.

'Thew halted at the last door on the left and turned to face the group. "Well, this right here is it. Look, I know it's a weird setup and I don't know how it works, but it is what it is. So you better decide for yourselves who goes in first and do your thing. There's all you need in the cupboards inside I guess if you want to bathe or whatever. I'm going to sit back in the lounge. I hope you find what you are looking for, but let me say that you all look fine to me, even you in the chair. And I hope that means something because I have brand new eyes that aren't worn out and they still see the truth. Plenty of folks worse off than you in the world, I'm sure." And with that he pushed past them all, climbed over Ava's chair and disappeared, leaving behind a piquant trail of cologne.

Jacob exhaled slowly, trying to maintain a sense of calm even though he hadn't felt this nervous since before the birth of Ava. His mind tried to recap the past few days that led up to this moment, when hope surfaced and a doorway had become ajar, an exit now possible from the prison of his own mind in which he had been a captive for six years.

He put the pieces together. His daughter insisted on going to church, which lead to Gabe and learning of this place. His odd relationship with Mr Derby, without whom the journey would not have been possible. Ishara, who his daughter dragged along and eventually enabled them to buy their way into the game. All played their part in the series of events and coincidences that led to the here and now. It was meant to be.

And Mary? Jacob could only assume that she still had some part to play in this, a role that meant the story didn't end after this adventure was over. They were both the same, lonely characters with heartbreak following them, uncertainty ahead of them, wanting the author of their scripts to weave their tales together and bind two separate stories into one.

"Mary, I think you and Zach should go first," Gabe said. "Unless anybody else thinks otherwise?" Nobody put their hand up to disagree. "We will all get our turn. This is it. I can't believe it's actually happening. See you on the other side little Zach."

Jacob looked Mary in the eye and grabbed her hand, giving it a big squeeze which then turned into a hug. "This is the moment our lives change forever. Take care in there and good luck." He found it hard to release her but eventually relaxed his grip.

"That's very sweet of you. Here goes," she said as she put her hand on Zach's shoulder and directed him through the doorway.

The bathroom was a poorly chosen shade of green somewhat between that of somebody's backyard lawn and the colour of mould that had the privilege of thriving on a piece of bread for a few days too long. Mary decided that mould was the more fitting resemblance. Dewy cobwebs occupied the dank corners of the room, and it seemed like a twisted joke that the purpose of this filthy room was for people to walk out cleaner than when they went in.

Standing next to a tall, thin cupboard which had once been protected by some sort of paisley green, plastic stick-on veneer that was now peeling off was the vanity unit. Solid porcelain, hot and cold taps in need of a polish, and home to a multi-coloured piece of soap that was made up of the stuck together remnants of other pieces of old soap. Above this vanity unit was a mirror. The mirror.

Although the room didn't seem to have been used recently, a mist adhered to the silver surface as if a hot tap had only just been switched off, fine droplets gathering and forming on a discrete area. It created a shape which may or may not have been a symbol but as hard as Mary looked, she could not fully focus and define it. It didn't change, but it possessed the strangest property such that her vision seemed to slide over it, and the more she concentrated, the less its shape made sense to her.

Trying to peer behind it and view her own reflection, she seemed different, as if looking at a mirage of herself, lines slightly bending and disappearing before reappearing again. She looked away and knelt down next to Zach. This would be the last time she would speak to her boy as he was.

"My beautiful boy," in soft tones she whispered the same words of reassurance that she had uttered thousands of times for his comfort, but mainly for hers. His father had left them both and she wanted him to know that he meant everything to her and she wasn't going anywhere.

"We are going to get your father back, yes we are. When we are done here you will be just like every other little boy and your daddy will come home. He will come home to us and we will be a family again just like we used to be." She started welling up and laughed at how silly she was. Zach stared at her with a blank look, but Mary read something in it that may or may not have been there and compelled her to explain her tears. "I'm not sad baby, mommy is crying because she is happy," she said.

Imagining a future of summers where she would be the perfect mom and bring trays of soft drink from the kitchen outside to Zach and his friends when they came over to play in the back yard, to having conversations over the dinner table discussing how his day at school was, or watching Diah and Zach forming a close father and son bond that she could see develop and thrive was a life of normalcy she yearned for. It was all she had ever wanted.

He would be just like every other little boy out there. Only… she didn't want him to be just like every other little boy out there. She wanted her special boy. The son she had always known and loved. What would he be like when that which made him special was taken from him? How would he be affected? What if she didn't love him, and even worse, *what if one day he didn't need her anymore?* That scared her more than anything. It scared her even more than not having Diah back in her life.

Mary welled up again, this time they were real tears of sadness, and in that second her dream of Diah's return to her was released forever. She knew in her heart that she had lost him long ago and he would never come back, no matter whether Zach was better or not and so she had to just accept it once and for all, refusing to let him haunt her thoughts anymore.

She would always see Diah in her boy, and there was no way she was going to change him at the risk of losing that. Her decision made, slowly, gently, she took her son's hand, the boy who needed her, and turned and walked him out of the room.

The bathroom door opened slowly and when Jacob saw Mary's face appear and she led her son out he could see that something hadn't gone to plan. He had never seen somebody so despondent and he instinctively ran over to her to console her.

"Mary! What is it? What happened in there? How is Zach?" He pressed her but then gave her space to speak if she chose. The worst case scenario ran through his mind. It was all untrue. There were no miracles, never were and never would be. The anticlimax hit him with a thud, the knowledge that there was going to be no change to his or his daughter's life would lead a normal person to think that he was no better or worse off now than he was before, but that was so far from the truth.

The status quo remaining the status quo meant he would forever live the consequences of the horrific accident plus be the subject of blame by his daughter for the failed expedition.

Mary reached over to him and touched his shoulder. "You two go in," she said.

"But? What happened in there?" he asked.

"Exactly what I wanted to happen," she replied. "Now go." She and Zach made way as Ava and Jacob entered the room.

Ava looked around and then turned to her father. "You aren't going to watch me take a shower so once we figure this thing out you are going to leave, right, old man?"

Ava had no intention of letting whatever was about to happen affect the way she felt about her father and what he had done to her and her mother. Her mother. Now there was something she had not considered as part of all this.

Whether she could wish herself to walk again or not was one thing, but changing the past could surely not be possible and she doubted there was a miracle available that could resurrect her mother. Or was there? The thought that she might be able to bring her mother back buckled her over in her chair as if a freight train had delivered this significant option with full force to her.

She noticed the mirror, eyes drawn to the undefinable shape, her vision blurring as the mysterious vortex of moisture she now gazed upon rippled before her. She became aware of an infinite number of future universes available to her and how to command the fulfilment of only one of them, requiring the distillation of her infinite possible choices into a single decision.

The mirror seemed to breathe, approaching her and then retreating again almost like the flow of waves on a beach, disorienting her and preventing her from choosing how to wield the power, what were her choices again? She felt that they were quite important, if only she could remember..

She saw something in the mirror and her father appeared beside her and she remembered where she was, who she was, and it all came flooding back. She knew her options. Should she choose the resurrection of herself, or surrender her selfishness and attempt the resurrection of her mother and her family?

The crescendo of the moment screamed in her ears like she was caught up in a hurricane, wind whistling like screams through the bathroom, or was that Zach howling outside the door she could hear? Momentarily distracted by the shrieking on the other side of the door, she refocused on the maelstrom she was enveloped by and could begin to make out something from the chaos.

Like tendrils penetrating her mind, some unknown force seemed to extract the decision out of her and her choice was made. She knew what she had to do to make it happen, she now understood how it all worked and a swirling force surrounded her and it felt as if she was accelerating forward on a rollercoaster that had reached its zenith and was plummeting as gravity took control.

"It's happeniii…" Her eyes wide, she looked across for her father and couldn't find him. She was lost.

And then…

Wed 23 Sept 1959 **7:59am**
Ira's Warehouse, Crescendo

Aaban ran his fingers through Faith's hair as Father Emmanuel trembled before him.

"The lamb has spoken, the journalist has spoken, and now it is my turn to have the privilege of addressing the camera. It is like after the final performance of a wonderful play, where the actors have all spoken their lines, the show is over and it is time for the applause and the accolades to be bestowed. The proud writer of the script appears on stage last and for the loudest applause. I have been writing the script and now it is time to collect my recognition for the masterpiece that I have toiled over." He took a bow to an imaginary audience, and stooped over to pick up an invisible rose that an admiring member of his audience had taken the time and care to purchase and throw to his feet. He savoured the smell of the rose that was not there and cast it away, to bow again.

"Camera on please. The finale needs to be captured," he said in a businesslike tone to one of his men. He turned to the lens and once again smiled, adopting the persona of judge, jury and executioner.

"I ask you all a question. How can one commit a crime even more heinous than misplacing belief and directing it towards a poor imitation of perfection like the others who have suffered punishment today? Having no belief at all!" He said the words with a sneer and spat towards Faith.

"Oh how foolish you must feel now. Completely denying the existence of something and being proven wrong. Silly girl, your foundations have crumbled around you and now you are here, about to learn a harsh, valuable lesson. I have captured all I need from you on camera. You shall be my first and ultimate prize!"

He pulled Faith's head back and put a long, serrated blade to her throat. Father Emmanuel screamed.

And then..

Wed 23 Sept 1959 **8:00am**
Jacob & Company, The House

And then, stillness.

Wed 23 Sept 1959 **8:00am**
Ira's Warehouse, Crescendo

And then, emptiness.

Wed 23 Sept 1959 **8:00am**
Jacob & Company in Despair

Stillness. The swirling maelstrom of energy and hope dissipated even quicker than it had developed, leaving Ava dizzy in her chair and nauseous to an extent comparable to the events of a few days ago.

Something wasn't quite right. Ava could sense something different, something had happened that she couldn't put her finger on and so she calmed herself down and searched within herself to ensure firstly that she was okay and then took the time to survey her surroundings.

She looked to her right and found her father collapsed and half hanging over the bathtub, his feet splayed at unnatural angles. He seemed to be breathing okay and was probably unconscious. She didn't need to worry herself over him. She looked to her left and saw the mirror, as plain as a mirror could be, doing nothing peculiar at all except reflecting the face of a scared and bewildered girl.

She remembered the journey, the house and the reason why she was there in that filthy bathroom and she excitedly grabbed at her legs with both hands, squeezing as hard as she could. Nothing. She began to hit them, harder, harder. Still nothing. She began to pound on them with as much force as she could muster until she was panting for air and they still did not provide any sense of feeling.

Concentrating as hard as she could, she attempted to wiggle her toes. Something must have gone wrong. Maybe it just had been so long since she had been able to walk that it would just take some time to build up the muscles and nerves again. It would be folly to think that she could just get up and walk straight away on her withered limbs, presently barely more than skin on bone. Frustrated, she sat for a minute and became aware that something else was awry and contributing to her discontent.

The small flame which carried the higher power within her that had begun to smoulder a few days ago had been extinguished. The warmth, the tingling, the awareness had disappeared and left but a distant memory of its existence in the space that it had once occupied and could only mean one thing. God was no longer present.

Had Zach been right? It had actually happened. She recalled hearing his cries right at the crescendo of her imminent metamorphosis a few moments ago.

She gasped, a sharp intake of air and Ava realised she had been holding her breath for some time, trying to still her body sufficiently so that she could make more sense of what was happening within her.

"No! No!!! This can't be happening! I should be walking, I should be walking!" she wailed uncontrollably, once again pounding upon her useless legs. She had already foreseen her future and in it she was happy, just a regular girl who could walk to the shops, ride a bike and play sport if she wanted to and now the future she had invested in had been whisked out from under her.

She could hear her father stirring next to her, body beginning to slowly straighten out from its misshapen slump and before she knew it Jacob sprang upright, nothing but concern and excitement on his face directed towards his daughter as he leaned over her and kissed her forehead and then hugged her tightly such that she didn't have the chance to recoil.

"Sweetheart! Can you walk? Did it work? Are you okay?" His desperate eyes gave away that he was asking for reasons more than just enquiring on his daughter's welfare. The mending of his relationship with his daughter rested on her ability to walk again and all blame for the accident expunged.

This was it. This was the moment he had been waiting years for. All wrongs made right. Now was his chance to earn fatherhood and his daughter back.

Hope turned to horror as Ava grabbed him by his shirt with one hand and struck him repeatedly but ineffectively with the flat of her other.

"No! Can't you feel it, or not feel it anymore ? It was fading inside me and now it's gone. I was so close!" Her face grimaced at what could have been. "So close but now I think what Zach said has come true and there is no hope. God is gone. Gone or dead, the outcome is still the same for me. I need to be alone." She had never ever been this angry or upset, not even after the accident. She was about to have everything again, and it was all taken away.

A soft knock followed by a squeak sounded from a handle and Gabe opened the door to the room and glanced around, relieved to see the two occupants up and about. "Hey, how are you guys in here?" A second glance exposed the tension between the father and daughter which led to a frowned look of apology on his face for walking into a private moment. Ava grunted, annoyed at the universe.

"We are just dandy thanks! And you? You know what has just happened, don't you? It's all over. Whatever force or power there was, it has gone. And that means I am the same, Simon will always be the same, we are all the same, broken and unfixable."

She thumped her fist against the wall, venting her fury and a concerned Mary appeared with a pale Zach by her side who looked like he had been to hell and back. After satisfying themselves that nobody was hurt they took stock of the situation.

Physically the group were all as they were prior to this new development, but there was that something unquantifiable inside them that was now missing, restoring them to their original state as of a few days ago. It was like they had been listening to a poorly wired stereo for so long that they didn't notice there was a background hum until it actually stopped. And now that the hum had stopped its absence was deafening. That feeling of God inside them was gone.

"Y'all still here?" 'Thew's croaky voice floated closer and closer to them from the corridor and echoed through the bathroom as he poked his head in. "Seems all kinda peaceful inside here now, doesn't it?" He pointed into his chest, then noticed the mirror hanging above the vanity. "Huh. Lookie there. Well, I guess that's that. I got my miracle but I'm guessing you didn't get yours." When these words were uttered he became very aware that the money from Ishara in his back pocket might no longer belong to him anymore, since technically the deal made was for three miracles.

He held himself assertively and squared up to the city folk, worried they might use their tricks to steal away the money that was now rightfully his. His goal now was to get them out of his house before they appealed for their cash.

"You-you ain't getting your money back you know, I got it fair and square and you know I told you that you were all fine in the beginning, so I hope you all aren't too unhappy. You still got a lot more than most people you know. Good luck, God bless, and you can get out of my house now. The party is over, nothing more to see here. Now git!"

He walked absentmindedly down the corridor to the living room, already forgetting about his visitors and they could hear him mutter to himself. "Don't worry mom, I'll get you out of your room shortly. Maybe just five more minutes." A pause. "Maybe ten..." He disappeared into the kitchen, the sound of cupboards opening and closing indicating that he was not going to waste any time reflecting on what had just happened.

The group looked at each other, despondently made their way down the corridor and out through the back door of the strange home, walking around the congregation of tents to find a suitable space on the ground to sit on an attempt to absorb the situation and what it meant for them now.

As they appeared from around the back of the house, a hundred pairs of disappointed eyes belonging to the faces of one hundred lost souls stared at them. Their reason for being there had now been snuffed out and they were adrift on a sea of the unknown with nowhere to go and no lure of hope to guide them.

"What do we do now?" a voice emerged from the crowd and nothing but shaking heads and shrugging shoulders was the reply. Some of the crowd were packing up slowly, but unsure where they were going to go or what to do. Others sat solemnly in groups while others hugged and cried at their missed chance.

Ava broke down again and recounted her story of what happened in the bathroom to the others but before she managed to reach the end of her story, Gabe interjected angrily.

"I knew I should have gone in first with Simon. First of all Mary goes in and doesn't know her backside from her elbow and wastes valuable time, and then I'm gentleman enough to let Ava go in. Me, the guy who is the reason you are all here, puts himself last and gets nothing!" His face was bright red and he looked wild. Incensed, he squeezed Simon's hand so tightly the boy let out a yelp.

"Hey!" Jacob stood up and addressed Gabe, pointing his finger menacingly at him and ready to let him have a piece of his mind, to an extent. "It wasn't about you, it was about Simon, supposedly. Nobody did anything wrong, we didn't know this was going to happen so you can't blame anybody. Yes, you let Zach and Ava go before you but that was the right thing to do under the circumstances at the time. I understand you are disappointed, as we all are. Hindsight is great but don't use it to hurt people who are close to you. Got it?" He sat down, satisfied with putting an out of line Gabe in his place. He looked over at Mary hoping to see that familiar look of admiration but she was looking at the ground, mind elsewhere.

"And to all of you, I'm sorry it didn't work out, we are all affected by this and at least we have each other. Let's take a moment to think about what this means for us, and what it really means is that nothing has changed. Can you believe it? God invades our very bodies then disappears, and yet we remain unchanged, completely."

"Well I don't think that's entirely true for me," Mary took exception to Jacob's words and snapped back into the conversation. "I know Zach may well be the same adorable little boy that he always was, but I have been monumentally affected by this. My whole outlook has been altered in ways I cannot describe, both spiritually and in relation to my inner self. I have let go of demons, I have let go of desires and hopes and I am content inside, in fact I have never felt so much at peace. The last few years I have been yearning for what I thought would make me happy again, but when it came to the crunch I realised I was happier to accept my life from its current perspective." She hugged Zach and smiled, happy that her little boy was always going to be her little boy. Her words resonated around them all and they saw that they too had become different people and viewed things from an altered standpoint. They sat there in silence for a while, one thought flooding their minds. God was gone. Impossibly and incomprehensively dead.

Interrupting their thoughts, a puffing and panting rotund figure approached their group from around a makeshift tent constructed of blankets, stepped around Ava and placed a hand on Jacob's shoulder from behind. Jacob jumped with fear but smiles of delight and surprise instantly appeared on everybody's faces as they recognised the man who had penetrated their circle.

"What the! Oh hello! It's so good to see you! What are you doing here?"

A moustached mouth spoke. "So how did you lot expect to get back home at the end of all this then eh?" The figure expelled smoke from his pipe as he spoke to the group, causing Ishara to cough and laugh simultaneously.

"Mr Derby!"

"The one and only!"

Wed 23 Sept 1959 *4:15pm*
Ira's Warehouse, Departed

A feeling of emptiness pervaded the rotting warehouse room, and not just because the clammy, fetid room hosted a group of deathly silent people, captors and captives alike, but a new emptiness resided inside each and every one of them that imbued a melancholy sense of holy loss.

Aaban stood shakily behind Faith, keen blade still pressed firmly against her neck, a single droplet of blood winding its way down the contours of her nape as the unexpected nonexistence of the divine presence inside prompted him to flinch and pierce her skin.

The knife was drawn away slowly as a sense of bereavement pervaded the hellion and for a moment Aaban stood frozen to the spot, all previous grandeur and bravado washed away, leaving a deflated, lost and bewildered man.

"No, it can't be. What has just happened? My Lord has…disappeared?" He looked around the room as if expecting to find the missing presence hiding in a corner.

"Not disappeared. Dead." *And boy, what a timely death,* she thought, relief washing over her body like a cool breeze in the musty room, her rigid muscles relaxing somewhat. But she wasn't out of the woods yet.

"You can feel it, the consciousness of something foreign within you has gone surely, because I can't sense it any more. Everything you have done, every crime you committed in the name of your Lord has been for nothing. Your whole cruel misguided plan to win favour as a devoted soldier has now just made you a common brutal criminal." Ira's croaky words cut his old boss just like the knife he was still holding in his quivering hand. The knife dropped to the floor. And still nobody moved.

After thirty seconds of feeling like the universe had paused, Faith kept her eyes on the motionless Aaban and slowly bent her knees, crouching to the ground, right hand stretched out feeling around the bloody floor before grasping the knife. Her movements were clearly noticeable and she became incredibly paranoid that Aaban was simply allowing her to do this and luring her into a trap. She slowly stood up again. Aaban remained in a trance and she ducked under his grip and backed away quickly, knife raised threateningly though her hand was shaking terribly.

"Hey, cut me free." Ira was still tied up and an uncertain Faith did not feel that it was a prudent idea to release the man who involved her in this mess in the first place. Her suspicious mind raced. Who knows, he could still be working with the bad guys and it was all just a set up to win Faith's trust in him which could be exploited at a later stage when he was free from his bonds.

"They have my family! Please, I must help them." Faith looked at the man and his face was so badly beaten she knew there was no way he could be involved on the side of the men who had done this. She didn't really care at this stage what happened to her, she was too exhausted, the constant surge of adrenaline had left her with nothing in the tank. She cut him free and then stood back, knife still held tightly out in front of her.

A couple of Aaban's men who were standing in the shadowy corners of the room were commanded to only spring to action after receiving an instruction or gesture from their boss. Having received nothing of the sort so far but sensing the situation slipping from the grasp of their inanimate leader they took the initiative to step in and they closed in on Ira.

"Stop," Aaban raised his hand, finally snapping back into the present reality and his men halted and hesitantly awaited further direction. He spoke slowly, in a low, deliberate tone. "Ira, I do not have your family. You know I love your wife and son, we have been very close for years. Please believe I am not a monster. I was just doing the bidding I was destined to do, the actions of today were not mine and since the Lord is no more, you are released and I must now take time to reconsider my place in this realm of existence." He turned to his men and with a flamboyant gesture of a bloody hand, he commanded "Let them go. Let them all go. Unlock the door. This is over."

The heavy bolt of the rusty door was released and it swung open, allowing cool air that did not have the stench of death upon it to flow into the room refreshingly. Ira and Faith hesitantly took a few steps towards the door, and then when they realised it was not a trick they hobbled as fast as they could down the slippery stairs and were met with gloriously warm sunlight. Faith broke down and hugged Ira whilst sobbing, salty tears causing the many cuts and bruises on his face to sing in agony but his mind channelled out the pain and directed his thoughts to more practical things because they were not out of the woods yet.

"Let's get as far away from here as possible. I know Aaban, he may change his mind at any second and I don't want to risk being around if he does. Are you okay? Once again I am sorry for involving you. Let's move now, can you walk?" She was touched at his concern and felt a warmth towards this poor man who was beaten within an inch of his life and still had no concern for his own welfare.

"Yes, I'm fine. Let's go." The pair limped their way unhindered out of the grounds of the warehouse and slowly made their way back towards civilisation, turning around frequently to look for followers, but none were to be seen.

Wed 23 Sept 1959   *7:55am*
The Man No More

Smash!

"Oh dear, clumsy me," Doris reprimanded herself as a stray elbow of hers nudged a half empty jar of cookies from off of the front counter. She was feeling a little discombobulated this morning and so she had tried to tackle the problem head on by plowing into a cleaning frenzy, maybe a little too enthusiastically.

"Can't even eat the poor little crunchy guys, such a waste." She bent over to pick up the dustpan and nearly provided herself with a black eye in the process, her tired looking face narrowly missing the tall plastic tube standing next to the coffee machine which she used to bang the spent grounds from the machine into.

Precisely half way through sweeping up glass and crumbs of varying shades of brown into a garbage bag, she heard a cough coming from a table and with a start she straightened herself up and left the remaining pile on the floor to be cleaned up later. If somebody were to have been observing her closely, they would have seen her sunny façade appear a little strained for an instant before resuming its usual buoyant demeanour.

She had oiled the front door hinges yesterday with canola and then used a butterknife to unscrew the bell and immediately felt liberated and alive. Not even one day into her liberation and she realised that the squeaky door and accompanying bell actually served a valuable purpose. She cursed herself under her breath for allowing a customer to not only enter the cafe without receiving a greeting, but to actually make their way to a table without being shown to one and offered a coffee on the way.

Was it 8am already? The elderly man must have arrived, probably pulling out his pocket square and placing his hat down this very minute.

For the next few moments she would not be able to fully relax knowing there was a small area of her domain where there was cajoling evidence of her clumsiness in the form of biscuits and the shards of their container only half cleaned up and lying visible to her customers. Trying to put it out of her mind with a grunt, she raised her eyebrows and prepared herself to give an eager greeting to the man.

The long back table that seated six had not one person but five sitting there and as Doris apologised profusely for her delay she noticed that her regular customer was not amongst the group. Barely acknowledging one another, the group paid no attention to her and even though repeated attempts to offer hot drinks and delicious pies were put to them they proffered no order, obliviously self-contained in a morose bubble.

As per the previous couple of days the group was made up of a cross-section of society, the only thing binding them together in any way was that today apart from being exceptionally glum, they were all wearing grey or black and not the usual dizzying mosaic of colours and styles of the previous mornings. The gentleman who for years had been waiting for friends that never arrived was now disconcertingly the absentee, and the waitress connected the dots and did not feel happy about the final picture that emerged.

Had he finally said whatever he had needed to say to the group, only to vanish shortly afterwards leaving behind sadness and confusion?

For the remainder of the day the sombre group turned over members as new joiners entered the café as some departed, all emanating the same low key mood of resigned despondency. There was a more noticeable mix of emotions as time progressed, certainly some responded differently to others with denial and anger prominent themes presenting themselves, although grief was the dominant force. A tear or two was shed, and Doris' main role for the day was to hand out tissues to those whose emotions got the better of them.

Over the course of the day the six seater table must have had over thirty visitors squeeze in, squash over, hold hands, cry, argue, sit down, stand up again and leave, gradually the numbers depleting to a few remainders.

Eventually the shadows grew longer and the natural light in the café diminished as the sun fell behind the horizon and as the orange glow disappeared there was one last remaining person in the café who looked at their watch, gathered up their belongings and left Doris alone and puzzling over what had just transpired.

As they pulled the front door open and stepped out into the evening. She raced out after them and shouted down the street.

"He's gone forever, isn't he?" she asked, already knowing the answer.

They turned around slowly and did nothing more than nod their head half-heartedly before continuing on their way, pulling their jacket tight around them.

She would see neither the elderly gentleman nor his friends again, and it wouldn't be long before she realised what a significant part of her life he had become over the last few days. At the beginning of each new morning she would feel a lingering void inside, but 1contentness that she had the chance to witness his long absent friends arrive to acknowledge him and enjoy his brief presence before his sad departure.

Doris grabbed the dustpan and broom and finished cleaning up the forgotten broken cookie jar before taking off her apron and turning the lights off, sitting in the darkness for an hour or so lost in her thoughts and mulling over the man before a chill overcame her.

Some secret part within her had been exposed over the past few days and revealed new desires, challenged her mindset and made her rethink her position immersed in the humble drudgery of servitude where she had visualised herself belonging forever. How could the presence of one man as old as time have that effect on her?

Her stomach rumbling, she snapped out of her contemplative state and helped herself to a take-away container full of left over cherry pie which she placed sideways into her handbag before sighing as she locked the door behind her and left for home, the end of just another day.

Wed 23 Sept 1959 9:15am
The Company Departs

"What on earth are you doing here? You didn't fly back to town?" the group echoed in chorus towards the portly, moustached figure who seemed a little more worse for wear than his usual immaculately presented self. Not normally one for being self-conscious about his appearance, on this rare occasion though Mr Derby nervously knew that his presentation was not optimal and perceived, albeit incorrectly, that the eyes being run over him were not doing so with the normal air of admiration but in judgment, and so did not lap up the attention with his normal vigour.

"Well you see, after you all disappeared on your little quest I returned to the helicopter and closed my eyes, you know just for a mere few minutes to return me to my normal levels of vitality and when I reopened them, lo and behold dusk was setting in. Quite the nap I assure you, one of my best in fact and I shall remember it for a while to come. Anyway this led me to second guess whether I should make the night journey back and during my thought process I asked myself how you would all return if I was not to fly you back? Without providing myself a satisfactory answer to this question, I decided that you would all be in a great predicament and thus decided to sleep in the helicopter until morning before then making my way to find this place you were all so keen to make your way to. A bit further away than I would have liked, to be honest. Speaking of, how did it all eventuate?" As he said this he noticed Ava still in her wheelchair and realised he had placed his foot in his own mouth. "Oh, I'm sorry."

Before any of the group could respond and feel pressure to uncomfortably relay the details of their failed mission, Mr Derby looked around and began to usher them to stand up and march out of the sea of tents and into the trees in the direction of where they had all come from with a sense of urgency. "I don't have a great feeling about this place and think we should leave. Look around, the cold, hungry masses are uprising."

They had all been sitting in a circle engaged with themselves and had not noticed that the mood in the camp had turned. The atmosphere had already been tense with needy, impatient and desperate people waiting for something extraordinary to happen that would change their lives forever, and now that that opportunity had disappeared, an ugliness had settled in.

Small commotions that could be heard amongst friends and families escalated into full-blown arguments as the realisation that there were going to be no miraculous events sank in and the disappointment turned into finger pointing and blaming. Anger inevitably became directed towards the small house that had been the destination of all the hopeful travellers as if it was decided that it was the cause of their problems and now branches and rocks were being hurled at the boarded up abode.

"Time to go. Now!" Jacob pushed Ava as quickly he could in the direction that they had all come from and the poor girl was getting thrown from side to side as her chair was shoved forcefully over the rough terrain. Gabe had picked up Simon and hurled him over his shoulder, the boy holding onto his crutches with dear life as he crashed through some low hanging branches and leaves grazed over his back.

Arriving at the road from where they had come from, a gun shot rang out from the direction of the house and this propelled them down the road until they were spent and gasping for breath.

Mr Derby doubled over and proceeded to cough so hoarsely that it sounded as if he had smoked for most of his life, which he of course had. Wheezing and shaking his head as if to suggest that no human being should ever have to travel at such speeds without the use of a car or plane, he plonked himself down on the arm of Ava's chair until he was sufficiently recovered to be able to stand upright once more.

Jacob shook his head as he paced up and down with his hands on his hips breathing deeply, his hair once again resuming the slightly mad appearance that it usually took on.

"Seriously? Resorting to violence for not being blessed with the power to win the lottery, for not being bestowed the amazing gift of always being able to find a car park? Surely the most significant takeaway of what has just happened is a bit bigger picture than that. God, and I mean the actual, ancient God has died with all of mankind as a witness."

Ava fumed at him. "Well you didn't have much to gain or lose did you from this trip, so you can just walk away without having your hopes crushed. As you can clearly see, I am not walking away and so I know exactly why those people are reacting the way they are reacting. You should just keep your mouth shut until you have something to say that makes sense."

"Everybody, everybody, we can discuss mankind's emotional response to this new turn of events in the helicopter. I think we should make haste because I do not want to be on this road and have to face any of those people back there who are probably also going to be on their way back to town by whichever means they got here, and would most likely involve coming this way," Mr Derby said sternly and the father and daughter dropped their bickering for the moment.

Continuing on solidly and only stopping once to finish off their remaining supplies, they spotted a white monogrammed handkerchief tied to a bush. Mr Derby leaned over and untied the marker and stuffed it firmly into his jacket pocket after mopping his brow with it. "Always over prepare and make life easy for yourself. That's my lesson to you for the day, especially if you have a bad memory and no sense of direction such as myself," he grinned.

Following the carefully placed marker off-road, soon thereafter the trees thinned out and the helicopter loomed into view as Mr Derby paused once again for breath before heaving himself up into the flying bird. "We shall leave in five. Or how about right now?

"You keep the strangest company," Mary told Jacob as she walked over to him with a shy smile on her face and indicated the round man who was now performing some checks within the aircraft. "I wonder what other mysteries and interesting facts you have shrouded around you? I think I might almost miss you once we get back to civilisation and we go our separate ways."

She smiled at him but was it just a smile, or a little more? Jacob blushed as he swept his hair back away from his face. "Well, nobody has ever accused me of being interesting before so I am thankful." He waved his hand in front of his face in a side to side motion. "Nothing much behind this façade other than what you can see. I'm a simple man, simple desires, simple thoughts."

"Well, you can stop that right there mister because trust me, no man is simple. I never have any idea what is going on in their heads. I have no idea what is going on in yours either," she looked away.

Jacob stuttered, his blood pressure rising and threatening to smother all thought processes and cause him to collapse. "Uh, I err. Yes, I have thoughts, about things, depends on what you are talking about I suppose." He threw a bag into the helicopter in an attempt to appear normal, however the bag came toppling back out and spilled over the ground. Mary laughed.

"Come on you, let's get you in before you cause some sort of disaster and set the place on fire. You adorable, clumsy oaf." Jacob climbed into the vehicle so that his red face was hidden from view.

"You really are something else Mary, you know that? Now what am I going to do with you? Hmm. I think you have given me…I mean, I think I'll… going to…write something for you, no never mind," he trailed off, unable to finish what he was saying or look directly at her and so took his seat.

She really had taken a hold of him in a very short time and he wanted her to know that, but it had been so long since he had the urge to express himself in this way that he knew he couldn't do it with a few clumsy sentences which would just come out wrong and do himself a disservice. Some time and thought would have to go into it to ensure a clear message was communicated. His mind hummed into action, inspiration aplenty.

Within moments everybody was inside the helicopter and crammed against one another, though this time the mood was very different compared to the nervous excitement of yesterday's trip into the unknown.

As the roar of the rotors whirred into life overhead, nothing was said, nothing was done as everybody dealt with the events of the morning in their own way and clearly nobody was in the state of mind to share thoughts or feelings just yet. Jacob whistled to himself and was the only one who displayed any sign of life as he proceeded to pull out a pen and notepad from his satchel and began to scribble away.

"Why are you so happy? Glad your daughter still can't walk? Is that it? And what are you writing? Why on earth would you be writing anything? And stop whistling!" Ava yelled out across the seats to her father. Jacob stopped whistling, however he continued to scratch away with his pen at something, pausing to think, looking around out the window and then scribbling away some more. More than once his eyes darted across to Mary as if checking something with her, and then he continued.

The flight was just as bumpy on the way back as it was on the way to their original destination, however, time stretched into an eternity and seemed to take far longer and Jacob wondered if they were flying into the wind or maybe flying slower to conserve fuel, if that was how helicopters worked. He did remember Mr

359

Derby saying the range was only just sufficient to get there and back again. Hopefully he had calculated accurately.

Jacob continued his scrawling for the next hour or so, protectively guarding it with his hand like a schoolboy during a test, should anybody glance in his direction.

Finally the backed up traffic of the freeway entrance passed below them and shortly after the large open space of the airfield came into view and Mr Derby set the bird down in precisely the same spot they had all climbed into it yesterday and in a much more delicate fashion than the last time.

He climbed down awkwardly, one hand hanging onto his hat at all times so that the still spinning rotors could not blow it away, and swiftly headed towards the hangar where he was intercepted by two men in mechanics outfits who rushed out. An enthusiastic conversation began before ending with a few handshakes and the nodding of heads before all parties disbanded, seemingly happy with the outcome of the discussion which to any onlookers would presumably have been about the borrowing of the helicopter by a novice without the owner's consent.

Mr Derby noticed that Ava and Jacob were once again engaged in a one-sided argument. The daughter, who even though confined to a wheelchair, seemed the more imposing and dominant of the pair and was waving her arms and pointing at her father while using language that was more appropriate on a construction site than next to an expensive flying machine surrounded by a group including children.

"Hey, hey you two, ease on up now. Ava, Ava! Come on, that is no way to speak to your own father." Mr Derby placed himself in between them and gently grabbed the reluctant girl by the arm and indicated that she should follow him, leading her away towards some not too distant fuel pumps where there was a dilapidated vinyl office chair that he lowered himself into and they were eye to eye.

"I'm not sure where to begin Ava, but let me start by saying that your father loves you very much and it hurts him when you treat him like this. I have known him for many years, and he speaks about you often. In fact, nearly every time that I have spoken with him he mentions you...or your mother..." Ava looked up at the man in front of her with the same anger in her eyes that would normally be reserved for her father.

"And what would you know huh? I have never even heard of you before. Dad may talk about me to you but he has certainly never spoken about you to me. What do you want?" Her temper began to boil over.

"Look, look. I know what happened to you all in that car accident years ago. I also know that yes, you lost your mother in that accident but your father lost the love of his life and the love of his daughter. I can see why you are angry at him, a split second with such terrible consequences, but what is done is done, time cannot be reversed and lived over again. Knowing his responsibility for the loss he has caused to his own family is punishment enough for him, don't you think?"

"Never. I have lost the use of my legs for the rest of my life because of him and so I have the rest of my life to remind him and make him pay." Her mood was foul now and she was getting tired of this man pressing her.

"Ava, you are so young and so angry. If you let this hatred take over you will be a bitter and unhappy woman for the rest of your life and will lose all your friends and everybody you care about. Nothing can change the past, you have a whole life ahead of you with your father, so would you rather constantly hurt him even though he is doing so much to make things up to you? That is the behaviour of one ungrateful and unworthy person. He has no friends, no self-esteem and you are kicking him while he is down? That is one low, low act by a daughter and you should be ashamed of yourself. He has given you everything, his time, his limited finances, his help, his devotion, has he not? He would, and does, do anything for you, even though you treat him like you do."

Ava sat silent for a minute before reluctantly mumbling the words "Yes, I suppose."

"And I can see now that he is pretty close to the end of his tether, and when that snaps do you really think that you will be okay should you drive him away? He has tried and tried to reconcile with you and is on the verge of giving up. I can guarantee you do not want to lose your mother *and* your father. You will regret it. Maybe not tomorrow, maybe not next week or even next year, but there will come a time when you look back and realise the mistake you have made. Trust me I know." He shuffled uncomfortably on the office chair and took a deep breath, as if about to offload the weight of the world.

"Every morning at precisely the same time I visit my mother in the Hillside Aged Care facility. There were many years when I didn't speak to her and now I am making up for lost time, wondering how I could ever have been so stupid when I was younger. As the years have passed, I have almost forgotten what it was that came between us, and it seems so irrelevant and petty that I am ashamed at my petulance. But, I do what I can to repair the damage and clear my conscience, so now I make sure I am there for her just as she was always there for me in my youth, and just like your father is always there for you now."

It wasn't hard for Ava to take a glimpse into the future and foresee hers mirroring Mr Derby's. She mumbled back to him.

"Look, I know you are right but it would just be weird now if I forgave him and acted all nice. It's just a habit now for me to be cruel to him and I'm aware I'm doing it and how much it hurts him, and though it used to bring me pleasure it's wearing me down. I am a reasonable girl Mr Derby, I can see the person I'm becoming and I don't like it. I have to stop, don't I?" She looked at the ground. "I have to stop."

Mr Derby was right of course. It had been far too long to hold a grudge, even if it originally was founded. She was sad inside, still legitimately hurting from the loss of years ago, that would never go away. Without her even realising it, the sense of loss of her absent mother had now spread and extended to her father as she pushed him away further and further.

He was almost about to disappear from her life too and it was in that moment that she decided to give in, go to him and tell him she missed him and loved him. She wanted to tell him she was sorry for all the horrible things she had said and done, and all she wanted was to be his daughter again, and for him to be her father, all forgiven and forgotten.

Tears running down her face, she brushed them away and wheeled across the tarmac with an overwhelming sense of relief as the colossal weight that had been on her shoulders for six years was finally about to be unburdened. Trying to push the wheels around quicker than her coordination allowed, she slipped and almost fell forward, laughing as she did so, wiping her eyes excitedly and starting up again totally oblivious to her grazed hands.

Looking over towards the helicopter she could see that the van had started up and had begun to move, past the hangars and picking up speed at a terrific rate. Where was her dad going?

Looking to her right she could see a figure running clumsily, and there was Mary screaming something towards the van and waving her arms around frantically chasing it in an attempt to will it to stop. The old machine found something within itself to hurtle along with more pace than it knew it had and screamed across the concrete. Ava put her hands to her head. Something was wrong.

Less than five seconds later the van her father was driving ploughed straight into the solid metal base of the airport's windsock and tore itself in half, glass and debris flying everywhere, the noise of the collision as loud as a thunderclap.

Ava could hear Mary's scream before the sound of her own drowned it out.

Wed 23 Sept 1959 ***11:15am***
Jacob and Mary

Watching Ava disappear into the distance with Mr Derby, Jacob had a chance to cool off from the dressing down he had just received from his daughter, completely oblivious this time as to what the cause was or even what she had said. The altercations occurred so frequently he had become numb to the message being conveyed and he was almost at the point of not caring.

There was absolutely nothing he could do to alter her perception of him, so he didn't see the value in trying to be her father for another second longer, it just wasn't what she wanted. From now on he would provide food and lodging and not risk giving any of himself to her to harm.

The confirmation of the existence of God three days ago had brought an edge of hope to Jacob's world but that edge had instead betrayed him and sliced him deeply. His hope extended to a future where the best of humanity was laid bare and that people would forgive, forget, move on, love, cherish and prosper. That his daughter would forgive, forget and move on.

What God had actually exposed was not the keen edge of hope but the jagged, rusted, vile edge of the worst of humanity's traits, their dark and ugly forms emerging and coiling tightly around the world, the more primal instincts of hatred, jealousy, greed and violence taking a stranglehold until all hope was choked out.

With infinite unexplored possibilities opened and questions arising from this unpredicted holy status quo, humanity was unsure of how to react and what behavioural expectations were to accompany the new world order. God was raw, powerful, historic, bloody, and terrible biblical times had returned. A once civilised society was on the brink of reverting to blood sacrifice and primitive order.

Somehow finding humour in this observation, Jacob acknowledged that Ava had been part of the dark and ugly blood sacrifice mindset long before God had made an appearance and so there was no noticeable behavioural change. He sighed, and watching Mr Derby and Ava from afar, he stood there with his arms folded and a frown on his face until he felt a slap on the back.

"I don't know what would be more difficult, having a child with an emotional deficit like Zach or one whose emotions are constantly fixed at extreme levels like Ava. I can see that you and I are equally challenged by opposite ends of the spectrum," Mary said. "You okay?"

"Mm not sure. I think I'm at breaking point right now, only one more daughter's outburst away from crumbling and becoming dead inside. I don't think I can do this anymore. The last few days have just been too much for me with losing my job,

God appearing, the miracle place failing me, the death of God, so I'm sure it's not long until something else bad happens."

Mary put her arm around him and pulled him close. "You and I are kindred spirits you know, we are on very similar paths, affected by the same people in our lives though in different ways and we have both been through significant life events. Just, hang in there okay? Promise me. I don't know what I would do without you now Jacob. You are a great man."

Jacob looked up at her. "Really? You don't know what you would do without me? I feel the same about you Mary. There is something about you that just makes me feel like things are going to be alright. I haven't told you this but you actually remind me of my wife and I know Ava thinks the same. You are so alike that it frightens me but excites me greatly at the same time, like something has awakened that I thought would always remain asleep inside of me. I don't suppose you would consider maybe going out for an old fashioned dinner date with me after this is all over?"

The words came out naturally almost without thought behind them, as if they just knew it was the right time to come out and ask her. Jacob would normally have been petrified in this situation, but his nerves were nowhere to be found. This woman standing before him must surely feel as connected to him as he was to her, they were the missing pieces of the puzzle for each other, both looking for something and that search was now over. He took a deep breath and awaited her reply eagerly.

"Um Jacob, I am really flattered and I do like you too, however, a comparison to your wife is really not the right thing to mention to a girl and it comes across as a little artificial, you know, like you don't really like me for me, you like me because I'm like her? What, you want me to style my hair like her and wear her old outfits? I don't think so. Look, let's just take a step back and start again and see how things go, okay? I'm not saying no, I'm just saying not now. Significant life events can often bring people together and create feelings that may not actually be there. Let's give it time and a chance to see what is real and what isn't."

The situation had now become monumentally awkward and she winced as soon as she saw the deadpan look on Jacob's face when her answer didn't fall in the favourable direction he was expecting. She knew he needed to be treated with kid gloves but for something as serious as this the straight up truth without mincing words was the only way to handle it and get the point across without giving false hope.

"Hey! Where are you going?" she called after him as he slowly turned around as if in a trance and walked off in the direction of the van. "Jacob?" Mary let him go, thinking he needed some time to process and have a think about things.

Jacob was barely aware of his movements, a fog surrounded him and caused confusion, disorienting him and his thoughts, compelling him to put one foot in front of the other and move away from the situation. This was it, the moment where he finally broke. The culmination of everything that had happened in the last few days had swallowed him up and consumed him. The last ounce of self-esteem and worth had escaped his body and he was sinking into the abyss where hopefully it would all be over soon.

With no heaven or hell there was no future risk of an afterlife to inflict any shameful reminders about who he was in this plane of existence, a failure of a man. He would fall into a quiet oblivion and no longer exist to be a burden or to be burdened. There could be no lower point in this worthless life of his.

As he stepped further into the fog, the light grew dim and the air pressure around him altered and grew cold as those now familiar tendrils of sound travelled across space and through dimensions to reach out, the vibrations around his ears phasing in and out and that faint voice of his lost wife soothing and caressing his emotions. Though he couldn't quite make out the words he could sense her pleading for him to remove himself from pain, cross through space and dimensions to join her forever.

He knew inside himself that she was long gone, and that this and the previous communications had been nothing but a trick of his own mind because death equalled death and nothing more, there could be no reaching out from the beyond, but still he heeded her dark beckoning and reached into his pocket, pulling out the keys to the van.

"Where are you going Jacob? Come back would you and let's talk shall we?" Mary shouted across the tarmac. She saw Jacob climb into the van and begin to drive, towards nothing in particular. "Where on earth are you going?" she asked herself, and then with a burst of adrenaline hitting her she realised what was about to happen.

Leaning forward and huddled over the steering wheel, Jacob put his foot down on the accelerator and the van lurched forward as if enjoying the chance to be put to the test. Although being propelled horizontally, he felt like he was falling and could not stop even if he wanted to. He involuntarily clutched at the side of the van to stop his apparent descent but he continued to fall, fall, faster and faster. It would all be over soon. He was about to finish properly what should have happened on the night of the accident all those years ago.

A large vertical shape loomed in the distance and now his foot was flat to the floor on the accelerator closing the distance as quickly as possible. This was the only way. He would not trouble anybody anymore and he could not be troubled.

He wondered if Faraday and Carol from his office would feel any sense of loss that he was gone. He doubted they would even have a care either way about the news. Ava would definitely not care, and Mary probably wouldn't either now that he had screwed things up. He pushed the accelerator flat to the floor, closed his eyes and waited for peace.

Wed 23 Sept 1959 *5:30pm*
The First Separation

A bitter wind worked its way through the streets, delivering a biting iciness as a lingering reminder of its visit to all that it touched before moving on in search of the next victim.

"I think we win the award for most tragic looking couple right now, and Halloween is still over a month away," a shivering Faith laughed as Ira and herself collapsed in a bruised and battered heap on the side of the road. A surge of adrenaline and the desire to get as far away from the warehouse as possible was what got them to back to the relative safety of civilisation, and that meant that for these two individuals from universes apart, their colliding worlds must now move on and re-enter their original orbits.

"I guess I'm out of a job hey? Or do you think I should turn up next Monday and pretend like nothing happened," Ira joked, and his face contorted into a half smile, half painful grimace. "Ouch, I have to stop being so funny," he laughed again at this, and the same reaction resulted.

"How are you able to make jokes right now? Were you just in the same warehouse as I was? Or was all that just a regular day at the office for you? After that, we must be in shock and should probably get to a hospital as soon as possible in all seriousness, you especially," Faith commented. She was shaking all over, and trying to fool herself into believing that it was just because of the cold but was not succeeding.

"But..?" Ira questioned Faith, sensing that she was not going to follow her own recommendation. She was too stubborn, too strong willed and too dedicated to work, all the reasons he selected her to be part of his plan in the first place. He guessed that she was probably going to go back to the office to get the day's events down onto paper.

"I'm going to head to the office and basically type out the contents of my brain while it's still fresh. It will be therapeutic for me and boy do I need some therapy right now. I saw a lot of bad today done to a lot of good people and I want to make sure that they get a write up that honours their bravery and completely and accurately tells the world exactly what happened in that warehouse today." She would never forget the smell of that warehouse and memories started flooding back. She felt her gorge rise.

"So Aaban will get what he deserves, if he can be found."

"Yes."

"I imagine I am going to be part of that story," Ira pondered. Faith nodded. "Yes."

"So I also imagine the police will be paying me a visit soon then. I am at peace with that." He looked at the sky, vainly trying to foresee the future for him and his family. He had so far shielded them from his hidden life, but there was no more hiding what he was. *Was.*

"Look, the things you did over the last couple of days were for the powers of good, not evil. I can see what your plan was, and yes it did backfire. I vow to you I will tell your story truthfully, that you are a good man who was trying to do a good thing. Your family will be proud of you," Faith promised. They both knew that the future for Ira did not look good, but neither felt the need to acknowledge this.

"I can't wait to hug my boy, kiss my wife. Go to church, ask for forgiveness, cleanse myself and start again as a new man, whether behind bars or not. I'm not entirely sure of who I am anymore, but I know darnn sure of who I am going to be."

"I know how you feel," Faith whispered to the air. "I was so sure of who I was as a person, and now.." she shrugged her shoulders and lifted her hands to the sky. "..No idea. For me there never was religion, no God, only fools and the downtrodden could commit belief towards that. And yet they were right and I was wrong."

"But now there is no God for you again," Ira mused. "So are you back to being an atheist?"

"There wasn't a God, then there was, and now there isn't again. Does that make us all atheists now? I mean, God actually, really, one hundred percent does not exist now. No debate, no discussion, I mean, nobody can argue about that. I am back to square one so in theory I should not be any different, but I can already tell it isn't going to be that simple."

Both herself and Ira lay back onto the grass and stared at the sky, glimpsing flashes of blue where the clouds thinned and revealed the heavens above. Faith spoke again, a thousand questions filling her head now that she had room to take in all that had happened.

"So there really should be no such thing as religion now. No need for churches or praying, well, there never was anyway I suppose, according to what we learned. No fighting, no more wondering. Mankind should really be able to focus on getting things done now, unhindered by archaic religious mindsets.

Think to back in the day when Galileo was around and the church threatened him with torture and death for his maverick theory that the earth was not the centre of the universe because it directly contradicted their teachings. Not to mention all the other discoveries discredited or kept under wraps for fear of the wrath of the church. How far did that set back science? Imagine if hundreds of years ago, God appeared in the same way and the events happened just as they did these past few days, the truths were revealed, and all of those fearful scientists throughout history were thereafter able to divulge their findings without being labelled as a witch, a heretic or in league with the devil. Imagine where the human race would be now. Mindblowing.

All religious shackles are now off. This is the point in time when humanity resets back to a common point, unites and agrees on something once and for all and moves on. Having said that, I get the feeling that now that God has come and gone, there is just going to be more weird stuff happening."

"Wow, that's what you are thinking about? After all we just went through all I am thinking about right now is how much my wife is going to kill me when I get home!" Ira laughed. He nodded pensively and tried to answer Faith.

"Who knows what changes we will see? I think the human response on an individual level would be quite unpredictable and random, maybe some people will change the direction of their lives one hundred and eighty degrees, maybe some will change five degrees. On an aggregate level though, all those individual changes will probably net out to zero and humanity will appear completely unchanged. My prediction is that mankind will still bicker, fight, disagree, have wars, and display the usual traits that a self-proclaimed intelligent species shouldn't."

Faith rolled over and slowly stood up, brushing the grass off herself and did a few stretches, allowing her time to think about Ira's words before responding.

"My thoughts are that I am one of those one hundred and eighty degree people, and then I have done another one hundred and eighty degrees on top of that. What a brief but intense way to rock the world, God! And what a personal and natural way to make a grand entrance into our existence, completely not how people would ever have predicted. For God to make that huge reveal just in those final moments of life, you know I think that was a sign of love for us, a last minute gift to keep us from eternally bickering about what the truth really was, to enjoy the splendour and converge to become a united species again. Only time will tell to see if it worked."

"So what you are saying is that you completely disagree with me on what the outcome of all this will mean to mankind," Ira laughed.

"Hey Ira, I could talk all day about how much I disagree with you, but it's probably time to cut this off at the pass before we are still here tomorrow discussing it. You know everybody is going to be dissecting this for centuries. I'll get myself back to the office to blurt it all out on paper before my goldfish memory forgets it all. I am just exhausted, physically and mentally but don't want to switch off just yet." She turned to face him and spoke sincerely as she placed her hands on his shoulders.

"Ira, I hate you but I love you. Fate brought us together and our paths must now diverge but mark my words they will meet again. Come here."

They hugged in the twilight, and although dirty, bloody and aching, an energy coursed through the both of them and they clung to each other with streaming tears leaving grimy trails on their cheeks, washing away the final remnants of the people that they used to be.

Slowly separating, Ira and Faith looked into each other's eyes and they would turn and walk away, cleansed and ready to continue on with their journeys in the new world, bound forever now somehow by those few shared moments in time.

Faith walked half a dozen steps when she heard whistling. Turning, she watched Ira limping away painfully, the uplifting melody he was generating through his cracked and dry lips at stark odds with his broken appearance. The man was about to walk into a firestorm no doubt at home, but the man bristled with excitement and anticipation.

"You know, I'm going to bill you for all the therapy I'm going to need after this!" she yelled after him, her voice cutting through the air and carrying a smile along with it.

His whistling stopped.

Wed 23 Sept 1959 *12:00pm*
Jacob Emerges

A dark fog swirled through the air and a blind Jacob panicked, hands flailing around in search of something physical to reassure him that he was not floating inside a cloud. "Why would I be here inside a cloud?" he wondered. Was he still in the helicopter and Mr Derby had taken them up too high? No, there was a deathly silence around him with no loud whirr of the rotors spinning above him.

Gradually, his mind retraced its steps back to the van colliding with the windsock pole and finally connected the dots. "I'm dead. I'm dead!" Panic set in. The opaque fog began to thin, becoming a white blur as misty, esoteric shapes swirled and danced into view. "Oh, thank God," he muttered to himself as his senses reawakened, and the awareness of incredible pain snapped him to full consciousness.

He felt as though he had been sawn clean through and his body split down from his left shoulder to his right hip. His legs felt as though they had been hit with sledgehammers up through the base of his feet, compacting his shins and femur. Eyes focusing completely now, he could see a steering wheel inches from his face and a large rusted metal pole behind him and to the right, starting beneath the van and climbing high into the sky.

"That should not be there," he commented in a daze.

"He's alive! He's alive!" a familiar female voice rang out, and he could see to his left a face peering at him through where the driver side window should have been.

"Jacob!" the door to the van opened with a yank and he felt an arm reach across and undo the seatbelt. He fell awkwardly to the side and out of the van onto the ground. The pain coursed through his body, something inside of him did not feel right. The woman knelt down next to him and stroked his head gently whilst scolding him angrily.

"Are you okay? I mean, what on earth were you thinking? I cannot believe you did that, and your seatbelt was on anyway you silly, infuriating man. Luckily the old bucket of bolts wasn't really going that fast. Thankfully you seem all right."

She lifted his head up into her lap and continued to stroke him. He looked at her and just as the spark of recognition filled his eyes and he knew who she was, he faded back into unconsciousness.

Within the void of his unconscious mind he could sense time's passage, though the pace at which it advanced was obscured, as immeasurable as tracking the speed of a shadow in the dark of night. Seconds passed, or were they years, aeons?

Emerging from beyond the silence, he could almost feel it calling out to him before he could hear it, a thousand distant echoes streaming across an unknown universe, lapping softly against the alpha waves of his mind like ripples at a lake's edge. That voice again. But no, not *the* voice. Not her voice. This was someone else.

Curiosity awakened him from the dream, his now flickering open eyes focused on identifying the dark shapes above him, turning them into recognisable features - mouths, noses, scared faces. And out of the many faces before him, all he saw was hers. The owner of the voice.

"You.."

Reconnecting mind and body, with resolve and determination normally beyond his limits he moved his unfeeling right hand towards where his jacket pocket should be, and guessing that the blind limb had found its target, closed his numb fingers around the contents, but with a gasp his strength failed him and his arm fell uselessly to the ground. Eyes straining to his left, he saw with relief that he was holding a crumpled and now bloody piece of paper.

"For…you…" he said, looking at her.

Puzzled eyes glanced towards the paper, and an uncertain hand reached out and prised it from his weak grip.

"A note?" her welling eyes asked him. Shaking hands unfolded the composition with undisguised anticipation, silence prevailing while the contents were absorbed. A tear fell.

"A poem."

Wed 23 Sept 1959   *12:19pm*
The poem

'As I pen these words, it is not my hand that wields the instrument that weaves my thoughts onto paper, but the strongest and yet most delicate part of me, beating inside.

Narratives of my soul reminding me of times past have been overwritten by you, releasing memories once sublime, reducing them to nothingness, just as a dream's existence fades when the majesty of the sun diminishes slumber to a lingering wisp of unconscious reflection.

Nostalgia became the kingdom I ruled with naïve devotion, echoes of the past became my wearying subjects whose longing appeals to comfort their tenderness blinded me from the seeking of new realms over which to reign and flourish.

Enter you, the invader, softly treading the lonely shadows of my lands and setting adrift my burdens of the past, as silently as the suppressed whisper upon my lips that threatens to release to you those words I fear are not ready to be consumed.

Now I feel you near, but oh that I wish my senses speak to me untruly, and the need to look over my shoulder for you compels me no more, myself just a fallen victim to a false reality manifested of my own desires, the peril threatened by your occupation unfounded.

Gallant in the face of inescapable defeat I concede I am overrun at last, my vulnerable landscape swept desolate, and all that stands in my world is I, and you, the lone essentia to which my musings surrender, fed enduringly by your coruscating brilliance.

Undreaming, au courant, I fathom your incursion was no siege on my defenceless heart, contrarily, thy designs were to coalesce yours and mine as one, elucidating the folly that I had permitted time precious to unravel in absence of you, the most beautiful part of me.

Yielding gently as a frail bough suffering the burden of winter snow, my disquiet now thaws as the embers of our newly shared moments glow resplendent, and a realization burns that all that life may deliver upon me will not affect me, for nothing delivered can matter when all that matters is you.

Entwined and cradled inseparably in each other's arms, eyes unable to break gaze, I walk my lands alongside you, and I breathe in every fundamental joy of life you emanate, and my every action in this new kingdom is destiny.

Now, that which controls the hand wielding the instrument that weaves my thoughts onto paper draws a line through time

----

and from this point I give myself to you, the sweetest of surrenders, so, dearest, take care of that which is now yours and will always be yours, that most delicate part of me beating inside, until time precious delivers my final moment.'

Wed 23 Sept 1959 *12:20pm*
The Second Separation

Mary's soft hands trembled and the tattered poem slipped from her grasp, floating lazily to the ground like an autumn leaf on a breezy day. Where there was a tear in her eye earlier there were now many. She reached out for the poem and clutched it tightly to her heart.

"You.. you wrote that for me?" She knew the answer, of course he did, but she couldn't believe that plain, uninteresting Mary who had a son with special needs could inspire those simply wonderful words from another human being and she was at a loss.

"My eyes have never laid upon something so beautiful. Thank you."

"And neither have mine." Jacob opened his mouth to reply and was glad to hear his voice project although he was aware how feeble his response was. Never quite as good with the verbal word as the written word. He was sure he was fully conscious now and this was happening in reality.

He followed up his cheesy line with another that he internally rebuked himself for as being completely unnecessary. "Sorry the handwriting was messy. I wrote it mostly in the helicopter."

Mary laughed and bent over to kiss Jacob on the forehead, sensing his mortification and playing along. "The handwriting was terrible, you got that right. I would love to know why you just handed me a shopping list?" She frowned and scrunched her eyes up at the piece of paper as if deciphering it. Milk, eggs, bread…A bit odd, no?"

She waved the paper around with a comical puzzled look on her face and her cheeky smile brought Jacob completely back to the present and as she hugged him tightly he made an effort to sit up but could do no more than cough uncontrollably. The group gathered around him, unsure of what to do.

The tender moment passed, and solemn concern for the man having a coughing fit was once again on everybody's mind. The majority vote of the group was to move him from the unrecognisable van to somewhere more comfortable where his condition could be assessed. Jacob winced and was visibly happy when Mary pressed herself close against him in an effort to stand him up, allowing him to close his eyes and appreciate her touch.

"Don't move him! He may have internal injuries or the like. Let me dash off to get the airfield medic." Mr Derby's voice boomed as he rushed off on his new mission of great importance, a trail of pipe smoke following behind him as usual.

The entrance of Mr Derby into Jacob's range of perception meant that where before he could only see Mary, the rest of party now became visible and he became self-conscious that he was the centre of attention and froze with embarrassment, cringing on the inside that all had witnessed his delivery of the poem, intended to be a personal and private matter.

What had he done? He asked himself this partially as a rhetorical question, but mostly because he could actually barely recall what he had actually done. Eyes darting about to survey the carnage of the van, and tuning himself into the pain he was feeling, he pieced the situation together again, locking it into his memory this time.

As was his nature he prepared himself for the offering of a profuse apology, however just as a standard grovelling paragraph was about to be delivered, Ava stepped forward into his field of vision with a look of fear and concern in her eyes that Jacob had never seen. The look of love on her face was for him? Something was different. This was not the girl that he knew as his daughter here and now. This was the look of his daughter as he knew her long ago. The daughter who used to love her father. He squinted to focus and make sure he was not seeing things.

"Dad!" The smile on her face exuded relief and she gave him a hug so tight that every cell of his body cried out in agony, but this was one hug that Jacob would not be short-changing himself on by bringing it to a premature close because of something as minor as acute and extraordinary pain. He looked up at her quizzically and shrugged. His words to her came out slowly, disjointed.

"Hi baby, seems like I am such a loser I can't even kill myself properly. Your dad couldn't even do that right. I just wanted...it would have been nice to see your mom again. Doing to myself exactly what I did to her would mean the circle would be complete, self-imposed justice would have been served."

"Don't say that! How could you say something so horrible. We are a family and I still need you. I need you dad. There, I said it." The words that would have been impossible for her to say only an hour ago were now spilling out of her like water from a burst dam. "I am so sorry I have been an absolutely terrible daughter and actually a terrible person in general. This is me saying that things are going to change. They have to." Her look was so sincere, so genuine that Jacob believed her.

"Are you saying all this because I tried to end it? The extremes I go to just to win my own daughter's love. Just be yourself Ava, don't change your view just because I didn't want the guilt anymore."

"No, no! I had already decided. Dear Mr Derby made me see who I had become and painted a view of the future that I did not want. It's time to move on. I can't punish you forever for an accident. An animal ran in front of the car, there was nothing you could do and I accept that now."

Jacob closed his eyes and groaned. The moment he had dreaded had arrived. It was time for him to come clean and stop lying to himself and those he loved.. "Ava, I fell asleep at the wheel. There was no animal." The words he had so carefully protected for so long had now been released and the feeling of purging something so dark and insidious from inside him was exhilarating but he knew this would ruin the reconciliation he had hoped for for so long.

"What?" Ava's deadpan look indicated that this did not compute.

"Nothing ran in front of the car Ava. I was asleep. I opened my eyes and there was the tree. I am solely to blame for everything."

After a long moment of contemplation and reflection during which time Jacob knew he had lost his daughter again so quickly after having rediscovered her, he was about to speak but Ava spoke first.

"I'm not sure what to do with that information just yet, I have to say. It took so much to shift my frame of mind to where it is right now, so do I just throw that all away and despise you again? Or do I bundle up that new knowledge with all the other bad stuff and compartmentalise it and put it away forever so that I can move forward. I don't know the answer, but I might have to just let everything sink in naturally and deal with it when the time is right for me. But for now, I am just happy that you are alive. Truly. I miss you dad. I want to be your daughter again."

"Come here baby and give your father another hug. I will be a much better dad, I promise. I'm sorry I've been such a no hoper and an embarrassment."

"Shut up. You are not." As they held each other, for that moment Jacob felt himself growing stronger, an invincibility binding with his broken body and making the pain an irrelevant afterthought. He allowed himself to open up and let the love of his daughter flow through him and fill the void left by the departure of God, to him it was an even more beautiful feeling inside.

"I, I think I am okay. I think I can stand. I don't feel so bad any more, mostly bruising all over that hurts but nothing serious. I am ninety nine percent sure." Ava slowly helped him to his feet and after a few wobbles he steadied and took a step forward successfully. He hugged her, six years' worth of lost hugs, all caught up in a moment.

A small silver bus with the name of the airport emblazoned on the side in red and blue pulled up and groaned to a halt alongside the group, a smell of diesel filling the air. A hydraulic door opened with a sound that reminded Jacob of the hiss of his old school bus door opening, and through a puff of smoke Mr Derby emerged, followed by a gentleman who looked to all appearances to be a mechanic, a leather doctor's case in his grip the only suggestion that he was the medic spoken of earlier. Jacob threw up both hands, warding off the medical specialist.

"I'm okay, just sore all over but nothing more than that to worry about. And if there is something worse going on internally, probably nothing you could do about it, sorry." The medic shrugged and raised his eyebrows to indicate no offence was taken.

Looking at the group and sensing that the exhausted bunch were at their physical and emotional limits, Mr Derby decided to step in and get things moving. "Well if that's the case, I am going to suggest we all hop aboard this bus and move onwards and upwards with our lives, as unchanged as they sadly may be after the expedition you just undertook. I know hopes were high, but let me tell you all, as unchanged as your lives might feel and as disappointing as that might feel to you, I can assure you that as people you have learned a lot about yourselves and those around you and your lives will never be the same as a result of this. Now get on the darned bus so we can get out of here and back to our homes." He jumped enthusiastically into the drivers' seat and beckoned them in whilst bouncing up and down like an excited child, a big grin curling his moustache even higher at the tips.

Ishara reached out to pat Jacob on the back, who nodded and the both of them assisted Ava onto the bus. The rest of the weary group climbed aboard slowly and collapsed onto the vinyl seats as if they were the most comfortable furniture they had ever had the pleasure to lounge upon.

"And don't worry, I am a much better driver than I am a helicopter pilot," Mr Derby looked back at his passengers with a wink. The decision was made to drop Gabe and Simon off first at St Paul's where the group had met such a short time ago but the bus shuddered to a halt some streets away from the destination.

"Looks like this will have to do," Mr Derby informed the group who all peered ahead to obtain a glimpse of what was going on out front. The street was still a parking lot, stationary cars facing all directions, mostly empty although a few contained occupants who had clearly left their cars and upon their return were now frustrated at wanting to drive away found themselves boxed in from all sides.

Peering down the road, the occupants of the bus could see a general flow of pedestrian traffic making its way towards St Pauls almost as if hypnotised and drawn in by some compelling force.

"There are more people around here now than before when God was still alive," Ava observed. "Doesn't that seem a little odd? I mean, God no longer exists, so technically there is absolutely no point in ever visiting a church again. Those people who thought that they were closer to God by doing so now know that this is no longer possible? And yet...." she waved her hand out in front of her to showcase the illogical behaviour being demonstrated before them.

"I just actually think that when all is said and done, God or no God, people are always going to continue to go to church, pray even though it's ineffective, believe in an afterlife even though one doesn't exist, and will probably create some new higher power to believe in eventually because that just seems to be what humans need." Ishara's opinion that the human race was pitiful, needy, and weakened further by the use of religion as a crutch was more than evident.

"We can't accept that humans might just be the supreme species now in the universe and have no other being to defer to, nothing higher to believe in and nothing but ourselves to rely on to provide us with hope and to have faith in for the future. Taking full responsibility for our own actions and not having an esoteric entity out there to blame, worship, or guide our thoughts and actions means that we are all alone, and our fate now lies in our own hands. Who thinks we are ready to handle that? No way. Look at the misguided lost souls who spend their Sundays going to church, they aren't strong enough to survive on their own. They will be like little chicks who have their incubator heat lamp taken away. Once that shining light up above that warms them and provides that security is gone they will perish. Just watch."

She stopped, aware that all eyes were on her, a few jaws wide open. "What? You know it's true. You watch, the weak will continue to worship God even after death, rather than take responsibility for their own lives. Pointless."

Gabe stepped forward and put his arm around Ishara, partly to calm her down, partly to simply stop her talking so that he and Simon would be able to say their farewells and leave. She sheepishly complied, aware that she had probably just come across as a little unhinged and with an undertone of a superiority complex. She visibly shrivelled before their eyes and Gabe laughed, patting her on the back affectionately to say it was okay and actually found it amusing.

"I love a girl with a strong opinion," he laughed. His arm remained around Ishara as he sighed and glanced at his watch with a weary look. "Well, I have to say this has been the most interesting couple of days of my life, but it is time to get back to reality and soldier on with this little guy, and you must all be ready to head home and jump into a nice hot shower or bath, I know I can't wait," he said, removing his arm from Ishara so that he could use it to ruffle Simon's hair, the young boy not even bothering to attempt to sweep it back into place, knowing it most likely would not be long until it was ruffled again.

Jacob stepped forward and extended his hand. "Gabe, I cannot thank you enough, really. From the other night dealing with the guy on my van, to even sharing with us the existence of the miracle destination. Just life-changing. You did not have to tell us strangers about it, you did not have to bring us strangers along, and yet you did." Jacob continued to shake Gabe's hand wholeheartedly and Gabe grinned.

"Jacob, if it wasn't for you, we wouldn't have even come close to getting there and back again. It was a pleasure meeting you and your daughter, and everybody here, I mean just think, not long ago you were all new faces to me and already I am finding it difficult to say goodbye. And for me, a guy who used to flit around from group to social group, that is a big deal. My life will be forever changed, not from the journey, but from what I learned from being with each of you all."

He gave a round of emotional hugs and handshakes and began to lead Simon up the hill, waving to the group. Simon excitedly turned around and waved too, only semi-interested in what was going on before concentrating on keeping up with Gabe.

Ishara looked up the hill sadly watching her infatuation leave before something clicked in her head and she plucked up the courage to run after him. The group watched her legs take quick, petite steps until she caught up and lay a hand upon his shoulder, spinning him around with surprise. A few words were had, a few laughs were laughed, and shortly after a beaming face walked down the hill. Seeing the inquisitive faces, she knew she had to satisfy their curiosity and share details of the interaction.

"What? We just talked, that's all!" she said coyly. "And maybe, *maybe* we will be catching up for a drink or something soon, nothing to get too excited about," she said excitedly as she rolled her eyes to the bemusement of the group.

"He's a good catch, well done!" Ava wheeled over and congratulated her friend. "He wasn't really my type as you of all people could tell, but it was fun competing for him, no? Keep me posted on how it all goes okay, I think you may chew him up and spit him out like all the others? I almost feel sorry for the guy. Come on, let's get back and see if Mr Derby can do a three point turn in a bus," she chuckled.

"Actually, I think I might walk from here. I want some time to think about a few things that presented themselves to me over the last couple of days, and there's nothing better for that than a nice evening stroll. I've got a lot going on in my head and it would be good for me to have a think about myself, the universe and my parents, most likely. I've never appreciated how lucky I am to have them, and for all they have given me. I am going to be a very different daughter from now on. And friend. Are we cool?" Ava nodded.

The girls held hands and gave each other a kiss, their bond tightening and they were once again two school friends against the world before Ishara branched off and commenced her pleasant walk of contemplation home.

Wed 23 Sept 1959 *2:28pm*
The Third Separation

A slight drizzle started to fall, as if sensing the onset of a melancholy mood settling over the diminishing party as they approached an end to a significant moment shared together. Jacob had always disliked being outside in the rain because it decreased the amount of freedom he had to move, act and do what he wanted to do, while increasing the necessity of mindfulness and reducing efficiencies.

One hand was constantly occupied grasping an umbrella, leaving only one hand for all other duties. The simple act of walking involved attention focused downwards and the observation of many detours where crooked, deviating paths were the only means to avoid the deeper puddles, the risk of his already wet shoes and socks becoming even more uncomfortable.

And yet now, looking to his left at Mary beside him he was oblivious to his saturated hair pressed flat against his face, droplets of water streaming down his cheeks, every second step falling into a pool of water on the road which could have been the size and depth of a lake for all he noticed.

He finally understood the romance of a rainy day, and looking up to the heavens he gave in and took his coat off, moving closer to Mary, raising it over her head in a selfless gesture to shield her from the rain at his own expense.

She smiled at him, blissfully ignorant of her makeup running and politely waved away the coat so that she could instead reach out for his hand which she held tightly and the two of them proceeded onwards. Jacob never wanted this moment to end and wished that the bus they were walking towards was on the other side of the world.

They all hopped back on board and after some cringe-worthy manoeuvring by Mr Derby, the vehicle continued its journey towards Mary's house. The two were sitting next to each other still holding hands, now participating in an awkward silence, eventually broken by Mary turning and grabbing Jacob's other hand followed by a look that told him that she needed to talk.

"You know, I have missed my husband every day since he left, but I think it has taken meeting you to realise that there is a future for me out there where I can move on and be content living my life without him. I was always so focused on missing him, beating myself up and thinking about getting him back that I never saw that I was living by my own means successfully and doing a pretty good job of it. I know how you feel about me Jacob, and if you just give me some time to get my head together I would be happy to see where things go, but not just yet. I could possibly have my arm twisted into dinner and movies sometimes, if you don't mind Zach coming along?" she said with a sincere smile.

"I would like nothing more. You make me very happy Mary, I look forward to seeing what the future holds." Jacob wondered how they could both have such a conversation whilst they both looked a hideous soggy sight. He was aware of a big pool of water forming under him and dripping off the seat, running down the aisle as the bus came to a halt at Mary's house.

"Take care everybody," Mary said to the bus as a whole, holding Zach's hand and leading him off gently. She took a step back up and planted a big kiss and hug on Mr Derby. "And thank you, you mysterious, amazing man. Now I know who to call if I ever need assistance for absolutely anything. Except for a helicopter flight, don't be offended but I may look elsewhere for that if I ever need one."

Mr Derby smiled. "That is fine Mary, I would too!" and he chuckled so wholeheartedly it turned into another coughing fit. After patting him on the back until his red face returned to a more normal shade, Mary backed away down the steps and walked herself and Zach down the driveway to her home where she grabbed her son's hand and used it to wave at the bus.

Voluntarily, he waved his other hand also and mouthed the words "goodbye" to the bus. The response from the remaining passengers was frantic wide eyed waving, cheers of encouragement so loud they were heard through the harsh grating of the bus changing gears.

Mary picked the boy up and looked into his eyes, excited at the changes that he seemed to be undergoing and couldn't wait to discover the extent to which he may be developing. Using one hand to unlock the front door, the other still holding him, she swung it open wide and entered.

"My darling, darling boy. How big and smart you are becoming! Mummy loves you very much. What an exciting adventure we just had, you were so brave! Let's get you into a nice hot bath and then I will make us a nice snack. Sounds good? Yes it does, doesn't it. Mummy likes seeing her wonderful boy eat."

Content to be resuming her domestic maternal duties she nuzzled into him as the door closed behind them and they returned to their familiar world.

Wed 23 Sept 1959 **6:00pm**
Faith's New Beginning

Closing the office door behind her ever so gently as she entered, the slightest click of the latch falling into place betrayed her arrival and Maxwell looked up from what he was doing with annoyance. A sharp intake of breath accompanied by a combined look of excitement and relief on his face gave way to a smile as he lunged out of Faith's chair and strode across the room, the two of them meeting in the middle in an embrace.

Faith was more than aware that she looked a dishevelled sight but was so overcome by the sight of a familiar face that she sank to her knees and started wiping tears from her eyes. "I can't believe I'm back," she muttered as Maxwell led her to a couch in the corner where she lay down.

"What happened? Are you okay? Where were you? After not hearing from you since yesterday afternoon I feared the worst. I tried calling your home, I visited, knocked on your door till my knuckles were red, worried that some crazy got you or one of your connectors or something! I'm leaping to the most pessimistic conclusions at the moment."

"I'm okay, well, physically at least. Actually, you didn't fear the worst. The worst was much, much worse than any sane mind could imagine. What I went through was terror, pure, distilled terror." She started shaking, and she attempted to pull herself together to try to describe to Maxwell the events that had befallen her over the last twenty four hours. The words came in no order, no logical sequence or timeline, they just fell from her as if the memories needed to be purged, but eventually every last cleansing word was spoken and she lay there, staring at the ceiling for minutes afterward.

Maxwell remained silent, trying his best to absorb what he had just heard and make sense of it all. Aaban's motivation for what he had done, Ira's involvement of Faith in the backfiring plan of salvation for himself and the people he had taken, how it had all unravelled when the inconceivable happened and God, worshipped since mankind's dawn, ceased to exist.

He sat down next Faith and stroked her hair, a taboo act even given their flirtatious relationship, however, the suffering that this girl had experienced instilled within him a deep sense of nurturing and he just wanted her to be okay. To his surprise, she brushed his hand away and she looked up at him with clarity, her head slightly shaking. "Maxwell. This all has to stop. This -you and me thing-, whatever it is. It's not right and we both know it can never happen. You are married, we have had our fun here in the office but I am strong enough now to say that I can draw a line in the sand and say it finishes here. Yes?"

He wanted to tell her that he didn't know what she was suggesting, that he wasn't aware of any "you and me thing" that needed to be stopped but he withdrew his hand and nodded. "I know, it is wrong and I feel ashamed, now. I'm clearly not as strong as you are or reluctant to put an end to those adorable looks I receive, but it is the mature thing to do before it has the chance to get out of hand. And you look too damn cute to resist when you cry. I just want you to be okay and feel safe right now, more than anything." An understanding passing between them and Faith extended her hand in friendship.

"Boss," she said seriously.

He extended his hand. "*Senior* Journalist," he said with an even more serious air.

After about five seconds had passed, Faith's expression slowly rolled through a variety of comical expressions, commencing with non-plussed, then confused, followed by enlightened and finally jubilation mixed with a little bit of disbelief, at which Maxwell cracked up.

"Senior! Really? Oh thank you! Do you mean it?" She lunged towards him and broke the agreement that they had literally just shook hands on, but Maxwell thought that given the occasion one last hug was permissible.

"Well, let's be honest, it's the role you have really been doing for a long time now but without the recognition, apart from the odd cat-stuck-in-a-tree story. But don't get your hopes up for a huge pay rise or back pay or anything. It's a title change, you will get a new desk nameplate but that is mostly as far as the glory goes I am afraid."

"Yes, yes I know, we are on a budget, times are tough etcetera etcetera. Thank you Maxwell, I appreciate this, really I do." She was beaming.

"You have really proven yourself these last few days, over the last year in fact. Now that we are talking shop, starting from tomorrow I really want you to bed down the events of the last few days. I think you have made a great start, and I don't know of anybody anywhere else who has had the exposure to the connectors as you, or who has aggregated as much information that was communicated at the time of God's appearance. Let's build on that."

"I will. I look forward to it. I just want to try to make sense of it all." She looked at the ground in thought, then back up to her boss. "Maxwell, is there any hope for the human race at all? Do you think God achieved whatever it was that was intended by the revelation?"

"Who can say? I feel like we are now more off the rails than ever as a race as a result. God was dying in a way on earth anyway, fewer and fewer followers, and more people questioning the reality of religion with only hearsay evidence available to validate it. Maybe your connector put it the most simply. The aim was just to reset the truth, nothing more, nothing less. And this was the last opportunity to do it. And now we know the truth, it is up to us to do with it what we will." He sighed.

"I am just sad to think that for the rest of our careers, there will never, ever be a story as big or groundbreaking as this. It's all downhill from here for us career-wise, unless there is another God that appears, or a resurrection of some kind."

Faith shrugged her shoulders. "Looks like back to boring old political news then."

"Don't count on it, I think there will be enough repercussions from all this to provide us with news from around the world for years. Anyway my dear, I am going to head off now and I am really looking forward to making a start tomorrow with renewed enthusiasm. Are you okay, though? You do look terrible, and I am concerned for you. Do you need a hospital, a drink, anything? I might subtly suggest a shower."

"No, you go. I'm physically fine, and I do feel better after unloading everything that happened to me onto you. I'm going to potter around here for a bit."

"As you wish. Take care and I will see you whenever you can make it in tomorrow. Sleep in, make sure you are okay, it will be a busy day but if you aren't up for it then you do whatever you need to do to take care of yourself after all that happened."

"Yes boss!" Maxwell walked slowly out of the office and closed the door gently behind him.

Alone in the office, Faith swivelled around in her chair, centred her being, harnessed her spirituality, placed her hands upon her typewriter and typed. And typed. Unplanned. Her subconscious was the author, a masterful narrative spouting forth via her fingers, through the keyboard and onto paper, weaving a story that needed to be told. Her chakras were aligned and her energy flows were streaming uninhibited. There was always a first time for everything.

Pausing to light a stick of incense, she then continued.

"Today was just another day, but little did this senior journalist know exactly what was in store when she strode into the office on the morning of 20 September, 1959...."

She had finally found her novel.

Wed 23 Sept 1959 3:08pm
The Fourth Separation

"Well that just leaves us oldies then, hey Jacob?" Mr Derby joked.

"What am I, chopped liver? Ava interjected.

"You are an old soul Ava, you beautiful girl. You don't quite fit the mould of those people around you, in a good way mind you. You possess the maturity to nurture your own thoughts and opinions without the influence or concern of others. Just like me! Maybe it rubs some the wrong way but you stay true to yourself and that is a quality that takes some many years to develop. So yes, you join the oldies club."

The effort of turning the big steering wheel was starting to take a toll on him and he exhaled with a big wheeze as he negotiated a tight corner.

They sat in silence for some minutes until the bus bumped, rattled and finally pulled over at the laneway where the two men had met daily, but seemed aeons ago now. The silence continued as the men realised they had met a crossroads in their relationship. Jacob was the first to speak.

"So as you know, I lost my job a few days ago and I'm afraid that our daily meetings may be over for good. I'm not sure how I feel about that, I never really thought about it much but I believe I have become quite attached to you Mr Derby." Jacob was beyond skirting issues and putting on a manly front, surprising himself greatly since this is what he had a grand record of doing historically. It was so much easier just saying what you intend to say and get it out there without requiring people to read between the lines.

"My dear chap I will of course miss you too, however, there is such an invention I believe called the telephone, or if you do find yourself awake and out of bed at 8:45am then you know where to find me. My preference is of course to discuss matters of importance and non-importance at a pub over a whisky or a port depending on my mood. You are more than welcome to join." He pulled out a pouch of tobacco and proceeded to pack his pipe absentmindedly, expert hands moving quickly and automatically performing the correct movements until a puff of smoke emerged from the corner of his mouth. He extended his hand.

"Until next time old chap. And goodbye to you old Ava. Take care of your father hey?" He winked at them both and climbed up into the bus, cranking the engine. The door squeaked close and just as the bus was about to take off down the road, Ava made such a racket that Jacob thought she had gone absolutely mad.

Waving her arms at the bus and screeching loudly, Mr Derby looked towards the noise and hit the brakes before the bus could really take flight. The door squeaked open.

"My goodness girl, what on earth is the matter. Well, what is it?"

"Sorry Mr Derby, I was just wondering, after all this time, I would die if I didn't find out. I have to know."

"Know what? Well? Spit it out!" He mocked impatience with a semi smile.

"Well, you are Mr Derby as we all know. But what is your first name? My father never told me so I might as well ask it from you."

"That's because your father didn't know."

"Well, what is it?"

"It's Derville."

"Derville?"

"Yes, Derville. And on that note, goodbye young lady," he laughed as he closed the door and careened down the road and around the corner out of sight.

"What an unusual man." Ava observed. "I am simply besotted with him!" she laughed as they passed the well-kept hedge, onwards along the unpainted picket fence that was missing some pickets and leaning over at an unnatural gravity-defying angle, finally arriving at their home.

Opening the door, Jacob walked down the corridor and stopped after a few steps. The first thing that went through his mind was how his house looked that little bit more familiar now during this time of day. He noticed that the sun was at the angle so that it streamed in through the small ornate stained glass window on his left, and projected the same glorious array of colours and patterns on the right hand side of the hall as the day he arrived home after losing his job.

The shadows formed by the furniture were falling at angles less strange to him than before, areas that he was used to being in darkness were now bathed in light, and that was just fine. Areas that were bathed in light were now in darkness.

The rules had been turned on their head but he was now getting used to the new rules. What was a temporary alternate reality before was now what the world be like forevermore, and he was okay with that. He had lost everything, but he had regained a once lost daughter.

Walking over to the corner of the room where he had dropped his work briefcase oh so long ago, he stared down at the beaten leather bag as seriously as if it contained dark secrets of the universe inside, threatening to escape and release themselves upon the world.

He stooped over to unbuckle the brass fasteners and reached slowly inside. He retrieved the silver photo frame containing the picture of his family that he had taken home from work and carefully made room on the mantle, displaying it such that all the other frames occupied secondary positions. Jacob nodded his head.

"Honey, can I make you a sandwich?"

A voice responded from down the corridor.

"Yes please! And Dad?"

"Yes?"

"Thank you!"

And Jacob got to work, his home feeling more like home now than it had in a long time. Today was just another day, but he had a pretty good feeling about those to come.